Robert Burns, James Logie Robertson

Burns selected Poems

Robert Burns, James Logie Robertson

Burns selected Poems

ISBN/EAN: 9783337208882

Printed in Europe, USA, Canada, Australia, Japan

Cover: Foto ©Andreas Hilbeck / pixelio.de

More available books at **www.hansebooks.com**

Clarendon Press Series

BURNS

SELECTED POEMS

EDITED

WITH INTRODUCTION, NOTES, AND
A GLOSSARY

BY

J. LOGIE ROBERTSON, M.A.

Oxford

AT THE CLARENDON PRESS

1889

PREFATORY NOTE.

It is hoped that this Selection from the poetry of Burns, while fairly representative of his best work, will serve also to shew the versatility of his genius. *The Jolly Beggars* and *Holy Willie's Prayer* it has been found necessary to exclude altogether,—brilliant and characteristic specimens of his poetical quality though they are. From the admitted poems an occasional line here, or stanza there, has, for one reason or another, also been dropped. It is with the utmost reluctance that the Editor has ventured upon any alteration of the Text. These alterations are few, and of the slightest.

The Selection has been divided into ' Poems ' and ' Songs,' and each series arranged as accurately as possible in strict chronological order. It is not only that such an arrangement reveals the development of the Author's poetical faculty : it also casts a suggestive light upon the history of his life. Special attention has been paid to the Notes. Here only I have offered, as the occasion required, and the space at my disposal permitted, some remarks on the characteristics of Burns's style, and on his indebtedness to the Scottish and English poets of the eighteenth century.

Care has been taken, by collation with the various editions, to give the most approved Text ; and where

variations of value occur, they have been quoted in the
Notes.   The form, or spelling, of the words of the Text
is for the most part Burns's own.   It is to be noted, however, that there is considerable difference in respect of
verbal form between the Kilmarnock and the Edinburgh
Editions of his Poems.   Some deference has occasionally
been shewn to familiar usage—'bonnie,' for example, has
been substituted for 'bonie.'

The Glossary, it is believed, is full; it is as correct as
I have been able to make it.   The derivation of the
principal words has been given only where it seemed safe,
or at least reasonable.

The Introduction is not more than it professes to be—
a clear outline of the life of Burns.   I have, however,
given a prominence, usually denied, to his early train-
ing.   The outline is to some extent necessarily supple-
mented in the Notes,—for the Poems are largely
autobiographical.   The best life of Burns, indeed, is
still to be found in his poems and letters.

In regard to the pronunciation of Scottish words, it
would, I think, be of little service to lay down hard and
fast rules, even if it were possible to do so.   The form is
for the most part phonetic, and the rhyme will often sug-
gest the pronunciation.   The student who has mastered
the language of Chaucer should find it an easier task to
master that of Burns, pronunciation and all.

J. LOGIE ROBERTSON.

LOCKHARTON TERRACE, SLATEFORD, N.B.
27th December, 1888.

INTRODUCTION.

A RACE of yeomen or small farmers of the name of Burnes
had been resident in Kincardineshire for at least two cen-
turies when, in 1748, William, the third son of one of them,
reluctantly left his father's house at Clochnahill, and travelled
southward in search of a livelihood. He was then twenty-
six years of age, and beyond health and a general knowledge
of agricultural work carried from his native county little else
that was likely to be of service to him, except a certificate
which truthfully testified that he was the son of an honest
farmer and a very well-inclined lad himself. He got as far
south as Edinburgh, and then turning his face westward,
after a wandering life of nine years in all, settled at last on
a small croft of seven acres on the right bank of the Doon,
about two miles south from the town of Ayr. Here, on the
edge of the public road, in the hamlet of Alloway, he built
with his own hands, out of the rudest materials, a cottage of
two rooms, to which in the following December he brought
home his young wife, Agnes Brown, from the adjoining
parish of Maybole. In this clay cabin Robert Burns, their
eldest child, was born on the twenty-fifth day of January,
1759. Three more children were born, and then, after a
tenancy of the croft of over eight years, William Burnes
was induced in the interest of his young and increasing
family to take a bold step. His croft maintained a cow,
and yielded vegetables for the Ayr market, but he had early
found it necessary to improve its slender gains by taking
wages as a jobbing gardener. His principal employer was
the Provost of Ayr, and this gentleman happening to have a
farm to let in the neighbourhood, William Burnes ventured

upon a lease of it at a yearly rental of about £40. That the provost had faith in the industry and probity of his gardener is very clear from the circumstance that he not only granted the lease but also advanced a loan of £100 to his tenant to enable him to stock the farm. The transference from the clay cottage and the seven-acre croft at Alloway to the seventy-acre farm of Mount Oliphant at the Whitsunday term of 1766 looked like prosperity, but it was in truth the commencement of an accumulation of woes which was at last to overwhelm William Burnes, and which threatened to include his family in his fate. Debt, which thus early hung upon the Burnes household, dragged almost every member of it down to the veriest drudgery for the next eighteen years. Yet the drudgery was lightened by family affection, and dignified by the practice of some of the noblest virtues.

In May, 1766, Robert was a few months over his seventh year. The period of infancy was past, and the boy, running about his father's door bare-headed and bare-footed in the summer months, had already begun to make acquaintance with the external world in the roadside hamlet and its neighbourhood. The same influences of scenery and boyish companionship which modified the development of his nature in Alloway continued to supplement the more powerful influence of a very careful home-training at Mount Oliphant. The farm was only two miles in a south-easterly direction from the croft, and as it lay on a gently-rising eminence it commanded a wide extent of the same character of landscape with which Burns's young eye had been familiar, and took in besides the new and attractive feature of a glimpse of sea. But the boy had not broken actual contact with the locality of his birth: the little school was there, and though his attendance was not so regular as it had been when he lived just across the road from the school-door, he still kept up for a couple of years longer an emulative connexion with his former school-fellows. The establishment of that humble school had been the work of his father just one year before the removal to Mount Oliphant. In March, 1765, William Burnes, with the concurrence of four of his neighbours, the fathers of young families like himself, had gone to Ayr to engage a competent tutor for the Alloway children. Such a tutor or teacher he found in John Murdoch, then a youth of eighteen, whom he engaged in an inn on the strength of his penmanship and a recommendation from the Rector of Ayr Academy. Murdoch taught the little school at Alloway for about three years, and from the nature of his engagement became as intimate with the parents of his pupils as with the pupils themselves. He was guaranteed a minimum salary, and was boarded in the house of each of his five employers in turn. Murdoch found in William Burnes a man at once intelligent and informed much above his station, of rare strength of character, and of deep, if somewhat stern, religious feeling. Many years afterwards, when he had made wide experience of the world, he wrote of him as the man who, of all men he ever knew, stood highest in his esteem. He found a miniature copy of the father in the son. The boy was an apt pupil in everything that required intellect; it was only in the more mechanical arts of singing and writing that he was backward and slow. Murdoch's teaching, so far as it went, was good; his method was excellent. 'The books most commonly used in the school were the *Spelling Book*, the *New Testament*, the *Bible* (sic), *Mason's Collection of Prose and Verse*, and *Fisher's English Grammar*. They committed to memory the hymns and other poems of that *Collection* with uncommon facility. This facility was partly owing to the method pursued by their father and me in instructing them, which was to make them thoroughly acquainted with the meaning of every word in each sentence that was to be committed to memory. . . As soon as they were capable of it I taught them to turn verse into its natural order, sometimes to substitute synonymous expressions for poetical words, and to supply all the ellipses.' To this testimony of Murdoch to the proficiency of young

Burns and his brother Gilbert, may be added the poet's own
impressions of those early school-days. He tells us in the
longest, as it is one of the best pieces of his own prose, his
autobiographical letter to Dr. Moore, how the first bit of
literature to give him pleasure was 'the Vision of Mirza.' It
was Addison too, whom he met in *Mason's English Collection*, and not a Scottish author, that was his first favourite in
poetry; and it is significant of the religious atmosphere in
which he was bred that the poem which sounded the earliest
music in his boyish ears was the hymn beginning 'How are
Thy servants bless'd, O Lord!' It is interesting to have
Burns's own statement of his schoolboy accomplishments :
' I made,' he says, 'an excellent English scholar ; and by the
time I was ten or eleven years of age, I was a critic in sub-
stantives, verbs, and particles.'

It was William Burnes, however, that was in the true sense
of the word his children's schoolmaster. Regularly of a
winter evening, after the farm-work for the day—in which the
children early bore a part—was ended, the student's candle
was lighted in the lonely farmhouse, and the family sat down
to mental toil. The girls went to no other school. Arith-
metic and religion were the subjects of instruction most
congenial to the father. To him they were equally exact
sciences. He drew up in the form of a catechism for his
children a compendium of religious belief, in which the
Calvinism is of a surprisingly milder type than was then in
vogue in Scotland. It was not his father's Calvinism that the
future poet attacked in satires of tremendous trenchancy.
William Burnes's piety is to be looked for in 'the saint, the
father, and the husband' of the *Cottar's Saturday Night.*
But school was not confined to the hours of evening. At all
times and seasons in the working day, whenever a fitting
opportunity offered, the father engaged his elder children,
and especially Robert, in the discussion of topics of lasting
interest, or imparted to them the results of his own reading
and observant experience. Burns was afterwards distin-

guished for his conversational powers,—for the freshness and pregnancy of his remarks : contemporaries who knew him have said, indeed, but with exaggeration, that his talk was more wonderful than his poetry. There can be little doubt that his habit of independent thought and his vigorous mode of expression were developed by the practice and personal example of his father. One disadvantage of life at Mount Oliphant was the want of society. It was a very isolated life. The boys found no playmates in the adjoining farms. These were mostly in the hands of shopkeepers, who preferred to live beside their business in town. They were thus thrown for companionship upon their father. And Robert at least was not only doing a man's work in the fields and the farmyard in his boyhood, but was thinking a man's thoughts and speaking the language of manhood as well.

It was at Mount Oliphant, too, that the door of the supernatural world opened to the imaginative mind of young Burns. An old relative, Betty Davidson, domiciled in the family before they left Alloway, had a store of ghostly and ghastly stories, which was exhaustless, though continually drawn upon. Her disclosure of the apocrypha of the invisible world around him made such a powerful impression on the mind of Robert as to give him, despite the efforts of a singularly robust reason, a permanent belief in its reality, and in its realism as portrayed by old Betty. She, doubtless, was the granny in the *Address to the Deil*, who was so fearfully intimate with the haunts and habits of the Evil One. And to her certainly we owe the diablerie of *Tam o' Shanter*.

With Murdoch's departure from Alloway in the end of 1767 the real school-days of Robert Burns came to an end. But the work of instruction did not cease : the father borrowed books of history and geography, poetry and philosophy; and careful reading, intensive rather than extensive, went on at home. In 1772 Robert and Gilbert went week about for a quarter in summer, when the lads could be best spared from farm-work, to the parish school of Dalrymple, about three miles off, for the purpose of improving their handwriting. And in the succeeding year Robert was boarded for a few weeks with Murdoch, who was now rector of the academy at Ayr, and with him revised his knowledge of English grammar, and began to read French. He took to French with what might almost be called instinctive liking. In a day or two he was engrossed in *Les Aventures de Télémaque.* To the last years of his life Burns was fond rather than vain of his acquaintance with French, and too frequently—both for those who knew the language and those who did not—brought into his conversation, and his correspondence, and even his poetry, a little bit of purple from that gay and gallant speech. The duties of the farm recalled him from those agreeable studies. As Mr. Murdoch has painted it—' The plains of Mount Oliphant began to whiten, and Robert was summoned to relinquish the pleasing scenes that surrounded the grotto of Calypso, and, armed with a sickle, to seek glory by signalizing himself in the fields of Ceres ; and so he did, for although but about fifteen, I was told that he performed the work of a man.' A new experience was awaiting him in those same harvest fields. He fell in love with his partner, a girl of about his own age, all as charmingly told in his rhymed *Epistle to Mrs. Scott, Gudewife of Wauchope-House,* and, even more charmingly, in his prose autobiographical *Letter to Dr. Moore.* It was this 'sonsy lass,' Nelly Kirkpatrick by name, the daughter of a country blacksmith, that made Burns a poet,—or, more correctly, in his own words, ' that roused the forming strain.' In praise of her he wrote his first song, composing it to a tune which he had heard her sing among the sheaves. From this time forward he was never a stranger to the grand passion. His heart was ' eternally lighted up by some goddess or other.'

It was about the year 1774 that William Burnes first began to feel the acute pressure of poverty. He was now the father of seven children, and, besides being poor, was ageing fast. His generous landlord was dead, and he had now to deal with a factor, whose brutal manners and pitiless threats are temperately described in *The Twa Dogs.* Burns's prose description of him has more heat : ' My indignation yet [1787] boils at the threatening, insolent epistles from the scoundrel tyrant, which used to set us all in tears.' The chief cause of these difficulties, next to the heavy loan from the landlord with which the lease at Mount Oliphant had begun, was the natural sterility of the farm. It was entirely worked by the family, who over-exerted themselves to make it productive, and lived as sparingly as anchorites. The hard work of this period, which should have been the happiest of his life, together with poor fare, and the mental distress arising from a knowledge of his father's circumstances that was only too sympathetic, developed in the boy-ploughman that melancholy to which he was constitutionally inclined, and brought on those headaches from which he continued to suffer intermittently all his life after.

The year 1775 is memorable in the life of Burns for his three-months' residence at Kirkoswald, a village about ten miles to the south-west, whither he had gone to learn mensuration and land-surveying. His residence here, besides bringing him acquainted with the wild, free life of smuggling farmers inhabiting the sea-board, gave him most of the qualifications necessary for the duties of an excise officer. On his return from Kirkoswald he seems to have joined a night dancing-school—in defiance unfortunately of the express wishes of his father. Previous to this act of rebellion, as he himself has styled it, he felt himself to be ' the most ungainly, awkward being in the parish.' It was partly to ' give his manners a brush ' that he went to the dancing-school. But there were other reasons, some of them desperate enough : ' Abandoned of view or aim in life, with a strong appetite for sociability (as well from native hilarity as from a pride of observation and remark) and a constitutional hypochondriac

taint which made me fly solitude—Add to these incentives to
social life my reputation for bookish knowledge, a certain
wild, logical talent, and a strength of thought something like
the rudiments of good sense, [which] made me generally
a welcome guest ; [and] 'tis no great wonder that where two
or three were met together there [too] was I.'

The poetical fruits of Mount Oliphant were some five
pieces,—all songs, the best of which certainly is *O Tibbie, I
hae seen the day.* But the poet was further qualifying for
future effort by the fitful but close study of a collection of
approved songs which he carried with him beside the cart
and behind the plough.   His reading, also, towards the close
of the Mount Oliphant period became pretty extensive, and
included Shakespeare, Pope, Thomson, Shenstone, and Allan
Ramsay.   His literary correspondence, too, with former
schoolfellows was getting to be so large that 'though he had
not three-farthings' worth of business in the world,' every
post brought him letters ; and, to crown all, he was the
confidant of love-sick swains and 'in the secret of half the
amours in the parish.'

He was now in his nineteenth year.   At the Whitsunday
term of 1777 the family removed from Mount Oliphant to
the farm of Lochlie, some ten or twelve miles to the north-
east, in the parish and near the village of Tarbolton.   It was
then a moorland farm, surrounded by low, dreary hills which
shut in the view.   Its extent was almost double that of
Mount Oliphant, and the annual rent, at twenty shillings an
acre, was £130.   Unfortunately there was no definite arrangement in writing with the landlord, and a dispute by and by
arising on a question of tenant rights, the case was submitted
to arbitrators, whose decision completed the ruin and has-
tened the death of William Burnes.   The tragic event
occurred in February, 1784 : and three months later the
family removed to Mossgiel.   The tenancy of Lochlie thus
lasted exactly seven years.   It was an eventful time in the life
of Burns, extending as it did through the period of his early

manhood, from his nineteenth to his twenty-sixth year. In
its social and literary aspects his life here was a continuation
of his later life at Mount Oliphant. It flowed on, he says,
'much in the same tenour till my twenty-third year.' There
were, however, important developments. At Halloween,
1780, he founded a Bachelors' Club, of some eight or twelve
young men in a similar station of life, and of kindred disposition with himself, and inaugurated a series of monthly
meetings, in the house of John Richard, at Tarbolton, by
proposing as a subject of debate, ' What kind of wife ought a
poor young farmer to marry?' The object of the Club was
avowedly to forget 'cares and labours in Mirth and Diversion.' There was a peculiarity in his personal appearance
at this time which is significant. ' He wore the only tied
hair in the parish, and in the church, his plaid, which was of
a particular colour, I think *fillemot*, he wrapped in a particular manner round his shoulders.' (*Account by David
Sillar.*) His manners had lost shyness and ungainliness.
He was self-possessed, free, and 'facile in addressing the
fair sex.' In 1781 he became a freemason,—' which,' says
Gilbert Burns, ' was his first introduction to the life of a boon
companion.' Yet, the brother goes on to say, ' I do not
recollect'—he is speaking of the Lochlie period—'to have
ever seen him intoxicated; nor was he at all given to
drinking. . . . His expenses never in any one year [from
1777 to 1786] exceeded his slender income [£7 a year,
the wages allowed him by his father]. His temperance and
frugality were everything that could be wished.'

In the year of his admission into St. David's Lodge, he
proposed marriage to Alison Begbie, a farmer's daughter
in domestic service in the neighbourhood. Her ultimate
refusal of his addresses plunged him into the deepest
melancholy, and had disastrous effects upon his future
conduct. It was during the courtship that he composed the
first of his famous love-songs, *Mary Morison* (sc. Alison
Begbie). In the same year he made an effort to break from

the bondage of the farm. Lint was at this time a common crop, and from growing it in his father's fields at Lochlie, and selling it to the flax-manufacturers, Burns caught at the idea of manufacturing it himself. Accordingly he entered into partnership with a second cousin, Peacock by name, a flax-spinner at Irvine on the Ayrshire coast; but Peacock was dishonest, to begin with; and, to end with, their factory went on fire, leaving at least one of the partners 'not worth sixpence in the world.' This futile attempt to make a livelihood by flax-dressing lasted some six months; and meanwhile he formed a firm friendship with Richard Brown, a seaman of frank manners but loose morals. This man's mind was 'fraught with courage, independence, and magnanimity. . . I loved him; I admired him to a degree of enthusiasm. . . His knowledge of the world was vastly superior to mine, and I was all attention to learning . . . but he spoke of a certain . . . failing with levity, which hitherto I had regarded with horror. Here his friendship did me a mischief.' (*Burns's Letter to Dr. Moore.*) Brown, however, has the credit of having been the first to recognize the poetical genius of Burns, and to encourage him to cultivate it. On his return to the plough in 1782 the young poet began with something like seriousness and system to act on his friend's advice. The poetical fruits of the Lochlie period include (besides *Mary Morison*) *An Autumn Song to Peggy*, *My Nannie O*, *Winter: a Dirge*, and the two poems on the subject of *Poor Mailie*, with considerably over a score of other pieces of varying merit. They have this in common, that they express the experiences of his everyday life.

Mossgiel, to which the family removed at Whitsunday, 1784, lies rather more than two miles from Lochlie and within one mile of the market town of Mauchline. It then consisted of nearly one hundred and twenty acres, which the brothers Robert and Gilbert leased conjointly from Mr. Gavin Hamilton, a writer in Mauchline, at a yearly rental of £90. The poet's connexion with this farm was to last only about two years. The history of those years has been very graphically sketched by each of the brothers. Part of the poet's account may be given. ' I entered,' he says, ' on this farm with a full resolution *Come, go to, I will be wise!* I read farming books, I calculated crops, I attended markets ; and, in short, in spite of the devil, the world, and the flesh, I believe I should have been a wise man ; but the first year from unfortunately buying-in bad seed, the second from a late harvest, we lost half of both our crops. This overset all my wisdom. . . . I now began to be known in the neighbourhood as a maker of rhymes. The first of my poetic offspring that saw the light '—he means by circulation in MS.—' was a burlesque lamentation on a quarrel '—*tulyie* is the word in the British Museum holograph—' between two reverend Calvinists, both of them dramatis personæ in my *Holy Fair*. . . . With a certain side of both clergy and laity it met with a roar of applause. *Holy Willie's Prayer* next made its appearance.' During the period marked by these satirical assaults upon the local clergy and ' orthodox ' church-goers, Burns was an enthusiastic student of native poets— Ramsay, and especially, Fergusson. He speaks of Fergusson's Scottish Poems as inspiring him with emulating vigour. Now, too, occurred his *liaison* with Jean Armour, the daughter of a master-mason in Mauchline. ' It was agreed between them,' says Gilbert, ' that they should make a legal acknowledgment of an irregular and private marriage, that he should go to Jamaica to push his fortune, and that she should remain with her father till [he had] the means of supporting a family.' The Armours, represented by the father, would, however, hear of no such agreement. They repelled his advances, and repudiated his offers of reparation. They cancelled his engagement by cutting his name from the written acknowledgment of marriage which he had presented to Jean. ' When he told me,' wrote Burns, referring to this incident, ' that the names were cut out of the paper, my heart died within me, and he cut my veins with

b

the news.'   Strange to say, it was at this very time that he
formed a romantic attachment with Mary Campbell—the
'Highland Mary' of his most impassioned love-lyric.   Particular reference is made to this attachment in the Notes.
Meanwhile, having withdrawn his name from the farm-lease,
without altogether withdrawing his services from the farm,
he set about the preparation of a volume of poetry, and
issued his 'Proposals for Publishing.'   His literary activity
at this time was astonishing in respect of both quantity and
quality of work.   Between the 1st of January and the appearance of the volume in the end of July, 1786, he was
producing upon an average five pieces per week, and the
productions included *The Twa Dogs, The Vision, Address to
the Unco Guid, The Holy Fair, To a Mountain Daisy*, and
A Dream.   The impetus which culminated in such astonishing activity had been gathering for some time.   In the two
last months of the preceding year he composed twelve pieces,
one of which—the cantata of *The Jolly Beggars*—contained
eight songs, while amongst the others were *Halloween, To a
Mouse, The Cotter's Saturday Night, Address to the Deil*,
and *Scotch Drink*.   At the same time that his volume was
passing through the Kilmarnock press he was casting des-
perately about for some means of earning a less precarious
livelihood than farming could in his experience of it provide.
He thought enviously of an appointment in the Excise, but
at last he arranged with a Dr. Douglas, of Port Antonio,
Jamaica, to serve for a term of three years, as overseer of
the negro labourers on his plantation in that island, at a
salary of £30 per annum.   He was to make the voyage on
board the *Nancy* (Captain Smith), advertised to sail from
the Clyde sometime in October.   His first intention, the
dictate of necessity, was to work his passage out; but the
unexpected pecuniary success of his book enabled him to
purchase a steerage passage.   The whole gain from the
edition [1]—which consisted of 574 copies, price 3*s.* each—

---

[1] Exhausted within a month from the date of issue.

amounted to £20. His fare to Jamaica was nine guineas. All his countrymen know how near Scotland came to losing him. His chest was already on the way to Greenock, and he himself, skulking in the country to escape a legal process which he believed the Armours had raised solely from revenge and covetousness, and which therefore he was determined to baffle, was on the point of setting out to join the *Nancy*, having already taken poetical farewell of his native Ayrshire, when an Edinburgh letter was put into his hand just in time to save him from the degradation of slave-driving, and from the obscurity of exile. This was Dr. Blacklock's letter to Burns's friend, the Rev. George Lawrie, minister of Loudon. It advised the poet to appeal to an Edinburgh audience with a new edition of his poems. The vision of fame, influential friends, and a possible independency by the pen, which this historical letter not unreasonably conjured up in the mind of the poet, was too powerfully attractive to be resisted. He was 'sheltering in the honoured shade' of Edinburgh in the ensuing November, with all thoughts of emigration completely, if only temporarily, swept like a hideous nightmare from his mind. Henry Mackenzie, the author of *The Man of Feeling*—sometimes styled the Scottish Addison—was the first to hail Burns from the arena of letters as a genius of no ordinary rank. He introduced him to the reading public, ten days after his arrival in Edinburgh, by an appreciative criticism of his *Poems* in No. 97 of *The Lounger*.

Burns responded to the heartiness with which Edinburgh received him by a brilliant appearance in both fashionable and literary circles. 'The town is at present all agog with the ploughman poet,' wrote Mrs. Cockburn, then a shrewd old lady, now best known as the authoress of the popular version of *The Flowers of the Forest*: '[he] receives adulation with native dignity, and is the very figure of his profession, strong but coarse ; yet he has a most enthusiastic heart of love. He has seen Duchess Gordon and all the gay world.'

The Duchess of Gordon was then queen of the gay world in the northern capital: she was even more charmed with his conversation than with his poetry. Professor Dugald Stewart was perhaps the best—he was the least assuming—representative of wisdom and learning : 'From his conversation,' he writes of Burns, 'I should have pronounced him to be fitted to excel in whatever walk of ambition he had chosen to exert his abilities.' The Professor was no less commendatory of the poet's manners : 'The attentions he received during his stay in town from all ranks and descriptions of persons were such as would have turned any head but his own. . . . He retained the same simplicity of manner and appearance . . . nor did he seem to feel any additional self-importance from the number and rank of his new acquaintance.' Among observant eyes in Edinburgh fixed with curiosity on the newcomer were those of Walter Scott, then a lad of fifteen. His description of the face and figure of Burns is an important supplement to Nasmyth's well-known portrait. 'His person,' writes Scott, 'was strong and robust . . . His features are represented in Mr. Nasmyth's picture, but to me it conveys the idea that they are diminished as if seen in perspective. I think his countenance was more massive than it looks in any of the portraits. . . There was a strong expression of sense and shrewdness in all his lineaments ; the eye alone, I think, indicated the poetical character and temperament. It was large, and of a dark cast, which glowed (I say literally *glowed*) when he spoke with feeling or interest. I never saw such another eye in a human head, though I have seen the most distinguished men of my time.' Nasmyth's picture of the poet represents him as he appeared in what Lockhart has called 'the first heyday of his reputation.' He is dressed in a blue coat, buff waistcoat with broad blue stripes, tight buckskin breeches, and top-boots.

Among his other friends Burns was fortunate in finding a patron, at once so generous and so honourable, in the Earl of Glencairn. To this nobleman he owed the introduction to

Creech the bookseller, which made the new edition of his *Poems* the great pecuniary success it proved to be. This edition, known as the First Edinburgh Edition, appeared about the middle of April, 1787, and was twice re-printed the same year. For the first impression there were no fewer than fifteen hundred subscribers, many of whom took several copies, and paid more than the selling price. With part of the money he now proceeded to gratify a desire he had for some time been ardently cherishing. ' I have no dearer aim,' he wrote, on the 22nd March, 1787, . . . 'than to make leisurely pilgrimages through Caledonia, to sit on the fields of her battles, to wander on the romantic banks of her rivers, and to muse by the stately towers or venerable ruins once the honoured abode of her heroes.' He set out on a Border tour in May ; in the end of June he began a tour in the West Highlands ; and on the 25th of August he started on his great tour in the North Highlands. Returning to Edinburgh about the middle of September, he set off a fortnight later for a final tour among the Ochils and neighbourhood, and was back for the winter on the 20th October. It was in December of the same year that he became entangled with Clarinda. This was his romantic name for Mrs. McLehose, a lady of about his own age, of independent means, and living separate from a heart-less husband. A remarkable series of some sixty love-letters passed between the pair in the short space of three months. In March, 1788, the poet broke away from Edin-burgh and the fascinations of Clarinda—whom, however, he never ceased to respect—and shortly afterwards was legally married to Jean Armour. The Church at Mauchline con-firmed the marriage in the following August, and in Decem-ber the married pair began their home life together at Ellisland, a small farm on the estate of Dalswinton, some five or six miles up the Nith from Dumfries. This, the last of the farms with which he had practical acquaintance, he leased from Patrick Millar, Esquire, brother of the Lord

Justice Clerk, at a rent of £50 for each of the first three years, and £70 per annum thereafter. The lease was executed in March, the month in which he at last came to a pecuniary settlement with his tardy publisher. There is no doubt of Creech's blameworthiness in keeping Burns hanging so long idly in Edinburgh. Gilbert Burns shared to the extent of £180 in the profits of the Edinburgh Edition; with the remainder, some £300, the poet set up house and stocked his farm.

The Ellisland period stretches over three and a half years. The first part of this short period was perhaps the happiest time in the poet's life. He was full of literary hopes and wise resolutions in a home of his own. He had a generous landlord, and a prettily-situated farm. His neighbours were kindly, when he knew them better; at first indeed they were rather puzzled with the phenomenon of a live poet in their midst; 'they look upon me,' he wrote, half-amused and half-annoyed, 'as if I were a hippopotamus come to Nithside.' Above all, his inspiration and power of utterance were unimpaired. Some excellent poetical work was done at Ellisland, notably *To Mary in Heaven* in 1789, and *Tam o' Shanter* in 1790. The farm, however, proved to be rather barren, and its hold upon his regular industry was greatly weakened by the long-looked-for appointment in the Excise. He received his commission some time in November, 1789. The salary was only £50, but it was certain, and there was hope of a Supervisorship, worth £200 a-year. The duties involved a great deal of fatiguing riding, and frequent absences from his farm. They led him also into the practice of an indiscriminate conviviality, to which he was previously-from a disposition genuinely social—only too strongly inclined. At last he threw up his farm, at the Martinmas term of 1791, and came to live in a small house of three rooms, forming part of a building in the Wee Vennel, in the town of Dumfries. His excise duties here were confined to the port, and kept him from the wholesome and inspiring contact with nature which he had so largely enjoyed in the landward district at Ellisland. His income was never more than £70. The second year of his residence in Dumfries is memorable for his imprudent expressions of sympathy with the French Revolution, then in progress, and for the happy commencement of his correspondence with George Thomson. His imprudence was severely noticed by the Board of Excise ; he was reprimanded, after inquiry into his conduct, and cautioned in such a way that he must have felt that promotion in his new profession was not likely to come for a long time. It was not alone his employers whom he displeased by his unguarded sayings on matters political. Many of his former friends and acquaintances both in Dumfries and elsewhere were, or affected to be, scandalized by his conduct. He became reckless, almost desperate ; against his better knowledge, fell into dissipated habits ; and at last so enfeebled his constitution that it was unable to throw off a cold he had contracted during the New Year festivities of 1796. He had previously removed from the Wee Vennel to the Mill Vennel, to a ' self-contained ' house of two storeys. It was in this house he died on the 21st of July, 1796, after a vain endeavour to derive benefit from sea-bathing by a fortnight's residence at Brow-on-Solway. He had never ceased writing poetry, and even during the later stages of his fatal illness he produced some of his tenderest lyrics. Perhaps the most notable of his compositions in the town of Dumfries were *Scots wha hae*, 1793, and *A Man's a Man for a' That*, 1795. In 1792-3 he had superintended the issue of the Second Edinburgh Edition of his Poems, published in two volumes, in February, by Creech.

CHRONOLOGY TO ELUCIDATE THE HISTORY OF BURNS.

—◆—

1748. William Burnes leaves Clochnahill, Kincardineshire.
1749. Employed in the work of laying out the Meadows, Edinburgh.
1750. Gardener to the Laird of Fairly in Dundonald Parish, Ayrshire.
1752. Gardener to Mr. Crawford, of Doonside, in the same county.
1757. Settles on a croft of seven acres in Alloway Parish. Marries Agnes Brown, from Maybole, in December.
1759. Birth of ROBERT BURNS, on the 25th January.
1765. Engagement of John Murdoch, at Whitsunday.
1766. The Burnes family remove to Mount Oliphant, in May.
1767. Murdoch's connexion with Alloway, as a teacher, ceases, probably in November.
1772. Robert attends Dalrymple Parish School for a quarter in summer.
1773. Boarded for about three weeks with Murdoch, now Rector of Ayr Academy. Revises English grammar, and begins to read French. Composes his first poem, a song—*Handsome Nell.*
1774. Robert the principal labourer on his father's farm.
1775. A few months at Kirkoswald, learning land-surveying. Attends a dancing-school, contrary to his father's wishes.
1777. The family remove from Mount Oliphant to the farm of Lochlie in Tarbolton Parish, at Whitsunday.
1780. Robert founds a Social Club at Tarbolton.

1781. He proposes marriage to Alison Begbie, and is rejected. Joins a Masonic Lodge in July. Shortly after, becomes a flax-dresser at Irvine, where he makes the acquaintance of Richard Brown.

1782. Back from Irvine, in January, to farm-work at Lochlie. Writing poetry.

1784. Death of his father, aged 62, in February. The family remove at Whitsunday from Lochlie to Mossgiel. Burns begins his satirical attacks on clerical hypocrisy.

1785. Acquaintance with Jean Armour. Composition of *Halloween*, *Cotter's Saturday Night*, *The Jolly Beggars*, &c. A year of great literary productivity.

1786. Disowned by the Armours (some time in spring). Episode of 'Highland Mary.' First edition of his *Poems* published at Kilmarnock, on 31st July. Prepares for emigration to Jamaica. Dr. Blacklock's letter of invitation, or advice. Burns enters Edinburgh, evening of 28th November. His *Poems* reviewed by Henry Mackenzie in *The Lounger* of 9th December. Is received into the world of rank and fashion, and welcomed by the literati. [This was his most productive year. To it belong *The Twa Dogs*, *The Holy Fair*, *The Brigs of Ayr*, &c.]

1787. First Edinburgh Edition of his *Poems* published, on 18th April, and the book re-printed twice in the same year. Tour in the Border Counties, begun early in May. Tour in the West Highlands, begun end of June. His great tour in the North Highlands, from 25th August to 16th September. Excursion to the Ochils in the end of Autumn. The 'Clarinda' episode, beginning on 6th December of this year, and ending rather abruptly in March of the next.

1788. Married to Jean Armour, in May. Enters in May upon a lease of Ellisland in Dumfriesshire. His marriage confirmed by the Church at Mauchline in August. A home at last established at Ellisland in December, by the arrival of his wife and child.

1789. Enters on duty as an officer of Excise in October.

1790. *Tam o' Shanter* written.

1791. Removes from Ellisland at Martinmas to the second storey of a house in the Wee Vennel (in Bank Street), in the town of Dumfries. His salary from the Excise, now his only source of income, about £50 a year,—never more than £70.

1792. His sympathy with the French Revolution, now in progress. Correspondence with George Thomson begins, in September. Order by the Board of Excise to inquire into Burns's political conduct, in December. Hope of promotion in the Excise put back, if not put out.

1793. Second Edinburgh Edition of his *Poems* published (2 vols.), in February. Removes from the flat in the Wee Vennel to a ' self-contained ' house of two storeys, and attics, in the Mill Vennel (now Burns Street), in May. *Scots wha hae* composed in this year.

1795. *A Man's a Man for a' That* written.

1796. Fatal illness. Tries sea-bathing at Brow-on-Solway, early in July. Returns home so weak as to be scarcely able to stand, on the 18th. Death on Thursday morning, the 21st. Burial at noon, Monday, the 25th, in St. Michael's Churchyard.

CONTENTS.

—♦—

SONGS.

POEMS.

Winter.

A DIRGE.

THE wintry west extends his blast,
 And hail and rain does blaw;
Or the stormy north sends driving forth
 The blinding sleet and snaw;
While, tumbling brown, the burn comes down, 5
 And roars frae bank to brae;
And bird and beast in covert rest,
 And pass the heartless day.

The sweeping blast, the sky o'ercast,
 The joyless winter-day   10
Let others fear,—to me more dear
 Than all the pride of May:
The tempest's howl, it soothes my soul,
 My griefs it seems to join;
The leafless trees my fancy please,   15
 Their fate resembles mine!

Thou Power Supreme, whose mighty scheme
 These woes of mine fulfil,
Here firm I rest—they must be best,
 Because they are Thy Will!   20
Then all I want (O do Thou grant
 This one request of mine!)
Since to enjoy Thou dost deny,
 Assist me to resign!

B

A Prayer in the Prospect of Death.

O THOU unknown Almighty Cause
    Of all my hope and fear!
In whose dread presence, ere an hour,
    Perhaps I must appear!

If I have wandered in those paths   5
    Of life I ought to shun—
As something loudly in my breast
    Remonstrates I have done—

Thou know'st that Thou hast formèd me
    With passions wild and strong;   10
And list'ning to their witching voice
    Has often led me wrong.

Where human weakness has come short,
    Or frailty stept aside,
Do Thou, All-Good!—for such Thou art—   15
    In shades of darkness hide.

Where with intention I have erred,
    No other plea I have
But—Thou art good; and Goodness still
    Delighteth to forgive.   20

Death and Dying Words of Poor Mailie.

AS Mailie, an' her lambs thegither,
  Was ae day nibblin on the tether,
Upon her cloot she coost a hitch,
An' owre she warsled in the ditch:
There, groanin, dying, she did lie,   5
When Hughoc he cam' doytin by.

Wi' glowrin een, an' lifted han's,
Poor Hughoc like a statue stan's;
He saw her days were near-hand ended,
But, wae 's my heart ! he could na mend it!   10
He gapèd wide, but naething spak.
At length poor Mailie silence brak.

'O thou, whase lamentable face
Appears to mourn my woefu' case !
My dying words attentive hear,   15
An' bear them to my Master dear.

'Tell him, if e'er again he keep
As muckle gear as buy a sheep,
Oh, bid him never tie them mair
Wi' wicked strings o' hemp or hair !   20
But ca' them out to park or hill,
An' let them wander at their will;
So may his flock increase, an' grow
To scores o' lambs an' packs o' woo' !

'Tell him, he was a master kin',   25
An' aye was guid to me an' mine;
An' now my dying charge I gie him,
My helpless lambs I trust them wi' him.

'Oh, bid him save their harmless lives
Frae dogs, an' tods, an' butchers' knives !   30
But gie them guid cow-milk their fill,
Till they be fit to fend themsel';
An' tent them duly e'en an' morn,
Wi' teats o' hay, an' rips o' corn.

'An' may they never learn the gates   35
Of ither vile, wanrestfu' pets—
To slink thro' slaps, an' reave, an' steal
At stacks o' pease, or stocks o' kail.

B 2

So may they, like their great forbears,
For monie a year come thro' the sheers :   40
So wives will gie them bits o' bread,
An' bairns greet for them when they're dead.

'My poor toop-lamb, my son an' heir,
Oh, bid him breed him up wi' care!
An' if he live to be a beast,   45
To pit some havins in his breast !

'An' neist, my yowie, silly thing,
Gude keep thee frae a tether string !
An' aye keep mind to moop an' mell
Wi' sheep o' credit like thysel' !   50

'And now, my bairns, wi' my last breath,
I lea'e my blessin' wi' you baith :
An' when you think upo' your mither,
Mind to be kind to ane anither.

'Now, honest Hughoc, dinna fail   55
To tell my master a' my tale ;
An' bid him burn this cursèd tether,
An', for thy pains, thou'se get my blether.'

This said, poor Mailie turned her head,
And closed her een amang the dead.   60

Poor Mailie's Elegy.

LAMENT in rhyme, lament in prose,
    Wi' saut tears tricklin down your nose ;
Our bardie's fate is at a close,
            Past a' remead ;
The last sad cape-stane o' his woe 's   5
            Poor Mailie 's dead !

It 's no the loss o' warl's gear,
That could sae bitter draw the tear,
Or mak our bardie, dowie, wear
    The mournin weed: 10
He 's lost a friend an neebor dear
    In Mailie dead.

Thro' a' the toun she trotted by him ;
A lang half-mile she could descry him ;
Wi' kindly bleat, when she did spy him, 15
    She ran wi' speed ;
A friend mair faithfu' ne'er came nigh him
    Than Mailie dead.

I wat she was a sheep o' sense,
An' could behave hersel' wi' mense ; 20
I 'll say 't, she never brak a fence
    Thro' thievish greed.
Our bardie, lanely, keeps the spence
    Sin' Mailie 's dead.

Or, if he wanders up the howe, 25
Her livin image in her yowe
Comes bleatin till him, owre the knowe,
    For bits o' bread ;
An' down the briny pearls rowe
    For Mailie dead. 30

She was nae get o' moorlan tips,
Wi' tauted ket, an' hairy hips ;
For her forbears were brought in ships
    Frae yont the Tweed :
A bonnier fleesh ne'er crossed the clips 35
    Than Mailie's—dead.

Wae worth the man wha first did shape
That vile wanchancie thing—a rape!
It mak's guid fellows girn an' gape,
                    Wi' chokin' dread;   40
An' Robin's bonnet wave wi' crape
                    For Mailie dead.

Oh, a' ye bards on bonnie Doon,
An' wha on Ayr your chanters tune,
Come, join the melancholious croon   45
                    O' Robin's reed !
His heart will never get aboon
                    His Mailie dead!

Man was made to Mourn.

A DIRGE.

WHEN chill November's surly blast
        Made fields and forests bare,
One evening, as I wandered forth
        Along the banks of Ayr,
I spied a man, whose agèd step   5
        Seemed weary, worn with care;
His face was furrowed o'er with years,
        And hoary was his hair.

'Young stranger, whither wand'rest thou?'
        Began the reverend sage;   10
'Does thirst of wealth thy step constrain,
        Or youthful pleasure's rage?
Or haply, pressed with cares and woes,
        Too soon thou hast began
To wander forth, with me to mourn   15
        The miseries of man!

'The sun that overhangs yon moors,
  Out-spreading far and wide,
Where hundreds labour to support
  A haughty lordling's pride;—   20
I've seen yon weary winter-sun
  Twice forty times return;
And every time has added proofs
  That man was made to mourn.

'O man! while in thy early years,   25
  How prodigal of time!
Mis-spending all thy precious hours,
  Thy glorious youthful prime!
Alternate follies take the sway,
  Licentious passions burn;   30
Which tenfold force gives Nature's law,
  That man was made to mourn.

'Look not alone on youthful prime,
  Or manhood's active might;
Man then is useful to his kind,   35
  Supported in his right:
But see him on the edge of life,
  With cares and sorrows worn;
Then age and want—oh, ill-matched pair!—
  Shew man was made to mourn.   40

'A few seem favourites of fate,
  In pleasure's lap caress'd;
Yet think not all the rich and great
  Are likewise truly blest.
But oh! what crowds in every land,   45
  All wretched and forlorn,
Through weary life this lesson learn,
  That man was made to mourn.

'Many and sharp the num'rous ills
  Inwoven with our frame;   50
More pointed still we make ourselves—
  Regret, remorse, and shame!
And man, whose heaven-erected face
  The smiles of love adorn,—
Man's inhumanity to man   55
  Makes countless thousands mourn!

'See yonder poor, o'erlaboured wight,
  So abject, mean, and vile,
Who begs a brother of the earth
  To give him leave to toil;   60
And see his lordly fellow-worm
  The poor petition spurn,
Unmindful tho' a weeping wife
  And helpless offspring mourn.

'If I'm designed yon lordling's slave—   65
  By Nature's law designed—
Why was an independent wish
  E'er planted in my mind?
If not, why am I subject to
  His cruelty or scorn?   70
Or why has man the will and power
  To make his fellow mourn?

'Yet let not this too much, my son,
  Disturb thy youthful breast;
This partial view of humankind   75
  Is surely not the last!
The poor, oppressèd, honest man,
  Had never, sure, been born,
Had there not been some recompense
  To comfort those that mourn.   80

' O Death ! the poor man's dearest friend,
The kindest and the best !
Welcome the hour my agèd limbs
Are laid with thee at rest !
The great, the wealthy fear thy blow,   85
From pomp and pleasure torn ;
But, oh ! a blest relief for those
That weary-laden mourn ! '

Epistle to Davie, a Brother Poet.

WHILE winds frae aff Ben Lomond blaw.
        An' bar the doors wi' drivin' snaw,
An' hing us owre the ingle,
I set me down to pass the time,
An' spin a verse or twa o' rhyme,   5
    In hamely westlin jingle.
While frosty winds blaw in the drift,
    Ben to the chimla lug,
I grudge a wee the great-folk's gift,
    That live sae bien an' snug :   10
        I tent less, and want less,
            Their roomy fire-side :
        But hanker and canker
            To see their cursèd pride.

It 's hardly in a body's pow'r   15
To keep, at times, frae being sour,
    To see how things are shar'd ;
How best o' chiels are whyles in want,
While coofs on countless thousands rant,
    And ken na how to wair't;   20

But Davie, lad, ne'er fash your head,
　　Tho' we hae little gear;
We're fit to win our daily bread,
　　As lang's we're hale and fier:
　　　　Mair spier na, nor fear na;　　　25
　　　　Auld age ne'er mind a feg;
　　　　The last o''t, the warst o''t,
　　　　Is only but to beg.

To lye in kilns and barns at e'en,
When banes are craz'd, and bluid is thin,　　30
　　Is, doubtless, great distress;
Yet then content could make us blest;
E'en then sometimes we'd snatch a taste
　　Of truest happiness.
The honest heart that's free frae a'　　35
　　Intended fraud or guile,
However fortune kick the ba',
　　Has aye some cause to smile,
　　　　An' mind still you'll find still
　　　　A comfort this nae sma';　　　40
　　　　Nae mair then we'll care then,
　　　　Nae farther we can fa'.

What tho', like commoners of air,
We wander out, we know not where,
　　But either house or hall?　　　45
Yet nature's charms, the hills and woods,
The sweeping vales, an' foaming floods,
　　Are free alike to all.
In days when daisies deck the ground,
　　And blackbirds whistle clear,　　　50
With honest joy our hearts will bound
　　To see the coming year:

On braes when we please, then,
    We 'll sit an' sowth a tune;
Sync rhyme till 't, we 'll time till 't,   55
    And sing 't when we hae done.

It 's no in titles nor in rank;
It 's no in wealth like Lon'on bank,
    To purchase peace and rest;
It 's no in makin' muckle mair: 60
It 's no in books; it 's no in lear,
    To make us truly blest:
If happiness hae not her seat
    An' centre in the breast,
We may be wise, or rich, or great,   65
    But never can be blest;
        Nae treasures, nor pleasures,
            Could make us happy lang;
        The heart aye 's the part aye,
            That makes us right or wrang.   70

Think ye, that sic as you and I,
Wha drudge an' drive thro' wet an' dry,
    Wi' never-ceasing toil;
Think ye, are we less blest than they,
Wha scarcely tent us in their way,   75
    As hardly worth their while?
Alas! how oft in haughty mood,
    God's creatures they oppress!
Or else, neglecting a' that 's good,
    They riot in excess!   80
        Baith careless and fearless
            Of either heaven or hell!
        Esteeming and deeming
            It a' an idle tale!

Then let us cheerfu' acquiesce ;   85
Nor make our scanty pleasures less,
　By pining at our state ;
And, even should misfortunes come—
I, here wha sit, hae met wi' some,
　An 's thankfu' for them yet.   90
They gie the wit of age to youth ;
　They let us ken oursel' ;
They make us see the naked truth,
　The real guid and ill.
　　　Tho' losses an' crosses   95
　　　Be lessons right severe,
　　　There 's wit there, ye 'll get there,
　　　Ye 'll find nae other where.

But tent me, Davie, ace o' hearts !
(To say aught less wad wrang the cartes,   100
　And flattery I detest)
This life has joys for you and I ;
An' joys that riches ne'er could buy ;
　An' joys the very best.
There 's a' the pleasures o' the heart,   105
　The lover an' the frien' ;
Ye hae your Meg, your dearest part,
　And I my darling Jean !
　　　It warms me, it charms me,
　　　To mention but her name ;   110
　　　It heats me, it beets me,
　　　An sets me a' on flame !

O all ye Powers who rule above !
O Thou whose very self art love !
　Thou know'st my words sincere !   115

The life-blood streaming thro' my heart,
Or my more dear immortal part,
  Is not more fondly dear!
When heart-corroding care and grief
  Deprive my soul of rest,   120
Her dear idea brings relief
  And solace to my breast.
      Thou Being, All-seeing,
        Oh, hear my fervent prayer!
      Still take her, and make her   125
        Thy most peculiar care!

All hail, ye tender feelings dear!
The smile of love, the friendly tear,
  The sympathetic glow!
Long since this world's thorny ways   130
Had number'd out my weary days
  Had it not been for you!
Fate still has blest me with a friend
  In every care and ill;
And oft a more endearing band,   135
  A tie more tender still.
      It lightens, it brightens
        The tenebrific scene,
      To meet with, and greet with
        My Davie or my Jean.   140

O how that name inspires my style!
The words come skelpin, rank and file,
  Amaist before I ken!
The ready measure rins as fine
As Phœbus and the famous Nine   145
  Were glowrin owre my pen.

My spav'et Pegasus will limp,
  Till ance he's fairly het;
And then he'll hilch, and stilt, and jimp,
  And rin an unco fit;   150
      But lest then the beast then
      Should rue this hasty ride,
      I'll light now, and dight now
      His sweaty wizen'd hide.

Death and Doctor Hornbook.

SOME books are lies frae end to end,
    And some great lies were never penn'd:
Ev'n ministers, they hae been kenn'd,
      In holy rapture,
A rousing whid at times to vend,   5
      And nail 't wi' Scripture.

But this that I am gaun to tell,
Which lately on a night befell,
Is just as true's the Deil's in hell
      Or Dublin city: 10
That e'er he nearer comes oursel'
      'S a muckle pity.

The clachan yill had made me canty,
I was na fou, but just had plenty;
I stacher'd whyles, but yet took tent aye   15
      To free the ditches;
An' hillocks, stanes, an' bushes, kenn'd aye
      Frae ghaists an' witches.

The rising moon began to glow'r
The distant Cumnock hills out-owre :   20
To count her horns, wi' a' my pow'r,
    I set mysel' ;
But whether she had three or four,
    I could na tell.

I was come round about the hill,   25
An' todlin' down on Willie's mill,
Setting my staff wi' a' my skill
    To keep me sicker;
Tho' leeward whyles, against my will,
    I took a bicker.   30

I there wi' Something did forgather,
That pat me in an eerie swither;
An awfu' scythe, out-owre ae shouther,
    Clear-dangling, hang;
A three-tae'd leister on the ither   35
    Lay, large an' lang.

Its stature seem'd lang Scotch ells twa,
The queerest shape that e'er I saw,
For fient a wame it had ava;
    And then its shanks,   40
They were as thin, as sharp an' sma'
    As cheeks o' branks.

'Guid-e'en,' quo' I; 'Friend ! hae ye been mawin'
When ither folk are busy sawin'?'
It seem'd to mak' a kind o' stan',   45
    But naething spak';
At length says I, 'Friend, wh'are ye gaun?
    Will ye go back?'

It spak' right howe,—'My name is Death,
But be na fley'd.' Quoth I, 'Guid faith,   50
Ye're maybe come to stap my breath ;
          But tent me, billie ;
I red ye weel, tak' care o' skaith,—
          See, there's a gully !'

'Guidman,' quo' he, 'put up your whittle ;   55
I'm no design'd to try its mettle ;
But if I did, I wad be kittle
          To be mislear'd ;
I wad na mind it, no' that spittle
          Out-owre my beard.'   60

'Weel, weel !' says I, 'a bargain be't ;
Come, gie's your hand, an' sae we're gree't :
We'll ease our shanks an' tak' a seat—
          Come, gie's your news ;
This while ye hae been mony a gate,   65
          At mony a house.'

'Ay, ay !' quo' he, an' shook his head,
'It's e'en a lang, lang time indeed
Sin' I began to nick the thread,
          An' choke the breath :   70
Folk maun do something for their bread,
          An' sae maun Death.

'Sax thousand years are near-hand fled
Sin' I was to the butching bred,
An' mony a scheme in vain's been laid,   75
          To stap or scar' me ;
Till ane Hornbook's ta'en up the trade,
          An' faith ! he'll waur me.

'Ye ken Jock Hornbook i' the clachan—
Deil mak' his king's-hood in a spleuchan!   80
He 's grown sae weel acquaint wi' Buchan
    An' ither chaps,
The weans haud out their fingers laughin'
    And pouk my hips.

' See, here 's a scythe, and there 's a dart,   85
They ha'e pierced mony a gallant heart;
But Doctor Hornbook, wi' his art
    And cursèd skill,
Has made them baith they 'll hardly scart,
    An' far less kill.   90

''Twas but yestreen, nae farther gane,
I threw a noble throw at ane;
Wi' less, I 'm sure, I 've hundreds slain;
    But deil-ma-care,
It just play'd dirl on the bane,   95
    But did nae mair.

' Hornbook was by, wi' ready art,
And had sae fortify'd the part,
That when I lookèd to my dart,
    It was sae blunt,   100
Fient haet o't wad ha'e pierced the heart
    Of a kail-runt.

' I drew my scythe in sic a fury,
I nearhand cowpit wi' my hurry,
But yet the bauld Apothecary   105
    Withstood the shock;
I might as weel ha'e try'd a quarry
    O' hard whin-rock.

C

'Ev'n them he canna get attended,
Altho' their face he ne'er had kenn'd it,   110
Just spit in a kail-blade, and send it;
   As soon 's he smells 't,
Baith their disease, and what will mend it,
   At once he tells 't.

'And then a' doctor's saws an' whittles,   115
Of a' dimensions, shapes, an' mettles,
A' kinds o' boxes, mugs, an' bottles,
   He 's sure to hae ;
Their Latin names as fast he rattles
   As A B C.   120

'Calces o' fossils, earths, and trees ;
True sal-marinum o' the seas ;
The farina of beans and pease,—
   He has 't in plenty;
Aqúa-fontis, what you please,   125
   He can content ye.'

'Wae 's me for Johnnie Ged's Hole now,'
Quoth I, 'if that thae news be true !
His braw calf-ward whare gowans grew,
   Sae white and bonnie—   130
Nae doubt they'll rive it wi' the plew;
   They'll ruin Johnnie !'

The creature grain'd an eldritch laugh,
And says, 'Ye needna yoke the pleugh,
Kirk-yards will soon be till'd eneugh,   135
   Tak' ye nae fear:
They 'll a' be trench'd wi' mony a sheugh
   In twa-three year.

'Whare I kill'd ane, a fair strae death,
By loss o' blood or want of breath,   140
This night I'm free to tak' my aith
          That Hornbook's skill
Has clad a score i' their last claith,
          By drap an' pill.

'An honest wabster to his trade,   145
Whase wife's twa nieves were scarce weel-bred,
Gat tippence-worth to mend her head
          When it was sair;
The wife slade cannie to her bed,
          But ne'er spak' mair.   150

'A countra laird had ta'en the batts,
Or some curmurring in his guts,
His only son for Hornbook sets,
          An' pays him well;
The lad, for twa guid gimmer pets,   155
          Was laird himsel'.

'That's just a swatch o' Hornbook's way;
Thus goes he on from day to day,
Thus does he poison, kill, an' slay,
          An's weel paid for't;   160
Yet stops me o' my lawfu' prey
          Wi' his curst dirt.

'But hark! I'll tell you of a plot,
Though dinna ye be speakin' o' 't;
I'll nail the self-conceited sot,   165
          As dead's a herrin';
Neist time we meet, I'll wad a groat,
          He gets his fairin'!'

But just as he began to tell,
The auld kirk-hammer strak the bell   170
Some wee short hour ayont the twal,
      Which rais'd us baith :
I took the way that pleas'd mysel',
      And sae did Death.

Epistle to John Lapraik.

WHILE briers an' woodbines budding green,
    An' paitricks scraichin loud at e'en,
An' morning poussie, whiddin seen,
      Inspire my muse,
This freedom in an unknown frien'   5
      I pray excuse.

On Fasten-e'en we had a rockin',
To ca' the crack and weave our stockin';
And there was muckle fun an' jokin',
      Ye need na doubt ;   10
At length we had a hearty yokin'
      At sang about.

There was ae sang amang the rest,
Aboon them a' it pleas'd me best,
That some kind husband had addrest   15
      To some sweet wife :
It thirl'd the heart-strings thro' the breast,
      A' to the life.

I 've scarce heard ought describe 't sae weel,
What gen'rous, manly bosoms feel ;   20
Thought I, 'Can this be Pope, or Steele,
      Or Beattie's wark ? '
They tauld me 'twas an odd kind chiel
      About Muirkirk.

It pat me fidgin fain to hear't,   25
And sae about him there I spier't;
Then a' that kent him round declared
            He had ingine;
That nane excell'd it, few came near't,
            It was sae fine;   30

That set him to a pint of ale,
An' either douce or merry tale,
Or rhymes an' sangs he'd made himsel',
            Or witty catches,—
'Tween Inverness and Teviotdale   35
            He had few matches.

Then up I gat, an' swoor an aith,
Tho' I should pawn my pleugh an' graith,
Or die a cadger pownie's death
            At some dyke-back,   40
A pint an' gill I'd gi'e them baith
            To hear your crack.

But, first an' foremost, I should tell,
Amaist as soon as I could spell,
I to the crambo-jingle fell,   45
            Though rude an' rough;
Yet crooning to a body's sel'
            Does weel eneugh.

I am nae poet, in a sense,
But just a rhymer like by chance,   50
An' hae to learning nae pretence,
            Yet what the matter?
Whene'er my Muse does on me glance,
            I jingle at her.

Your critic-folk may cock their nose,   55
And say, 'How can you e'er propose,
You wha ken hardly verse frae prose,
            To mak' a sang?'
But, by your leave, my learnèd foes,
            Ye 're maybe wrang.   60

What 's a' your jargon o' your schools,
Your Latin names for horns an' stools?
If honest Nature made you fools,
            What sairs your grammars?
Ye 'd better ta'en up spades and shools,   65
            Or knappin-hammers.

A set o' dull conceited hashes
Confuse their brains in college classes!
They gang in stirks, and come out asses,
            Plain truth to speak;   70
An' syne they think to climb Parnassus
            By dint o' Greek!

Gie me ae spark o' nature's fire,—
That 's a' the learning I desire;
Then tho' I drudge through dub an' mire   75
            At pleugh or cart,
My muse, though hamely in attire,
            May touch the heart.

Oh for a spunk o' Allan's glee,
Or Fergusson's, the bauld an' slee,   80
Or bright Lapraik's, my friend to be,
            If I can hit it!
That would be lear eneugh for me,
            If I could get it.

Now, sir, if ye hae friends enow,   85
Tho' real friends I b'lieve are few,
Yet, if your catalogue be fu',
    I 'se no insist;
But gif ye want ae friend that 's true,
    I 'm on your list.   90

I winna blaw about mysel';
As ill I like my fau'ts to tell ;
But friends, an' folk that wish me well,
    They sometimes roose me ;
Though I maun own, as monie still   95
    As far abuse me.

But Mauchline race, or Mauchline fair,
I should be proud to meet you there;
We 'se gie ae night's discharge to care
    If we forgather,   100
An' hae a swap o' rhymin' ware
    Wi' ane anither.

The four-gill chap, we 'se gar him clatter,
An' kirsen him wi' reekin' water ;
Syne we 'll sit down an' tak' our whitter,   105
    To cheer our heart;
An' faith, we 'se be acquainted better
    Before we part.

Awa ye selfish warly race,
Wha think that havins, sense, an' grace,   110
Ev'n love an' friendship, should give place
    To catch-the-plack !
I dinna like to see your face,
    Nor hear your crack.

But ye whom social pleasure charms,   115
Whose hearts the tide of kindness warms,
Who hold your being on the terms,
            'Each aid the others,'
Come to my bowl, come to my arms,
            My friends, my brothers !   120

But to conclude my lang epistle,
As my auld pen's worn to the gristle;
Twa lines frae you wad gar me fissle,
            Who am, most fervent,
While I can either sing or whistle,   125
            Your friend and servant.

Second Epistle to John Lapraik.

WHILE new-ca'd kye rowte at the stake,
    An' pownies reek in pleugh or braik,
This hour on e'enin's edge I take,
            To own I'm debtor
To honest-hearted auld Lapraik,   5
            For his kind letter.

Forjesket sair, with weary legs,
Rattlin' the corn out-owre the rigs,
Or dealing thro' amang the naigs
            Their ten hours' bite,   10
My awkwart Muse sair pleads and begs
            I wouldna write.

The tapetless ramfeezl'd hizzie,
She's saft at best, an' something lazy,
Quo' she, 'Ye ken, we've been sae busy   15
            This month an' mair,
That trowth my head is grown right dizzie,
            An' something sair.'

Her dowff excuses pat me mad ;
' Conscience !' says I, 'ye thowless jad !   20
I 'll write, an' that a hearty blaud,
          This vera night ;
So dinna ye affront your trade,
          But rhyme it right.

'Shall bauld Lapraik, the king o' hearts,   25
Tho' mankind were a pack o' cartes,
Roose you sae weel for your deserts,
          In terms sae friendly,
Yet ye 'll neglect to shaw your parts,
          An' thank him kindly ?'   30

Sae I gat paper in a blink,
An' down gaed stumpie in the ink :
Quoth I, ' Before I sleep a wink,
          I vow I 'll close it ;
An' if ye winna mak' it clink,   35
          By Jove I 'll prose it !'

Sae I 've begun to scrawl—but whether
In rhyme or prose, or baith thegither,
Or some hotch-potch that 's rightly neither,
          Let time mak' proof :   40
But I shall scribble down some blether
          Just clean aff-loof.

My worthy friend, ne'er grudge an' carp,
Tho' fortune use you hard an' sharp ;
Come, kittle up your moorland harp   45
          Wi' gleesome heart ;
Ne'er mind how Fortune waft an' warp :
          She 's but a flirt !

She's gi'en me monie a jirt an' fleg,
Sin' I could striddle owre a rig;   50
But, by the Lord, tho' I should beg
            Wi' lyart pow,
I'll laugh, an' sing, an' shake my leg,
            As lang's I dow!

Now comes the sax-an'-twentieth simmer   55
I've seen the bud upo' the timmer,
Still persecuted by the limmer
            Frae year to year;
But yet, despite the kittle kimmer,
            I, Rob, am here.   60

Do ye envy the city gent,
Behint a kist to lie and sklent,
Or purse-proud, big wi' cent. per cent.
            An' muckle wame,
In some bit brugh to represent   65
            A bailie's name?

Or is't the paughty, feudal thane,
Wi' ruffl'd sark an' glancing cane,
Wha thinks himsel' nae sheep-shank bane,
            But lordly stalks,   70
While caps and bonnets aff are ta'en,
            As by he walks?

O Thou wha gies us each guid gift!
Gie me o' wit an' sense a lift,
Then turn me, if Thou please, adrift   75
            Thro' Scotland wide;
Wi' cits nor lairds I wadna shift,
            In a' their pride!

Were this the charter of our state,
'On pain o' hell be rich an' great,'   80
Damnation then would be our fate,
　　　　Beyond remead ;
But, thanks to heaven, that's no the gate
　　　　We learn our creed.

For thus the royal mandate ran,   85
When first the human race began,—
'The social, friendly, honest man,
　　　　Whate'er he be,
'Tis he fulfils great Nature's plan,
　　　　An' none but he.'   90

O mandate glorious and divine !
The ragged followers of the Nine,
Poor thoughtless devils ! yet may shine
　　　　In glorious light,
While sordid sons of Mammon's line   95
　　　　Are dark as night.

Tho' here they scrape, an' squeeze, an' growl,
Their worthless nievefu' of a soul
May in some future carcase howl,
　　　　The forest's fright ;   100
Or in some day-detesting owl
　　　　May shun the light.

Lapraik and Burness then may rise
To reach their native kindred skies,
And sing their pleasures, hopes, an' joys,   105
　　　　In some mild sphere,
Still closer knit in friendship's ties
　　　　Each passing year !

Epistle to William Simson.

I GAT your letter, winsome Willie;
   Wi' gratefu' heart I thank you brawlie;
Though, I maun say't, I wad be silly,
      And unco vain,
Should I believe, my coaxin' billie,   5
      Your flatterin' strain.

But I 'se believe ye kindly meant it:
I sud be laith to think ye hinted
Ironic satire, sidelins sklented
      On my poor musie;   10
Tho' in sic phrasin' terms ye 've penn'd it,
      I scarce excuse ye.

My senses wad be in a creel,
Should I but dare a hope to speel
Wi' Allan, or wi' Gilbertfiel',   15
      The braes o' fame;
Or Fergusson, the writer-chiel,
      A deathless name.

(O Fergusson ! thy glorious parts
Ill suited law's dry musty arts!   20
My curse upon your whunstane hearts,
      Ye Enbrugh gentry !
The tythe o' what ye waste at cartes
      Wad stow'd his pantry!)

Yet when a tale comes i' my head,   25
Or lasses gie my heart a screed,
As whyles they're like to be my dead,
      (Oh, sad disease !)
I kittle up my rustic reed;
      It gies me ease.   30

Auld Coila now may fidge fu' fain,
She's gotten poets o' her ain,
Chiels wha their chanters winna hain,
            But tune their lays,
Till echoes a' resound again   35
            Her weel-sung praise.

Nae poet thought her worth his while
To set her name in measured style;
She lay like some unkenn'd-of isle
            Beside New Hollan',   40
Or whare wild meeting oceans boil
            Besouth Magellan.

Ramsay an' famous Fergusson
Gied Forth an' Tay a lift aboon;
Yarrow an' Tweed to monie a tune   45
            Owre Scotland rings;
While Irwin, Lugar, Ayr, an' Doon,
            Naebody sings.

Th' Illissus, Tiber, Thames, an' Seine,
Glide sweet in monie a tunefu' line;   50
But, Willie, set your fit to mine,
            An' cock your crest;
We'll gar our streams and burnies shine
            Up wi' the best!

We'll sing auld Coila's plains an' fells,   55
Her moors red-brown wi' heather-bells,
Her banks an' braes, her dens an' dells,
            Whare glorious Wallace
Aft bure the gree, as story tells,
            Frae southron billies.   60

At Wallace' name what Scottish blood
But boils up in a spring-tide flood!
Oft have our fearless fathers strode
          By Wallace' side,
Still pressing onward, red-wat shod,   65
          Or glorious died.

Oh sweet are Coila's haughs an' woods,
When lintwhites chant amang the buds,
And jinkin hares, in amorous whids,
          Their loves enjoy,   70
While through the braes the cushat croods
          With wailfu' cry!

Ev'n winter bleak has charms to me,
When winds rave thro' the naked tree;
Or frosts on hills of Ochiltree   75
          Are hoary grey;
Or blinding drifts wild-furious flee,
          Dark'ning the day!

O Nature! a' thy shows an' forms
To feeling pensive hearts hae charms!   80
Whether the summer kindly warms
          Wi' life an' light,
Or winter howls in gusty storms
          The lang dark night!

The muse, nae poet ever fand her,   85
Till by himsel' he learn'd to wander
Adown some trottin burn's meander,
          ˙An' no think lang;
Oh sweet to stray an' pensive ponder
          A heart-felt sang!   90

The warly race may drudge an' drive,
Hog-shouther, jundie, stretch, an' strive;
Let me fair Nature's face descrive,
      And I, wi' pleasure,
Shall let the busy grumbling hive   95
      Bum owre their treasure.

Fareweel, my rhyme-composing brither!
We 've been owre lang unkenn'd to ither:
Now let us lay our heads thegither,
      In love fraternal: 100
May envy wallop in a tether,
      Black fiend infernal!

While Highlandmen hate tolls and taxes;
While moorlan' herds like guid fat braxies;
While terra firma on her axis   105
      Diurnal turns,
Count on a friend, in faith an' practice,
      In ROBERT BURNS.

Epistle to Rev. John McMath.

WHILE at the stook the shearers cow'r
    To shun the bitter blaudin' show'r,
Or in gulravage rinnin' scour,
      To pass the time,
To you I dedicate the hour   5
      In idle rhyme.

My musie, tir'd wi' mony a sonnet
On gown, an' ban', an' douce black bonnet,
Is grown right eerie now she 's done it,
      Lest they should blame her, 10
An' rouse their holy thunder on it,
      And anathem her.

I own 'twas rash, an' rather hardy,
That I, a simple country bardie,
Should meddle wi' a pack sae sturdy,   15
          Wha, if they ken me,
Can easy, wi' a single wordie,
          Lowse hell upon me.

But I gae mad at their grimaces,
Their sighin', cantin', grace-proud faces,   20
Their three-mile prayers, an' half-mile graces,
          Their raxin' conscience,
Whase greed, revenge, and pride disgraces
          Waur nor their nonsense.

There's Gawn, misca'd waur than a beast,   25
Wha has mair honour in his breast
Than mony scores as guid 's the priest
          Wha sae abus'd him :
An' may a bard no crack his jest
          What way they 've us'd him? 30

See him, the poor man's friend in need,
The gentleman in word an' deed,
An' shall his fame an' honour bleed
          By worthless skellums,
An' not a Muse erect her head   35
          To cowe the blellums?

O Pope, had I thy satire's darts,
To gie the rascals their deserts !
I 'd rip their rotten hollow hearts,
          An' tell aloud   40
Their jugglin' hocus-pocus arts
          To cheat the crowd.

God knows I 'm no the thing I should be,
Nor am I even the thing I could be,
But twenty times I rather would be   45
          An atheist clean,
Than under gospel colours hid be
          Just for a screen.

An honest man may like a glass,
An honest man may like a lass,   50
But mean revenge, an' malice fause
          He 'll still disdain,
An' then cry zeal for gospel laws,
          Like some we ken.

They take religion in their mouth;   55
They talk o' mercy, grace, an' truth,
For what?—to gie their malice skouth
          On some puir wight,
An' hunt him down, owre right an' ruth,
          To ruin streicht.   60

All hail, Religion! maid divine!
Pardon a muse sae mean as mine,
Who in her rough imperfect line
          Thus daurs to name thee;
To stigmatize false friends of thine   65
          Can ne'er defame thee.

Tho' blotch't an' foul wi' mony a stain,
An' far unworthy of thy train,
With trembling voice I tune my strain
          To join with those   70
Who boldly dare thy cause maintain
          In spite of foes,

D

In spite o' crowds, in spite o' mobs,
In spite o' undermining jobs,
In spite o' dark banditti stabs   75
   At worth an' merit,
By scoundrels, even wi' holy robes,
   But hellish spirit.

O Ayr! my dear, my native ground,
Within thy presbyterial bound   8o
A candid liberal band is found
   Of public teachers,
As men, as Christians too, renown'd,
   An' manly preachers.

Sir, in that circle you are nam'd;   85
Sir, in that circle you are fam'd;
An' some, by whom your doctrine's blam'd,
   (Which gies ye honour)
Even, sir, by them your heart's esteem'd,
   An' winning manner.   9o

Pardon this freedom I have ta'en,
An' if impertinent I 've been,
Impute it not, good sir, in ane
   Whase heart ne'er wrang'd ye,
But to his utmost would befriend   95
   Ought that belang'd ye.

Halloween.

UPON that night when fairies light
  On Cassilis downans dance,
Or owre the lays, in splendid blaze,
 On sprightly coursers prance;
Or for Colean the rout is ta'en,   5
 Beneath the moon's pale beams;

There up the cove to stray and rove,
  Amang the rocks and streams
      To sport that night :

Amang the bonnie winding banks   10
  Where Doon rins wimplin clear,
Where Bruce ance ruled the martial ranks,
  An' shook his Carrick spear ;
Some merry, friendly country-folks
  Together did convene,   15
To burn their nits, an' pou their stocks
  An' haud their Halloween
      Fu' blithe that night.

The lasses feat, an' cleanly neat,
  Mair braw than when they 're fine ;   20
Their faces blithe fu' sweetly kythe,
  Hearts leal, an' warm, an' kin' :
The lads sae trig, wi' wooer-babs
  Weel knotted on their garten ;
Some unco blate, an' some wi' gabs   25
  Gar lasses' hearts gang startin'
      Whyles fast at night.

Then, first and foremost, through the kail,
  Their stocks maun a' be sought ance ;
They steek their een, an' grape an' wale, 30
  For muckle anes an' straught anes.
Poor hav'rel Will fell aff the drift,
  An' wander'd through the bow-kail,
An' pou't, for want o' better shift,
  A runt was like a sow-tail,   35
      Sae bow't that night.

D 2

Then, straught or crookèd, yird or nane,
  They roar an' cry a' throu'ther;
The vera wee-things, toddlin, rin
  Wi' stocks out-owre their shouther;   40
An' gif the custok 's sweet or sour,
  Wi' joctelegs they taste them;
Syne cozily, aboon the door,
  Wi' cannie care they 've placed them
          To lie that night.   45

The auld guidwife's weel-hoordet nits
  Are round an' round divided,
An' monie lads' an' lasses' fates
  Are there that night decided:
Some kindle couthie side by side,   50
  An' burn thegither trimly;
Some start awa wi' saucy pride,
  An' jump out-owre the chimlie
          Fu' high that night.

Jean slips in twa wi' tentie e'e;   55
  Wha 'twas, she wadna tell;
But this is Jock, an' this is me,
  She says in to hersel':
He bleez'd owre her, and she owre him,
  As they wad never mair part;   60
Till fuff! he started up the lum,
  An' Jean had e'en a sair heart
          To see 't that night.

Poor Willie, wi' his bow-kail runt,
  Was brunt wi' primsie Mallie;   65
An' Mary, nae doubt, took the drunt,
  To be compar'd to Willie:

Mall's nit lap out wi' pridefu' fling,
  An' her ain fit it brunt it ;
While Willie lap, and swoor by jing   70
  'Twas just the way he wanted
        To be that night.

Nell had her lover in her min',
  She pits hersel' an' Rob in ;
In loving bleeze they sweetly join,   75
  Till white in ase they're sobbin' :
Nell's heart was dancin' at the view,
  She whisper'd Rob to leuk for't :
Rob, stown'ins, prie'd her bonnie mou,
  Fu' cozie in the neuk for't,   80
        Unseen that night.

But Merran sat behint their backs,
  Her thoughts on Andrew Bell ;
She lea'es them gashin at their cracks,
  An' slips out by hersel' :   85
She thro' the yard the nearest tak's,
  An' for the kiln she goes then,
An' darklins grapet for the bauks,
  And in the blue-clue throws then,
        Right fear't that night.   90

An' aye she win't, an' aye she swat—
  I wat she made nae jaukin ;
Till something held within the pat,
  Guid Lord ! but she was quaukin' !
But whether 'twas the deil himsel',   95
  Or whether 'twas a bauk-en',
Or whether it was Andrew Bell,
  She did na wait on talkin'
        To spier that night.

Wee Jennie to her graunie says,   100
'Will ye go wi' me, graunie?
I 'll eat the apple at the glass
    I gat frae uncle Johnnie:'
She fuff't her pipe wi' sic a lunt,
    In wrath she was sae vap'rin',   105
She notic't na an aizle brunt
    Her braw new worset apron
            Out-thro' that night.

'Ye little skelpie-limmer's face!
    I daur you try sic sportin',   110
As seek the foul thief ony place,
    For him to spae your fortune!
Nae doubt but ye may get a sight!
    Great cause ye hae to fear it;
For mony a ane has gotten a fright,   115
    An' liv'd an' died deleeret,
            On sic a night.

'Ae hairst afore the Sherra-moor,
    I mind 't as weel 's yestreen—
I was a gilpey then, I 'm sure   120
    I was na past fyfteen:
The simmer had been cauld an' wat,
    An' stuff was unco green;
An' aye a rantin kirn we gat,
    An' just on Halloween   125
            It fell that night.

'Our stibble-rig was Rab M'Graen,
    A clever, sturdy fallow;
        *   *   *   *   *

            *   *   *   *   130

He gat hemp-seed, I mind it weel,
    An' he made unco light o' 't;
But mony a day was by himsel',
    He was sae sairly frighted
             That vera night.'   135

Then up gat fechtin' Jamie Fleck,
    An' he swoor by his conscience,
That he could saw hemp-seed a peck;
    For it was a' but nonsense :
The auld guidman raught down the pock,   140
    An' out a handfu' gied him;
Syne bade him slip frae 'mang the folk,
    Sometime when na ane see'd him,
             An' try't that night.

He marches thro' amang the stacks,   145
    Though he was something sturtin;
The graip he for a harrow tak's,
    And haurls at his curpin :
An' ev'ry now an' then he says,
    ' Hemp-seed I saw thee,   150
An' her that is to be my lass
    Come after me, an' draw thee,
             As fast this night.'

He whistl'd up Lord Lenox' March,
    To keep his courage cheery;   155
Altho' his hair began to arch,
    He was sae fley'd an' eerie :
Till presently he hears a squeak,
    An' then a grane an' gruntle;
He by his shouther gae a keek,   160
    An' tumbled wi' a wintle
             Out-owre that night.

He roar'd a horrid murder-shout,
    In dreadfu' desperation !
An' young an' auld come rinnin out,   165
    An' hear the said narration :
He swoor 'twas hilchin Jean M'Craw,
    Or crouchie Merran Humphie,
Till stop! she trotted thro' them a';
    An' wha was it but grumphie   170
            Asteer that night!

Meg fain wad to the barn gaen,
    To winn three wechts o' naething;
But for to meet the deil her lane,
    She pat but little faith in :   175
She gies the herd a pickle nits
    An' twa red-cheekit apples
To watch, while for the barn she sets,
    In hopes to see Tam Kipples
            That vera night.   180

She turns the key wi' cannie thraw,
    An' owre the threshold ventures;
But first on Sawnie gies a ca',
    Syne bauldly in she enters;
A ratton rattl'd up the wa',   185
    An' she cry'd Lord preserve her!
An' ran thro' midden-hole an' a'
    An' pray'd wi' zeal an' fervour,
            Fu' fast that night.

They hoy't out Will, wi' sair advice;   190
    They hecht him some fine braw ane;
It chanc'd the stack he faddom'd thrice,
    Was timmer-propt for thrawin';

He tak's a swirlie auld moss-oak
　　For some black grousome carlin;　　195
An' loot a winze, an' drew a stroke,
　　Till skin in blypes cam' haurlin
　　　　　Aff's nieves that night.

A wanton widow Leezie was,
　　As canty as a kittlen;　　200
But och! that night, amang the shaws,
　　She gat a fearfu' settlin!
She thro' the whins, an' by the cairn,
　　An' owre the hill gaed scrievin;
Whare three lairds' lan's met at a burn,　　205
　　To dip her left sark-sleeve in,
　　　　　Was bent that night.

Whyles owre a linn the burnie plays,
　　As through the glen it wimpl't;
Whyles round a rocky scaur it strays,　　210
　　Whyles in a wiel it dimpl't;
Whyles glitter'd to the nightly rays,
　　Wi' bickerin, dancin dazzle;
Whyles cookit underneath the braes,
　　Below the spreading hazle　　215
　　　　　Unseen that night.

Amang the brackens, on the brae,
　　Between her an' the moon,
The deil, or else an outler quey,
　　Gat up an' gae a croon:　　220
Poor Leezie's heart maist lap the hool;
　　Near lav'rock-height she jumpet,
But mist a fit, an' in the pool
　　Out-owre the lugs she plumpet,
　　　　　Wi' a plunge that night.　　225

In order, on the clean hearth-stane,
  The luggies three are ranged;
And ev'ry time great care is ta'en
  To see them duly changed:
Auld uncle John, wha wedlock's joys   230
  Sin' Mar's year did desire,
Because he gat the toom dish thrice,
  He heav'd them on the fire
              In wrath that night.

Wi' merry sangs, an' friendly cracks,   235
  I wat they did na weary;
And unco tales, an' funnie jokes —
  Their sports were cheap an' cheery;
Till butter'd sow'ns, wi' fragrant lunt,
  Set a' their gabs a-steerin';   240
Syne, wi' a social glass o' strunt,
  They parted aff careerin'
              Fu' blithe that night.

To a Mouse.

WEE, sleeket, cowrin, tim'rous beastie,
    Oh, what a panic's in thy breastie!
Thou needna start awa sae hasty,
              Wi' bickerin brattle!
I wad be laith to rin an' chase thee,   5
              Wi' murderin' pattle!

I'm truly sorry man's dominion
Has broken nature's social union,
And justifies that ill opinion
              Which makes thee startle   10
At me, thy poor earth-born companion,
              An' fellow-mortal!

I doubt na, whyles, but thou may thieve;
What then? poor beastie, thou maun live!
A daimen icker in a thrave   15
        'S a sma' request:
I 'll get a blessin' wi' the lave,
        An' never miss 't!

Thy wee bit housie, too, in ruin!
Its silly wa's the win's are strewin'!   20
And naething now to big a new ane
        O' foggage green!
An' bleak December's winds ensuin',
        Baith snell an' keen!

Thou saw the fields laid bare an' waste,   25
An' weary winter comin' fast,
And cozie here, beneath the blast,
        Thou thought to dwell,
Till crash! the cruel coulter past
        Out thro' thy cell.   30

That wee bit heap o' leaves an' stibble
Has cost thee mony a weary nibble!
Now thou 's turn'd out for a' thy trouble,
        But house or hald,
To thole the winter's sleety dribble,   35
        An' cranreuch cauld!

But, Mousie, thou art no thy lane
In proving foresight may be vain;
The best-laid schemes o' mice and men
        Gang aft a-gley,   40
An' lea'e us nought but grief an' pain
        For promis'd joy.

Still thou art blest, compar'd wi' me!
The present only toucheth thee;
But och! I backward cast my ee   45
    On prospects drear;
An' forward, though I canna see,
    I guess an' fear.

The Cotter's Saturday Night.

NOVEMBER chill blaws loud wi' angry sugh;
    The short'ning winter-day is near a close;
The miry beasts retreating frae the pleugh;
The black'ning trains o' craws to their repose:
The toil-worn Cotter frae his labour goes,—   5
This night his weekly moil is at an end,
Collects his spades, his mattocks, and his hoes,
Hoping the morn in ease and rest to spend,
And weary o'er the moor his course does hameward bend.

At length his lonely cot appears in view,   10
Beneath the shelter of an agèd tree;
Th' expectant wee-things, toddlin, stacher through
To meet their Dad, wi' flichterin noise and glee.
His wee bit ingle, blinkin bonnilie,
His clean hearthstane, his thriftie wifie's smile,   15
The lisping infant prattling on his knee,
Does a' his weary kiaugh and care beguile,
And makes him quite forget his labour and his toil.

Belyve the elder bairns come drapping in,
At service out, amang the farmers roun';   20
Some ca' the pleugh, some herd, some tentie rin
A cannie errand to a neibor town:
Their eldest hope, their Jenny, woman-grown,
In youthfu' bloom, love sparkling in her ee,

Comes hame, perhaps to shew a braw new gown, 25
Or deposite her sair-won penny-fee,
To help her parents dear, if they in hardship be.

With joy unfeign'd brothers and sisters meet,
An' each for other's welfare kindly spiers :
The social hours, swift-wing'd, unnotic'd fleet ;   30
Each tells the uncos that he sees or hears.
The parents, partial, eye their hopeful years ;
Anticipation forward points the view ;
The mother, wi' her needle and her sheers,
Gars auld claes look amaist as weel 's the new ;   35
The father mixes a' wi' admonition due.

Their master's and their mistress's command,
The younkers a' are warnèd to obey ;
And mind their labours wi' an eydent hand,
And ne'er, tho' out o' sight, to jauk or play :   40
'And O ! be sure to fear the Lord alway,
And mind your duty duly, morn and night !
Lest in temptation's path ye gang astray,
Implore His counsel and assisting might :   44
They never sought in vain that sought the Lord aright.'

But hark ! a rap comes gently to the door ;
Jenny, wha kens the meaning o' the same,
Tells how a neibor lad came o'er the moor,
To do some errands, and convoy her hame.
The wily mother sees the conscious flame   50
Sparkle in Jenny's ee, and flush her cheek ;
With heart-struck anxious care, enquires his name,
While Jenny hafflins is afraid to speak :
Weel-pleas'd the mother hears it 's nae wild worthless
    rake.

Wi' kindly welcome Jenny brings him ben ;   55
A strappin' youth, he takes the mother's eye ;
Blythe Jenny sees the visit 's no ill ta'en ;
The father cracks of horses, pleughs, and kye.
The youngster's artless heart o'erflows wi' joy,
But blate and laithfu', scarce can weel behave ;   60
The mother, wi' a woman's wiles, can spy
What makes the youth sae bashfu' an' sae grave ;
Weel-pleas'd to think her bairn 's respected like the
    lave.

O happy love, where love like this is found !
O heartfelt raptures, bliss beyond compare !   65
I 've pacèd much this weary mortal round,
And sage experience bids me this declare—
If Heaven a draught of heavenly pleasure spare,
One cordial in this melancholy vale,
'Tis when a youthful, loving, modest pair   70
In other's arms breathe out the tender tale,
Beneath the milk-white thorn that scents the evening
    gale.

Is there, in human form, that bears a heart,
A wretch, a villain, lost to love and truth,
That can, with studied, sly, ensnaring art,   75
Betray sweet Jenny's unsuspecting youth?
Curse on his perjur'd arts, dissembling smooth !
Are honour, virtue, conscience, all exil'd ?
Is there no pity, no relenting ruth,
Points to the parents fondling o'er their child,   80
Then paints the ruin'd maid, and their distraction
    wild ?

But now the supper crowns their simple board,
The halesome parritch, chief of Scotia's food :

The sowpe their only hawkie does afford,
That 'yont the hallan snugly chows her cood: 85
The dame brings forth in complimental mood,
To grace the lad, her weel-hain'd kebbuck fell;
And aft he 's prest, and aft he ca's it guid:
The frugal wifie, garrulous, will tell   89
How 'twas a towmond auld, sin' lint was i' the bell.

The cheerfu' supper done, wi' serious face
They round the ingle form a circle wide;
The sire turns o'er, with patriarchal grace,
The big ha'-Bible, ance his father's pride:
His bonnet rev'rently is laid aside,   95
His lyart haffets wearing thin and bare;
Those strains that once did sweet in Zion glide,
He wales a portion with judicious care;
And 'Let us worship God!' he says, with solemn
   air.

They chant their artless notes in simple guise;   100
They tune their hearts, by far the noblest aim;
Perhaps Dundee's wild warbling measures rise,
Or plaintive Martyrs, worthy of the name;
Or noble Elgin beets the heavenward flame,
The sweetest far of Scotia's holy lays: 105
Compar'd with these, Italian trills are tame;
The tickled ears no heartfelt raptures raise;
Nae unison hae they with our Creator's praise.

The priest-like father reads the sacred page,
How Abram was the friend of God on high;   110
Or Moses bade eternal warfare wage
With Amalek's ungracious progeny;
Or how the royal bard did groaning lie
Beneath the stroke of Heaven's avenging ire;

Or Job's pathetic plaint, and wailing cry ;   115
Or rapt Isaiah's wild, seraphic fire ;
Or other holy seers that tune the sacred lyre.

Perhaps the Christian volume is the theme,
How guiltless blood for guilty man was shed ;
How He, who bore in heaven the s<u>econ</u>d name, 120
Had not on earth whereon to lay His head :
How His first followers and servants sped ;
The precepts sage they wrote to many a land :
How he, who lone in Patmos banishèd,
Saw in the sun a mighty angel stand,   125
And heard great Bab'lon's doom pronounc'd by Heaven's
    command.

Then kneeling down, to Heaven's Eternal King
The saint, the father, and the husband prays :
Hope springs exulting on triumphant wing,
That thus they all shall meet in future days ;   130
There ever bask in uncreated rays,
No more to sigh, or shed the bitter tear,
Together hymning their Creator's praise,
In such society, yet still more dear ;   134
While circling time moves round in an eternal sphere.

Compar'd with this, how poor Religion's pride,
In all the pomp of method, and of art,
When men display to congregations wide
Devotion's every grace, except the heart !
The Power, <u>incens'd</u>, the pageant will desert,   140
The pompous strain, the sacerdotal stole ;
But haply, in some cottage far apart,
May hear, well-pleas'd, the language of the soul ;
And in His book of life the inmates poor enrol.

Then homeward all take off their sev'ral way; 145
The youngling cottagers retire to rest :
The parent pair their secret homage pay,
And proffer up to Heaven the warm request
That He who stills the raven's clam'rous nest,
And decks the lily fair in flow'ry pride, 150
Would, in the way His wisdom sees the best.
For them and for their little ones provide ;
But chiefly in their hearts with grace divine preside.

From scenes like these old Scotia's grandeur springs.
That makes her lov'd at home, rever'd abroad : 155
Princes and lords are but the breath of kings,
'An honest man's the noblest work of God:'
And certes, in fair virtue's heavenly road,
The cottage leaves the palace far behind ;
What is a lordling's pomp? a cumbrous load, 160
Disguising oft the wretch of human kind,
Studied in arts of hell, in wickedness refin'd !

O Scotia ! my dear, my native soil !
For whom my warmest wish to Heaven is sent !
Long may thy hardy sons of rustic toil 165
Be blest with health, and peace, and sweet content !
And oh may Heaven their simple lives prevent
From luxury's contagion, weak and vile !
Then, howe'er crowns and coronets be rent,
A virtuous populace may rise the while, 170
And stand a wall of fire around their much-loved isle.

O Thou ! who poured the patriotic tide
That streamed through Wallace's undaunted heart,
Who dared to nobly stem tyrannic pride,
Or nobly die, the second glorious part, — 175
(The patriot's God peculiarly Thou art,

E

His friend, inspirer, guardian, and reward!)
Oh never, never, Scotia's realm desert,
But still the patriot, and the patriot bard,   179
In bright succession raise, her ornament and guard!

Address to the Deil.

O THOU—whatever title suit thee,
    Auld Hornie, Satan, Nick, or Clootie—
Wha in yon cavern grim an' sootie,
        Clos'd under hatches,
Spairges about the brunstane cootie,   5
        To scaud poor wretches—

Hear me, auld Hangie! for a wee,
An' let poor damnèd bodies be;
I'm sure sma' pleasure it can gie,
        Ev'n to a deil,   10
To skelp an' scaud poor dogs like me,
        An' hear us squeel!

Great is thy pow'r, an' great thy fame;
Far kenn'd an' noted is thy name;
An' tho' yon lowin heugh's thy hame,   15
        Thou travels far;
An' faith! thou's neither lag nor lame
        Nor blate nor scaur.

Whyles rangin' like a roarin' lion,
For prey a' holes an' corners tryin';   20
Whyles on the strong-wing'd tempest flyin',
        Tirlin' the kirks;
Whyles in the human bosom pryin',
        Unseen thou lurks.

I've heard my rev'rend grannie say   25
In lanely glens ye like to stray,
Or, where auld ruin'd castles grey
       Nod to the moon,
Ye fright the nightly wand'rer's way
       Wi' eldritch croon.   30

When twilight did my grannie summon
To say her prayers, douce honest woman!
Aft yont the dyke she's heard you bummin
       Wi' eerie drone,
Or, rustlin' through the boortrees, comin'   35
       Wi' heavy groan.

Ae dreary, windy, winter night
The stars shot down wi' sklentin light,
Wi' you mysel' I gat a fright
       Ayont the lough ;   40
Ye like a rash-buss stood in sight,
       Wi' waving sough.

The cudgel in my nieve did shake,
Each bristled hair stood like a stake,
When wi' an eldritch, stoor quaick ! quaick !   45
       Amang the springs
Awa' ye squatter'd, like a drake,
       On whistlin' wings.

Let warlocks grim, an' wither'd hags,
Tell how wi' you, on ragweed nags,   50
They skim the muirs an' dizzy crags,
       Wi' wicked speed,
And in kirkyards renew their leagues
       Owre howket dead.

Thence countra wives, wi' toil an' pain,   55
May plunge an' plunge the kirn in vain ;
For oh ! the yellow treasure 's ta'en
        By witchin' skill ;
An' dawtet twal-pint Hawkie 's gane
        As yell 's the bill.   60

When thowes dissolve the snawy hoord,
An' float the jinglin' icy boord,
Then water-kelpies haunt the foord
        By your direction,
An' 'nighted travellers are allur'd   65
        To their destruction.

And aft your moss-traversing Spunkies
Decoy the wight that late an' drunk is :
The bleezin', curst, mischievous monkeys
        Delude his eyes,   70
Till in some miry slough he sunk is,
        Ne'er mair to rise.

Lang syne in Eden's bonnie yard
When youthfu' lovers first were pair'd,
An' all the soul of love they shar'd,   75
        The raptur'd hour,
Sweet on the fragrant flow'ry swaird,
        In shady bow'r,–

Then you, ye auld snick-drawin' dog !
Ye cam' to Paradise incog,   80
An' play'd on man a cursèd brogue,
        (Black be your fa' !)
An' gied the infant warld a shog,
        'Maist ruin'd a'.

D' ye mind that day when, in a bizz,   85
Wi' reeket duds an' reestet gizz
Ye did present your smootie phiz
     'Mang better folk,
An' sklented on the man of Uz
     Your spitefu' joke ?   90

An' how ye gat him i' your thrall,
An' brak him out o' house an' hall,
While scabs an' blotches did him gall
     Wi' bitter claw ;
An' lows'd his ill-tongu'd wicked scaul',   95
     Was warst ava ?

But a' your doings to rehearse,
Your wily snares an' fechtin' fierce,
Sin' that day Michael did you pierce,
     Down to this time,   100
Wad ding a Lallan tongue, or Erse,
     In prose or rhyme.

An' now, auld Cloots ! I ken ye 're thinkin'
A certain bardie's rantin', drinkin',
Some luckless hour will send him linkin'   105
     To your black pit ;
But faith ! he 'll turn a corner jinkin',
     An' cheat you yet.

But fare-you-weel, auld Nickie-ben !
Oh wad ye tak' a thought an' men' !   110
Ye aiblins might—I dinna ken—
     Still hae a stake ;
I 'm wae to think upo' yon den,
     Ev'n for your sake !

Scotch Drink.

L ET other poets raise a fracas
          'Bout vines, an' wines, an' drucken Bacchus,
An' crabbet names an' stories wrack us,
               An' grate our lug;
I sing the juice Scotch bere can mak' us,   5
               In glass or jug.

O thou, my muse, guid auld Scotch drink!
Whether thro' wimplin worms thou jink,
Or, richly brown, ream owre the brink
               In glorious faem,   10
Inspire me, till I lisp and wink,
               To sing thy name!

Let husky wheat the haughs adorn,
An' aits set up their awnie horn,
An' pease and beans at e'en or morn   15
               Perfume the plain;
Leeze me on thee, John Barleycorn,
               Thou king o' grain!

On thee aft Scotland chows her cood
In souple scones, the wale o' food;   20
Or tumblin' in the boiling flood
               Wi' kail an' beef;
But when thou pours thy strong heart's blood,
               There thou shines chief.

Food fills the wame, an' keeps us leevin';   25
Tho' life's a gift no worth receivin',
When heavy-dragg'd wi' pine an' grievin';
               But, oil'd by thee,
The wheels o' life gae down-hill, scrievin',
               Wi' rattlin' glee.   30

Thou clears the head o' doited Lear:
Thou cheers the heart o' drooping Care ;
Thou strings the nerves o' Labour sair
       At 's weary toil :
Thou even brightens dark Despair   35
       Wi' gloomy smile.

Aft, clad in massy siller weed,
Wi' gentles thou erects thy head ;
Yet humbly kind in time o' need,
      The poor man's wine,   40
His wee drap parritch, or his bread,
      Thou kitchens fine.

Thou art the life o' public haunts ;
But thee, what were our fairs and rants ?
Ev'n godly meetings o' the saunts,   45
      By thee inspir'd,
When gaping they besiege the tents,
      Are doubly fir'd.

That merry night we get the corn in,
O sweetly then thou reams the horn in !   50
Or reekin' on a New-year mornin'
      In cog or bicker,
An' just a wee drap sp'ritual burn in,
      An' gusty sucker !

When Vulcan gies his bellows breath,   55
An' ploughmen gather wi' their graith,
O rare ! to see thee fizz an' freath
      I' th' lugget caup !
Then Burnewin comes on like death
      At ev'ry chaup.   60

Nae mercy, then, for airn or steel;
The brawnie, bainie, ploughman chiel,
Brings hard owrehip, wi' sturdy wheel,
　　　　The strong forehammer,
Till block an' studdie ring and reel　　　　65
　　　　Wi' dinsome clamour.

When neibors anger at a plea,
An' just as wud as wud can be,
How easy can the barley-bree
　　　　Cement the quarrel!　　　　70
It 's aye the cheapest lawyer's fee
　　　　To taste the barrel.

Alake that e'er my muse has reason
To wyte her countrymen wi' treason!
But mony daily weet their weason　　　　75
　　　　Wi' liquors nice,
An' hardly, in a winter's season,
　　　　E'er spier her price.

Wae worth that brandy, burnin' trash!
Fell source o' mony a pain an' brash!　　　　80
Twins mony a poor, doylt, drucken hash
　　　　O' half his days;
An' sends, beside, auld Scotland's cash
　　　　To her warst faes.

Ye Scots, wha wish auld Scotland well!　　　　85
Ye chief, to you my tale I tell,
Poor plackless devils like mysel'!
　　　　It sets you ill,
Wi' bitter, dearthfu' wines to mell,
　　　　Or foreign gill.　　　　90

Fortune! if thou'll but gie me still
Hale breeks, a scone, an' whisky gill,
An' rowth o' rhyme to rave at will,
              Tak' a' the rest,
An' deal't about as thy blind skill   95
              Directs thee best.

The Auld Farmer's New-Year Morning Saluta-tion to his Auld Mare Maggie,

ON GIVING HER THE ACCUSTOMED RIPP OF CORN TO HANSEL IN THE NEW YEAR.

A GUID New Year I wish thee, Maggie!
      Hae—there's a ripp to thy auld baggie!
Tho' thou's howe-backit now, and knaggie,
              I've seen the day
Thou could hae gaen like ony staggie   5
              Out-owre the lay.

Tho' now thou's dowie, stiff, an' crazy,
An' thy auld hide as white's a daisie,
I've seen thee dappl't, sleek, an' glaizie,
              A bonny gray: 10
He should been tight that daur't to raize thee
              Ance in a day.

Thou ance was i' the foremost rank,
A filly buirdly, steeve, an' swank,
An' set weel down a shapely shank   15
              As e'er tread yird;
An' could hae flown out-owre a stank
              Like ony bird.

It's now some nine-an'-twenty year
Sin' thou was my guid-father's meere :   20
He gied me thee, o' tocher clear,
        An' fifty mark ;
Though it was sma', 'twas weel-won gear,
        An' thou was stark.

When first I gaed to woo my Jenny,   25
Ye then was trottin' wi' your minnie :
Though ye was trickie, slee, an' funnie,
        Ye ne'er was donsie ;
But hamely, tawie, quiet, an' cannie,
        An' unco sonsie.   30

That day ye pranc'd wi' muckle pride
When ye bure hame my bonnie bride :
An' sweet an' gracefu' she did ride,
        Wi' maiden air !
Kyle Stewart I could bragget wide   35
        For sic a pair.

Tho' now ye dow but hoyte and hobble,
An' wintle like a saumont-coble,
That day ye was a jinker noble
        For heels an' win' !   40
An' ran them till they a' did wauble
        Far, far behin'.

When thou an' I were young and skiegh,
An' stable-meals at fairs were driegh,
How thou wad prance, an' snore, an' skriegh,   45
        An' tak' the road !
Town's bodies ran, an' stood abiegh,
        An' ca't thee mad.

When thou was corn't, an' I was mellow,
We took the road aye like a swallow : 50
At brooses thou had ne'er a fellow
For pith and speed ;
But every tail thou pay't them hollow,
Where'er thou gaed.

The sma', droop-rumpl't, hunter cattle 55
Might aiblins waur't thee for a brattle ;
But sax Scotch mile thou try't their mettle,
An' gar't them whaizle :
Nae whip nor spur, but just a wattle
O' saugh or hazle. 60

Thou was a noble fittie-lan',
As e'er in tug or tow was drawn !
Aft thee an' I, in aught hours gaun,
On guid March weather,
Hae turn'd sax rood beside our han', 65
For days thegither.

Thou never braing't, an' fetch't, an' flisket ;
But thy auld tail thou wad hae whisket,
An' spread abreed thy weel-fill'd brisket
Wi' pith an' power, 70
Till spritty knowes wad rair't and risket,
An' slypet owre.

When frosts lay lang, an' snaws were deep,
An' threatened labour back to keep,
I gied thy cog a wee bit heap 75
Aboon the timmer ;
I ken'd my Maggie wad na sleep
For that or simmer.

In cart or car thou never reestet;
The steyest brae thou wad hae fac't it;   80
Thou never lap, an' stenn'd, an' breastet,
   Then stood to blaw;
But, just thy step a wee thing hastet,
   Thou snoov't awa.

My pleugh is now thy bairn-time a',   85
Four gallant brutes as e'er did draw;
Forbye sax mae I 've sell't awa,
   That thou hast nurst:
They drew me thretteen pund an' twa,
   The vera warst.   90

Mony a sair daurg we twa hae wrought,
An' wi' the weary warl' fought!
An' mony an anxious day I thought
   We wad be beat!
Yet here to crazy age we 're brought,   95
   Wi' something yet.

And think na, my auld trusty servan',
That now perhaps thou 's less deservin',
An' thy auld days may end in starvin';
   For my last fow,   100
A heapet stimpart—I 'll reserve ane
   Laid by for you.

We 've worn to crazy years thegither;
We 'll toyte about wi' ane anither;
Wi' tentic care I'll flit thy tether   105
   To some hain'd rig,
Whare ye may nobly rax your leather
   Wi' sma' fatigue.

The Twa Dogs.

'TWAS in that place o' Scotland's isle,
   That bears the name o' auld King Coil.
Upon a bonnie day in June,
When wearing thro' the afternoon,
Twa dogs, that were na thrang at hame,   5
Forgather'd ance upon a time.

The first I'll name, they ca'd him Cæsar,
Was keepet for his Honour's pleasure :
His hair, his size, his mouth, his lugs,
Shewed he was nane o' Scotland's dogs;   10
But whalpet some place far abroad,
Whare sailors gang to fish for cod.

His lockèd, letter'd, braw brass collar
Shewed him the gentleman and scholar :
But, though he was o' high degree,   15
The fient a pride, nae pride had he ;
But wad hae spent an hour caressin'
Ev'n wi' a tinkler-gipsy's messan.
At kirk or market, mill or smiddie,
Nae tawted tyke, though e'er sae duddie,   20
But he wad stand as glad to see him,
An' snuff'd at stanes an' hillocks wi' him.

The tither was a ploughman's collie,
A rhyming, ranting, roving billie,
Wha for his friend an' comrade had him,   25
And in his freaks had Luath ca'd him,
After some dog in Highland sang,
Was made lang syne—Lord knows how lang.

He was a gash an faithfu' tyke,
As ever lap a sheugh or dyke.   30
His honest, sonsie, baws'nt face,
Aye gat him friends in ilka place.
His breast was white, his tousie back
Weel clad wi' coat o' glossy black;
His gawsie tail, wi' upward curl,   35
Hung owre his hurdies wi' a swirl.

Nae doubt but they were fain o' ither,
And unco pack an' thick thegither;
Wi' social nose whyles snuff'd and snowket;
Whyles mice an' moudieworts they howket;   40
Whyles scour'd awa in lang excursion,
An' worry'd ither in diversion;
Until wi' daffin weary grown,
Upon a knowe they sat them down,
And there began a lang digression   45
About the lords o' the creation.

CÆSAR.

I 've aften wonder'd, honest Luath,
What sort o' life poor dogs like you have;
An', when the gentry's life I saw,
What way poor bodies liv'd ava.   50

Our Laird gets in his rackèd rents,
His coals, his kain, an' a' his stents:
He rises when he likes himsel';
His flunkies answer at the bell;
He ca's his coach, he ca's his horse;   55
He draws a bonnie silken purse
As lang 's my tail, whare, through the steeks,
The yellow-letter'd Geordie keeks.

Frae morn to e'en it's nought but toiling
At baking, roasting, frying, boiling;   60
An', tho' the gentry first are stechin,
Yet ev'n the ha' folk fill their pechan
Wi' sauce, ragoûts, and sic like trashtrie,
That's little short o' downright wastrie.
Our Whipper-in, wee blastet wonner!   65
Poor worthless elf, it eats a dinner
Better than ony tenant man
His Honour has in a' the lan':
An' what poor cot-folk pit their painch in,
I own it's past my comprehension.   70

LUATH.

Trowth, Cæsar, whyles they're fash't eneugh:
A cotter, howkin in a sheugh,
Wi' dirty stanes biggin a dyke,
Baring a quarry, and sic like,
Himsel', a wife, he thus sustains,   75
A smytrie o' wee duddie weans,
An' nought but his han'-darg to keep
Them right an' tight in thack an' rape.

An' when they meet wi' sair disasters,
Like loss o' health or want o' masters,   80
Ye maist wad think a wee touch langer
An' they maun starve o' cauld and hunger;
But, how it comes I never kent yet,
They're maistly wonderfu' contented;
An' buirdly chiels an' clever hizzies   85
Are bred in sic a way as this is.

C/ESAR.

But then to see how ye're neglecket,
How huff'd, and cuff'd, and disrespecket!
Lord, man! our gentry care as little
For delvers, ditchers, an' sic cattle;   90
They gang as saucy by poor folk
As I wad by a stinking brock.

I've noticed, on our Laird's court-day,
An' mony a time my heart's been wae,
Poor tenant bodies, scant o' cash,   95
How they maun thole a factor's snash;
He'll stamp an' threaten, curse an' swear
He'll apprehend them, poind their gear;
While they maun stan', wi' aspect humble,
An' hear it a', an' fear an' tremble!   100
I see how folk live that hae riches;
But surely poor folk maun be wretches

LUATH.

They're nae sae wretched's ane wad think;
Tho' constantly on poortith's brink,
They're sae accustomed with the sight,   105
The view o''t gies them little fright.

Then chance and fortune are sae guided,
They're aye in less or mair provided;
An' tho' fatigu'd wi' close employment,
A blink o' rest's a sweet enjoyment.   110

The dearest comfort o' their lives,
Their grushie weans an' faithfu' wives;
The prattling things are just their pride,
That sweetens a' their fire-side.

An' whyles twalpennie-worth o' nappy 115
Can mak' the bodies unco happy :
They lay aside their private cares,
To mind the Kirk and State affairs;
They 'll talk o' patronage and priests,
Wi' kindling fury i' their breasts, 120
Or tell what new taxation 's comin',
An' ferlie at the folk in Lon'on.

As bleak-fac'd Hallowmas returns
They get the jovial, rantin' kirns,
When rural life, of every station, 125
Unite in common recreation;
Love blinks, Wit slaps, an' social Mirth
Forgets there 's Care upo' the earth.

That merry day the year begins
They bar the door on frosty win's ; 130
The nappy reeks wi' mantling ream,
An' sheds a heart-inspiring steam ;
The luntin pipe, an' sneeshin mill,
Are handed round wi' right guid will ;
The cantie auld folks crackin crouse, 135
The young anes ranting through the house—
My heart has been sae fain to see them
That I for joy hae barket wi' them.

Still it 's owre true that ye hae said,
Sic game is now owre aften played ; 140
There 's monie a creditable stock
O' decent, honest, fawsont folk
Are riven out baith root an' branch,
Some rascal's pridefu' greed to quench,

F

Wha thinks to knit himsel' the faster   145
In favour wi' some gentle master,
Wha, aiblins thrang a-parliamentin',
For Britain's guid his saul indentin'—

CÆSAR.

Haith, lad, ye little ken about it:
For Britain's guid!—guid faith, I doubt it!   150
Say rather, gaun as Premiers lead him,
An' saying ay or no's they bid him;
At operas an' plays parading,
Mortgaging, gambling, masquerading;
Or maybe, in a frolic daft,   155
To Hague or Calais takes a waft,
To mak a tour, an' tak a whirl,
To learn *bon ton* an' see the worl'.

There, at Vienna or Versailles,
He rives his father's auld entails;   160
Or by Madrid he takes the rout,
To thrum guitars, an' fecht wi' nowt;
Or down Italian vista startles,
Love-making amang groves o' myrtles:
Then bouses drumly German water,   165
To mak himsel' look fair an' fatter.
For Britain's guid!—for her destruction!
Wi' dissipation, feud, an' faction.

LUATH.

Hech, man! dear sirs! is that the gate
They waste sae mony a braw estate?   170
Are we sae foughten an' haràss'd
For gear to gang that gate at last?

Oh would they stay aback frae courts,
An' please themsel's wi' country sports,
It wad for every ane be better,   175
The laird, the tenant, an' the cotter !
For thae frank, rantin' ramblin' billies,
Fient haet o' them 's ill-hearted fellows ;
Except for breakin' o' their timmer,
Or speakin' lightly o' their limmer,   180
Or shootin' o' a hare or moor-cock,
The ne'er-a-bit they 're ill to poor folk.

But will ye tell me, master Cæsar,
Sure great folk's life 's a life o' pleasure ?
Nae cauld nor hunger e'er can steer them,   185
The vera thought o' 't need na fear them.

CÆSAR.

Lord, man ! were ye but whyles whare I am,
The gentles—ye wad ne'er envy 'em.
It 's true they need na starve or sweat,
Thro' winter's cauld, or simmer's heat ;   190
They 've nae sair wark to craze their banes,
An' fill auld age wi' grips an' granes :
But human bodies are sic fools,
For a' their colleges and schools,
That when nae real ills perplex them   195
They mak' enow themsels to vex them ;
An' aye the less they hae to sturt them,
In like proportion less will hurt them.

A country fellow at the pleugh,
His acres tilled, he 's right eneugh ;   200

F 2

A country girl at her wheel,
Her dizzens done, she's unco weel :
But gentlemen, an' ladies warst,
Wi' ev'ndown want o' wark are curst.
They loiter, lounging, lank, an' lazy;   205
Though deil haet ails them, yet uneasy ;
Their days insipid, dull an' tasteless:
Their nights unquiet, lang an' restless.

An' ev'n their sports, their balls, an' races,
Their galloping through public places,   210
There's sic parade, sic pomp, an' art,
The joy can scarcely reach the heart.
The men cast out in party matches,
Then sowther a' in deep debauches:
Ae night they're mad wi' drink, an' roarin',   215
Neist day their life is past endurin'.
The ladies arm-in-arm in clusters,
As great an' gracious a' as sisters;
But hear their absent thoughts o' ither,
They're a' run deils an' jads thegither.   220
Whyles, o'er the wee bit cup an' platie,
They sip the scandal-potion pretty ;
Or lee-lang nights, wi' crabbet leuks
Pore owre the devil's pictured beuks ;
Stake on a chance a farmer's stackyard,   225
An' cheat like ony unhanged blackguard.

There's some exceptions, man an' woman ;
But this is gentry's life in common.

By this the sun was out o' sight,
An' darker gloamin brought the night: 230

The bum-clock hummed wi' lazy drone ;
The kye stood rowtin i' the loan ;
When up they gat, and shook their lugs,
Rejoiced they were na men, but dogs ;
An' each took aff his several way,   235
Resolv'd to meet some ither day.

*The Author's Earnest Cry and Prayer to the Scotch
Representatives in the House of Commons.*

YE Irish lords, ye knights an' squires,
   Wha represent our brughs an' shires,
An' doucely manage our affairs
            In parliament,
To you a simple poet's pray'rs   5
            Are humbly sent.

Tell them wha hae the chief direction
Scotland an' me 's in great affliction,
E'er sin' they laid that curst restriction
            On aqua-vitæ ;   10
An' rouse them up to strong conviction,
            An' move their pity.

Stand forth, an' tell yon Premier youth
The honest, open, naked truth :
Tell him o' mine an' Scotland's drouth,   15
            His servants humble :
The muckle deevil blaw you south,
            If ye dissemble !

Does ony great man glunch an' gloom ?
Speak out, an' never fash your thumb !   20

Let posts an' pensions sink or soom
        Wi' them wha grant them;
If honestly they canna come,
        Far better want them.

In gath'rin' votes you were na slack;   25
Now stand as tightly by your tack;
Ne'er claw your lug, an' fidge your back,
        An' hum an' haw;
But raise your arm, an' tell your crack
        Before them a'.   30

Paint Scotland greetin' owre her thrissle;
Her mutchkin stowp as toom 's a whissle;
An' curst excisemen in a bussle
        Seizin' a stell,
Triumphant crushin't like a mussel   35
        Or limpet shell.

Then on the tither hand present her,
A blackguard smuggler right behint her,
An' cheek-for-chow a chuffie vintner
        Colleaguing join,   40
Pickin' her pouch as bare as winter
        Of a' kind coin.

Is there, that bears the name o' Scot,
But feels his heart's bluid rising hot
To see his poor auld mither's pot   45
        Thus dung in staves,
An' plunder'd o' her hindmost groat
        By gallows knaves?

God bless your Honours ! can ye see 't—
The kind, auld, cantie carlin greet,   50
An' no get warmly to your feet,
      An' gar them hear it,
An' tell them wi' a patriot heat,
      Ye winna bear it ?

Some o' you nicely ken the laws,   55
To round the period an' pause,
An' wi' rhetòric clause on clause
      To mak' harangues ;
Then echo through Saint Stephen's wa's
      Auld Scotland's wrangs.   60

Arouse, my boys ! exert your mettle,
To get auld Scotland back her kettle ;
Or faith ! I 'll wad my new pleugh-pettle,
      Ye 'll see 't or lang,
She 'll teach you, wi' a reekin' whittle,   65
      Anither sang.

This while she 's been in crankous mood,
Her lost Militia fired her bluid ;
(Deil nor they never mair do guid,
      Played her that pliskie !)   70
An' now she 's like to rin red-wud
      About her whisky.

An' Lord ! if ance they pit her till 't,
Her tartan petticoat she 'll kilt,
An', durk an' pistol at her belt,   75
      She 'll tak' the streets,
An' rin her whittle to the hilt
      I' th' first she meets !

For Godsake, sirs ! then speak her fair,
An' straik her cannie wi' the hair,   8o
An' to the muckle house repair
          Wi' instant speed,
An' strive wi' a' your wit and lear
          To get remead.

Auld Scotland has a raucle tongue;   85
She's just a devil wi' a rung ;
An' if she promise auld or young
          To tak' their part—
Though by the neck she should be strung,
          She'll no desert.   9o

An' now, ye chosen Five-and-Forty,
May still your mither's heart support ye;
Then, tho' a Minister grow dorty,
          An' kick your place,
Ye'll snap your fingers, poor an' hearty,   95
          Before his face.

God bless your Honours a' your days
Wi' sowps o' kail and brats o' claise,
In spite o' a' the thievish kaes
          That haunt Saint Jamie's ! 100
Your Humble poet sings an' prays
          While Rab his name is.

POSTSCRIPT.

L ET half-starv'd slaves in warmer skies
      See future wines rich-clust'ring rise ;
Their lot auld Scotland ne'er envies,   1o5
          But, blythe and frisky,
She eyes her freeborn martial boys
          Tak' aff their whisky.

What though their Phœbus kinder warms,
While fragrance blooms and beauty charms, 110
When wretches range, in famish'd swarms,
          The scented groves;
Or, hounded forth, dishonour arms
          In hungry droves.

Their gun's a burden on their shouther; 115
They downa bide the stink o' powther;
Their bauldest thought's a hank'ring swither
          To stand or rin,
Till, skelp! a shot—they're aff, a' throu'ther,
          To save their skin!   120

But bring a Scotchman frae his hill,
Clap in his cheek a Highland gill,
Say—' Such is royal George's will,
          An' there's the foe!'
He has nae thought but how to kill   125
          Twa at a blow.

Nae cauld faint-hearted doubtings tease him;
Death comes, wi' fearless eye he sees him;
Wi' bluidy hand a welcome gies him;
          An', when he fa's,   130
His latest draught o' breathin' lea'es him
          In faint huzzas.

Sages their solemn een may steek,
An' raise a philosophic reek,
An' physically causes seek   135
          In clime and season;
But tell me whisky's name in Greek—
          I'll tell the reason.

Epistle to James Smith.

DEAR Smith, the sleëst pawkie thief
     That e'er attempted stealth or rief!
Ye surely ha'e some warlock-breef
          Owre human hearts;
For ne'er a bosom yet was prief   5
          Against your arts.

For me, I swear by sun an' moon,
An' every star that blinks aboon,
Ye've cost me twenty pair o' shoon
          Just gaun to see you;   10
An' ev'ry ither pair that's done,
          Mair ta'en I'm wi' you.

That auld capricious carlin, Nature,
To mak' amends for scrimpet stature,
She's turned you off, a human creature   15
          On her first plan,
And, in her freaks, on every feature
          She's wrote the Man.

Just now I've ta'en the fit o' rhyme,
My barmie noddle's working prime,   20
My fancy yerket up sublime
          Wi' hasty summon:
Hae ye a leisure-moment's time
          To hear what's comin'?

Some rhyme a neibor's name to lash;   25
Some rhyme (vain thought!) for needfu' cash;
Some rhyme to court the countra clash,
          An' raise a din;
For me, an aim I never fash;
          I rhyme for fun.   30

The star that rules my luckless lot
Has fated me the russet coat,
An' damn'd my fortune to the groat ;
   But, in requit,
Has blest me with a random shot   35
   O' countra wit.

This while my notion 's ta'en a sklent
To try my fate in guid black prent ;
But still the mair I 'm that way bent,
   Something cries 'Hoolie !   40
I red you, honest man, tak' tent !
   Ye 'll shaw your folly.

'There's ither poets, much your betters,
Far seen in Greek, deep men o' letters,
Hae thought they had ensur'd their debtors   45
   A' future ages ;
Now moths deform in shapeless tatters
   Their unknown pages.'

Then farewell hopes of laurel-boughs
To garland my poetic brows !   50
Henceforth I 'll rove where busy ploughs
   Are whistlin' thrang,
An' teach the lanely heights an' howes
   My rustic sang.

I 'll wander on, wi' tentless heed   55
How never-halting moments speed,
Till fate shall snap the brittle thread ;
   Then, all unknown,
I 'll lay me with th' inglorious dead,
   Forgot and gone !   60

But why o' death begin a tale?
Just now we 're living, sound an' hale;
Then top and maintop crowd the sail,
        Heave Care o'er-side!
And large, before Enjoyment's gale,   65
        Let 's tak' the tide.

This life, sae far 's I understand,
Is a' enchanted fairy-land,
Where Pleasure is the magic wand
        That, wielded right,   70
Mak's hours like minutes, hand in hand,
        Dance by fu' light.

The magic wand then let us wield;
For, ance that five-an'-forty 's speel'd,
See crazy, weary, joyless Eild,   75
        Wi' wrinkl'd face,
Come hostin', hirplin' owre the field,
        Wi' creepin' pace.

When ance life's day draws near the gloamin',
Then farewcel vacant, careless roamin';   80
An' farewcel cheerfu' tankards foamin',
        An' social noise;
An' farewcel dear deluding woman,
        The joy of joys!

O Life! how pleasant, in thy morning,   85
Young Fancy's rays the hills adorning!
Cold-pausing Caution's lesson scorning,
        We frisk away,
Like schoolboys at th' expected warning,
        To joy an' play.   90

We wander there, we wander here,
We eye the rose upon the brier,
Unmindful that the thorn is near,
      Among the leaves;
And, tho' the puny wound appear,   95
      Short while it grieves.

Some, lucky, find a flowery spot,
For which they never toil'd nor swat;
They drink the sweet and eat the fat,
      But care or pain;   100
And haply eye the barren hut
      With high disdain.

With steady aim some fortune chase;
Keen hope does ev'ry sinew brace;
Thro' fair, thro' foul, they urge the race,   105
      An' seize the prey;
Then cannie, in some cozie place,
      They close the day.

And others, like your humble servan',
Poor wights! nae rules nor roads observin',   110
To right or left eternal swervin',
      They zig-zag on;
'Till, curst with age, obscure and starvin',
      They aften groan.

Alas! what bitter toil an' straining—   115
But truce with peevish, poor complaining!
Is fortune's fickle Luna waning?
      E'en let her gang!
Beneath what light she has remaining
      Let 's sing our sang.   120

My pen I here fling to the door,
And kneel, ye Powers! and warm implore,
'Tho' I should wander Terra o'er
      In all her climes,
Grant me but this, I ask no more,   125
      Aye rowth o' rhymes.

'Gie dreeping roasts to countra lairds,
Till icicles hing frae their beards ;
Gie fine braw claes to fine life-guards
      And maids of honour ;   130
An' yill an' whisky gie to cairds,
      Until they sconner.

'A title, Dempster merits it ;
A garter gie to Willie Pitt ;
Gie wealth to some be-ledger'd cit,   135
      In cent. per cent.;
But give me real, sterling wit,
      And I'm content.

'While ye are pleas'd to keep me hale,
I'll sit down o'er my scanty meal,   140
Be 't water-brose or muslin-kail,
      Wi' cheerfu' face,
As lang 's the muses dinna fail
      To say the grace.'

An anxious ee I never throws   145
Behint my lug, or by my nose ;
I jouk beneath misfortune's blows
      As weel 's I may ;
Sworn foe to sorrow, care, and prose,
      I rhyme away.   150

O ye douce folk that live by rule,
Grave, tideless-blooded, calm an' cool,
Compar'd wi' you—oh, fool ! fool ! fool !
   How much unlike !
Your hearts are just a standing pool, 155
   Your lives a dyke !

Nae hare-brain'd sentimental traces
In your unletter'd nameless faces ;
In *arioso* trills and graces
   Ye never stray ; 160
But *gravissimo* solemn basses
   Ye hum away.

Ye are sae grave, nae doubt ye 're wise ;
Nae ferly tho' ye do despise
The hairum-scairum ram-stam boys, 165
   The rattling squad :
I see you upward cast your eyes—
   Ye ken the road !

Whilst I—but I shall haud me there ;
Wi' you I 'll scarce gang onywhere : 170
Then, Jamie, I shall say nae mair,
   But quat my sang,
Content wi' you to mak' a pair,
   Whare'er I gang.

The Vision.

DUAN FIRST.

THE sun had clos'd the winter day,
 The curlers quat their roarin' play,
And hunger'd maukin ta'en her way
   To kail-yards green,

While faithless snaws ilk step betray   5
　　　Whare she has been.

The thresher's weary flingin-tree
The lee-lang day had tirèd me ;
And when the day had clos'd his ee,
　　　Far i' the west,   10
Ben i' the spence, right pensivelie,
　　　I gaed to rest.

There, lanely by the ingle-cheek,
I sat and ey'd the spewing reek,
That fill'd, wi' hoast-provoking smeek,   15
　　　The auld clay biggin' ;
An' heard the restless rattons squeak
　　　About the riggin'.

All in this mottie, misty clime,
I backward mus'd on wasted time,   20
How I had spent my youthfu' prime,
　　　An' done nae-thing,
But stringing blethers up in rhyme,
　　　For fools to sing.

Had I to guid advice but harket,   25
I might, by this, hae led a market,
Or strutted in a bank an' clarket
　　　My cash-account ;
While here, half-mad, half-fed, half-sarket,
　　　Is a' th' amount.   30

I started, mutt'ring 'blockhead ! coof !'
An' heav'd on high my wauket loof,
To swear by a' yon starry roof,
　　　Or some rash aith,
That I henceforth wad be rhyme-proof   35
　　　Till my last breath—

When click! the string the snick did draw;
An' jee the door gaed to the wa';
An' by my ingle-lowe I saw,
          Now bleezin bright,   40
A tight outlandish hizzie braw
          Come full in sight.

Ye need na doubt I held my whisht;
The infant aith, half-form'd, was crusht;
I glowr'd as eerie's I'd been dusht   45
          In some wild glen;
When sweet, like modest Worth, she blusht
          An' steppèd ben.

Green, slender, leaf-clad holly boughs
Were twisted, gracefu', round her brows;   50
I took her for some Scottish Muse
          By that same token;
And come to stop those reckless vows,
          Would soon been broken.

A hare-brain'd, sentimental trace   55
Was strongly markèd in her face;
A wildly-witty, rustic grace
          Shone full upon her;
Her eye, ev'n turned on empty space,
          Beamed keen with honour.   60

Down flowed her robe, a tartan sheen,
Till half a leg was scrimply seen;
An' such a leg! my bonnie Jean
          Could only peer it;
Sae straught, sae taper, tight, an' clean—   65
          Nane else came near it.

G

Her mantle large, of greenish hue,
My gazing wonder chiefly drew;
Deep lights and shades, bold-mingling, threw
  A lustre grand ;   70
And seem'd, to my astonish'd view,
  A well-known land.

Here rivers in the sea were lost;
There mountains to the skies were tost:
Here tumbling billows mark'd the coast 75
  With surging foam ;
There distant shone Art's lofty boast,
  The lordly dome.

DUAN SECOND.

With musing-deep, astonish'd stare,
I view'd the heavenly-seeming fair ; 80
A whisp'ring throb did witness bear
  Of kindred sweet,
When with an elder sister's air
  She did me greet.

'All hail, my own inspirèd bard ! 85
In me thy native Muse regard;
Nor longer mourn thy fate is hard,
  Thus poorly low ;
I come to give thee such reward
  As we bestow.   90

'Know, the great genius of this land
Has many a light aërial band,
Who, all beneath his high command,
  Harmoniously,
As arts or arms they understand, 95
  Their labours ply.

'They Scotia's race among them share :
Some fire the soldier on to dare ;
Some rouse the patriot up to bare
   Corruption's heart;   100
Some teach the bard, a darling care,
   The tuneful art.

'Some, bounded to a district space,
Explore at large man's infant race
To mark the embryotic trace   105
   Of rustic bard ;
And careful note each opening grace,
   A guide and guard.

'Of these am I—Coila my name;
And this district as mine I claim,   110
Where once the Campbells, chiefs of fame,
   Held ruling pow'r :
I mark'd thy embryo tuneful flame,
   Thy natal hour.

'With future hope I oft would gaze   115
Fond on thy little early ways,
Thy rudely caroll'd, chiming phrase,
   In uncouth rhymes,
Fir'd at the simple, artless lays
   Of other times.   120

'I saw thee seek the sounding shore,
Delighted with the dashing roar ;
Or when the North his fleecy store
   Drove through the sky,
I saw grim Nature's visage hoar   125
   Struck thy young eye.

G 2

'Or when the deep-green-mantled earth
Warm cherish'd every floweret's birth,
And joy and music pouring forth
      In every grove,   130
I saw thee eye the general mirth
      With boundless love.

'When ripen'd fields and azure skies
Called forth the reapers' rustling noise,
I saw thee leave their evening joys,   135
      And lonely stalk,
To vent thy bosom's swelling rise
      In pensive walk.

'When youthful love, warm-blushing, strong,
Keen-shivering shot thy nerves along,   140
Those accents, grateful to thy tongue,
      Th' adorèd Name,
I taught thee how to pour in song,
      To sooth thy flame.

'I saw thy pulse's maddening play   145
Wild send thee Pleasure's devious way,
Misled by Fancy's meteor ray,
      By passion driven;
But yet the light that led astray
      Was light from Heaven.   150

'I taught thy manners-painting strains,
The loves, the ways of simple swains,
Till now o'er all my wide domains
      Thy fame extends;
And some, the pride of Coila's plains,   155
      Become thy friends.

'Thou canst not learn, nor can I show,
To paint with Thomson's landscape glow;
Or wake the bosom-melting throe
     With Shenstone's art;   160
Or pour, with Gray, the moving flow
     Warm on the heart.

' Yet all-beneath th' unrivall'd rose
The lowly daisy sweetly blows;
Tho' large the forest's monarch throws   165
     His army shade,
Yet green the juicy hawthorn grows
     Adown the glade.

'Then never murmur nor repine;
Strive in thy humble sphere to shine;   170
And, trust me, not Potosi's mine,
     Nor kings' regard,
Can give a bliss o'ermatching thine,
     A rustic bard.

'To give my counsels all in one—   175
Thy tuneful flame still careful fan;
Preserve the dignity of Man,
     With soul erect;
And trust the Universal Plan
     Will all protect.   180

'And wear thou *this!*' She solemn said,
And bound the holly round my head:
The polish'd leaves and berries red
     Did rustling play;
And, like a passing thought, she fled   185
     In light away.

Address to the Unco Guid.

O YE wha are sae guid yoursel',
    Sae pious and sae holy,
Ye've nought to do but mark and tell
    Your neibours' faults and folly !
Whase life is like a weel-gaun mill,   5
    Supplied wi' store o' water;
The heapet happer's ebbing still,
    An' still the clap plays clatter;—

Hear me, ye venerable core,
    As counsel for poor mortals   10
That frequent pass douce Wisdom's door
    For glaikit Folly's portals.
I, for their thoughtless, careless sakes,
    Would here propone defences —
Their donsie tricks, their black mistakes,   15
    Their failings and mischances.

Ye see your state wi' theirs compared,
    And shudder at the niffer ;
But cast a moment's fair regard,—
    What mak's the mighty differ ?   20
Discount what scant occasion gave,
    That purity ye pride in,
And (what's aft mair than a' the lave)
    Your better art o' hidin'.

Think, when your castigated pulse   25
    Gi'es now and then a wallop,
What ragings must his veins convulse
    That still eternal gallop !

Wi' wind and tide fair i' your tail,
   Right on ye scud your sea-way;   30
But in the teeth o' baith to sail,
   It mak's an unco lee-way.

See Social Life and Glee sit down,
   All joyous and unthinking,
Till, quite transmugrify'd, they're grown   35
   Debauchery and Drinking:
Oh would they stay to calculate
   Th' eternal consequences!
Or, your more dreaded hell to state,
   Damnation of expenses!   40

Ye high, exalted, virtuous dames,
   Tied up in godly laces,
   Before ye gi'e poor Frailty names
   Suppose a change o' cases;
Suppose for sin convenience snug,   45
   A treacherous inclination—
But, let me whisper i' your lug,
   Ye 're aiblins nae temptation.

Then gently scan your brother man,
   Still gentler sister woman;   50
Tho' they may gang a kennin wrang,
   To step aside is human:
One point must still be greatly dark,
   The moving why they do it!
And just as lamely can ye mark   55
   How far perhaps they rue it.

Who made the heart, 'tis He alone
   Decidedly can try us;
He knows each chord—its various tone,
   Each spring—its various bias: 60

Then at the balance let 's be mute,
    We never can adjust it;
What 's done we partly may compute,
    But know not what 's resisted.

The Holy Fair.

UPON a simmer Sunday morn,
    When Nature's face is fair,
I walkèd forth to view the corn,
    An' snuff the caller air.
The rising sun owre Galston muirs   5
    Wi' glorious light was glintin';
The hares were hirplin' down the furs;
    The lav'rocks they were chantin'
            Fu' sweet that day.

As lightsomely I glowr'd abroad   10
    To see a scene sae gay,
Three hizzies, early at the road,
    Cam' skelpin' up the way;
Twa had manteeles o' dolefu' black,
    But ane wi' lyart lining;   15
The third, that gaed a-wee aback,
    Was in the fashion shining
            Fu' gay that day.

The twa appear'd like sisters twin,
    In feature, form, an' claes;   20
Their visage wither'd, lang, an' thin,
    An' sour as ony slaes:
The third cam' up, hap-stap-an'-lowp,
    As light as ony lambie,
An' wi' a curchie low did stoop,   25
    As soon as e'er she saw me,
            Fu' kind that day.

Wi' bonnet aff quoth I 'Sweet lass,
  I think ye seem to ken me;
I'm sure I've seen that bonnie face,   30
  But yet I canna name ye.'
Quo' she, an' laughin' as she spak',
  An' tak's me by the hands,
'Ye, for my sake, ha'e gi'en the feck
  Of a' the ten commands   35
          A screed some day.

'My name is Fun—your cronie dear,
  The nearest friend ye hae;
An' this is Superstition here,
  An' that's Hypocrisy.   40
I'm gaun to Mauchline Holy Fair,
  To spend an hour in daffin':
Gin ye'll go there, yon runkled pair,
  We will get famous laughin'
          At them this day.'   45

Quoth I 'With a' my heart I'll do't;
  I'll get my Sunday's sark on,
An' meet you on the holy spot;
  Faith, we'se ha'e fine remarkin'!'
Then I gaed hame at crowdie-time   50
  An' soon I made me ready;
For roads were clad, frae side to side,
  Wi' monie a wearie body
          In droves that day.

Here farmers gash, in ridin' graith,   55
  Gaed hoddin' by their cotters;
There swankies young, in braw braid-claith,
  Are springin' o'er the gutters.

The lasses, skelpin' barefit, thrang,
  In silks an' scarlets glitter,   60
Wi' sweet-milk cheese in mony a whang,
  An' farls bak'd wi' butter
          Fu' crump that day.

When by the plate we set our nose,
  Weel heapèd up wi' ha'pence,   65
A greedy glowr Black Bonnet throws,
  An' we maun draw our tippence.
Then in we go to see the show:
  On ev'ry side they're gath'rin',
Some carryin' deals, some chairs an' stools,   70
  An' some are busy blethrin',
          Right loud that day.

Here stands a shed to fend the show'r
  An' screen our countra gentry;
There racer Jess, an' twa-three mair,   75
  Are blinkin' at the entry.
Here sits a raw o' tittlin' jads,
  Wi' heavin' breasts an bare neck;
An' there a batch o' wabster lads,
  Blackguardin' frae Kilmarnock   80
          For fun this day.

Here some are thinkin' on their sins,
  An' some upo' their claes ;
Ane curses feet that fyl'd his shins,
  Anither sighs an' prays :   85
On this hand sits a chosen swatch,
  Wi' screw'd-up grace-proud faces ;
On that a set o' chaps at watch,
  Thrang winkin' on the lasses
          To chairs that day.   90

Oh happy is that man an' blest!
Nae wonder that it pride him!
Whase ain dear lass, that he likes best,
Comes clinkin' down beside him!
Wi' arm repos'd on the chair-back,　　　　95
He sweetly does compose him;
Which by degrees slips round her neck,
An's loof upon her bosom,
　　　　Unken'd that day.

Now a' the congregation o'er　　　　100
Is silent expectation;
For Moodie specls the holy door,
Wi' tidings o' damnation.
Should Hornie, as in ancient days,
'Mang sons o' God present him,　　　　105
The vera sight o' Moodie's face,
To 's ain het hame had sent him
　　　　Wi' fright that day.

Hear how he clears the points o' faith
Wi' rattlin' an' thumpin'!　　　　110
Now meekly calm, now wild in wrath,
He's stampin' an' he's jumpin'!
His lengthen'd chin, his turned-up snout,
His eldritch squeel an' gestures,
Oh how they fire the heart devout,　　　　115
Like cantharidian plaisters,
　　　　On sic a day!

But hark! the tent has changed its voice;
There's peace an' rest nae langer;
For a' the real judges rise—　　　　120
They canna sit for anger.

Smith opens out his cauld harangues
    On practice and on morals;
An' aff the godly pour in thrangs,
    To gi'e the jars an' barrels   125
            A lift that day.

What signifies his barren shine
    Of moral pow'rs and reason?
His English style, an' gesture fine,
    Are a' clean out o' season.   130
Like Socrates or Antonine,
    Or some auld Pagan heathen,
The moral man he does define,
    But ne'er a word o' faith in,
            That's right that day.   135

In guid time comes an antidote
    Against sic poison'd nostrum;
For Peebles, frae the water-fit,
    Ascends the holy rostrum:
See, up he's got the Word o' God,   140
    An' meek an' mim has view'd it,
While Common-sense has ta'en the road,
    An' aff, an' up the Cowgate,
            Fast, fast that day.

Wee Miller neist the guard relieves,   145
    An' orthodoxy raibles,
Tho' in his heart he weel believes
    An' thinks it auld wives' fables:
But faith! the birkie wants a manse,
    So cannily he hums them;   150
Altho' his carnal wit an' sense
    Like hafflins-wise o'ercomes him
            At times that day.

Now butt an' ben the change-house fills
  Wi' yill-caup commentators;   155
Here's cryin' out for bakes an' gills,
  An' there the pint-stowp clatters;
While thick an' thrang, an' loud an' lang,
  Wi' logic an' wi' Scripture,
They raise a din that in the end   160
  Is like to breed a rupture
         O' wrath that day.

Leeze me on drink! it gi'es us mair
  Than either school or college;
It ken'les wit, it waukens lair,   165
  It pangs us fu' o' knowledge:
Be't whisky gill, or penny wheep,
  Or ony stronger potion,
It never fails, on drinkin' deep,
  To kittle up our notion   170
         By night or day.

The lads an' lasses, blythely bent
  To mind baith saul an' body,
Sit round the table, weel content,
  An' steer about the toddy.   175
On this ane's dress, an' that ane's leuk,
  They're makin' observations;
While some are cozie i' the neuk,
  An' forming assignations
         To meet some day.   180

But now the Lord's ain trumpet touts,
  Till a' the hills are rairin',
And echoes back return the shouts:
  Black Russell is na spairin':

His piercin' words, like highlan' swords,   185
  Divide the joints an' marrow ;
His talk o' hell, whare devils dwell,
  Our vera sauls does harrow
            Wi' fright that day.

A vast, unbottom'd, boundless pit,   190
  Fill'd fu' o' lowin' brunstane,
Whase ragin' flame an' scorchin' heat
  Wad melt the hardest whunstane !
The half-asleep start up wi' fear,
  An' think they hear it roarin',   195
When presently it does appear
  'Twas but some neibor snorin'
            Asleep that day.

'Twad be owre-lang a tale to tell
  How mony stories past,   200
An' how they crouded to the yill
  When they were a' dismist ;
How drink gaed round, in cogs an' caups,
  Amang the furms an' benches ;
An' cheese an' bread, frae women's laps,   205
  Was dealt about in lunches
            An' dawds that day.

In comes a gawsie, gash guidwife,
  An' sits down by the fire,
Syne draws her kebbuck an' her knife ;   210
  The lasses they are shyer.
The auld guidmen about the grace
  Frae side to side they bother,
Till some ane by his bonnet lays
  An' gi'es them 't like a tether,   215
            Fu' lang that day.

Wacsucks for him that gets nac lass,
  Or lasses that hac naething!
Sma' need has he to say a grace,
  Or melvie his braw claithing!   220
O wives, be mindfu' ancc yoursel'
  How bonnie lads ye wanted,
An' dinna for a kebbuck-heel
  Let lasses be affronted
        On sic a day!   225

Now Clinkumbell wi' rattlin' tow
  Begins to jow an' croon;
Some swaggcr hame the best they dow,
  Some wait the afternoon.
At slaps the billies halt a blink,   230
  Till lasses strip their shoon:
Wi' faith an' hope, an' love an' drink,
  Thcy're a' in famous tune
        For crack that day.

To a Mountain Daisy.

WEE, modest, crimson-tippèd flow'r!
    Thou's met me in an evil hour;
For I maun crush amang the stoure
        Thy slender stem;
To spare thee now is past my pow'r,   5
        Thou bonnie gem!

Alas! it's no thy neibor sweet,
The bonnie lark, companion meet,
Bending thee 'mang the dewy wcet,
        Wi' spreckl'd breast,   10
When upward springing blythe to grect
        The purpling east.

Cauld blew the bitter biting north
Upon thy early humble birth ;
Yet cheerfully thou glinted forth   15
          Amid the storm,
Scarce rear'd above the parent earth
          Thy tender form.

The flaunting flow'rs our gardens yield,
High shelt'ring woods and wa's maun shield;   20
But thou, beneath the random bield
          O' clod or stane,
Adorns the histie stibble-field,
          ·   Unseen, alane.

There, in thy scanty mantle clad,   25
Thy snawy bosom sunward spread,
Thou lifts thy unassuming head
          In humble guise ;
But now the share uptears thy bed,
          And low thou lies !   30

Such is the fate of artless maid,
Sweet flow'ret of the rural shade !
By love's simplicity betray'd,
          And guileless trust ;
Till she, like thee, all soil'd is laid   35
          Low i' the dust.

Such is the fate of simple bard,
On life's rough ocean luckless starr'd !
Unskilful he to note the card
          Of prudent lore,   40
Till billows rage, and gales blow hard,
          And whelm him o'er !

Such fate to suffering Worth is given,
Who long with wants and woes has striven.
By human pride or cunning driven   45
      To mis'ry's brink,
Till wrench'd of every stay but Heaven,
      He, ruined, sink!

Ev'n thou who mourn'st the Daisy's fate,
That fate is thine—no distant date;   50
Stern Ruin's ploughshare drives elate
      Full on thy bloom,
Till crush'd beneath the furrow's weight
      Shall be thy doom!

Despondency.

AN ODE.

OPPRESS'D with grief, oppress'd with care,
    A burden more than I can bear,
  I set me down and sigh;
O life! thou art a galling load
Along a rough, a weary road,   5
  To wretches such as I!
Dim-backward as I cast my view,
  What sick'ning scenes appear!
What sorrows yet may pierce me through,
  Too justly I may fear!   10
    Still caring, despairing,
      Must be my bitter doom;
    My woes here shall close ne'er
    But with the closing tomb!

Happy, ye sons of busy life,
Who, equal to the bustling strife,
  No other view regard!

Ev'n when the wishèd end's denied,
Yet, while the busy means are plied.
They bring their own reward :   20
Whilst I, a hope-abandon'd wight,
    Unfitted with an aim,
Meet ev'ry sad returning night
    And joyless morn the same.
        You, bustling and justling,   25
            Forget each· grief and pain :
        I, listless, yet restless,
            Find ev'ry prospect vain.

How blest the solitary's lot,
Who, all-forgetting, all-forgot,   30
    Within his humble cell,
The cavern, wild with tangling roots,
Sits o'er his newly-gather'd fruits,
    Beside his crystal well !
Or, haply, to his ev'ning thought,   35
    By unfrequented stream,
The ways of men are distant brought,
    A faint collected dream ;
        While praising, and raising
            His thoughts to heav'n on high,   40
        As wand'ring, meand'ring,
            He views the solemn sky.

Than I, no lonely hermit plac'd
Where never human footstep trac'd,
    Less fit to play the part,   45
The lucky moment to improve,
And just to stop, and just to move,
    With self-respecting art :

But ah! those pleasures, loves, and joys,
  Which I too keenly taste,   50
The Solitary can despise,
  Can want, and yet be blest!
    He needs not, he heeds not,
      Or human love or hate,
    Whilst I here must cry here   55
      At perfidy ingrate!

Oh enviable early days,
When dancing thoughtless pleasure's maze
  To care, to guilt unknown!
How ill exchang'd for riper times,   60
To feel the follies, or the crimes,
  Of others, or my own!
Ye tiny elves that guiltless sport,
  Like linnets in the bush,
Ye little know the ills ye court,   65
  When manhood is your wish!
    The losses, the crosses,
      That active man engage;
    The fears all, the tears all,
      Of dim-declining age!   70

Epistle to a Young Friend.

I LANG hae thought, my youthfu' friend,
    A something to have sent you,
Tho' it should serve nae ither end
    Than just a kind memento;
But how the subject theme may gang   5
    Let time and chance determine;
Perhaps it may turn out a sang,
    Perhaps turn out a sermon.

Ye 'll try the world soon, my lad;
And, Andrew dear, believe me,   10
Ye 'll find mankind an unco squad,
And muckle they may grieve ye:
For care and trouble set your thought,
Ev'n when your end 's attained;
And a' your views may come to nought,   15
Where ev'ry nerve is strained.

I 'll no say men are villains a';
The real harden'd wicked,
Wha hae nae check but human law,
Are to a few restricket: 20
But och! mankind are unco weak,
An' little to be trusted;
If self the wavering balance shake,
It 's rarely right adjusted!

Yet they wha fa' in fortune's strife,   25
Their fate we should na censure;
For still th' important end of life
They equally may answer;
A man may hae an honest heart,
Tho' poortith hourly stare him;   30
A man may tak' a neibor's part,
Yet hae nae cash to spare him.

Aye free aff han' your story tell,
When wi' a bosom crony;
But still keep something to yoursel'   35
Ye scarcely tell to ony.
Conceal yoursel' as weel 's ye can
Frae critical dissection;
But keek thro' every other man,
Wi' sharpen'd, sly inspection.   40

The sacred lowe o' weel-plac'd love,
    Luxuriantly indulge it;
But never tempt th' illicit rove,
    Tho' naething should divulge it:
I waive the quantum o' the sin,   45
    The hazard of concealing:
But och! it hardens a' within,
    And petrifies the feeling!

To catch dame Fortune's golden smile,
    Assiduous wait upon her;   50
And gather gear by ev'ry wile
    That's justified by honour,—
Not for to hide it in a hedge,
    Nor for a train attendant,
But for the glorious privilege   55
    Of being independent.

The fear o' hell 's a hangman's whip
    To haud the wretch in order;
But where ye feel your honour grip,
    Let that aye be your border;   60
Its slightest touches—instant pause;
    Debar a' side pretences;
And resolutely keep its laws,
    Uncaring consequences.

The great Creator to revere,   65
    Must sure become the creature;
But still the preaching cant forbear,
    And ev'n the rigid feature:
Yet ne'er, with wits profane to range,
    Be complaisance extended;   70
An atheist laugh 's a poor exchange
    For Deity offended!

When ranting round in pleasure's ring,
　Religion may be blinded;
Or if she gie a random sting,   75
　It may be little minded;
But when on life we're tempest-driven ·
　A conscience but a canker—
A correspondence fix'd wi' Heaven
　Is sure a noble anchor!   80

Adieu, dear amiable youth!
　Your heart can ne'er be wanting:
May prudence, fortitude, and truth
　Erect your brow undaunting!
In ploughman phrase, 'God send you speed' 85
　Still daily to grow wiser;
And may ye better reck the rede
　Than ever did th' adviser!

A Dream.

GUID-MORNIN' to your Majesty!
　　May Heaven augment your blisses
On every new birthday ye see,
　A humble poet wishes!
My bardship here, at your levee,   5
　On sic a day as this is,
Is sure an uncouth sight to see
　Amang thae birthday dresses
　　　　　　Sae fine this day.

I see ye 're complimented thrang   10
　By mony a lord an' lady;
'God save the King!' 's a cuckoo sang
　That 's unco easy said aye;

The poets, too, a venal gang,
    Wi' rhymes weel-turn'd an' ready,   15
Wad gar you trow ye ne'er do wrang,
    But aye unerring steady,
                On sic a day.

For me! before a monarch's face,
    Ev'n there I winna flatter;   20
For neither pension, post, nor place
    Am I your humble debtor :
So, nae reflection on your grace
    Your kingship to bespatter,
There's mony waur been o' the race,   25
    And aiblins ane been better
                Than you this day.

'Tis very true, my sov'reign king,
    My skill may weel be doubted;
But facts are chiels that winna ding   30
    An' downa be disputed :
Your royal nest, beneath your wing,
    Is e'en right reft an' clouted,
And now the third part o' the string,
    An' less, will gang about it   35
                Than did ae day.

Far be 't frae me that I aspire
    To blame your legislation,
Or say ye wisdom want, or fire,
    To rule this mighty nation;   40
But faith! I muckle doubt, my Sire,
    Ye've trusted ministration
To chaps wha in a barn or byre
    Wad better fill'd their station,
                Than courts yon day.   45

And, now ye 've gi'en auld Britain peace
  Her broken shins to plaister,
Your sair taxation does her fleece
  Till she has scarce a tester:
For me, thank God! my life 's a lease,   50
  Nae bargain wearin' faster,
Or faith! I fear that wi' the geese
  I shortly boost to pasture
          I' the craft some day.

I 'm no mistrusting Willie Pitt   55
  When taxes he enlarges,
(An' Will 's a true guid fallow's get,
  A name not envy spairges),
That he intends to pay your debt,
  An' lessen a' your charges;   60
But God-sake! let nae saving fit
  Abridge your bonnie barges
          An' boats this day.

Adieu, my Liege! may Freedom geck
  Beneath your high protection;   65
An' may ye rax Corruption's neck,
  And gie her for dissection!
But, since I 'm here, I 'll no neglect,
  In loyal, true affection,
To pay your Queen, wi' due respect,   70
  My fealty an' subjection
          This great birthday.

Hail, Majesty most Excellent!
  While nobles strive to please ye,
Will ye accept a compliment   75
  A simple poet gies ye?

Thae bonnie bairntime Heaven has lent,
　Still higher may they heeze ye
In bliss, till fate some day is sent,
　For ever to release ye　　　　　　　　　80
　　　　　　Frae care that day.

For you, young potentate o' Wales,
　I tell your Highness fairly,
Down Pleasure's stream, wi' swelling sails,
　I'm tauld ye're driving rarely ;　　　　85
But some day ye may gnaw your nails,
　An' curse your folly sairly,
That e'er ye brak Diana's pales,
　Or rattl'd dice wi' Charlie,
　　　　　　By night or day.　　　　　90

Yet aft a ragged cowt's been known
　To mak' a noble aiver ;
So ye may doucely fill a throne
　For a' their clish-ma-claver :
There, him at Agincourt wha shone,　　95
　Few better were or braver ;
And yet, wi' funny, queer Sir John,
　He was an unco shaver
　　　　　　For mony a day.

Ye, lastly, bonnie blossoms a',　　　　100
　Ye royal lasses dainty,
Heaven mak' you guid as weel as braw,
　An' gie you lads a-plenty !
But sneer na British boys awa,
　For kings are unco scant aye,　　　　105
An' German gentles are but sma',—
　They're better just than want aye
　　　　　　On onie day.

God bless you a'! Consider now,
  Ye 're unco muckle dautet ;   110
But, ere the course o' life be through,
  It may be bitter sautet ;
An' I hae seen their coggie fou
  That yet hae tarrow't at it ;
But or the day was done, I trow,   115
  The laggen they hae clautet
        Fu' clean that day.

A Bard's Epitaph.

IS there a whim-inspirèd fool,
  Owre fast for thought, owre hot for rule,
Owre blate to seek, owre proud to snool?
        Let him draw near;
And owre this grassy heap sing dool,   5
        And drap a tear.

Is there a bard of rustic song
Who, noteless, steals the crowds among,
That weekly this arena throng?
        Oh pass not by!   10
But, with a frater-feeling strong,
        Here heave a sigh.

Is there a man whose judgment clear
Can others teach the course to steer,
Yet runs himself life's mad career   15
        Wild as the wave?
Here pause—and, thro' the starting tear,
        Survey this grave.

The poor inhabitant below
Was quick to learn and wise to know,   20

And keenly felt the friendly glow,
    And softer flame ;
But thoughtless follies laid him low,
    And stain'd his name !

Reader, attend ! Whether thy soul   25
Soars fancy's flights beyond the pole,
Or darkling grubs this earthly hole
    In low pursuit,
Know prudent, cautious self-control
    Is wisdom's root.   30

In Recommendation of Willie Chalmers.

W I' braw new branks in mickle pride,
    And eke a braw new brechan,
My Pegasus I 'm got astride,
    And up Parnassus pechin' ;
Whiles owre a bush wi' downward crush   5
    The doited beastie stammers ;
Then up he gets, and off he sets
    For sake o' Willie Chalmers.

I doubt na, lass, that weel kenn'd name
    May cost a pair o' blushes ;   10
I am nae stranger to your fame,
    Nor his warm urgèd wishes.
Your bonnie face, sae mild an' sweet,
    His honest heart enamours,
An' faith ye 'll no be lost a whit,   15
    Tho' wair'd on Willie Chalmers.

Auld Truth hersel' might swear ye 're fair,
    And Honour safely back her,
And Modesty assume your air,
    And ne'er a ane mistak' her :   20

And sic twa love-inspiring een
  Might fire even holy palmers ;
Nae wonder then they 've fatal been
  To honest Willie Chalmers.

I doubt na fortune may you shore   25
  Some mim-mou'd pouther'd priestie,
Fu' lifted up wi' Hebrew lore,
  An' band upon his breastie :
But oh ! what signifies to you
  His lexicons and grammars ;   30
The feeling heart 's the royal blue,
  An' that 's wi' Willie Chalmers.

Some gapin', glow'rin' countra laird
  May warsle for your favour,
May claw his lug, an' straik his beard,   35
  An' hoast up some palaver.
My bonnie maid, before ye wed
  Sic clumsy-witted hammers,
Seek Heaven for help, and barefit skelp
  Awa wi' Willie Chalmers !   40

The Brigs of Ayr.

'TWAS when the stacks get on their winter hap,
    And thack and rape secure the toil-won crap ;
Potato-bings are snuggèd up frae skaith
O' coming Winter's biting, frosty breath ;
The bees, rejoicing o'er their summer toils,   5
Unnumber'd buds and flow'rs' delicious spoils,
Seal'd up with frugal care in massive waxen piles,
Are doom'd by man, that tyrant o'er the weak,
The death o' devils, smoor'd wi' brimstone reek :

The thundering guns are heard on every side,   10
The wounded coveys, reeling, scatter wide;
The feather'd field-mates, bound by Nature's tie,
Sires, mothers, children, in one carnage lie :
(What warm poetic heart but inly bleeds,
And execrates man's savage, ruthless deeds!)   15
Nae mair the flow'r in field or meadow springs;
Nae mair the grove with airy concert rings,
Except perhaps the Robin's whistling glee,
Proud o' the height o' some bit half-lang tree ;
The hoary morns precede the sunny days,   20
Mild, calm, serene, wide spreads the noontide blaze,
While thick the gossamour waves wanton in the rays.

'Twas in that season, when a simple Bard,
Unknown and poor—simplicity's reward—
Ae night, within the ancient brugh of Ayr,   25
By whim inspir'd, or haply prest wi' care,—
He left his bed, and took his wayward route,
And down by Simpson's wheel'd the left about :
(Whether impell'd by all-directing Fate
To witness what I after shall narrate ;   30
Or whether, rapt in meditation high,
He wander'd out, he knew not where nor why).
The drowsy Dungeon-clock had number'd two,
And Wallace Tower had sworn the fact was true ;
The tide-swoln firth, with sullen-sounding roar,   35
Through the still night dash'd hoarse along the shore :
All else was hush'd as Nature's closèd e'e ;
The silent moon shone high o'er tower and tree ;
The chilly frost, beneath the silver beam,
Crept gently crusting o'er the glittering stream—   40

When lo ! on either hand the list'ning Bard,
The clanging sugh of whistling wings is heard ;
Two dusky forms dart thro' the midnight air,
Swift as the gos drives on the wheeling hare ;
Ane on th' Auld Brig his airy shape uprears.   45
The ither flutters o'er the rising piers :
Our warlock Rhymer instantly descried
The Sprites that owre the Brigs of Ayr preside.
(That bards are second-sighted is nae joke,
And ken the lingo of the sp'ritual folk ;   50
Fays, spunkies, kelpies, a', they can explain them,
And ev'n the vera deils they brawly ken them.)
Auld Brig appear'd of ancient Pictish race,
The vera wrinkles Gothic in his face :
He seem'd as he wi' Time had warstl'd lang,   55
Yet, teughly doure, he bade an unco bang.
New Brig was buskit in a braw new coat,
That he at Lon'on, frae ane Adams, got ;
In 's hand five taper staves as smooth 's a bead,
Wi' virls and whirlygigums at the head.   60
The Goth was stalking round with anxious search,
Spying the time-worn flaws in ev'ry arch ;
It chanc'd his new-come neibor took his ee,
And e'en a vex'd and angry heart had he !
Wi' thieveless sneer to see his modish mien,   65
He, down the water, gies him this guid-e'en : ·

AULD BRIG.

I doubt na, frien', ye 'll think ye 're nae sheepshank
Ance ye were streekit owre frae bank to bank !
But gin ye be a brig as auld as me—
Tho' faith that day, I doubt, ye 'll never see—   70
There 'll be, if that day come, I 'll wad a boddle,
Some fewer whigmaleeries in your noddle.

NEW BRIG.

Auld Vandal! ye but show your little mense,
Just much about it wi' your scanty sense:
Will your poor narrow footpath of a street,   75
Where twa wheelbarrows tremble when they meet,
Your ruin'd formless bulk o' stane an' lime
Compare wi' bonnie brigs o' modern time?
There 's men of taste would tak' the Ducat stream,
Tho' they should cast the very sark and swim,   80
Ere they would grate their feelings wi' the view
O' sic an ugly Gothic hulk as you.

AULD BRIG.

Conceited gowk! puff'd up wi' windy pride!
This mony a year I 've stood the flood and tide;
And, tho' wi' crazy eild I 'm sair forfairn,   85
I 'll be a brig when ye 're a shapeless cairn!
As yet ye little ken about the matter,
But twa-three winters will inform ye better.
When heavy, dark, continued, a'-day rains
Wi' deepening deluges o'erflow the plains;   90
When from the hills where springs the brawling Coil,
Or stately Lugar's mossy fountains boil,
Or where the Greenock winds his moorland course,
Or haunted Garpal draws his feeble source,
Arous'd by blustering winds an' spotting thowes,   95
In mony a torrent down the snaw-broo rowes;
While crashing ice, borne on the roaring spate,
Sweeps dams, an' mills, an' brigs, a' to the gate;
And from Glenbuck down to the Ratton-key
Auld Ayr is just one lengthen'd, tumbling sea—   100
Then down ye 'll hurl, de'il nor ye never rise!
And dash the gumlie jaups up to the pouring skies!

A lesson sadly teaching to your cost
That Architecture's noble art is lost!

NEW BRIG.

Fine architecture, trowth, I needs must say't o''t ! 105
The Lord be thankit that we've tint the gate o''t !
Gaunt, ghastly, ghaist-alluring edifices,
Hanging with threat'ning jut, like precipices ;
O'er-arching mouldy gloom-inspiring coves,
Supporting roofs fantastic, stony groves ;   110
Windows and doors in nameless sculpture drest,
With order, symmetry, or taste unblest ;
Forms like some bedlam statuary's dream,
The craz'd creations of misguided whim ;
Forms might be worshipp'd on the bended knee, 115
And still the second dread command be free,—
Their likeness is not found on earth, in air, or sea!
Mansions that would disgrace the building taste
Of any mason reptile, bird, or beast ;
Fit only for a doited monkish race,   120
Or frosty maids forsworn the dear embrace,
Or cuifs of later times, wha held the notion
That sullen gloom was sterling true devotion ;
Fancies that our guid brugh denies protection,— 124
And soon may they expire, unblest wi' resurrection !

AULD BRIG.

O ye, my dear-remember'd ancient yealings,
Were ye but here to share my wounded feelings !
Ye worthy Proveses, an' mony a Bailie,
Wha in the paths o' righteousness did toil aye ;
Ye dainty Deacons, an' ye douce Conveeners,   130
To whom our moderns are but causey-cleaners ;

Ye godly Councils wha hae blest this town;
Ye godly Brethren o' the sacred gown,
Wha meekly gae your hurdies to the smiters;   134
And (what would now be strange) ye godly Writers;
A' ye douce folk I 've borne aboon the broo,—
Were ye but here, what would ye say or do?
How would your spirits groan in deep vexation,
To see each melancholy·alteration;
And, agonizing, curse the time and place   140
When ye begat the base degenerate race!
Nae langer rev'rend men, their country's glory,
In plain braid Scots hold forth a plain braid story;
Nae langer thrifty citizens, an' douce,
Meet owre a pint, or in the Council-house;   145
But staumrel, corky-headed, graceless gentry,
The herryment and ruin of the country;
Men, three-parts made by tailors and by barbers,
Wha waste your weel-hain'd gear on curst new brigs
  and harbours!

NEW BRIG.

Now haud you there! for faith ye 've said enough, 150
And muckle mair than ye can mak' to through.
As for your priesthood, I shall say but little,
Corbies and clergy are a shot right kittle;
But, under favour o' your langer beard,
Abuse o' magistrates might weel be spar'd: 155
To liken them to your auld-warld squad,
I must needs say, comparisons are odd.
In Ayr, wag-wits nae mair can hae a handle
To mouth 'a citizen,' a term o' scandal;
Nae mair the Council waddles down the street,   160
In all the pomp of ignorant conceit;

I

Men wha grew wise priggin' owre hops an' raisins,
Or gather'd liberal views in bonds and seisins.
If haply Knowledge, on a random tramp,
Had shor'd them with a glimmer of his lamp,   165
And would to Common-sense for once betray'd them,
Plain dull Stupidity stept kindly in to aid them.

WHAT farther clishmaclaver might been said,
What bloody wars, if sprites had blood to shed,
No man can tell; but all before their sight   170
A fairy train appear'd in order bright :
Adown the glittering stream they featly danc'd;
Bright to the moon their various dresses glanc'd;
They footed o'er the watery glass so neat,
The infant ice scarce bent beneath their feet;   175
While arts of minstrelsy among them rung,
And soul-ennobling bards heroic ditties sung.
Oh, had M'Lauchlan, thairm-inspiring sage,
Been there to hear this heavenly band engage,
When thro' his dear strathspeys they bore with High-
     land rage !   180
Or when they struck old Scotia's melting airs,
The lover's raptured joys or bleeding cares,
How would his Highland lug been nobler fir'd,
And ev'n his matchless hand with finer touch inspir'd !
No guess could tell what instrument appear'd,   185
But all the soul of Music's self was heard;
Harmonious concert rung in every part,
While simple melody pour'd moving on the heart.

The Genius of the Stream in front appears,
A venerable Chief advanc'd in years,   190
His hoary head with water-lilies crown'd,
His manly leg with garter-tangle bound.

Next came the loveliest pair in all the ring,
Sweet female Beauty hand in hand with Spring;
Then, crown'd with flowery hay, came Rural Joy, 195
And Summer with his fervid beaming eye;
All-cheering Plenty, with her flowing horn,
Led yellow Autumn wreath'd with nodding corn ;
Then Winter's time-bleach'd locks did hoary show
By Hospitality with cloudless brow.   200
Next follow'd Courage with his martial stride,
From where the Feal wild-woody coverts hide ;
Benevolence, with mild benignant air,
A female form, came from the towers of Stair ;
Learning and Worth in equal measures trode   205
From simple Catrine, their long-lov'd abode ;
Last, white-robed Peace, crown'd with a hazel wreath,
To rustic Agriculture did bequeath
The broken iron instruments of death ;
At sight of whom our sprites forgat their kindling
    wrath.   210

A Prayer for a Reverend Friend's Family.

O THOU dread Power who reign'st above !
    I know thou wilt me hear,
When for this scene of peace and love
    I make my prayer sincere.

The hoary sire—the mortal stroke,   5
    Long, long be pleased to spare,
To bless his little filial flock,
    And show what good men are.

She, who her lovely offspring eyes
    With tender hopes and fears—   10

Oh, bless her with a mother's joys,
But spare a mother's tears!

Their hope, their stay, their darling youth,
In manhood's dawning blush—
Bless him, thou God of love and truth,   15
Up to a parent's wish!

The beauteous, seraph sister-band,
With earnest tears I pray,
Thou know'st the snares on ev'ry hand
Guide Thou their steps alway.   20

When soon or late they reach that coast,
O'er life's rough ocean driven,
May they rejoice, no wanderer lost,
A family in heaven!

Tam Samson's Elegy.

HAS auld Kilmarnock seen the deil?
  Or great Mackinlay thrawn his heel?
Or Robertson again grown weel,
          To preach an' read?
'Na, waur than a'!' cries ilka chiel,   5
          'Tam Samson 's dead!'

Kilmarnock lang may grunt an' grane,
An' sigh, an' sab, an' greet her lane,
An' cleed her bairns, man, wife, an' wean,
          In mourning weed;   10
To Death she 's dearly paid the kane—
          Tam Samson 's dead!

The brethren o' the mystic level
May hing their head in woefu' bevel,
While by their nose the tears will revel   15
      Like ony bead;
Death's gi'en the lodge an unco devel—
      Tam Samson's dead!

When Winter muffles up his cloak,
And binds the mire like a rock;   20
When to the loughs the curlers flock
      Wi' gleesome speed,
Wha will they station at the cock?—
      Tam Samson's dead!

He was the king o' a' the core   25
To guard, or draw, or wick a bore,
Or up the rink like Jehu roar
      In time o' need;
But now he lags on Death's hog-score—
      Tam Samson's dead!   30

Now safe the stately sawmont sail,
And trouts be-dropp'd wi' crimson hail,
And eels weel kenn'd for souple tail,
      And geds for greed,
Since dark in Death's fish-creel we wail   35
      Tam Samson dead!

Rejoice, ye birring paitricks a';
Ye cootie muircocks, crousely craw;
Ye maukins, cock your fud fu' braw,
      Withouten dread;   40
Your mortal fae is now awa'—
      Tam Samson's dead!

That woefu' morn be ever mourn'd
Saw him in shootin' graith adorn'd,
While pointers round impatient burn'd,   45
        Frae couples freed ;
But och ! he gaed and ne'er return'd !
        Tam Samson's dead !

In vain auld age his body batters ;
In vain the gout his ankles fetters ;   50
In vain the burns cam' down like waters,
        An acre braid !
Now ev'ry auld wife, greetin', clatters
        'Tam Samson's dead !'

Owre mony a weary hag he limpit,   55
An' aye the tither shot he thumpit,
Till coward Death behint him jumpit,
        Wi' deadly feide ;
Now he proclaims, wi' tout o' trumpet,
        'Tam Samson's dead !'   60

When at his heart he felt the dagger,
He reel'd his wonted bottle-swagger,
But yet he drew the mortal trigger
        Wi' weel-aim'd heed ;
'Lord, five !' he cry'd, an' owre did stagger— 65
        Tam Samson's dead !

Ilk hoary hunter mourn'd a brither ;
Ilk sportsman-youth bemoan'd a father :
Yon auld gray stane, amang the heather,
        Marks out his head,   70
Whare Burns has wrote, in rhyming blether,
        Tam Samson's dead !'

There low he lies in lasting rest!
Perhaps upon his mould'ring breast
Some spitefu' muirfowl bigs her nest,   75
        To hatch and breed;
Alas! nae mair he'll them molest!
        Tam Samson's dead!

When August winds the heather wave,
And sportsmen wander by yon grave,   80
Three volleys let his memory crave
        O' pouther an' lead,
Till Echo answer frae her cave
        'Tam Samson's dead!'

Heaven rest his saul whare'er he be!   85
Is the wish o' mony mae than me:
He had twa fauts, or maybe three,
        Yet what remead?
Ae social honest man want we—
        Tam Samson's dead?   90

PER CONTRA.

Go, Fame, and canter like a filly,
Through a' the streets an' neuks o' Killie;
Tell every social honest billie
        To cease his grievin',   95
For, yet unskaith'd by Death's gleg gullie,
        Tam Samson's leevin'!

A Winter Night.

WHEN biting Boreas, fell and doure,
    Sharp shivers thro' the leafless bow'r;
When Phœbus gi'es a short-liv'd glow'r
        Far south the lift,
Dim-darkening through the flaky show'r,   5
        Or whirling drift;

Ae night the storm the steeples rocked,
Poor Labour sweet in sleep was locked,
While burns, wi' snawy wreaths up-choked,
        Wild-eddying swirl,   10
Or, thro' the mining outlet bocked,
        Down headlong hurl:

List'ning the doors' an' winnocks' rattle,
I thought me on the ourie cattle,
Or silly sheep, wha bide this brattle   15
        O' winter war,
And thro' the drift, deep-lairing, sprattle
        Beneath a scaur.

Ilk happing bird, wee, helpless thing,
That, in the merry months o' spring,   20
Delighted me to hear thee sing,
        What comes o' thee?
Whare wilt thou cow'r thy chittering wing,
        An' close thy ee?

Ev'n you, on murdering errands toil'd,   25
Lone from your savage homes exil'd,—
The blood-stained roost, and sheep-cote spoil'd,
        My heart forgets,

While pitiless the tempest wild
   Sore on you beats.   30

Now Phœbe, in her midnight reign,
Dark-muffled, view'd the dreary plain ;
Still crowding thoughts, a pensive train,
   Rose in my soul,
When on my ear this plaintive strain,   35
   Slow, solemn, stole :—

' Blow, blow, ye winds, with heavier gust !
And freeze, thou bitter-biting frost !
Descend, ye chilly, smothering snows !
Not all your rage, as now united, shows   40
More hard unkindness, unrelenting,
Vengeful malice unrepenting,
Than heaven-illumin'd Man on brother Man bestows !
See stern Oppression's iron grip,
Or mad Ambition's gory hand,   45
Sending, like bloodhounds from the slip,
Woe, want, and murder o'er a land !
Ev'n in the peaceful rural vale,
Truth, weeping, tells the mournful tale,
How pampered Luxury, Flattery by her side,   50
The parasite empoisoning her ear,
With all the servile wretches in the rear,
Looks o'er proud property, extended wide ;
And eyes the simple rustic hind,
Whose toil upholds the glittering show,   55
A creature of another kind,
Some coarser substance, unrefined,
Placed for her lordly use thus far, thus vile, below.
Where, where is Love's fond, tender throe,

With lordly Honour's lofty brow,   60
The powers you proudly own?
Is there, beneath Love's noble name,
Can harbour, dark, the selfish aim,
To bless himself alone?
Mark maiden-innocence a prey   65
To love-pretending snares;
This boasted Honour turns away,
Shunning soft Pity's rising sway,
Regardless of the tears and unavailing prayers!
Perhaps, this hour, in Misery's squalid nest,   70
She strains your infant to her joyless breast,
And with a mother's fears shrinks at the rocking blast!
Oh! ye, who, sunk in beds of down,
Feel not a want but what yourselves create,
Think, for a moment, on his wretched fate   75
Whom friends and fortune quite disown!
Ill-satisfied keen Nature's clam'rous call,
Stretched on his straw he lays himself to sleep,
While, through the ragged roof and chinky wall,
Chill o'er his slumbers piles the drifty heap!   80
Think on the dungeon's grim confine,
Where Guilt and poor Misfortune pine!
Guilt, erring man, relenting view;
But shall thy legal rage pursue
The wretch, already crushèd low   85
By cruel fortune's undeservèd blow?
Affliction's sons are brothers in distress;
A brother to relieve, how exquisite the bliss!'

I heard nae mair, for Chanticleer
    Shook off the pouthery snaw,   90
And hail'd the morning with a cheer,
    A cottage-rousing craw.

But deep this truth impressed my mind—
Thro' all His works abroad,
The heart benevolent and kind   95
The most resembles God.

Address to Edinburgh.

E DINA ! Scotia's darling seat!
All hail thy palaces and tow'rs,
Where once beneath a monarch's feet
Sat Legislation's sovereign pow'rs !
From marking wildly-scattered flow'rs,   5
As on the banks of Ayr I stray'd,
And singing, lone, the lingering hours,
I shelter in thy honoured shade.

Here Wealth still swells the golden tide,
As busy Trade his labours plies ;   10
There Architecture's noble pride
Bids elegance and splendour rise !
Here Justice, from her native skies,
High wields her balance and her rod ;
There Learning, with his eagle eyes,   15
Seeks Science in her coy abode.

Thy sons, Edina ! social, kind,
With open arms the stranger hail ;
Their views enlarged, their liberal mind,
Above the narrow, rural vale ;   20
Attentive still to Sorrow's wail,
Or modest Merit's silent claim ;
And never may their sources fail,
And never envy blot their name !

Thy daughters bright thy walks adorn,   25
    Gay as the gilded summer sky,
Sweet as the dewy milk-white thorn,
    Dear as the raptured thrill of joy!
Fair Burnet strikes th' adoring eye,
    Heaven's beauties on my fancy shine;   30
I see the Sire of Love on high,
    And own His work indeed divine.

There, watching high the least alarms,
    Thy rough, rude fortress gleams afar;
Like some bold veteran, grey in arms,   35
    And marked with many a seamy scar:
The ponderous wall and massy bar,
    Grim-rising o'er the rugged rock,
Have oft withstood assailing war,
    And oft repell'd th' invader's shock.   40

With awe-struck thought, and pitying tears.
    I view that noble, stately dome,
Where Scotia's kings of other years,
    Famed heroes! had their royal home:
Alas, how changed the times to come!   45
    Their royal name low in the dust,
Their hapless race wild-wandering roam!
    Though rigid law cries out 'twas just.

Wild beats my heart to trace your steps,
    Whose ancestors, in days of yore,   50
Through hostile ranks and ruined gaps
    Old Scotia's bloody lion bore:
Ev'n I who sing in rustic lore,
    Haply my sires have left their shed,

And faced grim Danger's loudest roar,   55
Bold-following where your fathers led !

Edina ! Scotia's darling seat !
All hail thy palaces and tow'rs,
Where once beneath a monarch's feet
Sat Legislation's sovereign pow'rs !   60
From marking wildly-scatter'd flow'rs,
As on the banks of Ayr I stray'd,
And singing, lone, the lingering hours,
I shelter in thy honoured shade.

To a Haggis.

FAIR fa' your honest sonsie face,
   Great chieftain o' the pudding-race !
Aboon them a' ye tak' your place,
          Painch, tripe, or thairm :
Weel are ye wordy o' a grace   5
          As lang's my arm.

The groaning trencher there ye fill,
Your hurdies like a distant hill ;
Your pin wad help to mend a mill
          In time o' need ;   10
While thro' your pores the dews distil
          Like amber bead.

His knife see rustic Labour dight,
An' cut you up wi' ready sleight,
Trenching your gushing entrails bright,   15
          Like ony ditch ;
And then, oh what a glorious sight,
          Warm-reekin', rich !

Then horn for horn they stretch an' strive ;
Deil tak' the hindmost! on they drive ;   20
Till a' their weel-swalled kytes belyve
            Are bent like drums ;
Then auld guidman, maist like to rive,
            Bethanket hums.

Is there, that owre his French ragoût,   25
Or olio that wad staw a sow,
Or fricassée wad mak' her spew
            Wi' perfect sconner,
Looks down wi' sneering scornfu' view
            On sic a dinner?   30

Poor devil! see him owre his trash
As feckless as a wither'd rash,
His spindle-shank a guid whip-lash,
            His nieve a nit;
Thro' bloody flood or field to dash,   35
            Oh how unfit!

But mark the rustic haggis-fed!
The trembling earth resounds his tread!
Clap in his walie nieve a blade,
            He 'll mak' it whissle ;   40
An' legs, an' arms, an' heads will sned,
            Like taps o' thrissle.

Ye Pow'rs wha mak' mankind your care,
And dish them out their bill o' fare,
Auld Scotland wants nae skinking ware   45
            That jaups in luggies ;
But, if ye wish her gratefu' prayer,
            Gie her a Haggis !

To the Guidwife of Wauchope House.

I MIND it weel in early date,
  When I was beardless, young, and blate,
An' first could thrash the barn,
Or haud a yokin' at the pleugh,
An' tho' forfoughten sair eneugh,   5
Yet unco proud to learn—
When first amang the yellow corn
  A man I reckon'd was,
And wi' the lave ilk merry morn
  Could rank my rig and lass,   10
    Still shearing, and clearing
      The tither stookèd raw,
    Wi' claivers an' haivers
      Wearing the day awa.

E'en then a wish (I mind its pow'r)   15
A wish that to my latest hour
  Shall strongly heave my breast,
That I, for poor auld Scotland's sake,
Some usefu' plan or book could make,
  Or sing a sang at least.   20
The rough burr-thistle, spreading wide
  Amang the bearded bear,
I turn'd the weeder-clips aside,
  An' spar'd the symbol dear:
    No nation, no station,   25
      My envy e'er could raise;
    A Scot still, but blot still,
      I knew nae higher praise.

But still the elements o' sang,
In formless jumble, right an' wrang,   30
  Wild floated in my brain;

Till, on that hairst I said before,
My partner in the merry core,
  She rous'd the forming strain.
I see her yet, the sonsie quean,   35
  That lighted up my jingle,
Her witching smile, her pauky een,
  That gart my heart-strings tingle :
    I fir èd, inspirèd,
      At every kindling keek,   40
    But bashing, and dashing,
      I fearèd aye to speak.

Health to the sex! ilk guid chiel says,
Wi' merry dance in winter days,
  An' we to share in common !   45
The gust o' joy, the balm of woe,
The saul o' life, the heaven below,
  Is rapture-giving woman.
Ye surly sumphs, who hate the name,
  Be mindfu' o' your mither ;   50
She, honest woman, may think shame
  That ye 're connected with her.
    Ye 're wae men, ye 're nae men,
      That slight the lovely dears ;
    To shame ye, disclaim ye,   55
      Ilk honest birkie swears.

For you, no bred to barn and byre,
Wha sweetly tune the Scottish lyre,
  Thanks to you for your line !
The marled plaid ye kindly spare   60
By me should gratefully be ware ;
  'Twad please me to the nine.

I 'd be mair vauntie o' my hap
Douce hingin' owre my curple,
Than ony ermine ever lap,   65
Or proud imperial purple.
   Farewell then ! lang hale then,
      An' plenty be your fa' ;
   May losses and crosses
      Ne'er at your hallan ca' !   70

The Humble Petition of Bruar Water

TO THE NOBLE DUKE OF ATHOLE.

M Y lord, I know your noble ear
   Woe ne'er assails in vain ;
Emboldened thus, I beg you 'll hear
   Your humble slave complain,
How saucy Phœbus' scorching beams,   5
   In flaming summer pride,
Dry-withering, waste my foamy streams,
   And drink my crystal tide.

The lightly-jumpin' glowerin' trouts,
   That thro' my waters play,   10
If, in their random wanton spouts,
   They near the margin stray ;
If, hapless chance ! they linger lang,
   I 'm scorching up so shallow,
They 're left the whitening stanes amang,   15
   In gasping death to wallow.

Last day I grat wi' spite and teen,
   As poet Burns came by,
That to a bard I should be seen
   Wi' half my channel dry :   20

K

A panegyric rhyme, I ween,
  Ev'n as I was, he shor'd me ;
But had I in my glory been,
  He, kneeling, wad ador'd me.

Here, foaming down the skelvy rocks,   25
  In twisting strength I rin ;
There high my boiling torrent smokes,
  Wild-roaring o'er a linn :
Enjoying large each spring and well
  As nature gave them me,   30
I am, altho' I say 't mysel',
  Worth gaun a mile to see.

Would then my noble master please
  To grant my highest wishes,
He 'll shade my banks wi' tow'ring trees,   35
  And bonnie spreading bushes.
Delighted doubly then, my lord,
  You 'll wander on my banks,
And listen mony a grateful bird
  Return you tuneful thanks.   40

The sober lav'rock, warbling wild,
  Shall to the skies aspire ;
The gowdspink, music's gayest child,
  Shall sweetly join the choir ;
The blackbird strong, the lintwhite clear,   45
  The mavis mild and mellow ;
The robin pensive autumn cheer,
  In all her locks of yellow.

This too a covert shall ensure,
  To shield them from the storm ;   50
And coward maukin sleep secure,
  Low in her grassy form :

Here shall the shepherd make his seat,
  To weave his crown of flow'rs;
Or find a shelt'ring safe retreat   55
  From prone-descending showers.

And here, by sweet endearing stealth,
  Shall meet the loving pair,
Despising worlds with all their wealth
  As empty idle care;   60
The flowers shall vie in all their charms
  The hour of heav'n to grace,
And birks extend their fragrant arms
  To screen the dear embrace.

Here, haply, too at vernal dawn   65
  Some musing bard may stray,
And eye the smoking dewy lawn,
  And misty mountain grey;
Or by the reaper's nightly beam,
  Mild-chequering thro' the trees,   70
Rave to my darkly-dashing stream,
  Hoarse-swelling on the breeze.

Let lofty firs and ashes cool
  My lowly banks o'erspread,
And view, deep-bending in the pool,   75
  Their shadows' watery bed;
Let fragrant birks, in woodbines drest,
  My craggy cliffs adorn;
And, for the little songsters' nest,
  The close embow'ring thorn.   80

So may old Scotia's darling hope,
  Your little angel band,
Spring, like their fathers, up to prop
  Their honour'd native land!

So may thro' Albion's farthest ken,   85
  To social flowing glasses,
The grace be—'Athole's honest men,
  And Athole's bonnie lasses!'

On Scaring some Water-fowl in Loch Turit.

WHY, ye tenants of the lake,
    For me your watery haunt forsake?
Tell me, fellow-creatures, why
At my presence thus you fly?
Why disturb your social joys,   5
Parent, filial, kindred ties?
Common friend to you and me,
Nature's gifts to all are free:
Peaceful keep your dimpling wave,
Busy feed, or wanton lave;   10
Or, beneath the sheltering rock,
Bide the surging billow's shock.

Conscious, blushing for our race,
Soon, too soon, your fears I trace.
Man, your proud usurping foe,   15
Would be lord of all below;
Plumes himself in freedom's pride,
Tyrant stern to all beside.

The eagle, from the cliffy brow,
Marking you his prey below,   20
In his breast no pity dwells,
Strong necessity compels.
But man, to whom alone is giv'n
A ray direct from pitying Heav'n,
Glories in his heart humane--   25
And creatures for his pleasure slain!

In these savage liquid plains,
Only known to wand'ring swains,
Where the mossy riv'let strays
Far from human haunts and ways,   30
All on Nature you depend,
And life's poor season peaceful spend.

Or, if man's superior might
Dare invade your native right,
On the lofty ether borne,   35
Man with all his powers you scorn;
Swiftly seek, on clanging wings,
Other lakes and other springs;
And the foe you cannot brave,
Scorn at least to be his slave.   40

On Captain Grose's Peregrinations thro' Scotland.

HEAR, Land o' Cakes, and brither Scots,
     Frae Maidenkirk to Johnnie Groat's!
If there's a hole in a' your coats,
          I rede you tent it :
A chield's amang you takin' notes,   5
          And faith he'll prent it.

If in your bounds ye chance to light
Upon a fine, fat, fodgel wight,
O' stature short, but genius bright,
          That's he, mark weel;   10
And wow! he has an unco sleight
          O' cauk and keel.

By some auld houlet-haunted biggin',
Or kirk deserted by its riggin',
It's ten to ane ye'll find him snug in   15
    Some eldritch part,
Wi' deils, they say, Lord save's! colleaguin'
    At some black art.

Ilk ghaist that haunts auld ha' or chaumer,
Ye gipsy-gang that deal in glamour,   20
And you, deep read in hell's black grammar,
    Warlocks and witches—
Ye'll quake at his conjuring hammer,
    Ye midnight wretches!

It's tauld he was a sodger bred,   25
And ane wad rather fa'n than fled ;
But now he's quat the spurtle blade,
    And dogskin wallet,
And ta'en the—Antiquarian trade
    I think they call it.   30

He has a fouth o' auld nick-nackets :
Rusty airn caps and jinglin' jackets,
Wad haud the Lothians three in tackets
    A towmont guid ;
And parritch-pats and auld saut-backets,   35
    Before the Flood.

Forbye, he'll shape you aff fu' gleg
The cut of Adam's philibeg :
The knife that nicket Abel's craig—
    He'll prove you fully   40
It was a faulding jocteleg,
    Or lang-kail gully.

But wad ye see him in his glee,
For meikle glee and fun has he,
Then set him down, and twa or three   45
   Guid fellows wi' him ;
And port, O port! shine thou a wee,
   And then ye 'll see him !

Now, by the pow'rs o' verse and prose,
Thou art a dainty chield, O Grose !   50
Whae'er o' thee shall ill suppose,
   They sair misca' thee ;
I 'd take the rascal by the nose,
   Wad say 'Shame fa' thee ! '

Epistle to Dr. Blacklock.

WOW, but your letter made me vauntie !
  And are ye hale, and weel, and cantie ?
I kenn'd it still, your wee bit jauntie
   Wad bring ye to :
Lord send you aye as weel 's I want ye,   5
   And then ye 'll do.

But what d'ye think, my trusty fier ?
I 'm turned a gauger—peace be here !
Parnassian queans, I fear, I fear,
   Ye 'll now disdain me !   10
And then my fifty pounds a year
   Will little gain me.

Ye glaiket, gleesome, dainty damies,
Wha by Castalia's wimplin' streamies,
Lowp, sing, and lave your pretty limbies,   15
   Ye ken, ye ken,
That strang necessity supreme is
   'Mang sons o' men.

I hae a wife and twa wee laddies;
They maun ha'e brose and brats o' duddies;   20
Ye ken yoursel's my heart right proud is—
      I need na vaunt—
But I 'll sned besoms, thraw saugh woodies,
      Before they want.

Lord help me through this warld o' care!   25
I 'm weary sick o' 't late and air!
Not but I hae a richer share
      Than mony ithers;
But why should ae man better fare,
      And a' men brithers?   30

Come, firm Resolve, take thou the van,
Thou stalk o' carl-hemp in man!
And let us mind faint heart ne'er wan
      A lady fair;
Wha does the utmost that he can,   35
      Will whyles do mair.

But to conclude my silly rhyme,
(I 'm scant o' verse, and scant o' time)
To make a happy fireside clime
      To weans and wife—   40
That 's the true pathos and sublime
      Of human life.

Elegy on Captain Matthew Henderson.

O DEATH! thou tyrant fell and bloody!
    The meikle devil wi' a woodie
Haurl thee hame to his black smiddie
      O'er hurcheon hides,
And like stock-fish come o'er his studdie   5
      Wi' thy auld sides!

He's gane! he's gane! he's frac us torn!
The ae best fellow e'er was born!
Thee, Matthew, Nature's sel' shall mourn
    By wood and wild,   10
Where, haply, Pity strays forlorn,
    Frae man exil'd!

Ye hills, near ncibors o' the starns,
That proudly cock your cresting cairns!
Ye cliffs, the haunts of sailing earns,   15
    Where Echo slumbers!
Come, join, ye Nature's sturdiest bairns,
    My wailing numbers!

Mourn, ilka grove the cushat kens!
Ye haz'ly shaws and briery dens!   20
Ye burnies, wimplin' down your glens
    Wi' toddlin' din,
Or foaming strang, wi' hasty stens,
    Frae lin to lin!

Mourn, little harebells o'er the lea;   25
Ye stately foxgloves, fair to see;
Ye woodbines, hanging bonnilie
    In scented bow'rs;
Ye roses on your thorny tree,
    The first o' flow'rs!   30

At dawn, when ev'ry grassy blade
Droops with a diamond at his head;
At ev'n, when beans their fragrance shed
    I' the rustling gale—
Ye maukins, whiddin through the glade,   35
    Come join my wail!

Mourn, ye wee songsters o' the wood;
Ye grouse that crap the heather bud;
Ye curlews, calling thro' a clud;
      Ye whistling plover;   40
And mourn, ye whirring paitrick brood!
      He 's gane for ever!

Mourn, sooty coots, and speckled teals;
Ye fisher herons, watching eels;
Ye duck and drake, wi' airy wheels   45
      Circling the lake;
Ye bitterns, till the quagmire reels,
      Rair for his sake!

Mourn, clam'ring craiks, at close o' day,
'Mang fields o' flow'ring clover gay;   50
And, when ye wing your annual way
      Frae our cauld shore,
Tell thae far warlds wha lies in clay,
      Wham we deplore.

Ye houlets, frae your ivy bow'r,   55
In some auld tree or eldritch tow'r,
What time the moon, wi' silent glow'r,
      Sets up her horn,
Wail thro' the dreary midnight hour
      Till waukrife morn!   60

O rivers, forests, hills, and plains!
Oft have ye heard my canty strains;
But now, what else for me remains
      But tales of woe?
And frae my een the drapping rains   65
      Maun ever flow!

Mourn, Spring, thou darling of the year!
Ilk cowslip cup shall kep a tear:
Thou, Simmer, while each corny spear
                Shoots up its head,   70
Thy gay, green, flow'ry tresses shear
                For him that's dead!

Thou, Autumn, wi' thy yellow hair,
In grief thy sallow mantle tear!
Thou, Winter, hurling thro' the air   75
                The roaring blast,
Wide o'er the naked world declare
                The worth we've lost!

Mourn him, thou Sun, great source of light!
Mourn, empress of the silent night!   80
And you, ye twinkling starnies bright,
                My Matthew mourn!
For through your orbs he's ta'en his flight,
                Ne'er to return.

O Henderson! the man—the brother!   85
And art thou gone, and gone for ever?
And hast thou crost that unknown river,
                Life's dreary bound?
Like thee, where shall I find another,
                The world around!   90

Go to your sculptur'd tombs, ye Great,
In a' the tinsel trash o' state!
But by thy honest turf I'll wait,
                Thou man of worth!
And weep the ae best fellow's fate   95
                E'er lay in earth.

Tam o' Shanter.

A TALE.

WHEN chapman billies leave the street,
And drouthy neibors neibors meet,
As market-days are wearing late,
An' folk begin to tak the gate ;
While we sit bousing at the nappy,   5
An' getting fou and unco happy,
We think na on the lang Scots miles,
The mosses, waters, slaps, and styles,
That lie between us and our hame,
Where sits our sulky, sullen dame,   10
Gathering her brows like gathering storm,
Nursing her wrath to keep it warm.

This truth fand honest Tam o' Shanter,
As he frae Ayr ae night did canter
(Auld Ayr, whom ne'er a town surpasses   15
For honest men and bonny lasses.)

O Tam ! hadst thou but been sae wise
As ta'en thy ain wife Kate's advice !
She tauld thee weel thou was a skellum,
A bletherin', blusterin', drunken blellum,   20
That, frae November till October,
Ae market-day thou was na sober ;
That ilka melder wi' the miller,
Thou sat as lang as thou had siller ;
That every naig was ca'd a shoe on,   25
The smith and thee gat roarin' fou on ;
That at the Lord's house, even on Sunday,
Thou drank wi' Kirkton Jean till Monday.

She prophesied that, late or soon,
Thou wad be found deep drown'd in Doon,   30
Or catch'd wi' warlocks in the mirk
By Alloway's auld haunted kirk.

Ah, gentle dames! it gars me greet
To think how mony counsels sweet,
How mony lengthen'd sage advices,   35
The husband frae the wife despises!

But to our tale : Ae market-night
Tam had got planted unco right
Fast by an ingle, bleezing finely,
Wi' reaming swats, that drank divinely;   40
And at his elbow, souter Johnnie,
His ancient, trusty, drouthy crony :
Tam lo'ed him like a very brither;
They had been fou for weeks thegither.
The night drave on wi' sangs an' clatter;   45
And aye the ale was growing better :
The landlady and Tam grew gracious,
Wi' favours secret, sweet, and precious :
The souter tauld his queerest stories;
The landlord's laugh was ready chorus :   50
The storm without might rair and rustle,
Tam did na mind the storm a whistle.

Care, mad to see a man sae happy,
E'en drowned himsel' amang the nappy.
As bees flee hame wi' lades o' treasure,   55
The minutes wing'd their way wi' pleasure :
Kings may be blest, but Tam was glorious,
O'er a' the ills o' life victorious!

But pleasures are like poppies spread—
You seize the flower, its bloom is shed!   60
Or like the snow falls in the river—
A moment white, then melts for ever;
Or like the borealis race—
That flit ere you can point their place;
Or like the rainbow's lovely form—   65
Evanishing amid the storm.

Nae man can tether time nor tide;
The hour approaches Tam maun ride;
That hour, o' night's black arch the keystane,
That dreary hour Tam mounts his beast in;   70
And sic a night he took the road in
As ne'er poor sinner was abroad in.

The wind blew as 'twad blawn its last;
The rattling showers rose on the blast;
The speedy gleams the darkness swallow'd;   75
Loud, deep, and lang the thunder bellow'd:
That night, a child might understand,
The deil had business on his hand.

Weel mounted on his gray meare, Meg,
A better never lifted leg,   80
Tam skelpit on thro' dub and mire,
Despising wind and rain and fire—
Whiles holding fast his gude blue bonnet,
Whiles crooning o'er an auld Scots sonnet,
Whiles glow'ring round wi' prudent cares   85
Lest bogles catch him unawares.
Kirk-Alloway was drawing nigh,
Where ghaists and houlets nightly cry.

By this time he was cross the ford,
Where in the snaw the chapman smoor'd;   90
And past the birks aud meikle stane,
Where drunken Charlie brak 's neck-bane;
And thro' the whins, and by the cairn,
Where hunters fand the murder'd bairn;
And near the thorn, aboon the well,   95
Where Mungo's mither hanged hersel'.
Before him Doon pours all his floods;
The doubling storm roars through the woods;
The lightnings flash from pole to pole;
Near and more near the thunders roll;   100
When, glimmering thro' the groaning trees,
Kirk-Alloway seem'd in a bleeze;
Through ilka bore the beams were glancing,
And loud resounded mirth and dancing.

Inspiring bold John Barleycorn!   105
What dangers thou canst make us scorn!
Wi' tippenny we fear nae evil;
Wi' usquabae we'll face the devil!
The swats sae reamed in Tammie's noddle,
Fair play—he car'd na deils a boddle!   110
But Maggie stood right sair astonish'd,
Till, by the heel and hand admonish'd,
She ventur'd forward on the light;
And wow! Tam saw an unco sight!
Warlocks and witches in a dance!   115
Nae cotillon, brent new frae France,
But hornpipes, jigs, strathspeys, and reels,
Put life and mettle in their heels.
A winnock-bunker in the east,
There sat auld Nick in shape o' beast—   120

A towzie tyke, black, grim, and large!
To gie them music was his charge :
He screw'd the pipes, and gart them skirl
Till roof and rafters a' did dirl!
Coffins stood round, like open presses,   125
That shaw'd the dead in their last dresses;
And, by some devilish cantrip sleight,
Each in its cauld hand held a light,
By which heroic Tam was able
To note upon the haly table,   130
A murderer's banes in gibbet airns;
Twa span-lang, wee, unchristen'd bairns;
A thief new-cutted frae a rape—
Wi' his last gasp his gab did gape ;
Five tomahawks wi' blude red-rusted ;   135
Five scymitars wi' murder crusted ;
A garter which a babe had strangled ;
A knife a father's throat had mangled,
Whom his ain son of life bereft—
The grey hairs yet stack to the heft;   140
Wi' mair of horrible and awefu',
Which even to name wad be unlawfu'.

As Tammie glowr'd, amaz'd and curious,
The mirth and fun grew fast and furious :
The piper loud and louder blew;   145
The dancers quick and quicker flew;
They reel'd, they set, they cross'd, they cleekit,
Till ilka carlin swat and reekit,
And coost her duddies on the wark,
And linket at it in her sark !   150

Now Tam, O Tam! had they been queans
A' plump and strapping in their teens,

Their sarks, instead o' creeshie flannen,
Been snaw-white seventeen hunder linen;
Thir breeks o' mine, my only pair,   155
That ance were plush, o' guid blue hair,
I wad hae gi'en them off my hurdies,
For ae blink o' the bonnie burdies!

But wither'd beldams, auld and droll,
Rigwoodie hags wad spean a foal,   160
Louping an' flinging on a crummock,
I wonder didna turn thy stomach.

But Tam kent what was what fu' brawlie:
There was ae winsome wench and waulie,
That night enlisted in the core,   165
Lang after kenn'd on Carrick shore!
(For mony a beast to dead she shot,
And perish'd mony a bonnie boat,
And shook baith meikle corn and bear,
And held the country-side in fear.)   170
Her cutty sark, o' Paisley harn,
That while a lassie she had worn,
In longitude tho' sorely scanty,
It was her best, and she was vauntie.
Ah! little kent thy reverend grannie,   175
That sark she coft for her wee Nannie
Wi' twa pund Scots ('twas a' her riches)
Wad ever grac'd a dance of witches!

But here my muse her wing maun cour;
Sic flights are far beyond her power—   180
To sing how Nannie lap and flang
(A souple jade she was and strang)
And how Tam stood, like ane bewitch'd,
And thought his very een enrich'd!

L

Even Satan glowr'd, and fidg'd fu' fain, —— — 185
And hotch'd and blew wi' might and main ;
Till first ae caper, syne anither,
Tam tint his reason a'thegither,
And roars out 'Weel done, Cutty-sark!'
And in an instant all was dark :   190
And scarcely had he Maggie rallied,
When out the hellish legion sallied.

As bees bizz out wi' angry fyke
When plundering herds assail their byke ;
As open pussie's mortal foes   195
When pop ! she starts before their nose ;
As eager runs the market-crowd
When 'Catch the thief!' resounds aloud ;
So Maggie runs, the witches follow,
Wi' mony an eldritch skriech and hollow.   200

Ah Tam ! ah Tam ! thou 'll get thy fairin' !
In hell they 'll roast thee like a herrin' !
In vain thy Kate awaits thy comin'—
Kate soon will be a woefu' woman !
Now do thy speedy utmost, Meg,   205
And win the key-stane o' the brig ;
There at them thou thy tail may toss,
A running stream they dare na cross.
But ere the key-stane she could make,
The fient a tail she had to shake !   210
For Nannie, far before the rest,
Hard upon noble Maggie prest,
And flew at Tam wi' furious ettle ;
But little wist she Maggie's mettle !
Ae spring brought off her master hale,   215
But left behind her ain grey tail :

The carlin claught her by the rump,
And left poor Maggie scarce a stump !

Now, wha this tale o' truth shall read,
Each man and mother's son, take heed :   220
Whene'er to drink you are inclined,
Or cutty sarks rin in your mind,
Think !—ye may buy the joys o'er dear ;
Remember Tam o' Shanter's meare.

Lament of Queen Mary.

NOW Nature hangs her mantle green
      On every blooming tree,
And spreads her sheets o' daisies white
    Out o'er the grassy lea :
Now Phœbus cheers the crystal streams,   5
    And glads the azure skies ;
But nought can glad the weary wight
    That fast in durance lies.

Now lavcrocks wake the merry morn,
    Aloft on dewy wing ;   10
The merle, in his noontide bower,
    Makes woodland echoes ring ;
The mavis wild, wi' mony a note,
    Sings drowsy day to rest :
In love and freedom they rejoice,   15
    Wi' care nor thrall opprest.

Now blooms the lily by the bank,
    The primrose down the brae ;
The hawthorn 's budding in the glen,
    And milk-white is the slae :   20

L 2

The meanest hind in fair Scotlànd
  May rove thae sweets amang;
But I, the Queen of a' Scotlànd,
  Maun lie in prison strang.

I was the Queen o' bonnie France,   25
  Where happy I hae been;
Fu' lightly rase I in the morn,
  As blythe lay down at e'en:
And I'm the sovereign of Scotlànd,
  And mony a traitor there;   30
Yet here I lie in foreign bands,
  And never-ending care.

But as for thee, thou false woman,
  My sister and my fae,
Grim vengeance yet shall whet a sword   35
  That thro' thy soul shall gae:
The weeping blood in woman's breast
  Was never known to thee;
Nor th' balm that drops on wounds of woe
  Frae woman's pitying ee.   40

My son! my son! may kinder stars
  Upon thy fortune shine;
And may those pleasures gild thy reign
  That ne'er wad blink on mine!
God keep thee frae thy mother's faes,   45
  Or turn their hearts to thee;
And where thou meet'st thy mother's friend
  Remember him for me!

Oh soon to me may summer suns
  Nae mair light up the morn!   50
Nae mair to me the autumn winds
  Wave o'er the yellow corn!

And in the narrow house of death
Let winter round me rave ;
And the next flowers that deck the spring   55
Bloom on my peaceful grave!

On Pastoral Poetry.

HAIL, Poesie! thou nymph reserv'd!
   In chase o' thee what crowds hae swerv'd
Frae common sense, or sunk enerv'd
      'Mang heaps o' clavers!
And och! o'er aft thy joes hae starv'd,   5
     • Mid a' thy favours!

Say, lassie, why, thy train amang,
While loud the trump's heroic clang,
And sock or buskin skelp alang
      To death or marriage—   10
Scarce ane has tried the shepherd-sang
      But wi' miscarriage?

In Homer's craft Jock Milton thrives;
Eschylus' pen Will Shakespeare drives;
Wee Pope, the knurlin, till him rives   15
      Horatian fame ;
In thy sweet sang, Barbauld, survives
      Even Sappho's flame.

But thee, Theocritus, wha matches?
They're no herd's ballats, Maro's catches;   20
Squire Pope but busks his skinklin patches
      O' heathen tatters :
I pass by hunders, nameless wretches,
      That ape their betters.

In this braw age o' wit and lear   25
Will nane the shepherd's whistle mair
Blaw sweetly in its native air
        And rural grace,
And, wi' the far-fam'd Grecian, share
        A rival place?   30

Yes! there is ane—a Scottish callan!
There's ane! come forrit, honest Allan!
Thou need na jouk behint the hallan,
        A chiel sae clever;
The teeth o' Time may gnaw Tantallan,   35
        But thou's for ever.

Thou paints auld Nature to the nines
In thy sweet Caledonian lines:
Nae gowden stream thro' myrtles twines,
        Where Philomel,   40
While nightly breezes sweep the vines,
        Her griefs will tell!

In gowany glens thy burnie strays,
Where bonnie lasses bleach their claes;
Or trots by hazelly shaws and braes,   45
        Wi' hawthorns gray,
Where blackbirds join the shepherd's lays
        At close o' day.

Thy rural loves are Nature's sel';
Nae bombast spates o' nonsense swell;   50
Nae snap conceits, but that sweet spell
        O' witchin' love—
That charm that can the strongest quell,
        The sternest move.

SONGS.

—◆—

Mary Morison.

O MARY, at thy window be—
　　It is the wish'd, the trysted hour!
Those smiles and glances let me see,
　　That make the miser's treasure poor.
How blythely wad I bide the stoure,　　　5
　　A weary slave frae sun to sun,
Could I the rich reward secure—
　　The lovely Mary Morison.

Yestreen, when to the trembling string
　　The dance gaed thro' the lighted ha',　　10
To thee my fancy took its wing—
　　I sat, but neither heard nor saw.
Though this was fair, and that was braw,
　　And yon the toast of a' the town,
I sigh'd, and said amang them a'　　　15
　　'Ye are na Mary Morison.'

Oh, Mary, canst thou wreck his peace
　　Wha for thy sake wad gladly die?
Or canst thou break that heart of his,
　　Whase only faut is loving thee?　　　20
If love for love thou wilt na gie,
　　At least be pity to me shown;
A thought ungentle canna be
　　The thought o' Mary Morison.

An August Song to. Peggy.

N OW westlin winds and slaught'ring guns
⠀⠀Bring autumn's pleasant weather;
The moorcock springs on whirring wings
⠀⠀Amang the blooming heather:
Now waving grain, wide o'er the plain,⠀⠀⠀⠀⠀⠀5
⠀⠀Delights the weary farmer;
And the moon shines bright when I rove at night
⠀⠀To muse upon my charmer.

The partridge loves the fruitful fells;
⠀⠀The plover loves the mountains;⠀⠀⠀⠀⠀⠀10
The woodcock haunts the lonely dells,
⠀⠀The soaring hern the fountains:
Thro' lofty groves the cushat roves,
⠀⠀The path of man to shun it;
The hazel bush o'erhangs the thrush,⠀⠀⠀⠀⠀⠀15
⠀⠀The spreading thorn the linnet.

Thus ev'ry kind their pleasure find—
⠀⠀The savage and the tender;
Some social join, and leagues combine,
⠀⠀Some solitary wander.⠀⠀⠀⠀⠀⠀20
Avaunt—away the cruel sway,
⠀⠀Tyrannic man's dominion!
The sportsman's joy, the murdering cry,
⠀⠀The flutt'ring gory pinion!

But, Peggy dear, the ev'ning's clear,⠀⠀⠀⠀⠀⠀25
⠀⠀Thick flies the skimming swallow;
The sky is blue, the fields in view
⠀⠀All fading-green and yellow:

Come let us stray our gladsome way,
  And view the charms of Nature;   30
The rustling corn, the fruited thorn,
  And ev'ry happy creature.

We'll gently walk, and sweetly talk,
  Till the silent moon shine clearly;
I'll clasp thy waist, and, fondly prest,   35
  Swear how I love thee dearly:
Not vernal showers to budding flowers,
  Not autumn to the farmer,
So dear can be as thou to me,
  My fair, my lovely charmer!   40

'*My Nannie, O.*'

BEHIND yon hills where Lugar flows
    'Mang moors an' mosses many, O,
The wintry sun the day has clos'd,
  And I'll awa to Nannie, O.

The westlin wind blaws loud an' shrill;   5
  The night's baith mirk and rainy, O;
But I'll get my plaid, an' out I'll steal,
  An' owre the hill to Nannie, O.

My Nannie's charming, sweet, an' young;
  Nae artfu' wiles to win ye, O: 10
May ill befa' the flattering tongue
  That wad beguile my Nannie, O!

Her face is fair, her heart is true,
  As spotless as she's bonnie, O;
The op'ning gowan wat wi' dew   15
  Nae **purer** is than Nannie, O.

A country lad is my degree,
　An' few there be that ken me, O;
But what care I how few they be?
　I'm welcome aye to Nannie, O.   20

My riches a' 's my penny-fee,
　An' I maun guide it cannie, O;
But warl's gear ne'er troubles me,
　My thoughts are a' my Nannie, O.

Our auld guidman delights to view   25
　His sheep an' kye thrive bonnie, O;
But I 'm as blythe that hauds his pleugh,
　An' has nae care but Nannie, O.

Come weel, come woe, I care na by;
　I 'll tak what Heav'n will sen' me, O;   30
Nae ither care in life have I
　But live an' love my Nannie, O.

'*Rantin' Rovin' Robin.*'

THERE was a lad was born in Kyle,
　But whatna day o' whatna style,
I doubt it 's hardly worth the while
　To be sae nice wi' Robin.
　　Robin was a rovin' boy,   5
　　　Rantin', rovin', rantin', rovin';
　　Robin was a rovin' boy,
　　　Rantin' rovin Robin!

Our monarch's hindmost year but ane
　Was five-and-twenty days begun,   10
'Twas then a blast o' Janwar win'
　Blew hansel in on Robin.

The gossip keekit in his loof;
Quo' scho 'Wha lives will see the proof,
This waly boy will be nae coof—   15
    I think we'll ca' him Robin.

'He'll hae misfortunes great an' sma',
But aye a heart aboon them a';
He'll be a credit till us a'—
    We'll a' be proud o' Robin.'   20

Farewell to Ballochmyle.

THE Catrine woods were yellow seen,
    The flowers decay'd on Catrine lee;
Nae lav'rock sang on hillock green,
    But nature sickened on the ee.
Thro' faded groves Maria sang,   5
    Hersel' in beauty's bloom the while,
And aye the wild-wood echoes rang
    Fareweel the braes o' Ballochmyle!

Low in your wintry beds, ye flowers,
    Again ye'll flourish fresh and fair;   10
Ye birdies dumb in with'ring bowers,
    Again ye'll charm the vocal air.
But here, alas! for me nae mair
    Shall birdie charm or floweret smile;
Fareweel the bonnie banks of Ayr!   15
    Fareweel, fareweel, sweet Ballochmyle!

Meenie's ee.

AGAIN rejoicing Nature sees
    Her robe assume its vernal hues;
Her leafy locks wave in the breeze,
    All freshly steep'd in morning dews.

And maun I still on Meenie doat,   5
  And bear the scorn that's in her ee?
For it's jet jet black, an' it's like a hawk,
  An' it winna let a body be!

In vain to me the cowslips blaw,
  In vain to me the violets spring,   10
In vain to me in glen or shaw
  The mavis and the lintwhite sing.

The merry ploughboy cheers his team;
  Wi' joy the tentic seedsman stalks;
But life to me's a weary dream,   15
  A dream of ane that never wauks.

The wanton coot the water skims;
  Amang the reeds the ducklings cry;
The stately swan majestic swims,
  And ev'ry thing is blest but I.   20

The shepherd steeks his faulding slap,
  And o'er the moorlands whistles shrill;
Wi' wild, unequal, wand'ring step
  I meet him on the dewy hill.

And when the lark, 'tween light and dark,   25
  Blythe waukens by the daisy's side,
And mounts and sings on flittering wings,
  A woe-worn ghaist I hameward glide.

Come, Winter, with thine angry howl,
  And, raging, bend the naked tree;   30
Thy gloom will soothe my cheerless soul,
  When Nature all is sad like me!

Farewell the Bonnie Banks of Ayr.

THE gloomy night is gath'ring fast,
　　Loud roars the wild inconstant blast;
Yon murky cloud is foul with rain,
I see it driving o'er the plain.
The hunter now has left the moor,　　　　　　5
The scatter'd coveys meet secure,
While here I wander, prest with care,
Along the lonely banks of Ayr.

The Autumn mourns her ripening corn
By early Winter's ravage torn ;　　　　　　10
Across her placid azure sky
She sees the scowling tempest fly :
Chill runs my blood to hear it rave ;
I think upon the stormy wave,
Where many a danger I must dare,　　　　　　15
Far from the bonnie banks of Ayr.

'Tis not the surging billow's roar;
'Tis not that fatal deadly shore ;
Though death in every shape appear,
The wretched have no more to fear :　　　　　　20
But round my heart the ties are bound,
That heart transpierc'd with many a wound ;
These bleed afresh, those ties I tear,
To leave the bonnie banks of Ayr.

Farewell, old Coila's hills and dales,　　　　　　25
Her heathy moors and winding vales !
The scenes where wretched fancy roves,
Pursuing past unhappy loves !

Farewell, my friends! farewell, my focs!
My peace with these, my love with those :   30
The bursting tears my heart declare—
Farewell the bonnie banks of Ayr!

The Birks of Aberfeldy.

BONNIE lassie, will ye go,
   Will ye go, will ye go,
Bonnie lassie, will ye go
   To the birks of Aberfeldy?

Now simmer blinks on flowery braes,   5
And o'er the crystal streamlet plays,
Come let us spend the lightsome days
   In the birks of Aberfeldy.

The little birdies blythely sing,
While o'er their heads the hazels hing,   10
Or lightly flit on wanton wing
   In the birks of Aberfeldy.

The braes ascend like lofty wa's,
The foaming stream deep-roaring fa's,
O'erhung wi' fragrant spreading shaws—   15
   The birks of Aberfeldy.

The hoary cliffs are crown'd wi' flowers,
White o'er the linns the burnie pours,
And rising weets wi' misty showers
   The birks of Aberfeldy.   20

Let Fortune's gifts at random flee,
They ne'er shall draw a wish frae me,
Supremely blest wi' love and thee
   In the birks of Aberfeldy.

To Clarinda.

CLARINDA, mistress of my soul,
  The measured time is run!
The wretch beneath the dreary pole
  So marks his latest sun.

To what dark cave of frozen night   5
  Shall poor Sylvander hie?
Depriv'd of thee, his life and light,
  The sun of all his joy!

We part—but, by these precious drops
  That fill thy lovely eyes!   10
No other light shall guide my steps
  Till thy bright beams arise.

She, the fair sun of all her sex,
  Has blest my glorious day;
And shall a glimmering planet fix   15
  My worship to its ray?

Macpherson's Farewell.

FAREWELL, ye dungeons dark and strong,
  The wretch's destinie!
Macpherson's time will not be long
  On yonder gallows-tree.

  Sae rantingly, sae wantonly,   5
    Sae dauntingly gaed he;
  He played a spring, and danced it round,
    Below the gallows-tree.

O what is death but parting breath?
  On many a bloody plain   10
I've dared his face, and in this place
  I scorn him yet again!

Untie these bands from off my hands,
   And bring to me my sword,
And there's no a man in all Scotlànd   15
   But I'll brave him at a word.

I've lived a life of sturt and strife ;
   I die by treacherie :
It burns my heart I must depart
   And not avengèd be.   ' 20

Now farewell light, thou sunshine bright,
   And all beneath the sky !
May coward shame distain his name,
   The wretch that dares not die !

'*Of a' the Airts.*'

O F a' the airts the wind can blaw
      I dearly like the west,
For there the bonnie lassie lives,
   The lassie I lo'e best :
There's wild-woods grow, and rivers row,   5
   And mony a hill between ;
But day and night my fancy's flight
   Is ever wi' my Jean.

I see her in the dewy flowers,
   I see her sweet and fair ;   10
I hear her in the tunefu' birds,
   I hear her charm the air :
There's not a bonnie flower that springs
   By fountain, shaw, or green ;
There's not a bonnie bird that sings,   15
   But minds me o' my Jean.

The Lazy Mist.

THE lazy mist hangs from the brow of the hill,
　　Concealing the course of the dark winding rill ;
How languid the scenes, late so sprightly, appear,
As autumn to winter resigns the pale year !
The forests are leafless, the meadows are brown,　　5
And all the gay foppery of summer is flown :
Apart let me wander, apart let me muse,
How quick time is flying, how keen fate pursues !

How long I have lived—but how much lived in vain !
How little of life's scanty span may remain !　　10
What aspects old Time in his progress has worn !
What ties cruel Fate in my bosom has torn !
How foolish, or worse, till our summit is gained !
And downward, how weaken'd, how darken'd, how
　　pain'd !
Life is not worth having, with all it can give ;　　15
For something beyond it poor man sure must live.

Auld Lang Syne.

SHOULD auld acquaintance be forgot,
　　And never brought to mind ?
Should auld acquaintance be forgot,
　　And auld lang syne ?
　　　　For auld lang syne, my dear,　　5
　　　　For auld lang syne,
　　　　We 'll tak' a cup o' kindness yet,
　　　　For auld lang syne !

We twa hae run about the braes,
　　And pou'd the gowans fine ;　　10
But we 've wandered mony a weary foot
　　Sin' auld lang syne.

M

We twa hae paidl'd in the burn,
   Frae mornin' sun till dine ;
But seas between us braid hae roared   15
   Sin' auld lang syne.

And there 's a hand, my trustie fiere,
   And gie 's a hand o' thine ;
And we 'll tak' a right guid-willie waught
   For auld lang syne.   20

And surely ye 'll be your pint-stowp,
   And surely I 'll be mine ;
And we 'll tak' a cup o' kindness yet
   For auld lang syne.

'*Go, fetch to me a pint o' Wine.*'

GO, fetch to me a pint o' wine,
   And fill it in a silver tassie,
That I may drink, before I go,
   A service to my bonnie lassie.
The boat rocks at the pier o' Leith ;   5
   Fu' loud the wind blaws frae the ferry ;
The ship rides by the Berwick-law,
   And I maun leave my bonnie Mary.

The trumpets sound, the banners fly,
   The glittering spears are rankèd ready ;   10
The shouts o' war are heard afar,
   The battle closes thick and bloody !
It 's not the roar o' sea or shore
   Wad make me langer wish to tarry ;
Nor shouts o' war that 's heard afar—   15
   It 's leaving thee, my bonnie Mary.

'*John Anderson, my jo!*'

JOHN Anderson, my jo John,
   When we were first acquent,
Your locks were like the raven,
   Your bonnie brow was brent ;
But now your brow is beld, John,   5
   Your locks are like the snaw ;
But blessings on your frosty pow,
   John Anderson, my jo.

John Anderson, my jo John,
   We clamb the hill thegither;   10
And mony a canty day, John,
   We've had wi' ane anither :
Now we maun totter down, John,
   And hand in hand we'll go ;
And sleep thegither at the foot,   15
   John Anderson, my jo.

Willie's Browst.

O WILLIE brew'd a peck o' maut,
   And Rob and Allan cam' to see ;
Three blyther hearts, that lee-lang night,
   Ye wad na found in Christendie.
     We are na fou, we're nae that fou,   5
      But just a drappie in our ee ;
     The cock may craw, the day may daw,
      And aye we'll taste the barley bree.

Here are we met, three merry boys,
   Three merry boys, I trow, are we ;   10
And mony a night we've merry been,
   And mony mae we hope to be !

It is the moon, I ken her horn,
   That 's blinkin' in the lift sae hie ;
She shines sae bright to wyle us hame,   15
   But, by my sooth, she 'll wait a wee!

Wha first shall rise to gang awa,
   A craven, coward loon is he!
Wha first beside his chair shall fa',
   He is the king amang us three!   20

To Mary in Heaven.

THOU lingering star, with less'ning ray,
   That lov'st to greet the early morn,
Again thou usher'st in the day
   My Mary from my soul was torn.
O Mary! dear departed shade!   5
   Where is thy place of blissful rest?
Seest thou thy lover lowly laid?
   Hear'st thou the groans that rend his breast?

That sacred hour can I forget?
   Can I forget the hallowed grove,   10
Where, by the winding Ayr, we met,
   To live one day of parting love?
Eternity can not efface
   Those records dear of transports past ;
Thy image at our last embrace—   15
   Ah! little thought we 't was our last!

Ayr, gurgling, kiss'd his pebbled shore,
   O'erhung with wild-woods, thickening green;
The fragrant birch and hawthorn hoar
   Twin'd amorous round the raptur'd scene ;   20

The flowers sprang wanton to be prest;
The birds sang love on every spray;
Till too, too soon the glowing west
Proclaim'd the speed of wingèd day.

Still o'er these scenes my mem'ry wakes,   25
And fondly broods with miser care;
Time but th' impression stronger makes,
As streams their channels deeper wear.
My Mary! dear departed shade!
Where is thy place of blissful rest?   30
Seest thou thy lover lowly laid?
Hear'st thou the groans that rend his breast?

Banks and Braes o' Bonnie Doon.

YE banks and braes o' bonnie Doon,
    How can ye bloom sae fresh and fair?
How can ye chant, ye little birds,
    And I sae weary fu' o' care?
Thou 'll break my heart, thou warbling bird,   5
    That wantons thro' the flowering thorn;
Thou minds me o' departed joys,
    Departed never to return!

Aft hae I roved by bonnie Doon,
    To see the rose and woodbine twine;   10
And ilka bird sang o' its love,
    And fondly sae did I o' mine.
Wi' lightsome heart I pu'd a rose,
    Fu' sweet upon its thorny tree;
And my fause lover staw my rose,   15
    But ah! he left the thorn wi' me.

'*Oh, for Ane-an'-Twenty, Tam!*'

OH, for ane-an'-twenty, Tam!
   And hey, sweet ane-an'-twenty, Tam!
I 'll learn my kin a rattlin' sang,
   An I saw ane-and-twenty, Tam.

They snool me sair, and haud me down,   5
   And gar me look like bluntie, Tam;
But three short years will soon wheel roun'—
   An' then comes ane-an'-twenty, Tam.

A glieb o' lan', a claut o' gear,
   Was left me by my auntie, Tam;   10
At kith or kin I need na spier,
   An I saw ane-an'-twenty, Tam.

They 'll hae me wed a wealthy coof,
   Tho' I mysel' hae plenty, Tam;
But hear'st thou, laddie? there 's my loof!   15
   I 'm thine at ane-an'-twenty, Tam!

Sweet Afton.

FLOW gently, sweet Afton, among thy green braes,
   Flow gently, I 'll sing thee a song in thy praise:
My Mary 's asleep by thy murmuring stream,
Flow gently, sweet Afton, disturb not her dream.   4

Thou stock-dove whose echo resounds thro' the glen,
Ye wild whistling blackbirds in yon thorny den,
Thou green-crested lapwing, thy screaming forbear,
I charge you, disturb not my slumbering Fair.

How lofty, sweet Afton, thy neighbouring hills,
Far-mark'd with the courses of clear-winding rills!   10
There daily I wander as noon rises high,
My flocks and my Mary's sweet cot in my eye.

How pleasant thy banks and green valleys below,
Where wild in the woodlands the primroses blow!
There oft, as mild ev'ning weeps over the lea,   15
The sweet-scented birk shades my Mary and me.

Thy crystal stream, Afton, how lovely it glides,
And winds by the cot where my Mary resides;
How wanton thy waters her snowy feet lave,
As, gath'ring sweet flowerets, she stems thy clear
    wave!   20

Flow gently sweet Afton, among thy green braes,
Flow gently, sweet river, the theme of my lays;
My Mary's asleep by thy murmuring stream,
Flow gently, sweet Afton, disturb not her dream.

Song of Death on the Battle-field.

FAREWELL, thou fair day! thou green earth! and ye
    skies,
  Now gay with the broad setting sun!
Farewell, loves and friendships, ye dear tender ties!
  Our race of existence is run!

Thou grim king of terrors! thou life's gloomy foe!   5
  Go, frighten the coward and slave;
Go, teach them to tremble, fell tyrant! but know
  No terrors hast thou to the brave!

Thou strik'st the dull peasant—he sinks in the dark,
  Nor saves e'en the wreck of a name;   10
Thou strik'st the young hero—a glorious mark!
  He falls in the blaze of his fame!

In the field of proud honour, our swords in our hands,
Our king and our country to save—
While victory shines on life's last ebbing sands—   15
Oh, who would not die with the brave?

Parting Song to Clarinda.

A E fond kiss, and then we sever;
      Ae fareweel, and then forever!
Deep in heart-wrung tears I'll pledge thee,
Warring sighs and groans I'll wage thee.
Who shall say that Fortune grieves him,   5
While the star of hope she leaves him?
Me, nae cheerful twinkle lights me;
Dark despair around benights me.

I'll ne'er blame my partial fancy,
Naething could resist my Nancy;   10
But to see her was to love her,
Love but her, and love for ever.
Had we never lov'd sae kindly,
Had we never lov'd sae blindly,
Never met—or never parted,   15
We had ne'er been broken-hearted.

Fare-thee-weel, thou first and fairest!
Fare-thee-weel, thou best and dearest!
Thine be ilka joy and treasure,
Peace, enjoyment, love, and pleasure!   20
Ae fond kiss, and then we sever;
Ae farewell, alas! for ever!
Deep in heart-wrung tears I'll pledge thee,
Warring sighs and groans I'll wage thee!

The Lea-Rig.

WHEN o'er the hill the eastern star
　　Tells bughtin'-time is near, my jo;
And owsen frae the furrow'd field
　　Return sae dowf and weary O;
Down by the burn, where scented birks　　5
　　Wi' dew are hangin' clear, my jo,
I 'll meet thee on the lea-rig,
　　My ain kind dearie O.

In mirkest glen, at midnight hour,
　　I 'd rove, and ne'er be eerie·O,　　10
If thro' that glen I gaed to thee,
　　My ain kind dearie, O;
Altho' the night were ne'er sae wild,
　　And I were ne'er sae weary O,
I 'll meet thee on the lea-rig,　　15
　　My ain kind dearie O.

The hunter lo'es the morning sun,
　　To rouse the mountain deer, my jo;
At noon the fisher seeks the glen,
　　Alang the burn to steer, my jo;　　20
Gi'e me the hour o' gloamin grey,
　　It maks my heart sae cheery O,
To meet thee on the lea-rig,
　　My ain kind dearie O.

Highland Mary.

YE banks and braes and streams around
　　The castle o' Montgomery!
Green be your woods, and fair your flowers,
　　Your waters never drumlie!

There Simmer first unfald her robes,   5
  And there the langest tarry;
For there I took the last fareweel
  O' my sweet Highland Mary.

How sweetly bloom'd the gay green birk,
  How rich the hawthorn's blossom,   10
As underneath their fragrant shade
  I clasp'd her to my bosom !
The golden hours on angel wings
  Flew o'er me and my dearie :
For dear to me as light and life   15
  Was my sweet Highland Mary.

Wi' mony a vow and lock'd embrace
  Our parting was fu' tender ;
And, pledging aft to meet again,
  We tore oursel's asunder ;   20
But oh fell Death's untimely frost,
  That nipt my flower sae early !
Now green 's the sod, and cauld 's the clay,
  That wraps my Highland Mary !

Oh pale pale now those rosy lips,   25
  I aft hae kiss'd sae fondly !
And clos'd for aye the sparkling glance,
  That dwelt on me sae kindly !
And mouldering now in silent dust
  That heart that lo'ed me dearly !   30
But still within my bosom's core
  Shall live my Highland Mary.

Duncan Gray's Wooing.

DUNCAN GRAY cam' here to woo—
Ha, ha, the wooing o' 't!
On blythe Yule-night when we were fou --
Ha, ha, the wooing o' 't!
Maggie coost her head fu' high,   5
Look'd asklent and unco skeigh,
Gart poor Duncan stand abeigh;
Ha, ha, the wooing o' 't!

Duncan fleech'd, and Duncan pray'd—
Ha, ha, the wooing o' 't!   10
Meg was deaf as Ailsa Craig—
Ha, ha, the wooing o' 't!
Duncan sigh'd baith out and in,
Grat his een baith bleert an' blin',
Spak' o' lowpin o'er a linn;   15
Ha, ha, the wooing o' 't!

Time and chance are but a tide—
Ha, ha, the wooing o' 't!
Slighted love is sair to bide—
Ha, ha, the wooing o' 't!   20
Shall I, like a fool, quoth he,
For a haughty hizzie die?
She may gae to—France for me!
Ha, ha, the wooing o' 't!

How it comes let doctors tell   25
Ha, ha, the wooing o' 't!
Meg grew sick as he grew hale—
Ha, ha, the wooing o' 't!

Something in her bosom wrings,
For relief a sigh she brings;   30
And oh her een! they spak' sic things!
    Ha, ha, the wooing o' 't!

Duncan was a lad o' grace—
    Ha, ha, the wooing o' 't!
Maggie's was a piteous case—   35
    Ha, ha, the wooing o' 't!
Duncan could na be her death,
Swelling pity smoor'd his wrath;
Now they're crouse and canty baith:
    Ha, ha, the wooing o' 't!   40

'*Braw Braw Lads.*'

BRAW, braw lads on Yarrow braes,
    Ye wander thro' the blooming heather;
But Yarrow braes nor Ettrick shaws
    Can match the lads o' Galla Water.

But there is ane, a secret ane,   5
    Aboon them a' I lo'e him better;
And I 'll be his, and he 'll be mine,
    The bonnie lad o' Galla Water.

Altho' his daddie was nae laird,
    And tho' I hae na meikle tocher,   10
Yet, rich in kindest truest love,
    We 'll tent our flocks by Galla Water.

It ne'er was wealth, it ne'er was wealth,
    That coft contentment, peace, or pleasure;
The bands and bliss o' mutual love,   15
    O that 's the chiefest warld's treasure!

Wandering Willie.

HERE awa, there awa, wandering Willie,
　Here awa, there awa, haud awa' hame ;
Come to my bosom, my ain only dearie,
　Tell me thou bring'st me my Willie the same.

Winter winds blew loud and cauld at our parting ;　5
　Fears for my Willie brought tears to my ee :
Welcome now, Simmer, and welcome, my Willie,
　The Simmer to Nature, my Willie to me.

Rest, ye wild storms, in the cave of your slumbers !
　How your dread howling a lover alarms !　　10
Waken, ye breezes, row gently, ye billows,
　And waft my dear laddie ance mair to my arms !

But oh, if he's faithless, and minds na his Nannie,
　Flow still between us, thou wide roaring main !
May I never see it, may I never trow it,　　15
　But, dying, believe that my Willie's my ain !

The Soldier's Return.

WHEN wild War's deadly blast was blawn,
　　And gentle Peace returning,
Wi' mony a sweet babe fatherless,
　　And mony a widow mourning,
I left the lines and tented field,　　5
　　Where lang I 'd been a lodger,
My humble knapsack a' my wealth,
　　A poor and honest sodger.

A leal light heart was in my breast,
    My hand unstain'd wi' plunder;   10
And for fair Scotia, hame again,
    I cheery on did wander.
I thought upon the banks o' Coil,
    I thought upon my Nancy,
I thought upon the witching smile   15
    That caught my youthful fancy.

At length I reach'd the bonnie glen
    Where early life I sported;
I pass'd the mill and trysting thorn,
    Where Nancy aft I courted :   20
Wha spied I but my ain dear maid,
    Down by her mother's dwelling!
And turn'd me round to hide the flood
    That in my een was swelling.

Wi' alter'd voice quoth I 'Sweet lass,   25
    Sweet as yon hawthorn's blossom,
Oh happy, happy may he be,
    That's dearest to thy bosom!
My purse is light, I've far to gang,
    And fain would be thy lodger;   30
I've serv'd my king and country lang—
    Take pity on a sodger.'

Sae wistfully she gazed on me,
    And lovelier was than ever;
Quo' she, 'A sodger ance I lo'ed,   35
    Forget him shall I never:
Our humble cot and hamely fare—
    Ye freely shall partake it ;
That gallant badge, the dear cockade,
    Ye're welcome for the sake o''t.'   40

She gaz'd—she redden'd like a rose,
  Syne pale like ony lily;
She sank within my arms, and cried
  'Art thou my ain dear Willie?'
'By Him who made yon sun and sky   45
  By whom true love 's regarded,
I am the man; and thus may still
  True lovers be rewarded!

The wars are o'er, and I 'm come hame,
  And find thee still true-hearted!   50
Tho' poor in gear, we 're rich in love,
  And mair we 'se ne'er be parted.'
Quo' she 'My grandsire left me gowd,
  A mailen plenish'd fairly;
And come, my faithfu' sodger lad,   55
  Thou 'rt welcome to it dearly.'

For gold the merchant ploughs the main,
  The farmer ploughs the manor;
But glory is the sodger's prize,
  The sodger's wealth is honour.   60
The brave poor sodger ne'er despise,
  Nor count him as a stranger;
Remember he 's his country's stay,
  In day and hour of danger.

Bonnie Jean.

THERE was a lass, and she was fair,
  At kirk and market to be seen;
When a' our fairest maids were met,
  The fairest maid was bonnie Jean.

And aye she wrought her mammie's wark,   5
   And aye she sang sae merrilie;
The blythest bird upon the bush
   Had ne'er a lighter heart than she.

But hawks will rob the tender joys
   That bless the little lintwhite's nest;   10
And frost will blight the fairest flowers,
   And love will break the soundest rest.

Young Robie was the brawest lad,
   The flower and pride of a' the glen;
And he had owsen, sheep, and kye,   15
   And wanton naigies nine or ten.

He gaed wi' Jeanie to the tryste,
   He danced wi' Jeanie on the down;
And lang ere witless Jeanie wist,
   Her heart was tint, her peace was stown.   20

As in the bosom of the stream
   The moonbeam dwells at dewy e'en,
So trembling, pure, was tender love
   Within the breast of bonnie Jean.

And now she works her mammie's wark,   25
   And aye she sighs wi' care and pain;
Ye wist na what her ail might be,
   Or what wad make her weel again.

But did na Jeanie's heart loup light,
   And did na joy blink in her ee,   30
As Robie tauld a tale o' love
   Ae e'enin' on the lily lea?

The sun was sinking in the west,
  The birds sang sweet in ilka grove;
His cheek to hers he fondly laid,   35
  And whispered thus his tale o' love:

'O Jeanie fair, I lo'e thee dear;
  Oh canst thou think to fancy me?
Or wilt thou leave thy mammie's cot,
  And learn to tent the farms wi' me?   40

'At barn or byre thou shalt na drudge,
  Or naething else to trouble thee;
But stray amang the heather-bells,
  And tent the waving corn wi' me.'

Now what could artless Jeanie do?   45
  She had nae will to say him na:
At length she blushed a sweet consent,
  And love was aye between them twa.

'*Scots wha hae.*'

SCOTS, wha hae wi' Wallace bled,
  Scots, wham Bruce has aften led,
Welcome to your gory bed,
          Or to victorie!

Now's the day, and now's the hour;   5
See the front o' battle lour!
See approach proud Edward's power
          Chains and slaverie!

N

Wha will be a traitor knave?
Wha can fill a coward's grave?   10
Wha sae base as be a slave?
                    Let him turn and flee!

Wha for Scotland's king and law
Freedom's sword will strongly draw,
Free-man stand, or free-man fa',   15
                    Let him on wi' me!

By oppression's woes and pains!
By your sons in servile chains!
We will drain our dearest veins,
                    But they shall be free!   20

Lay the proud usurpers low!
Tyrants fall in every foe!
Liberty's in every blow!
                    Let us do, or die!

A Red Red Rose.

MY luve is like a red red rose
      That's newly sprung in June;
My luve is like the melodie
      That's sweetly played in tune.

As fair art thou, my bonnie lass,   5
      So deep in luve am I;
And I will luve thee still, my dear,
      Till a' the seas gang dry.

Till a' the seas gang dry, my dear,
      And the rocks melt wi' the sun;   10
And I will luve thee still, my dear,
      While the sands o' life shall run.

And fare-thee-well, my only luve!
And fare-thee-well a while!
And I will come again, my luve,   15
   Tho' 'twere ten thousand mile!

Ca' the Yowes.

C A' the yowes to the knowes,
   Ca' them where the heather grows,
Ca' them where the burnie rows,
   My bonnie dearie.

Hark the mavis' e'ning sang   5
Sounding Clouden's woods amang;
Then a-faulding let us gang,
   My bonnie dearie.

We 'll gae down by Clouden side,
Through the hazels spreading wide   10
O'er the waves that sweetly glide
   To the moon sae clearly.

Yonder 's Clouden's silent towers,
Where at moonshine's midnight hours.
O'er the dewy bending flowers,   15
   Fairies dance sae cheery.

Ghaist nor bogle shalt thou fear;
Thou 'rt to love and heaven sae dear,
Nocht of ill may come thee near,
   My bonnie dearie.   20

Fair and lovely as thou art,
Thou hast stown my very heart;
I can die—but canna part,
   My bonnie dearie.

Snaws of Age.

BUT lately seen in gladsome green
  The woods rejoic'd the day;
Thro' gentle showers the laughing flowers
  In double pride were gay;
But now our joys are fled   5
  On winter blasts awa;
Yet maiden May, in rich array,
  Again shall bring them a'.

But my white pow—nae kindly thowe
  Shall melt the snaws of age;   10
My trunk of eild, but buss or beild,
  Sinks in Time's wintry rage.
Oh age has weary days,
  And nights o' sleepless pain!
Thou golden time o' youthfu' prime,   15
  Why com'st thou not again?

'My Nannie's Awa'.

NOW in her green mantle blythe Nature arrays,
  And listens the lambkins that bleat o'er the braes,
While birds warble welcomes in ilka green shaw;
But to me it's delightless—my Nannie's awa.

The snawdrap and primrose our woodlands adorn,   5
And violets bathe in the weet o' the morn;
They pain my sad bosom, sae sweetly they blaw,
They mind me o' Nannie—and Nannie's awa.

Thou lav'rock that springs frae the dews of the lawn,
The shepherd to warn o' the grey-breaking dawn,   10
And thou, mellow mavis, that hails the night fa',
Give over for pity—my Nannie's awa.

Come Autumn, sae pensive, in yellow and grey,
And soothe me wi' tidings o' Nature's decay :
The dark dreary winter, and wild-driving snaw   15
Alane can delight me—now Nannie's awa.

'*A Man's a Man for a' that.*'

IS there, for honest poverty,
   That hings his head, an' a' that?
The coward-slave ! we pass him by,
   We dare be poor for a' that !
For a' that, an' a' that,   5
   Our toils obscure, an' a' that;
The rank is but the guinea's stamp,
   The man 's the gowd for a' that.

What though on hamely fare we dine,
   Wear hoddin grey, an' a' that?   10
Gi'e fools their silks, and knaves their wine,
   A man 's a man for a' that !
For a' that, an' a' that,
   Their tinsel show, an' a' that,
The honest man, though e'er sae poor,   15
   Is king o' men for a' that.

Ye see yon birkie, ca'd a lord,
   Wha struts, an' stares, an' a' that?
Tho' hundreds worship at his word
   He 's but a coof for a' that!   20
For a' that, an' a' that,
   His ribband, star, an' a' that—
The man o' independent mind,
   He looks an' laughs at a' that.

A prince can mak' a belted knight,   25
   A marquis, duke, an' a' that ;
But an honest man 's aboon his might –
   Guid faith! he mauna fa' that!
For a' that, an' a' that,
   Their dignities, an' a' that,   30
The pith o' sense an' pride o' worth
   Are higher rank than a' that.

Then let us pray that come it may,
   As come it will for a' that,
That sense and worth, o'er a' the earth,   35
   May bear the gree, an' a' that.
For a' that, an' a' that,
   It 's comin' yet, for a' that,
That man to man, the world o'er,
   Shall brothers be for a' that.   40

The Braw Wooer.

LAST May a braw wooer cam' doun the lang glen,
   And sair wi' his love he did deave me ;
I said there was naething I hated like men,—
   The deuce gae wi' 'm to believe me, believe me,
   The deuce gae wi 'm to believe me!   5

He spak' o' the darts in my bonnie black een,
  And vow'd for my love he was deein';
I said he might dee when he likèt, for Jean—
  The Lord forgie me for leein', for leein',
  The Lord forgie me for leein'!   10

A weel-stockèt mailen, himsel' for the laird,
  And marriage aff-hand, were his proffers:
I never loot on that I kenn'd it, or car'd,
  But thought I might hae waur offers, waur offers,
  But thought I might hae waur offers.   15

But what wad ye think? in a fortnight or less—
  The de'il tak' his taste to gae near her!
He up the lang loan to my black cousin Bess—
  Guess ye how, the jad! I could bear her, could bear
    her,
  Guess ye how, the jad! I could bear her.   20

But, a' the niest week as I petted wi' care,
  I gaed to the tryste o' Dalgarnock,
And wha but my fine fickle lover was there!
  I glowr'd as I'd seen a warlock, a warlock,
  I glowr'd as I'd seen a warlock.   25

But owre my left shouther I ga'e him a blink,
  Lest neibors might say I was saucy;
My wooer he caper'd as he'd been in drink,
  And vow'd I was his dear lassie, dear lassie,
  And vow'd I was his dear lassie.   30

I spier'd for my cousin fu' couthy and sweet,
  Gin she had recover'd her hearin',
And how her new shoon fit her auld schachl't feet—
  But heavens! how he fell a-swearin', a-swearin',
  But heavens! how he fell a-swearin'!   35

He begged, for gudesake, I wad be his wife,
Or else I wad kill him wi' sorrow:
So, e'en to preserve the poor body in life,
I think I maun wed him to-morrow, to-morrow,
I think I maun wed him to-morrow.   40

In the Cauld Blast.

O WERT thou in the cauld blast
    On yonder lea, on yonder lea,
My plaidie to the angry airt,
    I'd shelter thee, I'd shelter thee;
Or did misfortune's bitter storms   5
    Around thee blaw, around thee blaw,
Thy bield should be my bosom,
    To share it a', to share it a'.

Or were I in the wildest waste,
    Sae black and bare, sae black and bare,   10
The desert were a paradise,
    If thou wert there, if thou wert there;
Or were I monarch o' the globe,
    Wi' thee to reign, wi' thee to reign,
The brightest jewel in my crown   15
    Wad be my queen, wad be my queen.

Fairest Maid on Devon Banks.

FAIREST maid on Devon banks,
    Crystal Devon, winding Devon,
Wilt thou lay that frown aside
And smile as thou wert wont to do?

Full well thou know'st I love thee dear;   5
Couldst thou to malice lend an ear?
Oh did not love exclaim 'Forbear
  Nor use a faithful lover so'?

Then come, thou fairest of the fair!
Those wonted smiles, oh let me share!   10
And by thy beauteous self I swear
  No love but thine my heart shall know.

NOTES.

—◆—

Winter—A Dirge.

THE following extract is part of a note with which Burns intro-
duces this poem in his Commonplace Book : 'There is scarcely
any earthly object gives me more—I don't know if I should call it
pleasure, but something which exalts me, something which en-
raptures me—than to walk in the sheltered side of a wood or high
plantation on a cloudy winter day, and hear a stormy wind howling
among the trees and raving o'er the plain. It is my best season
for devotion ; my mind is rapt up in a kind of enthusiasm to Him
who, in the language of Scripture, "walks on the wings of the
wind." In one of those seasons, just after a tract of misfortune, I
composed the following song.'

It was probably composed at Lochlie (a dreary farm about
ten miles inland from Ayr) in the winter of 1781-2, when the poet
was just completing his 23rd year. The 'tract of misfortune'
seems to refer to his disastrous attempt to carry on business as
a flax-dresser at Irvine. 'My partner,' he says, in his well-known
autobiographical letter to Dr. Moore, 'was a scoundrel of the first
water [i. e. robbed him] ; and to finish the whole, as we were
giving a welcome carousal to the New Year [1782], the shop took
fire and burnt to ashes, and I was left, like a true poet, not worth
sixpence.' He returned to the thraldom of the farm at Lochlie, to
find that 'clouds of misfortune were gathering thick round [my]
father's head, and what was worst of all he was visibly far gone
in a consumption.' The old man died, bankrupt, just two years
later.

l. 9. *The sweeping blast, the sky o'ercast.* In all editions this line
is placed within inverted commas, on the authority of Burns himself, as a quotation from ' Dr. Young.' Presumably this is Young
of the *Night Thoughts,*—whose *Ocean, an Ode* (of some 300

verses) includes the following passage, which seems to have lingered vaguely in the memory of Burns :—

> 'The northern blast,
> The shattered mast,
> The syrt, the whirlpool, and the rock,
> The breaking spout,
> The stars gone out,
> The boiling strait, the monsters' shock,
>
> Let others fear ;
> To Britain dear
> Whate'er promotes her daring claim,' &c.

ll. 13-16. *The tempest's howl*, &c. Cp the last stanza of his
Song *Mecnie's ec*—p. 155 in this selection :—

> 'Come, Winter, with thine angry howl,
> And, raging, bend the naked tree;
> Thy gloom will soothe my cheerless soul
> When Nature all is sad like me.'

A Prayer in Prospect of Death.

In his Commonplace Book, under date August 1784, Burns has
recorded that this was 'a Prayer when fainting fits and other
alarming symptoms . . . *first* put nature on the alarm.' It was
probably composed at Lochlie early in the year 1782. Like the
preceding poem, and several other pieces written about the same
time (omitted in the present selection), it reflects some of the
peculiar features of the Calvinism in which Burns was reared.

Death and Dying Words of Poor Mailie.

The Commonplace Book of Burns explains that Mailie was 'my
ain (own) pet yowe.' The poem was composed at the ploughtail
on a spring afternoon in 1782. Gilbert Burns, the poet's brother,
remembered the occasion and the circumstances : '[Robert had]
bought a ewe and two lambs from a neighbour, and she was
tethered in a field adjoining the house at Lochlie. He and I were
going out with our teams, and our two younger brothers to drive
for us, at mid-day, when Hugh Wilson, a curious-looking, awkward
boy, clad in plaiding, came to us with much anxiety in his face, and
the information that the ewe had entangled herself in the tether,

and was lying in the ditch. Robert was much tickled with Hughoc's appearance and postures on the occasion. Poor Mailie was set to rights; and when we returned from the plough in the evening he repeated to me her Death and Dying Words pretty much as they now stand.'

The fitness of such a subject for humorous poetical treatment was doubtless suggested to Burns by Hamilton [1] of Gilbertfield's *Dying Words of Bonny Heck, a famous Greyhound.*

Carlyle sees in this and the next poem the first touches of a ' tender sportfulness' peculiar to Burns.

l. 1. *an' her lambs thegither.* With her lambs beside her. She alone was tethered. The verb is therefore properly singular—as in the first, or Kilmarnock, edition, although the plural form appears in the Commonplace Book.

l. 8. *Poor Hughoc.* Hughoc claims our pity because he was pitiful and yet powerless to help. The boy, Hugh Wilson, was employed to tend cattle on a neighbouring farm. -*oc* is the diminutive *ock*. Burns's own herdboy on his first farm of Mossgiel was called Davoc :—

> ' For men—I've three mischievous boys,
> Run deils for ranting an' for noise ;
> A gaudsman ane, a thresher t'other,
> Wee Davoc hauds the nowte in fother.'
>
> *The Inventory*, ll. 34-37.

ll. 17, 18. *Tell him, if e'er again*, &c. Burns made no secret of his poverty, and frequently made a jest of it. Occasionally there was some bitterness in the jest. There is none here. The humour is, of course, heightened by Mailie's supposed acquaintance with her master's purse.

l. 45. *to be a beast.* To be a full-grown ram.

ll. 53, 54. *An' when you think upo' your mither*, &c. This couplet expresses a touch of the 'tender sportfulness' to which Carlyle refers.

l. 58. *An', for thy pains*, &c. Payment of the messenger is by bequest (*legatum nuncupatione*, as a Scottish lawyer would say); and the nature of the legacy offers a humorous contrast to the solemnity of the occasion.

---

[1] Not to be confounded with the refined Hamilton of Bangour. He of Gilbertfield died an old man in Lanarkshire in 1751. He belonged to Fife, and had been a lieutenant in the army.

Poor Mailie's Elegy.

The news of Mailie's death, duly communicated by the commissioned herdboy, sends the poet into mourning. The ' Elegy ' is constructed quite on the model of *The Epitaph of Habbie Simson, the Piper of Kilbarchan*, which was the work of the middle Sempill [1], and long regarded as a standard of perfection. This minor 'makkar' was the first to introduce, if he did not invent, the stanza-form which Ramsay, Fergusson, and, above all, Burns so popularized in Scotland. He used it for the first time in *The Epitaph* here alluded to, a specimen stanza of which (with the spelling modernized) may be given :—

> ' At Clerk-plays when he wont to come
> His pipe play'd trimly to the drum ;
> Like bikes o' bees he garr'd it bum
> And tuned his reed ;
> Now all our pipers may sing dumb
> Sin' Habbie 's dead.'

l. 37. *Wae worth the man.* Literally, 'woful be the man.' ' Worth ' with this meaning seems to ask alliance with the German *werden* to be, or to become. The A.-S. *woerthan*, or *weordan* means ' to be.' Cp. Scott's use of the expression in the first canto of *The Lady of the Lake :*—

> ' Woe worth the chase, woe worth the day
> That costs thy life, my gallant gray ! '

Cp. also *The Dream* of William Dunbar, l. 56,—' Weill worth thé, sister,' &c.

Man was made to Mourn.

This poem is mainly an indignant protest against the inequalities of rank in human life. Nature made of one blood, and of one brotherhood, the whole human community, but the creation of class distinctions has broken the natural bond, and the great majority of mankind, subjected to the will and power of a few, find life scarcely worth living. Burns's Letters show that the mood of mind revealed in this poem was pretty habitual to him.

---

[1] Robert, son of Sir James, and father of Francis—all poets. Robert died in 1669 at an advanced age. The youngest Sempill is the best known, having written some very popular songs, one of which, ' *Maggie Lauder*,' is still a favourite.

Southey points out that this poem was composed to the cadence of an old Scottish elegy called *The Life and Age of Man*, which commences—

> ' Upon the sixteen hunder year
> Of God, and fifty-three,
> Fra Christ was born, that bought us dear,
> As writings testifie ;
>
> On January the sixteenth day,
> As I did ly alone,
> With many a sigh and sob did say—
> *Ah, man is made to moan !* '

' I had an old grand-uncle,' wrote Burns to Mrs. Dunlop, ' with whom my mother lived a while in her girlish years. The good old man, for such he was, was long blind ere he died, during which time his highest enjoyment was to sit down and cry, while my mother would sing the simple old song of *The Life and Age of Man*. It is this way of thinking, it is these melancholy truths [contained in the old Elegy and reproduced by Burns in *Man was made to Mourn*] that make religion so precious to the poor miserable children of men.' (*Correspondence*, 16th Aug., 1788.)

The poem was written probably in November, 1784, and certainly at Mossgiel, a small farm about one mile from Mauchline, to which the family had removed shortly after the death of the poet's father in February.

ll. 17-20. *The sun that overhangs yon moors*, etc. Both place and person are specified in the version given in the Commonplace Book :—

> ' Yon sun that hangs o'er Carrick moors
> That spread so far and wide,
> Where hundreds labour to support
> The lordly Cassilis' pride.'

l. 39. *age and want—oh, ill-matched pair !* Cp. Shakespeare, *As You Like It*, Act II. Sc. vii—

> 'Oppressed with two weak evils, age and hunger ' ;

and Gray, *Ode on a Distant Prospect of Eton College*—

> ' Lo ! Poverty—to fill the band—
> That numbs the soul with icy hand,
> And slow-consuming Age.'

ll. 59, 60. *Who begs a brother*, &c. 'He used to remark to me,' says Gilbert Burns, speaking of his brother, 'that he could not conceive a more mortifying picture of human life than a man seeking work. In casting about in his mind how the sentiment might be brought forward, the elegy, *Man was made to mourn*, was composed.'

l. 75. *This partial view of humankind*, i. e. this aspect of society which reveals the partiality of fortune towards the few, her injustice towards the many.

l. 78. *Had never, sure, been born.* Cp.

'Life is not worth having, with all it can give ;
For something beyond it poor man sure must live.'

Song—*The Lazy Mist* (p. 161 in this selection).

Epistle to Davie, a Brother Poet.

This was written at Mossgiel, probably in January 1785. 'Davie' was David Sillar, the son of a small farmer in the same parish of Tarbolton, Ayrshire. He was Burns's junior by one year ; and among other accomplishments (in addition to making rhymes) which recommended him to the favour of Burns, he possessed those of 'lover, ploughman, and fiddler.' He published a book of verse in 1789. He was at one time a grocer ; then a schoolmaster ; and latterly, as Bailie Sillar, administered the law at Irvine. He died in 1830, much respected, leaving behind him a good deal of property.

The stanza-form of this epistle is peculiar, and difficult to manage effectively. Burns seems to have mastered its intricacies at the first trial. It was a favourite measure of Allan Ramsay (*The Vision*—published 1724) and of Alexander Montgomery (*The Cherrie and the Slae*—running to 114 stanzas—published 1597). A specimen of Ramsay's craft in handling this measure may be given :—

'When Phoebus' head turns light as cork,
And Neptune leans upon his fork,
And limping Vulcan blethers ;
When Pluto glowers as he were wild,
And Cupid, Love's wee wingèd child,
Falls down and 'files his feathers ;

When Pan forgets to tune his reed,
   And flings it careless by,
And Hermes, wing'd at heels and head,
   Can neither stand nor lie ;
      When staggering and swaggering
      They stoiter home to sleep,
      While sentries at entries
      Immortal watches keep.'
              The Vision (spelling modernized).

l. 9. *the great-folk's gift.* Fortune's gift to them,—luxurious comfort.

l. 20. *ken na how to wair't.* This, of course, is the indefinite use of the neuter pronoun.

l. 24. *hale and fier.* The expression has descended, in pretty constant use all the way, from the old ' Makkaris ' ; e. g.

   ' Or cuir this wicht at heart be haill and feir
   Both thow and I most in the court appeir.'
         The Dream (William Dunbar, *circa* 1460-1513).

l. 25. *Mair spier na, nor fear na.* Burns gives this line to Ramsay, and his editors have followed him. It seems to be an incorrect recollection of a passage in Ramsay's *Vision*, which runs—

      ' Rest but a while content,
      Not fearful, but cheerful,
      And wait the will of fate,
      Which minds to, designds to,
      Renew your ancient state.'

ll. 46-48. *Yet nature's charms, the hills and woods*, &c. The same sentiment, expressed under similar conditions of poverty and obscurity, occurs in Goldsmith's *Traveller;* —

   ' Creation's heir, the world, the world is mine ! '

ll. 63-66. *If happiness hae not her seat*, &c. Cp. Goldsmith :- -

   ' Vain, very vain, my weary search to find
   That bliss which only centres in the mind.'
                  The Traveller.

ll. 107, 108. *Ye hae your Meg, your dearest part*, &c. Even ' Meg' has been drawn from her obscurity : she is identified with ' Margaret Orr, a servant at Stair House.' ' Jean ' is Jean Armour, the daughter of James Armour, master mason, Mauchline. She after-

O

wards became the poet's wife, and is celebrated as 'bonnie Jean.'
Burns first made her acquaintance in the summer of 1784.
Mauchline is a small market town about five miles south-east
of Lochlie.

ll. 119-122. Variation in MS.—which some will prefer to the
text :—

> 'In all my share[1] o' care an' grief,
>   Which fate has largely given,
> My hope, my comfort, an' relief,
>   Are thoughts of her and heaven.'

l. 138. *the tenebrific scene.* 'Tenebrific' is scarcely an improvement on 'tenebrious.' It may be put in the same category with
'frater-feeling,' and the more objectionable 'sapientipotent,' and
'terrae-filial'—the invention of Young. Burns, it must be con-
fessed, had a weakness in his English compositions for a word of
'learned length.' 'Can he [Burns, speaking of himself] descend
to mind the paltry concerns about which the terrae-filial race fret,
and fume, and vex themselves?'—*Correspondence* (15th Jan. 1783).

Death and Dr. Hornbook.

Composed at Mossgiel 'in seed-time, 1785'—as Burns himself
tells us; but not included in the Kilmarnock edition (31st July,
1786). It was first printed in the first Edinburgh edition (April,
1787). 'Dr. Hornbook' was John Wilson, schoolmaster of
Tarbolton, the next village to Mauchline. He had opened a small
store for the sale of drugs and groceries at Tarbolton, and pre-
sumed on his medical ambition to give medical advice. Burns
met him one evening at a masonic meeting, and listened impatiently
and not altogether silently to the 'bauld apothecary's' parade of
his knowledge and his nostrums. The poem was conceived during
the night-walk to Mossgiel, and next afternoon was recited in the
fields to Gilbert. The effect of the satire was to clear Wilson's
school of scholars and his shop of customers. He removed
to Glasgow, where he continued to teach till about the year 1807,
when he was appointed session-clerk to 'the Gorbals,' a suburb of
Glasgow. The office speedily became a lucrative one, and in his
latter days, according to Lockhart, he used to bless the hour
in which he provoked the castigation of Burns.

---

[1] Cp. Goldsmith—
> 'In all my griefs, and God has given my share.'—*Deserted Village.*

l. 5. *A rousing whid.* This is probably the first printed use of
'whid' in the sense of 'fib.' The earliest reading was—'great lies
and nonsense baith to vend.' To whid is less to lie than to equivocate.

l. 16. *free the ditches.* That is, to keep free or clear of them.

l. 20. *The distant Cumnock hills.* They lie south-east from
Tarbolton.

l. 26. *todlin' down on Willie's mill.* Tarbolton mill, a short
distance from the village on the road to Mossgiel. William Muir
was the miller.

l. 37. *lang Scotch ells twa.* An ell Scottish is an English yard
plus an inch. The effect of the apparition is to · sober him.
Previously he failed to account to his understanding by the use of
his senses for the number of the moon's horns. Now his senses
are steady enough to take a complete inventory of the features and
equipment of the apparition. At the same time his bold familiarity
of manner does not forsake him. The blended humour and truth-
fulness of the whole scene has been admitted even by Wordsworth.
Cp. Tam o'Shanter in similar circumstances :—

> 'The swats sae ream'd in Tammie's noddle,
> Fair play,—he cared na deils a boddle !'

l. 54. *there's a gully!* He will defend himself with assurance.

ll. 57, 58. *kittle to be mislear'd.* Chambers interprets it, 'difficult
to be put out of my art.' It probably means 'likely to be mischievous,' 'apt to be rude.'

l. 65. *been mony a gate.* 'An epidemical fever was then raging
in the country [around Tarbolton].'—*Note by* BURNS.

l. 73. *Sax thousand years are near-hand fled.* Burns follows the
orthodox Scripture chronology, which fixes the creation of man at
4004 B. C.

l. 77. *ane Hornbook's ta'en up the trade.* The hornbook, or child's
first book at school, which supplied Burns with a name for the
village schoolmaster (the prefixed 'Dr.' indicating the quack), is
described by Cowper :—

> 'Neatly secured from being soiled or torn
> Beneath a pane of thin translucent horn,
> A book (to please us at a tender age
> 'Tis called a book, though but a single page)
> Presents the prayer the Saviour deigned to teach,
> Which children use, and parsons—when they preach.'
> *Tirocinium.*

Shenstone, with whose verses Burns was well acquainted, also refers to the hornbook :—

'Their books of stature small they take in hand,
Which with pellucid horn securèd are
To save from fingers wet the letters fair.'
                                    The Schoolmistress.

l. 80. *mak' his king's-hood in a spleuchan!* A coarse imprecation. The king's-hood is the second stomach of a ruminating animal. A spleuchan is a tobacco-pouch.

l. 81. *weel-acqu aint wi' Buchan.* 'Buchan's *Domestic Medicine.'*— *Note by* BURNS. Dr. Wm. Buchan's book was, and may yet in some quarters be, the Scottish house-wife's *vade mecum* for all ailments. Buchan died in 1805.

l. 84. *ponk.* Death, as here delineated, though lean, is not a skeleton. He is skin and bone, naked but for patches of hair, and bearded. From being a terror, on whom none could look, he has become in broad day the familiar mockery of the children of Tarbolton, who point at him in derision and pluck the hair of his limbs as he passes. Death's case against Hornbook is that the latter cures where the former by long use and wont is entitled to kill, and that he kills where he is not wanted—that is, where the patient would naturally recover if Hornbook did not interfere. It is on the second count of the indictment that Death claims, and by implication carries, the sympathy of the poet.

ll. 123–125. *farina. Aqua.* The metre requires the accent on the first syllable of 'farina,' and a trisyllabic pronunciation of 'aqua.'

l. 127. *Johnnie Ged's Hole.* An open grave. Ged was the grave-digger.

l. 129. *His braw calf-ward.* The churchyard,—from its small size. A calf-ward is explained by Jamieson (*Scottish Dict.*) to be 'an enclosure for rearing calves.' Ged perhaps used the church-yard as a grazing-plot.

l. 139. *a fair strae death.* By a natural death in bed, as op-posed to death by violence or accident. 'Our simple forefathers,' says Jamieson, 'slept on beds of straw.'

l. 145. *An honest wabster to his trade.* An honest man, a weaver by trade, or occupation.

l. 165. *self-conceited sot.* Wilson was less self-conceited than self-complacent, if one may credit the anecdotes told of him. 'I

have often wondered,' he is reported to have said, 'what set
Robert Burns upon me, for we were aye on the best of terms.'
l. 171. *Some wee short hour ayont the twal*. One, two, or at
most three o'clock in the morning. 'Short' refers to the time
taken in striking the hour.

Epistle to John Lapraik.

This epistle bears date 1st April, 1785. The occasion that
produced it was exactly as stated in the epistle. 'It was at
a " rocking" (see Glossary) at our house [Mossgiel],' says Gilbert
Burns, 'when we had twelve or fifteen young people with their
rocks, that Lapraik's song ... was sung, and we were informed
who was the author. Upon this Robert wrote his first epistle to
Lapraik.' John Lapraik was a small farmer living, when Burns
sought his acquaintance, on the farm or croft of Muirsmill, near
Muirkirk in Ayrshire,—about fourteen miles due east of Mossgiel.
He was then fifty-eight years of age, and had a local reputation for
his rhymes. He seems to have been a kindly and very respectable old man. The song which so touched the sympathies of
Burns will be found in the collection of his pieces which Lapraik
published, on the strength of Burns's recommendation of them, in
1788. Lockhart thought it the best in the collection. It begins :—

'When I upon thy bosom lean,
And fondly clasp thee a' my ain,
I glory in the sacred ties
That made us ane wha ance were twain.
A mutual flame inspires us baith,
The tender look, the melting kiss,
Even years shall not destroy our love,
But only bring us change o' bliss.'

ll. 21, 22. *Can this be Pope, or Steele, or Beattie's wark?* This is
simply a compliment. Burns, though a generous, was no indis-
criminating critic. James Beattie (1735-1803), Professor of Moral
Philosophy at Aberdeen, wrote *The Minstrel*, a poem in the
Spenserian stanza, and an *Essay on the Nature of Truth*, by which
he was believed to have overthrown the Scepticism of Hume.

l. 28. *he had ingine*, i.e. he had genius (*ingenium*).
l. 45. *I to the crambo-jingle fell.* I took to rhyming. Crambo is
a play where one gives a word to which another finds a rhyme.

l. 50. *a rhymer like by chance,* i. e. happen to be only a kind of mere versifier.

l. 54. *I jingle at her.* I make rhymes to her.

ll. 79, 80. *Allan's glee, or Fergusson's.* Allan Ramsay (1686-1758) author of a pastoral drama, *The Gentle Shepherd,* and songs, tales, humorous satires, and epistles in the Scottish language. He was the most popular Scottish poet before Burns. Robert Fergusson (1750-1774), author of humorous poems chiefly descriptive of social life in or near Edinburgh,—such as *Leith Races, Hallowfair, The Daft Days,* &c. His best pieces are in Scotch. His most ambitious effort is *The Farmer's Ingle.* Burns greatly admired both, and was indebted to both in several ways. His criticism of their respective styles in these lines is to the point. Scott also touched off the characteristic of the elder bard by dubbing him ' the joyous Ramsay.'

l. 112. *catch-the-plack.* Money-making.

l. 123. *gar me fissle.* Literally, make me rustle. The metaphor is taken from the rustling agitation of a bush in the wind. He means he will be pleasurably excited.

Second Epistle to Lapraik.

Lapraik's answer has not been preserved. This is Burns's reply to it, and is dated April 21st, 1785.

l. 1. *new-ca'd kye rowte at the stake.* Absurdly translated ' newly driven kine' by most editors. It means ' cows, that have recently calved, low in their stalls.' The upright post to which the cow is fastened in the stall is ' the stake.'

l. 8. *Rattlin the corn out-owre the rigs,* i. e. sowing broad-cast.

l. 10. *Their ten hours' bite.* Fodder, a small quantity given about ten o'clock.

l. 13. *The tapetless ramfeezl'd hizzie.* Cowper, writing in August, 1787, says of Burns : ' His candle is bright but shut up in a dark lantern. I lent him to a very sensible neighbour of mine, but his uncouth dialect spoiled all ; and before he had read him through, he was quite *ramfeezled.*'

l. 20. ' *Conscience!* ' *says I,* &c. This remonstrance with the Muse reminds one of honest Launcelot's debate with his conscience before he ran away from the Jew's service. See *Merchant of Venice.*

l. 26. *Tho' mankind were a pack o' cartes.* The emphasis on *mankind.*

l. 32. *stumpie.* The quill was already 'worn to the gristle.'

l. 44. *Tho' fortune use you hard.* The reference may be a general one, but probably points to the loss of his little patrimonial farm which Lapraik sustained by the failure of an Ayr Bank, a few years previously.

Epistle to William Simson.

This epistle bears date, May 1785. Burns was still at Mossgiel. William Simson was the schoolmaster of Ochiltree, a village on the Lugar about eight miles south from Mossgiel. Hearing of Burns, whose reputation was fast spreading from parish to parish of Ayr-shire, and being himself a versifier, he sought the acquaintance of the farmer-poet of Mossgiel by means of a letter which has been lost. Simson is believed to have been of superior ability to Sillar and Lapraik.

l. 15. *Wi' Allan, or wi' Gilbertfiel'.* Allan Ramsay and Wm. Hamilton of Gilbertfield. See foot-note on page 189.

l. 17. *Fergusson, the writer-chiel.* Fergusson (see note, *Epistle to Lapraik,* l. 80) was educated at St. Andrew's University, but, through domestic poverty, was forced to become a copying-clerk in a law-office in Edinburgh. He became insane, and died miserably in a madhouse in Edinburgh in his 24th year.

l. 31. *Auld Coila.* Old Kyle, the middle of the three divisions of Ayr, in which Burns was born : 'There was a lad was born in Kyle.' See also *The Vision,* ll. 109, 110.

l. 58. *Whare glorious Wallace.* Many of the exploits of Sir William Wallace, the Scottish patriot, are connected with Ayr-shire—more particularly with Ayr, Cumnock, Irvine, Turnberry Hold, Leglane Woods, &c. 'In [my] boyish days,' wrote Burns to Mrs. Dunlop, herself a descendant of Wallace, 'I remember, in particular, being struck with that part of Wallace's story where the lines occur—

> Syne to the Leglen wood, when it was late,
> To make a silent and a safe retreat.

I chose a fine summer Sunday . . . and walked half-a-dozen of miles to pay my respects to the Leglen wood . . . and as I explored every *den and dell* where I could suppose my heroic countryman to have lodged, I recollect . . . that my heart glowed with a wish to be able to make a song on him in some measure equal to his merits.'—*Letters* (Nov. 1786). For Ayrshire memories of Wallace, see Scott's *Tales of a Grandfather*, chap. vii; and Blind Harry's *Wallace*, especially Bk. vii. It was Hamilton of Gilbertfield's spiritless version of the old minstrel's epic with which Burns was acquainted.

l. 65. *red-wat-shod.* A strong image—shod with blood. 'In this one word,' says Carlyle (*Essay on Burns*), 'a full vision of horror and carnage, perhaps too frightfully accurate for Art.' The expression occurs in the old romance of *Arthur*, published from the MS. of the Marquis of Bath in the Early English Text Society's issue for 1864 :—

> 'There men were wetschoede
> All of brayn and of blode.'
>
> *Arthur*, ll. 469, 470.

ll. 91, 92. *The warly race may drudge an' drive*, &c. 'I forget that I am a poor insignificant devil, unnoticed and unknown, stalking up and down fairs and markets, when I happen to be in them reading a page or two of mankind . . . whilst the men of business jostle me on every side as an idle encumbrance in their way.'—BURNS's *Letters* (15 Jan. 1783). In the poet's Letters one has often the anticipation, as here, of an image or sentiment which his poetry has made familiar.

l. 108. *In Robert Burns.* This is the first instance of the poet's use of that form of the family name which he has made famous. Previous to this, and occasionally afterwards till April 14, 1786, he signed 'Burness'—pronounced with the accent on the first syllable.

Epistle to Rev. John M°Math.

M°Math was a young clergyman of broad views, at this time—17th Sept. 1785—assistant to the aged minister of Tarbolton. He subsequently fell into dissipated habits, and died in Mull, one of the Western Islands, in 1825.

l. 8. *On gown, an' ban', an' douce black-bonnet*, i. e. on the wearers of these—minister and elder.

l. 25. *There's Gawn, misca'd*, &c. Mr. Gavin Hamilton, residing in Mauchline, was accused by the Kirk session there of absenting himself from divine service, neglecting family-worship, setting out on a journey on a Sunday, and otherwise breaking the

Fourth Commandment. He was cited to answer for his conduct. A member of the session, a hypocritical elder named William Auld, took a prominent part in the accusation, and by so doing drew down upon himself the severest and most daring of all the satires of Burns—*Holy Willie's Prayer.* A copy of this production, which ran through the district in MS., had been asked from the author himself by Mr. McMath, and the request was the occasion of this epistle.

l. 91. *Pardon this freedom,*—not of addressing him, but of complimenting him on the liberality of his religious views, his candour, and his winning manners.

Halloween.

The eve or vigil of All Hallows, or All Saints   held on the evening of the 31st October. Among the Scottish peasantry of the Lowlands the festival, in the words of Carlyle, has 'passed and repassed in rude awe and laughter since the era of the Druids.' The superstitious element of awe in its observance even among rustics has now, however, pretty well disappeared. Fun, and the forecasting of fortunes in the field of matrimony, are the principal objects of the ceremonies of the night.

The poem was probably composed either in view of, or shortly after, the Halloween of 1785. It appeared in the Kilmarnock edition with such clear and copious notes by the author that there is scarcely anything to be added to, or subtracted from them. The measure is that of *Christ's Kirk on the Green,* but the 'rhyme formula' is not quite the same. In *Christ's Kirk* it is *ab ab ab ab c*; here it is for the most part *ab ab cd cd e*.

l. 1. *Upon that night when fairies light.* Halloween, says Burns, 'is thought to be a night when witches, devils, and other mischief-making beings are all abroad on their baneful midnight errands ; particularly those aerial beings, the fairies, are said, on that night, to hold a grand anniversary.'

l. 2. *Cassilis downans.* 'Certain little, romantic, rocky, green hills in the neighbourhood of the ancient seat of the Earls of Cassilis.'—BURNS. The castle of Cassilis is situated on the lower Doon near the village of Dalrymple. The 'downans' are three or four in number, the highest about 300 feet above the level of the Doon, and rise so abruptly in the midst of a flat country as to require in the peasant mind some fairy marvel or other to account for their origin.

l. 5. *for Colean the rout is ta'en.* Colzean House, or Castle, one of the seats of the lords of Cassilis, is situated on the edge of a cliff on the Carrick (or southern) shore of Ayrshire. The caves, six in number—the largest being 50 ft. high—are situated just under the castle, and are supposed to be frequented by fairies.

l. 10. *the bonnie winding banks where Doon* &c. It was the celebration of the Halloween of his boyhood that Burns recollected while writing this poem. The scenery is near Alloway and Mount Oliphant.

l. 13. *shook his Carrick spear.* The ancestors of Bruce the Scottish patriot were earls of Carrick. Carrick is the southern of the three divisions of Ayrshire, Kyle and Cunningham being the other two.

l. 29. *Their stocks maun a' be socht.* 'The first ceremony of Halloween,' says Burns, ' is, pulling each a stock (or plant of kail). They must go out hand in hand, with eyes shut, and pull the first they meet with. Its being big or little, straight or crooked, is prophetic of the size and shape of the grand object of all their spells—the husband or wife. If any yird (or earth) stick to the root, that is tocher (or fortune) ; and the taste of the custoc (that is, the heart of the stem) is indicative of the natural.temper and disposition. Lastly, the stems, or to give them their proper appellation, the runts, are placed somewhere above the head of the door, and the Christian names of the people whom chance brings into the house are, according to the priority of placing the runts, the names in question.'

l. 46. *The auld guidwife's weel-hoordet nits.* ' Burning the nuts is a favourite charm. They name the lad and lass to each particular nut, as they lay them in the fire ; and according as they burn quietly together, or start from beside one another, the course and issue of the courtship will be.'—BURNS.

l. 79. *pric'd her bonnie mou'.* Kissed her.

l. 89. *And in the blue-clue throws then.* Burns gives the directions for this ceremony : 'Steal out, all alone, to the kiln [where the grain is dried before being ground in the mill], and, darkling, throw into the *pot* a clue of blue yarn ; wind it in a new clue off the old one ; and towards the latter end something will hold the thread : demand " wha hauds?" i. e. " Who holds?" and answer will be returned from the *kiln-pot*—the full name of your future spouse.' The pot, or pat, is simply the bottom of the kiln.

l. 102. *eat the apple at the glass.* 'Take a candle and go alone to

>

a looking-glass; eat an apple before it—and some traditions say
you should comb your hair all the time; the face of your conjugal
companion to be will be seen in the glass as if peeping over your
shoulder.'—BURNS.

l. 109. *skelpie-limmer's-face.* Burns explains this 'a technical
term in female scolding.' Minx comes near the meaning.

ll. 125, 126. *on Halloween it fell that night.* The battle of
Sheriffmuir was in 1715. A year or two before that event harvest
was late, and the festival of harvest-home was held on at least one
farm on 31st October. [It has been equally late, or later, on some
upland farms this year, 1888.]

l. 127. *Our stibble-rig was Rab M'Graen.* He was the leader of
the reapers.

l. 131. *He gat hemp-seed.* 'Steal out unperceived, and sow a
handful of hemp-seed, harrowing it with anything you can
conveniently draw after you. Repeat now and then, "Hemp-
seed, I saw [*sow*] thee! Hemp-seed, I saw thee! and him (or her)
that is to be my true-love, come after me and pou [*pull*] thee!"
Look over your left shoulder, and you will see the appearance of
the person invoked in the attitude of pulling hemp. Some
traditions say, "Come after me and shaw [*show*] thee!" . . . in
which case it simply appears. Others omit the harrowing, and
say, "Come after me and harrow thee!"'—BURNS.

l. 173. *To winn three wechts o' naething.* Burns has this note :—
'You go [alone and unseen] to the barn, and open both doors,
taking them off the hinges if possible—for there is danger that the
being about to appear may shut the doors and do you some
mischief. Then take that implement used in winnowing corn
which in our country dialect we call a *wecht*, and go through all
attitudes of letting down corn against the wind. Repeat it
three times, and [at] the third time a being will pass through
the barn, in at the windy door and out at the other, having the
figure in question with the dress and retinue marking the station
in life.'

l. 183. *first on Sawnie gies a ea'.* Calls to the herdboy, whom
she has bribed, to be on the outlook.

l. 192. *the stack he faddom't thrice.* 'Take an opportunity of
going unnoticed to a bere [barley] stack, and fathom [i. e. embrace]
it three times round. The last fathom of the last time you will
catch in your arms the appearance of your future . . . yoke-fellow.'
—BURNS's *Note.*

l. 193. *timmer-propt for thrawin.* Supported by poles or planks to prevent the stack from falling,—or because it was threatening to fall. To thraw is to twist. ' For ' is either ' against,' or ' because of.'

l. 206. To *dip her left sark-sleeve in.* ' You go out,' says Burns in a note, ' one or more (for this is a social spell) to a south-running spring or rivulet, where three lairds' lands meet, and dip your left shirt-sleeve. Go to bed in view of a fire, and hang your wet sleeve before it to dry. Lie awake, and some time near midnight an apparition, having the exact figure of the grand object in question [future wife, or husband] will come and turn the sleeve, as if to dry the other side of it.'

l. 208. *Whyles owre a linn,* &c. This stanza presents such a succession of views, exhaustive of the character of a Scottish ' burnie,' as for clearness, completeness, and rapidity has never perhaps been equalled.

l. 227. *The luggies three.* ' Take three dishes ; put clean water in one, foul water in another, and leave the third empty ; blindfold a person, and lead him to the hearth where the dishes are ranged. He dips the left hand,—if by chance in the clean water the future wife will come to the bar of matrimony a maid ; if in the foul, a widow ; if in the empty dish, it foretells ... no marriage at all. It is repeated thrice, and each time the arrangement of the dishes is altered.'—*Note by* BURNS.

l. 231. *Mar's year.* 1715, the year of a rebellion in favour of the Stuarts, raised by the Earl of Mar. It ended at Sheriff-Moor.

l. 239. *butter'd sow'ns wi' fragrant lunt.* With an appetizing smell, because served with butter, not milk. ' This,' says Burns, ' is always the Halloween supper.'

This long descriptive poem of *Halloween* is of all the productions of Burns the most difficult to be understood by an English reader. It contains a larger proportion of old Scottish words than any other piece he has composed. Many of these words are now all but obsolete, and some of them even in Burns's day were comparatively rare. But there was a merit in using them : ' thy bonnie auld words gar me smile,' wrote old Hamilton of Gilbertfield to young Allan Ramsay.

To a Mouse.

The tender pathos of Burns first unmistakeably revealed itself in this little poem. Yet Currie, the first and by no means the worst of Burns's editors, could not decide whether it 'should be considered as serious or comic'! It is remarkable that Carlyle should give an inferior place to this poem comparatively with the verses on the *Death of Mailie.* Burns's sympathy with nature, animate and in-animate—with the 'silly' sheep, the 'ourie' cattle, the wounded hare, 'happing' birds, wild-fowl, the 'auld' mare, the field mouse, the mountain daisy, &c.—was genuine and deep, and as fine as that of Wordsworth. This is one of the features of his genius which differentiate him from all antecedent Scottish poets, and from his contemporary Cowper,—with whom he had much in common. The occasion of this poem arose as usual from a commonplace enough event in his ordinary life. He was ploughing, in No-vember 1785, and the share happened to turn up the nest of a field mouse. The little creature was in panic haste to escape across the field, when John Blane, Burns's farm-servant, caught up the pattle or plough spade, and set off in pursuit. Burns called to him to let it alone, and was observed by Blane to fall into a thoughtful mood. The poem was composed that same day, exactly as it now stands.

l. 33. *turn'd out for a' thy trouble,* i.e. in return for.

l. 39, 40. *The best-laid schemes o' mice and men,* &c. This is now proverbial.

The Cotter's Saturday Night.

This poem begins with a description of a Scottish November evening in the open air of the country. Burns habitually drew from nature. The November weather of 1785 was around him when he composed the poem. Writing on 17th Feb. 1786 to his friend, John Richmond, who had just gone from Mauchline to fill a situation as clerk in Edinburgh, Burns says—' I have been very busy with the muses since I saw you, and have composed, among several others, "The Ordination". . . ."Scotch Drink," "The Cottar's Saturday Night," "An Address to the Devil," &c. I have likewise completed my poem on the Dogs, but have not shown it to the world.'

The poem is modelled, in regard to measure, theme, and treat-ment, on *The Schoolmistress* of Shenstone[1], and more especially

---

[1] Cp. stanzas 12-14 of this text of *The Cotter's Saturday Night* with stanzas 12 and 14 of *The Schoolmistress,*—not for sentiment but for style.

The Farmer's Ingle of Fergusson.   It could be ill spared from any collection of Burns's poetry less on account of its poetical merit than because of its historical and ethical value.   It contains many feeble lines, but in the descriptive parts it is a faithful transcript from peasant life, and in the reflective parts it bears testimony to the moral character of the author.   It reveals at once his religion and his patriotism.

More than half of the poem is in English, the transition from the vernacular occurring at those points in the description where the sentiment becomes more elevated.   An unusually elevated or serious train of thought in the mind of a Scottish peasant seems to demand for its expression the use of a speech which one may describe as Sabbath Scotch.

l. 8. *the morn,* i.e. to-morrow, the weekly day-of-rest.

l. 14. *His wee bit ingle blinkin bonnilie.* Cp. Fergusson's *Farmer's Ingle,*—

> ' The guidman, new come hame, is blithe to find,
>   When he out-owre the hallan flings his een,
> That ilka turn is handled to his mind ;
>   That a' his housie looks sae cosh and clean ;
> For cleanly house lo'es he tho' e'er so mean.'   (ll. 14-18.)

l. 22. *errand to a neibour town,* i. e. farm-town, or farm.

l. 68. *If Heaven a draught of pleasure,* &c.   A poetical rendering of the passage in Burns's Commonplace Book, under date April, 1783 :—' If anything on earth deserves the name of rapture or transport, it is the feeling of green eighteen in the company of the mistress of his heart when she repays him with an equal return of affection.'

ll. 79–80. *Is there no pity . . . points to the parents,* &c.   The relative is seldom omitted when it is in the nominative case.   Cp. Scott's *Lady of the Lake* :—

> ' With every hardy plant could bear
>   Loch Katrine's keen and searching air.'

l. 93. *The sire turns o'er with patriarchal grace,* &c.   William Burnes, the poet's father, is here delineated.

ll. 102, 3, 4. *Dundee . . . Martyrs . . . Elgin.* Favourite psalm tunes—still occasionally heard, but chiefly in rural churches.

ll. 122, 123. *How his first followers,* &c.   The reference in the former line is to the *Acts of the Apostles,* in the latter to the various *Epistles.*

l. 129. *Hope springs exulting*, &c. An acknowledged application of a line of Pope's couplet—

> ' See! from the brake the whirring pheasant springs
> And mounts exulting on triumphant wings.'
> *Windsor Forest.*

ll. 149, 150. *stills the raven's clamorous nest*, &c. These are Scriptural references—*Psalm* cxlvii. 9 ; and *Matthew* vi. 28.

l. 156. *Princes and lords are but the breath of kings.* A recollection of Goldsmith (*Deserted Village*)—

> ' Princes and lords may flourish or may fade,
> A breath has made them, as a breath has made ';

repeated in the song *A Man's a Man for a' that.*

l. 157. '*An honest man,*' &c. Pope's *Essay on Man.*

l. 167. *may Heaven their simple lives prevent from luxury.* A unique use of 'prevent'—meaning 'defend' or 'protect,' perhaps 'lead.'

l. 175. *die, the second glorious part.* The only alternative to a patriot in arms for his country—victory or ' a gory bed.' If he cannot 'do,' at least he can 'die.' See song *Scots wha hae.*

Address to the Deil.

This famous poem, scarcely less original in subject than in treatment, was composed at Mossgiel near the end of 1785. It was suggested to Burns, says his brother Gilbert, 'by running over in his mind the many ludicrous accounts and representations we have of Satan.' It embodies the ordinary Scottish-peasant conception of the appearance, habits, history and character of the devil. In his autobiographical letter to Dr. Moore, Burns writes—' In my infant and boyish days I owed much to an old woman who resided in the family, remarkable for her ignorance, credulity, and superstition. She had, I suppose, the largest collection in the country of tales and songs concerning *devils*, ghosts, fairies, *witches, kelpies, spunkies, wraiths, apparitions, cantraips.* . . . This cultivated the latent seeds of poetry, but had so strong an effect on my imagination that to this hour, in my nocturnal rambles, I sometimes keep a sharp look-out in suspicious places; and though *nobody can be more sceptical than I am in such matters*, yet it often takes an effort of philosophy to shake off these *idle terrors.*' The poem is more or less humorous, throughout, but the humour is here dashed with awe, there with indignation ; while a sudden infusion of pity and even tenderness, flowing unexpectedly and yet naturally from the last stanza, brings the *Address* to a most effective close. That Burns believed in a personal devil may well be doubted. The humorous satire of the piece is at the expense of popular Scottish Calvinism. The tenderness is for an imaginary being, supposed for the moment to be real, who is suffering the pains of eternal misery. The piece is anti-Calvinistic.

ll. 1, 2. *O thou, whatever title*, &c. Cp. Pope's *Dunciad* :—

> ' O Thou whatever title please thine ear,
> Dean, Drapier, Bickerstaff, or Gulliver.'
>
> (Bk. I. ll. 19, 20.)

l. 3. *yon cavern.* The place of torment. See l. 15.

l. 7. *auld Hangie.* Hangman—to whom condemned criminals are committed for the final execution of the law.

ll. 19-21. *raugin' like a roaring lion*, &c. References to the scripture text that describes Satan ' going about like a roaring lion seeking whom he may devour,' to his title of ' Prince of the Power of the air,' and to his natural hostility to churches.

l. 40. *Ayont the lough.* This adventure is probably a reminiscence of Lochlie.

l. 59. *twal-pint Hawkie.* Yielding twelve Scotch pints of milk (six gallons) and therefore a valuable cow, petted and highly prized.

l. 73. *Lang syne*, &c. The stanza beginning here was originally a compliment to his sweetheart Jean Armour, but just as he was going to press with his first volume, his relation to Jean was so far altered that he cancelled the compliment, and substituted the stanza of the text. The complimentary stanza went—

> ' Lang syne in Eden's happy scene
> When strappin' Adam's days were green
> And Eve was like my bonnie Jean,
> 　　　My dearest part,
> A dancin,' sweet, young handsome quean
> 　　　O' guileless heart.'

l. 99. *that day Michael did you pierce.* The reference is to *Paradise Lost* :—

> ' It [the sword of Michael] met
> The sword of Satan, with steep force to smite
> Descending, and in half cut sheer ; nor stayed,

But, with swift wheel reverse, deep entering, shared
All his right side. Then Satan first knew pain.'
(ll. 322-326.)

Scotch Drink.

This poem was probably composed early in 1786. Burns had now come to the close of his 27th year, and was entering upon the most productive period of his life as a poet. The next eighteen pieces in this collection were part of the production of 1786 - in some respects the most eventful year of his life. It was the great year of his domestic difficulties, of his first appearance as an author, of his flight from Mossgiel to Edinburgh, and of his recognition as the laureate of Scotland. *Scotch Drink* is a set-off to Fergusson's *Cauler Water*.

l. 1. *Let other poets*, &c. So Fergusson—

'The fuddlin' bardies, now-a-days,
Rin maukin-mad in Bacchus' praise,
And limp and stoiter thro' their lays
          Anacreontic.'
                              Cauler Water.

l. 3. *crabbet names an' stories.* Greek and Latin names and legends.

l. 6. *in glass or jug.* Whether whisky or ale.

l. 8. *Whether through wimplin' worms*, &c. Whether distilled or brewed.

ll. 31-36. *Thou clears the head*, &c. Cp. Horace :—

'Tu spem reducis mentibus anxiis,
Viresque et addis cornua pauperi
     Post te neque iratos trementi
          Regum apices neque militum arma.'
                              Car. iii. 21.

l. 37. *clad in massy siller weed*, i. e. served in silver mugs at the tables of the rich. Ale is meant.

ll. 41, 42. *His . . . parritch or his bread thou kitchens fine.* Small ale is meant. Cp. for similarity of opinion, Maggie Muckleback-it's reply to Monkbarns in Scott's *Antiquary* : 'An ye wanted fire and meat and claes, and were deeing o' cauld, and had a sair heart—whilk is warst o' a'—wi' just tippence i. your pouch, wadna ye be glad to buy a dram wi't, to be cilding and claes and a supper, and heart's ease into the bargain, till the morn's morning ?'.

P

l. 47. *When gaping they besiege the tents.* Surround the 'tent' (a kind of box-pulpit) at a Holy Fair, i. e. an open air religious service connected with the celebration of the Holy Communion. See Burns's *Holy Fair.*

l. 53. *a wee drap spiritual burn in,* with a little ardent spirits added to the ale.

l. 55. *Vulcan gies his bellows breath.* The blacksmith blows his bellows. At evening, after the day's work afield is over, the ploughmen bring their plough-irons for repair to the village smithy, where there is a gathering of rustics, who discuss the local news, and at times assist *Burn-the-wind,* as the blacksmith has been called, in the more mechanical and laborious part of his work.

ll. 71, 72. *It's aye the cheapest lawyer's fee to taste the barrel.* But it is never safe to predict what will come out of the *amphora.* Horace was equally bold to taste but less confident of the event :—

> 'Seu tu querelas sive geris jocos,
>   Seu rixam,' &c.—*Car.* iii. 21.

l. 84. *her warst faes.* The French.

ll. 85, 86. *Ye Scots ... ye chief, puir plackless,* &c. That is, ' Ye patriotic Scots, and especially those of you who are poor.'

l. 92. *Hale breeks, a scone, an' whisky gill, An' rowth o' rhyme.* The wish of Omar the Tentmaker (700 years before Burns) nearly corresponded :—

> 'A book of verses underneath the bough,
> A jug of wine, a loaf of bread, and thou
>   Beside me singing in the wilderness—
> And wilderness were paradise enow !'
>   *Rubaiyat* of Omàr Khayyam (E. Fitzgerald's).

The Auld Farmer's New-Year Morning Salutation to his Auld Mare.

In this *Salutation* the old farmer gives the history of 'an auld trusty servant,' and incidentally reveals the last thirty years or so of his own life. The mare has been associated with him in his joys and sorrows alike. She has even seemed to share them. (See stanzas 6, 9, 11, and 16.) He now makes a kind of ceremonious acknowledgment of her long and faithful sympathetic service.

l. 20. *my guid-father's meere.* Father-in-law's. The mare and fifty merks constituted the bride's dowry.

l. 21. *o' tocher clear.* Of clear dowry.

l. 23. *'twas weel-won gear.* The money, some £33 or £34, came from an honest household. Money honestly earned brings a blessing with it.

l. 35. *Kyle-Stewart I could bragget wide.* The central division of Ayrshire, viz. Kyle, was subdivided into districts, in one of which, King-Kyle by name, Burns was born, and to another of which, Stewart-Kyle, he had removed when his father went to Lochlie; Mossgiel was in Stewart-Kyle. Stewart-Kyle is that part of Ayrshire which lies between Irvine water and the river Ayr. 'Bragget' means 'challenged.'

ll. 43–46. *When thou and I,* &c. These lines are illustrative of the old Scots proverb—'A fou man and a hungry horse aye mak haste hame.'

l. 53. *every tail thou pay't them hollow.* Outran, or distanced every tail of them, every horse.

l. 57. *sax Scotch mile.* In miles, and especially pints, Scottish measure was considerably larger than English. But a pound Scots was only a shilling of English money.

l. 85. *My pleugh is now thy bairn-time a'.* My present plough-team of four horses are all thy offspring.

ll. 100–102. *For my last fow,* &c. Because I will reserve for you a good half-peck of my last bushel of corn.

The Twa Dogs.

The value of this poem lies largely in the fidelity of the views it affords of the social condition and character of the Scottish peasantry. It also furnishes the opinion entertained by the Scottish peasantry of the character and social life of their 'lairds.' Burns's philosophy of life is Goldsmith's. Happiness is independent of rank and wealth : it is a creation of the heart. (See *Epistle to Davie*, stanza 5.) It centres only in the mind. (See *The Traveller.*) He therefore counsels an intelligent contentment for all; and a kindlier sympathy between the working and the wealthy classes. The friendliness of the dogs is a humorous satire upon the relation in which their masters stand to each other.

l. 2. *That bears the name o' auld King Coil.* The district of Ayrshire lying between the rivers Ayr and Doon is called Coil, or Kyle, or King's Kyle. Here Burns was born—' There was a lad was born in Kyle.' History disowns King Coil, but tradition assigns him a place among the ancient British chieftains of Strath-clyde.

l. 12. *to fish for cod.* Newfoundland is meant.

l. 22. *And snuff'd at staues.* This is weak comparatively with the suppressed original. Burns's descriptions are no less realistic than the pictures of Wilkie. (*Sc.* 'Collessie Fair.')

l. 24. *A rhyming, ranting, roving billie.* This, of course, is the ploughman. It is Burns himself, who really owned a 'collie,' or sheep-dog, to which he had given the name of *Luath*,—after (as he tells us himself) 'Cuchullin's dog in Ossian's *Fingal*.' Cp. the song, *Rantin', rovin', Robin.*

l. 62. *the ha' folk.* The servants' hall.

ll. 65, 66. *wee blastit wonner ... it eats a dinner.* A diminutive meagre huntsman, a wonder to see. The dog's use of 'it' is here to be noted. So men speak of a dog : so Cæsar speaks of a man.

l. 78. *in thack an' rape.* Said primarily of stacks of corn in a stack-yard,—covered and secured from the weather. Applied to a household the expression means shelter, clothing, food—in short, the necessaries of life.

ll. 81, 82. *a wee touch langer an' they maun starve.* Cp. the common expression 'A word more, and I have done.'

l. 96. *thole a factor's snash.* A recollection of the farm life at Mount Oliphant : 'My indignation yet boils at the recollection of the scoundrel factor's insolent threatening letters, which used to set us all in tears.'—Burns's *Letter to Dr. Moore*, Aug. 1787.

l. 115. *twalpennie-worth o' nappy.* A quart of ale. A shilling Scots was only a penny sterling; a pound Scots, one-and-eight-pence. Scottish coins were withdrawn early last century, but money long continued to be calculated in the old way in Scotland.

l. 119. *patronage and priests.* Right of appointing ministers to parishes (then, and indeed till 1874, exercised by a landholder known as 'the patron'); and clergymen. Patronage was very unpopular in some quarters—it was a vexed question, often discussed, nearly everywhere.

l. 123. *bleak-faced Hallowmas.* See *Halloween*, p. 34.

l. 148. *his saul indentin'.* Dedicating his whole heart and life ; Luath does not finish the sentence.

l. 162. *fecht wi' nowt.* Bull-fighting is referred to. The language is, of course, that kind of sarcasm which calls a spade a spade.

l. 165. *drumly German water.* The German spas are referred to, then becoming fashionable. Mineral waters are not usually quite clear.

l. 192. *grips an' graues,* gripes and groans.

ll. 193, 194. *sic fools for a' their colleges.* Cp.

> 'They gang in stirks an' come out asses,
> Plain truth to speak.'
>
> (*First*) *Epistle to Lapraik*, ll. 69, 70.

l. 202. *Her dizzens done.* So many dozens of hanks of thread. spun by her.

l. 225. *a farmer's stackyard.* The whole year's crop on a farm.

l. 231. *The bum-clock hummed wi' lazy drone.* Cp. Gray's line—
'The beetle wheels his droning flight.'—*Elegy.*

The Author's Earnest Cry and Prayer.

Early in 1786 the Excise laws were being enforced with a rigour which alarmed the Scottish distillers, and those of the community who loved a dram. Burns joined in the outcry. His motto was 'Freedom and Whisky gang thegither.' The poem should be read after the verses in praise of Scotch Drink. It would be quite wrong to argue from these poems that Burns was an immoderate drinker. His brother Gilbert's testimony is that he was never intoxicated, nor 'at all given to drinking,' during the seven years of his early manhood, ending at his 28th birthday (Jan. 1786).

ll. 1, 2. *Ye Irish lords . . . wha represent our brughs,* &c. The eldest sons of Scottish peers were ineligible for election to the House of Commons.

l. 13. *you Premier youth.* Pitt—he was born in the same year as Burns, 1759.

l. 17. *blaw ye south,* i. e. out of Scotland, not again to represent that country.

l. 68. *Her lost Militia fired her bluid.* The reference is to the Scottish Militia Bill,—rejected by the Whigs because of the conditions with which it was burdened.

l. 81. *the muckle house.* Of Parliament,—called elsewhere in this poem 'St. Stephen's,' and 'St. Jamie's.'

l. 91. *Ye chosen Five-and-forty.* The number of representatives assigned to Scotland by the Articles of the Union, 1707.

l. 122. *Clap in his cheek a Highland gill.* That is, a gill of Highland whisky. The principal distillery in Scotland for several years was at Ferintosh in Cromartyshire. This distillery was exempt from duty—a privilege which Government bought back (in 1783) by paying the proprietor a sum of over £20,000.

l. 135. *causes seek.* To account, that is, for bravery.

Epistle to James Smith.

Smith was one of Burns's intimate friends. In 1786, when this letter was addressed to him, he was a shopkeeper (a draper) in Mauchline. His portrait is drawn in the third stanza. He died, even before Burns, in the West Indies, after an unsuccessful attempt to carry on business as a calico-printer in West Lothian. This poem is rich in revelation of the writer's natural disposition, his prospects, and his aims: it presents also his view of human nature, and of human life.

ll. 37-42. *This while my notion's ta'en a sklent,* &c. In the spring of 1786 Burns issued Proposals for publishing a volume of Scottish poems by subscription. The diffidence expressed in this stanza appears in his correspondence: 'Remember a poor poet militant in your prayers. He looks forward with fear and trembling to that (to him) important moment which stamps the die with—with— with, perhaps, [his] eternal disgrace.'—(*Letter,* of date 17th April, 1786.)

l. 133. *A title, Dempster merits it.* George Dempster, M.P., a patriotic Scotsman.

The Vision.

'The Vision' is of unequal merit. Some of the stanzas of which it consists Burns had the good taste to keep in manuscript. Many of the stanzas which he printed are here suppressed. It is divided into *Duans* in imitation of Macpherson's 'Ossian's *Cath-loda.*' It begins in Scotch, but the change from Scotch to English is skilfully effected before the first *Duan* ends. The whole of the second *Duan* is in English. The key upon which the poem ends is in remarkable contrast in its supernatural solemnity to the homely realistic strain with which it opens.

'The Vision' is to be regarded as a poetical representation of a great decision at which after full deliberation Burns arrives, to consecrate his hopes and energies—his whole soul—to poetry. The 'Muse' is his own nobler nature; the 'guid advice' of the fifth stanza is the expression of a mere worldly desire to be rich, to be, or to seem independent. 'It was not necessary,' says Carlyle, 'for Burns to be rich, to be, or to seem *independent*; but it *was* necessary for him to be at one with his own heart; to place what was highest in his nature highest also in his life. . . . Both poet and man of the world he must not be.' If he had acted consistently with this decision, it would have been well.

l. 2. *their roaring play.* Curling is often referred to as 'the roaring game.'

ll. 3, 4. *hunger'd maukin ta'en her way to kailyards green.* Cp. Thomson's *Winter* :—

> 'The foodless wilds
> Pour forth their brown inhabitants. The hare,
> Tho' timorous of heart, and hard beset
> By death in various forms, dark snares, and dogs,
> And more unpitying man, the garden seeks,' &c.

ll. 92-96. *many a light aërial band.* This idea of guardian spirits is a common one in poetry. It is a leading feature of Ramsay's *Vision*, with which Burns was doubtless acquainted. Milton imports it from classical mythology into his *Comus*. The name of the 'Muse,' Coila, was suggested to Burns by Ross, author of *The Fortunate Shepherdess*, who had named his muse 'Scota.' (See Burns's *Letter to Mrs. Dunlop*, 7 Mar. 1788.)

l. 111. *Campbells, chiefs of fame.* The Loudon branch of that family.

l. 121. *I saw thee seek the sounding shore.* At Mount Oliphant as a boy he was daily in sight of the sea. But Burns makes little reference to the sea, even in his songs. Perhaps his most effective use of sea imagery is in the lines—

> 'The wan moon is setting ayont the white wave,
> And time is setting with me O.'

ll. 139-144. *When youthful love*, &c. 'My passions, when once lighted up, raged like so many devils. till they got vent in rhyme ; and then the conning over my verses, like a spell, soothed all into quiet.'—(*Autobiographical Letter to Dr. Moore.*)

ll. 153, 154. *o'er all my wide domains thy fame extends.* He had yet published nothing, but his poems, passed about in MS., were already much talked of in the district of Kyle.

ll. 158-160. *paint with Thomson's landscape glow* &c. The landscape glow may be allowed to Thomson ; but Gray is not usually credited with 'warmth,' nor Shenstone with the power of 'melting.' In a letter to Dr. Moore, of date Jan. 1787, Burns repeats his criticism:—'In a language where Pope and Churchill have raised the laugh, and Shenstone and Gray drawn the tear, where Thomson and Beattie have painted the landscape, ... I am not vain enough to hope for distinguished poetic fame.'

l. 171. *not Potosi's mine.* Silver to the value of hundreds of millions of pounds sterling has been extracted from the mines in the mountains of Bolivia near the town of Potosi. (Bollaert's *Antiq. of S. America.*)

Address to the Unco Guid.

The ' Unco Guid' are those who never deviate from the path of rectitude, and never neglect duty. They are compared to a well-going mill, which never gets out of gear, does an immense amount of grinding, and is ready to do any amount more.

ll. 10–14. *counsel . . . propone defences.* Legal expressions. He will advocate their case, and advance a plea or two in their behalf.

l. 21. *what scant occasion gave.* Viz. 'the purity they pride in.' They were never assailed by temptation.

l. 48. *Ye're aiblins nae temptation.* In effect, you are never likely to be tempted, being without attractions.

l. 49 to the end. These generous lines express the various reasons that make charitable judgment even in the mind a duty. Cp. Gray's *Elegy*,

> ' No farther seek .   .   .   .   .   .
> To draw his frailties from their dread abode,—
> .   .   .   .
> The bosom of his Father and his God.'

l. 64. *know not what's resisted.* We are ignorant of the strength of the temptation.

The Holy Fair.

' Holy Fair,' says Burns, 'is a common phrase in the west of Scotland for a sacramental occasion.' The institution known by this name was a particular method, confined to rural districts, of celebrating the Lord's Supper. The celebration was annual, on a Sunday in summer; the religious services were partly conducted in the open air, in the neighbourhood of the church; several clergymen, four or five, came to assist the local minister; and

people flocked to the gathering from far and wide from various
and mingled motives. Burns's description of the manner in which
the sacred festival was ordinarily held, and of the abuses connected
with it, is graphic and by no means overstrained. It was Mauchline 'Holy Fair' from which he drew, but Mauchline was fairly
representative of rural Scotland in the matter of Holy Fairs.
Pennant, in his *Tour in Scotland* (1769), has the following
remarks on the conduct of the common people assembled at a Holy
Fair: 'There are in some places three thousand communicants
and as many idle spectators. Of the first, as many as possible
crowd each side of a long table, and the elements are rudely
shoven from one to another; and in some places before the day is
at an end, fights and other indecencies ensue. It is often made a
season of debauchery.' The fidelity of Burns's description, so far
as it goes, constitutes the satire of the poem. It is the satire of
exposure. It should not, however, be forgotten that genuine
Devotion was of the company at those gatherings as well as Fun,
Superstition, and Hypocrisy.

The *Holy Fair* is closely constructed on the lines of Fergusson's
Leith Races. Burns's Correspondence shows that in the spring of
1786 he was an enthusiastic student of Fergusson. 'Be so good as
send me Fergusson,' he writes in February to a friend in Edinburgh,
'and I will remit you the money.' 'Meeting with Fergusson's
Scottish Poems,' he writes in his Autobiographical Letter to Dr. Moore,
'I strung anew my wildly-sounding lyre with emulating vigour.'
In subject, plan, treatment, and measure, the *Holy Fair* more or less
strikingly resembles *Leith Races*. The latter poem opens thus :—

'In July month, ae bonny morn,
When nature's rokelay green
Was spread owre ilka rig o' corn
To charm our rovin' een,—
Glow'rin' about I saw a queen
The fairest 'neath the lift.'
She accosts the musing poet, and asks him if he does not mean to
see the Races. He asks in turn :—
'And wha are ye, my winsome dear,
That taks the gate sae early?
Where do ye win, if ane may speir?
For I right meikle ferly
That sic braw-buskit laughin' lass
Thir bonnie blinks should gie,

And loup like Hebe owre the grass,
    As wanton, and as free
        Frae dool this day.'
She replies—
        'I dwell amang the caller springs
        That weet the land o' cakes,
        And aften tune my canty strings
        At bridals and late wakes:
        They ca' me MIRTH.'

l. 5. *owre Galston muirs.* Galston parish adjoins that of Mauchline on the north side.

l. 15. *ane wi' lyart lining.* Hypocrisy's mantle had the white lining.

ll. 46-49. *Quoth I, 'With a' my heart I'll do't.'* An early MS. in the British Museum shows a different version—

        'Quoth I, I'll get my tither coat,
        And on my Sunday's sark,
        An' meet ye in the yard without
        At openin' o' the wark!'

l. 68. *in we go to see the show.* Mauchline 'Holy Fair' was held in the churchyard.

l. 75. *racer Jess.* A notorious female of the village—Jess Gibson by name—described as 'remarkable for her pedestrian feats.'

l. 80. *frae Kilmarnock.* The 'blackguard weaver-lads' had therefore come ten miles 'for fun that day.'

l. 87. *grace-proud faces.* Proudly conscious of being the special favourites of Heaven, the chosen people. Repeated from *Epistle to Rev. J. McMath* (stanza 4).

ll. 91-99. On this stanza Hogg, 'the Ettrick Shepherd,' has a charmingly characteristic note :—'This verse sets boldly out with a line of a *Psalm.* [*Ps.* cxlvi. 5.] It is the best description ever was drawn. *Unken'd that day* surpasses all.'

l. 102. *Moodie speels the holy door.* Ascends the 'tent,' or open-air pulpit. Moodie, Smith, Peebles, Miller, Russell were clergymen belonging to the district who had come to assist the minister of Mauchline, Rev. W. Auld (better known as 'Daddy Auld'), at the celebration of the Sacrament.

l. 103. *tidings o' damnation.* Originally 'salvation.' Altered at the suggestion of Rev. Dr. Hugh Blair, at one time Professor of Rhetoric, Edinburgh University.

l. 104. *as in ancient days.* (See *Book of Job*, chap. i.)

l. 131. *Antonine.* Marcus Aurelius (born A.D. 121).

l. 143. *aff an' up the Cowgate.* Clean away from the sound of the preacher's voice. The Cowgate was the street in Mauchline nearest to the scene of the 'Holy Fair.'

ll. 163-171. An incidental return to the subject of Scotch Drink. (See *ante.*) But the praise here is partly satirical.

l. 167. *penny-wheep.* William Langlande describes 'Rose the Regratour' as pouring together '*peni* ale and piriwhit for laborers and louh folk.'—(*Vision of Piers Ploughman.*)

l. 184. *Black Russell is na spairin.* His voice, it is said, could be heard a mile away. He was tall, dark, stern, and of a fierce temper. A favourite subject of his was the punishment of the wicked. He was popular, both in Kilmarnock, and afterwards in Stirling. In his younger years he had been a schoolmaster in Cromarty, where memories of him were still preserved in Hugh Miller's boyhood.

l. 188. *Our very sauls does harrow.* Burns acknowledges the quotation :

> 'I could a tale unfold whose lightest word
> Would harrow up thy soul.'
>
> (*Hamlet*, Act i. Sc. 5.)

l. 215. *gie's them 't like a tether.* Cp. *Epistle to McMath* :—

> 'Their three-mile prayers, an' half-mile graces.'

l. 226. *Clinkumbell.* The bell-ringer, the beadle. Cp. for blacksmith 'Burnewin'. The following variation is found—

> 'Then Robin Gib, wi weary jow,
> Begins to clink an' croon.'

To a Mountain Daisy.

This little gem, which anticipates some of the touches characteristic of Wordsworth, was produced in April, 1786. The subject, like that of the Field-mouse, was found at his feet in the fields, while he was ploughing. The Address properly ends with the sixth stanza. The remaining three stanzas, which look as if they were three successive afterthoughts, are not spoken to the daisy. The poet starts away from the immediate subject to pursue his own mournful reflections on the tragedy of human life. It is worthy of note that the last four stanzas are all but uniformly constructed on the same pattern of style, each beginning 'Such is the fate,' &c. (with a little variation) and ending 'till,' &c. It should also be noticed that the descriptive part of the poem is at least sprinkled with Scottish words, while the reflective portion is in English. With Burns there is never great indulgence in the use of Scotch when the sentiment is unusually elevated or tender.

l. 41. *billows rage, and gales blow hard.* The billows represent his own strong passions; the gales are the adverse circumstances of the outer world.

l. 49. *Ev'n thou who mourn'st the daisy's fate.* Gray's mournful lines were echoing in the mind of Burns as he composed this stanza :—

'For thee, who, mindful of the unhonoured dead,' &c. (to the end of the *Elegy*).

l. 51. *Stern ruin's ploughshare drives elate.* A recollection of an image in Young's *Night Thoughts* :—

'Final Ruin fiercely drives
His ploughshare o'er Creation.'—(*Night 9th.*)

Despondency.

Burns's despondency was not feigned. It was partly constitutional; but it was largely owing at this time (the spring of 1786) to domestic misery. He was toiling hard on an ungrateful farm, and actually maintaining himself on £7 a-year. And yet there seemed no escape that was not desperate from the bondage of the farm. He was unhappy in his love affair with Jean Armour. The Armours looked upon him as disreputable and forbade him their house ; and Jean had been induced to disown him. He was besides ostracised by the Church. There is something pathetic in this young man of twenty-seven warning the young from his own experience of the fears and tears of 'dim-declining age.'

l. 45. *Less fit to play the part.* The recurrence of an old idea. Thus, in 1781 he had written to his father :—'As for this world I despair of ever making a figure in it. I am not formed for the bustle of the busy, nor the flutter of the gay .... I am heartily tired of [this weary life] ; and, if I do not very much deceive myself, I could contentedly and gladly resign it.'

l. 56. *perfidy ingrate.* Jean Armour's conduct is here referred to. Under parental pressure she had consented to the destruction of the informal contract of her marriage with Burns.

Epistle to a Young Friend.

'Andrew' of this epistle was the son of Robert Aiken, a writer in Ayr, and a generous friend of the poet. There is in the advice which this poem contains much knowledge of human nature and the world. The date is May 1786.

ll. 37-40. These lines have been the subject of much misdirected censure. They inculcate a very necessary prudence in the conduct of life. A high authority counselled a union of the wisdom of the serpent with the harmlessness of the dove. Burns meant nothing dishonourable or disingenuous. He would not have his youthful friend 'wear his heart upon his sleeve for daws to peck at'; neither would he have him spy out the weaknesses of his fellows for the purpose of taking any mean or selfish advantage. The word 'sly' is not used in any mean sense.

l. 48. After this line came a stanza which Burns suppressed as likely to be misunderstood. The worldly wisdom of it at least is apparent :—

> 'If ye hae made a step aside—
>   Some hap mistake o'erta'en you,
> Yet still keep up a decent pride,
>   And ne'er owre far demean you ;
> Time comes wi' kind oblivious shade,
>   And daily darker sets it ;
> And if nae mair mistakes are made
>   The warld soon forgets it.'

A Dream.

This poem is introduced in the Kilmarnock edition with the following note :—'On reading in the public papers the Laureate's[1] Ode, with the other parade of June 4th, 1786, the author was no sooner dropt asleep than he imagined himself transported to the Birthday Levee, and, in his dreaming fancy, made the following Address.'

Mrs. Dunlop, the most candid and kindly of all the friends of Burns, had recommended the omission of the *Dream* from the Edinburgh edition on the score of prudence. The poet wrote to her on April 30th, 1787,—' You are right in your guess that I am not very amenable to counsel. Poets, much my superiors, have so flattered

1 William Whitehead was the Laureate from 1757-1788.

those who possessed the adventitious qualities of wealth and power that I am determined to flatter no created being either in prose or verse. . . . For my *Dream*, which has unfortunately incurred your loyal displeasure, I hope [soon] to have the honour of appearing at Dunlop [House] in its defence.' The measure is in all respects identical with that of Allan Ramsay's *Edinburgh's Salutation to the Marquis of Carnarvon.*

l. 1. *Guid mornin' to your majesty.* King George III, then near the middle of his long reign.

ll. 32, 33. *Your royal nest . . . is e'en right reft.* The allusion is to the loss of the American Colonies about three years previously. Their independence was acknowledged by Britain at the treaty which was concluded at Paris in September 1783.

ll. 62, 63. *Abridge your boats an' barges.* Referring to a parliamentary debate in the spring of 1786 on a proposal to give up 64-gun ships, and otherwise reduce the force of the navy.

l. 82. *young potentate o' Wales.* Afterwards George IV, then in his 24th year.

l. 89. *rattled dice wi' Charlie.* Charles James Fox, the great statesman.

l. 95. *him at Agincourt.* Henry V, the hero of the battle (1415).

l. 97. *queer Sir John.* Falstaff, as drawn by Shakespeare.

ll. 113, 114. *I hae seen their coggie fou that yet hae tarrow't at it.* 'To tarrow at a fou coggie' is said of a child who, being cross, refuses his food. The image seems to have been suggested by Ramsay's *Gentle Shepherd* (Act i. Sc. 2):—

> 'Like dawted wean, that tarrows at its meat,
> That for some feckless whim will orp an' greet ;
> The lave laugh at it, till the dinner's past,
> An' syne the fool thing is obliged to fast,
> Or scart anither's leavings at the last.'

A Bard's Epitaph.

The 'Bard' is generally identified as Burns himself. Wordsworth characterizes the confession of these lines as 'at once devout, poetical, and human.' They contain, he says, 'a history in the shape of a prophecy.' Burns's knowledge had too often little influence on his practice. 'If to know one's errors were a probability of mending them, I stand a fair chance,' he says, in a letter to Mr. Aiken, Oct. 1786.

In Recommendation of Willie Chalmers.

William Chalmers, or Chambers, was a solicitor in Ayr, who had asked Burns to write 'a poetical epistle to a young lady, his Dulcinea : I had seen her,' says Burns, 'but was scarcely acquainted with her, and wrote as follows.' This happened probably before he left Ayrshire for Edinburgh. We find him writing to Chambers about a month after his arrival in the Scottish capital, in such terms as prove a close companionship between them in 1786. It is not known how Chambers sped in his courtship. The poem was kept in MS. up to 1829, when it was printed by Lockhart in his *Life of Burns.*

l. 3. *My Pegasus I'm got astride.* Pegasus was the fabled horse of the Muses. Burns, of course, means that he is going to do his best for his friend, but fears that, unless he puts forth his utmost effort, he will break down. Parnassus was the supposed favourite haunt of Apollo and the Muses.

The Brigs of Ayr.

This and the next three pieces were composed in the interval between the publication of the Kilmarnock edition and the departure for Edinburgh. The publication was on the last day of July ; the departure for Edinburgh, from Mossgiel, was on the 27th November, 1786.

The *Brigs of Ayr* was partly written in compliment to Mr. John Ballantine, Provost of Ayr, and a banker by profession. Under his chief-magistracy a new bridge, intended to relieve the old one of all heavy traffic, was being built over the river Ayr sometime in September and October. The subject is treated in the manner and in the measure of Fergusson's *Dialogue between Brandy and Whisky,* and may have been suggested by that poet's *Mutual Complaint of Plainstanes and Causey.* The description with which Burns commences his poem, and the dialogue between the 'twa brigs,' are vigorously expressed and maintained ; but the conclusion is unsatisfactory both in matter and manner. The piece must be regarded as a fragment, which the poet either could not or would not finish in a way worthy of his best style. He makes an abrupt digression to the associations of the river Ayr.

l. 28. *down by Simpson's.* 'A noted tavern at the auld brig end.' —*Note by* BURNS.

ll. 33, 34. *Dungeon-clock . . . Wallace Tower.* 'The two steeples.'
—*Note by* BURNS. Both removed. There is a new Wallace Tower.

l. 53. *Auld Brig appeared of ancient Pictish race.* The old bridge
still stands, and so late as 1877 was reopened for vehicular traffic.
It is said to date from the 14th century. It consists of four lofty
arches, strongly built, but the path across is steep and narrow.
The new bridge is about a hundred yards below it.

l. 79. *tak' the Ducat stream.* 'A noted ford just above the Auld
Brig.'—*Note by* BURNS.

ll. 89-102. This passage was selected by Carlyle as a specimen
of graphic description : 'The last line is in itself a Poussin-picture
of the Deluge ! The welkin has, as it were, bent down with its
weight ; the *gumlie jaups* and the *pouring skies* are mingled
together ; it is a world of rain and ruin.' From Glenbuck to the
Ratton-quay is from source to mouth.

l. 115. *Forms might be worshipped.* That is, that might be,
worshipped.

l. 116. *And still the second dread command be free.* That is, be
unbroken, remain intact. 'Thou shalt not make unto thee any
likeness of anything,' &c.

l. 119. *any mason . . . beast.* Such as a beaver.

l. 136. *borne aboon the broo.* Carried across the water, or kept
out of the water.

l. 178. *M'Lauchlan, thairm-inspiring sage.* Clever performer on
the violin.

l. 202. *Where the Feal.* The Faile water is a tributary of the Ayr.
It passes the mansion of Coilsfield, the seat of the Montgomeries,
who were famous in battle.

l. 204. *A female form came from the towers of Stair.* This was
complimentary to Mrs. Stewart of Stair. See *Letters of Burns*—
to Mrs. Stewart, of date Oct. 1786.

l. 205. *Learning and Worth.* Professor Dugald Stewart, of Catrine, the well-known philosopher. 'I think his character . . . stands
thus—four parts Socrates, four parts Nathaniel, and two parts
Shakespeare's Brutus.'—Burns's *Letters.*

A Prayer for a Reverend Friend's Family.

The reverend friend was Mr. (afterwards Dr.) George Lawrie,
minister of the parish of Loudoun. Burns spent a night in the
manse (at the village of Newmilns, about ten miles east from

Kilmarnock) some time in October of 1786. His kindly reception by the minister's family, and the glimpse of domestic happiness which the visit afforded him, made such a lively impression upon his mind, at a time when he was feeling himself to be little better than a homeless outcast, that, as he himself said, he scarcely slept at all, but passed the night in thought and prayer. These verses were the substance of his prayer for the minister and his family. Mr. Lawrie was then in his 57th year; Mrs. Lawrie was alive; and the children consisted of a son, then a young man, afterwards his father's successor in the pastorate of the parish, and four daughters, the youngest a mere girl. Part of the evening was spent in music and dancing.

It was this 'reverend friend' to whom was sent Dr. Blacklock's famous letter, predicting success to the new Scottish poet if he should try his fortune with an Edinburgh publisher.

l. 5. *the mortal stroke.* Dr. Lawrie survived Burns for three years. He was 70 at his death.

ll. 21-24. Cp. the lines of the well-known hymn by Michael Bruce, composed about twenty years before Burns's 'Prayer':—

> 'A few short years of evil past,
> We reach the happy shore
> Where death-divided friends at last
> Shall meet to part no more.'
> *Scot. Paraph.* liii.

Tam Samson's Elegy.

Composed early in November. Samson was then sixty-three years old. He survived the 'Elegy' nine years. He was a well-to-do seedsman in Kilmarnock, which, in 1786, was a petty but ancient town of narrow streets and thatched houses, containing some three thousand people chiefly engaged in making blue bonnets, carpets, and shoes. Burns has a note on the origin of the 'Elegy':—'When this worthy old sportsman went out last muir-fowl season, he supposed it was to be, in Ossian's phrase, *the last of his fields*; and expressed an ardent wish to die and be buried in the muirs. On this hint the author'—spake.

l. 2. *great Mackinlay.* A popular preacher. He was ordained in April of this year (1786). Burns wrote a satirical poem on his Ordination.

l. 3. *Robertson again grown weel.* A preacher in Kilmarnock, unpopular partly because he read his sermons. He was ill at this time. Burns, with satirical humour, supposes that his recovery would be a calamity to the town.

l. 13. *brethren o' the mystic level.* Freemasons. Burns himself was first admitted, in St. David's (Tarbolton) Lodge, in July 1781.

l. 20. 'Mire' here is to be pronounced as a dissyllable.

l. 23. 'The cock,' or 'tee,' is the mark at each end of the curling 'rink,' or course of the stones. Other terms peculiar to the game occur in this and the next stanza. 'To wick' is to take an angle off a side shot, or lying stone. 'The hogscore' is a distance-length drawn across the 'rink,' over which every stone must come, or it is withdrawn from the rink.

l. 46. *Frae couples freed.* That is, uncoupled.

ll. 49-52. These lines mean that he was so enthusiastic a sportsman that neither age, nor disease, nor bad weather could keep him indoors in the shooting season. 'Batters' and 'fetters' are, of course, in the 'historical' present tense.

l. 56. *the tither shot he thumpit.* 'Banged off' the other shot.

l. 65. '*Lord, five!*' *he cried.* He forgot his own mortal wound in the success of his last shot: it brought down to his astonished delight five birds. Death was easy!

ll. 74, 75. An exquisite touch. Not in the first Edinburgh edition.

l. 91. The *Per Contra* may reasonably be supposed to be the result of Tam Samson's remonstrance on being described as dead. Killie is Kilmarnock—the local name.

A Winter Night.

This poem, like *The Brigs of Ayr*, is an unequal performance. The first portion is in vigorous Scotch, the second in bombastic English. The second stanza, descriptive of a snowstorm at night, is a masterpiece. The pathos of the fourth stanza repeats the sympathy expressed in the *Address to the Field Mouse*. Even the fox, the thief of 'the blood-stained roost,' comes in for a share of pity on such a night. The poem was published with a prefixed motto from Shakespeare's *King Lear*, beginning—

> 'Poor naked wretches, wheresoe'er you are,
> That bide the pelting of this pityless storm.'

l. 8. 'The rest of the labouring man is sweet.'

ll. 19–22. *Ilk happing bird . . . what comes o' thee?* Cowper had put the same question just the year before :

'How find the myriads, that in summer cheer
The hills and valleys with their ceaseless songs,
Due sustenance, or where subsist they now?'

and had answered it :

'In chinks and holes
Ten thousand seek an unmolested end,
.   .   .   . self-buried ere they die.'
Winter Morning Walk.

ll. 37, 38. *Blow, blow, ye winds . . . and freeze, thou frost.* The whole succeeding passage is a paraphrase, with comment, of the song in *As You Like It*, beginning—

'Blow, blow, thou winter wind!
Thou art not so unkind
As man's ingratitude.'

ll. 84–86. *Shall thy legal rage pursue*, &c. Nine days before his death, that is, on July 12th, 1796, Burns wrote :— 'A rascal of a haberdasher, to whom I owe a considerable bill . . . has commenced a process against me, and will infallibly put my emaciated body into jail.' The bill was only a few pounds. The haberdasher certainly embittered the closing hours of the life of Burns. In these lines the poet seems to plead against his own future misfortune.

Address to Edinburgh.

Written in Edinburgh in December, 1786, shortly after his arrival in that city.

l. 4. *Sat Legislation's sovereign powers.* The Scottish parliament was united to that of England in 1707.

ll. 5–8. The sentiment of this quatrain reappears no less poetically in the Dedication of the first Edinburgh Edition of his Poems :—'The Poetic Genius of my Country found me as the prophetic bard Elijah did Elisha—at the plough, and threw her inspiring mantle over me. . . . . I tuned my wild artless notes as she inspired. She whispered me to come to this Ancient Metropolis of Caledonia, and lay my song under your honoured protection.'

l. 22. *modest Merit's silent claim.* Cp. *Epistle to William Simson*, stanza 4th, *ante*,—' My curse upon your whunstane hearts,' &c.

l. 29. *Fair Burnet.* 'Heavenly Miss Burnet, daughter of Lord Monboddo, at whose house I have had the honour to be more than once.'—(Burns's *Letter to W. Chalmers*, Dec. 27th, 1786.) An aged Edinburgh lady, Mrs. Cockburn, authoress of the song *The Flowers of the Forest*, wrote to a friend about this time—' The town is at present all agog with the ploughman-poet. . . He has seen Duchess Gordon and all the gay world. His favourite, for looks and manners, is Bess Burnet—no bad judge, indeed.'

l. 34. *Thy rough rude fortress.* Edinburgh Castle, built on a crag.

l. 42. *that noble stately dome.* Holyrood Palace, a mile east from the Castle.

l. 47. *Their hapless race wild wandering roam.* The reference is generally to the exiled Stuarts, particularly to bonnie Prince Charlie, whose defeat at Culloden occurred forty years before Burns's visit to Edinburgh. In poetical sentiment Burns was a Jacobite, in politics a radical.

l. 52. *Old Scotia's bloody lion.* The Scottish blazon is a red lion rampant on a yellow field. ' The ruddy lion ramped in gold.'— Scott. In a letter to the Earl of Buchan Burns speaks of musing ' on those hard-contended fields where Caledonia, rejoicing, saw her bloody lion borne through broken ranks to victory and fame.'

To a Haggis.

First printed in the *Caledonian Mercury*, the first Scottish news-paper, on Dec. 20th, 1786. The last stanza is said to have been an impromptu grace said by the poet at a friend's table. The poem grew out of the grace.

To the Guidwife of Wauchope House.

This rhymed letter bears date March, 1787, and was written in answer to a rhymed letter from Mrs. Elizabeth Scott of Wauchope House, Roxburghshire, who was the wife of a laird, and dabbled in verse. The lady, by the way, was a niece of Mrs. Cockburn, mentioned above. It was first printed in Mrs. Scott's volume of verse, published in 1801.

The whole of this poem, but more especially the third stanza, may be illustrated by a passage from the Autobiographical Letter of Burns to Dr. Moore :—' This kind of life, the cheerless gloom of a hermit with the unceasing moil of a galley-slave, brought me to my 16th year ; a little before which period I first committed the sin of rhyme . . . In my 15th autumn my partner [in the harvest-field] was a bewitching creature, a year younger than myself. My scarcity of English denies me the power of doing her justice in that language, but you know the Scottish idiom—she was a bonnie, sweet, sonsie lass. In short, she, altogether unwittingly to herself, initiated me in that delicious passion which . . . I hold to be the first of human joys . . . Indeed, I did not know myself why I liked so much to loiter behind with her when returning in the evening from our labours, why the tones of her voice made my heart-strings thrill like an Æolian harp, and particularly why my pulse beat such a furious *rantann* when I looked and fingered over her little hand to pick out the cruel nettle-stings and thistles. Among her other love-inspiring qualities, she sung sweetly . . . Thus with me began love and poetry.'—(*Letter*, 2nd Aug. 1787.)

l. 60. *The marled plaid ye kindly spare.* In her letter Mrs. Scott had said—

'O gif I kenn'd but whar ye bide
I'd send to you a marled plaid ;
'Twad haud your shouthers warm an' braw,
An' douce at kirk or market shaw.'

l. 65. *Than ony ermine ever lap*, i. e. than any person whom ermine robes ever infolded, or wrapped.

The Humble Petition of Bruar Water.

The measure of this poem is built on the lines of Allan Ramsay's *Edinburgh's Salutation to Lord Carnarvon*, and the treatment of the subject is also very similar ; e. g. Ramsay has—

'O that ilk worthy British peer
Would follow your example !
My auld grey head I yet would rear
An' spread my skirts mair ample,' &c.

Burns's indebtedness to Ramsay has been greatly u. derrated, or altogether overlooked, by the critics. It was always heartily acknowledged by Burns himself. The concluding wish of the

Salutation expresses, much less gracefully and melodiously it is true, the same sentiment which is contained in the concluding wish of the *Humble Petition*.

The Bruar is an impetuous torrent in Blair Athole, rushing over falls to the Garry, a principal tributary of the Tay. It was in September, 1787, that Burns visited the Falls of Bruar in the course of his Highland Tour. He was invited to spend a couple of days at Athole House, and he repaid the invitation three days later with this delightful poem. 'It was,' he writes to Mr. (afterwards Professor) Walker, tutor to the Duke's children at Blair,—'it was the effusion of an half-hour. I do not mean it was extempore, for I have endeavoured to brush it up as well as Mr. Nicol's chat, and the jogging of the chaise, would allow. [Nicol, one of the masters of the Edinburgh High School, was his travelling companion.] It eases my heart a good deal, as rhyme is the coin with which a poet pays his debts of honour or gratitude. What I owe to the noble family of Athole of the first kind I shall ever proudly boast, what I owe of the last . . . I shall never forget. The little angel-band ! I declare I prayed for them very sincerely to-day at the Fall of Foyers.'—(*Letter*, 5th Sept. 1787.)

l. 34. *grant my highest wishes.* The petition was granted.

l. 82. *Your little angel-band.* Cp. with this the 'seraph-sister band' of the 5th stanza of the *Prayer for a Rev. Friend's Family,* (*ante*). Indeed, the scenes of the two poems may be compared (and contrasted) so far as the families, in the one case the minister of Loudoun's, in the other that of the Duke of Athole, are concerned. The Duke's household included four sons and three daughters, the youngest a mere infant.

ll. 87, 88. '*Athole's honest men and Athole's bonnie lasses !*' This had been Burns's toast at the dinner table at Blair, and was complimentary to the Duke's family. It gave great delight.

On Scaring some Water-Fowl.

A poem almost Wordsworthian in the intensity of its delicate sympathy with the lower creation. But the concluding lines are not in the style of Wordsworth. 'This,' says Burns, 'was the production of a solitary forenoon's walk from Oughtertyre House. I lived there, the guest of Sir William Murray, for two or three weeks, and was much flattered by my hospitable reception.' Loch Turrit is in a wild and lonely hollow among hills behind Ochtertyre

House, about two miles from Crieff in Perthshire. Another
Ochtertyre, also known to Burns, is near Stirling. The date of
the visit, and of the composition of the lines, was about the middle
of October, 1787.

ll. 3, 4. *Tell me, fellow-creatures, why At my presence thus you
fly?* Cp. the lines in the *Address to the Field Mouse*—

> 'I'm truly sorry man's dominion
> Has broken nature's social union,' &c.

l. 26. [*Glories in*] *creatures for his pleasure slain.* Burns had
no sympathy with field sport : it rather roused his indignation.
Before Wordsworth he counselled us—

> 'Never to blend our pleasure or our pride
> With sorrow of the meanest thing that feels.'

In a letter (4th May, 1789) to Mr. Alex. Cunningham, the poet
writes—'There is something in this business of destroying-for-
our-sport . . . . which I could never reconcile to my ideas of
virtue.'

On Captain Grose's Peregrinations in Scotland.

Francis Grose was the son of a wealthy jeweller who lived
at Richmond. He had held the commission of Captain in the
Surrey Militia, but, while still a young man, developed a taste for
antiquarian research, and about the 30th year of his age devoted
the rest of his life, some twenty years, to his favourite study.
After preparing and publishing *The Antiquities of England*, and some
works on military antiquities, he came to Scotland in the summer
of 1789 to write up the antiquities of the northern kingdom ; and
commenced work in Dumfriesshire. Burns had then been just a
year settled in his farm of Ellisland, a few miles up the Nith from
Dumfries. His nearest neighbour about a mile higher up the river
was Robert Riddell, Esq., of Friars Carse, a gentleman of antiquarian tastes, at whose table he first met Captain Grose. Mr.
Riddell's friendly interest in Burns resembled Mr. Throckmorton's
in Cowper; he allowed him the freedom of his grounds, and gave
him a key so that he could use the privilege at his convenience.

Grose's personal appearance is described in the second stanza
of this poem. The poem itself was one of the productions, says
Burns, 'of my leisure thoughts in my excise rides.' (*Letter to R.
Graham, Esq., of Fintry*, 9th Dec. 1789.) His appointment to an

Excise Division, in the middle of which lay his farm, was made about the time of his first acquaintance with Grose, that is, in the early part of autumn. The poem seems to have been first printed in the *Kelso Chronicle* on Sept. 4th, 1789, over an assumed name. It afterwards appeared in the *Scots Magazine* for Nov. 1791, and was of course included in the Edinburgh Edition of 1793. Grose died in Dublin in May 1791.

l. 1. *Land o' cakes.* That is, oatmeal cakes. First applied to Scotland, so far as I know, by Fergusson :—

> 'Oh soldiers ! for your ain dear sakes,
> For Scotland's, *alias* Land o' Cakes,
> Gie not her bairns sic deadly paiks,' &c.
>   *The King's Birthday in Edinburgh.*

l. 2. *Frae Maidenkirk to Johnny Groat's.* From end to end of the country. Kirkmaiden is in Wigtownshire, and is the most southerly parish in Scotland. The form *Maidenkirk* is a poetical licence.

l. 6. *he'll prent it,* i. e. his collection of notes.

l. 11. *he has an unco sleight o' cauk an' keel.* Grose's books were illustrated. The *Antiquities of Scotland* included nearly 200 views.

l. 26. *An' ane wad rather fa'n than fled.* That is, one who would rather have fallen than fled. See also the last line of this poem for the omission of the relative in the nominative case.

l. 32. *airn caps an' jinglin' jackets.* Iron headpieces, and coats of mail. These are plain ploughman's names—which, of course, are non-military. Cp. 'fecht wi' nowte' in the *Twa Dogs* for 'bull-fighting.'

Epistle to Dr. Blacklock.

The Rev. Thomas Blacklock, D.D., commonly known as the blind poet of literary Edinburgh, lived in that city in learned ease on an annuity for which he had reluctantly given up the living of Kirkcudbright parish. To this living, much against the wishes of the people, on account of his blindness, he had been presented by the Earl of Selkirk. He was blind from his infancy. Universal testimony, often in extravagant phrases, speaks of his cheerfulness of manner and benignity of disposition. He is described as 'an angel on earth.' Bishop Berkeley even was not more highly eulogized. Dr. Johnson, on his visit to Edinburgh, looked upon Blacklock, we are told, with reverence.

It was *his* letter to the minister of Loudoun that, more than anything else, induced Burns to give up the idea of emigrating to Jamaica, at least until he had tried his fortune with the publishers of Edinburgh. He remained till his death, in 1791, Burns's sincerest friend and warmest admirer. This Epistle, dated 'Ellisland, 21st Oct. 1789,' was in reply to a rhymed letter from Dr. Blacklock received in the preceding August. That letter concluded thus:—

> 'For me, with grief and sickness spent,
> Since I my journey homeward bent,
> Spirits depress'd no more I mourn,
> But vigour, life, and health return.
> No more to gloomy thoughts a prey,
> I sleep all night and live all day;
> By turns my book and friend enjoy,
> And thus my circling hours employ.
> Happy, while yet these hours remain,
> If Burns could join the cheerful train,
> With wonted zeal, sincere and fervent,
> Salute once more his humble servant,
>
> THOMAS BLACKLOCK.'

l. 8. *I'm turned a gauger! Peace be here!* The hope of an appointment in the Excise was entertained by Burns so early as the summer of 1786, that is, about the time when he was meditating emigration to Jamaica. 'I have been feeling all the various rotations and movements within, respecting the Excise. There are many things plead strongly against it . . . . All these reasons urge me to go abroad, and to all these reasons I have only one answer—the feelings of a father. This, in the present mood I am in, overbalances everything that can be laid in the scale against it . . . . Should you, my friends, my benefactors, be successful in your applications for me, perhaps it may not be in my power, in that way, to reap the fruit of your friendly efforts.' (*Letter to Mr. Robert Aiken*, presumably of date Oct. 1786.) In January, 1788, he wrote, 'I have almost given up the Excise idea.' In the succeeding spring, or rather summer, he took the farm of Ellisland. But the 'idea' still haunted his mind, and at last, through the influence of Mr. Graham of Fintry, one of the Commissioners of Excise, he received the appointment about a year after directly requesting it of him. The request was made in Sept. 1788. Writing in the same month and year to Miss Peggy Chalmers, the poet says—'If I could set all before your view, whatever disrespect you, in common with the world, have for this business [i. e. gauging] I know you would approve of my idea.' Shortly after beginning his duties as an officer of Excise he wrote on 1st Nov. 1789, to his friend Ainslie—'I know not how the word *exciseman,* or still more opprobrious *gauger,* will sound in your ears. I too have seen the day when my auditory nerves would have felt very delicately on this subject; but a wife and children are things which have a wonderful power in blunting that kind of sensations. Fifty pounds a year for life, and a provision for widows and orphans, you will allow, is no bad settlement for a poet. For the ignominy of the profession I have the encourage- ment which I once heard a recruiting sergeant give . . . in the streets of Kilmarnock: Gentlemen! for your further and better encouragement I can assure you that our regiment is the most blackguard corps under the crown, and consequently with us an honest fellow has the surest chance of preferment!'

ll. 9, 10. *Parnassian queans, I fear, I fear, ye'll now disdain me!* 'The Excise division which I have got is so extensive, no less than ten parishes to ride over! and it abounds besides with so much business, that I can scarcely steal a spare moment.' This to his intimate friend Richard Brown on 4th Nov. 1789; and to his patron Mr. Graham on the 9th—'Nor do I find my hurried life greatly inimical to my correspondence with the Muses. Their visits to me, indeed, . . . are short and far between; but I meet them now and then as I jog through the hills of Nithsdale, just as I used to do on the banks of Ayr.'

l. 13. *Ye glaiket . . . dannies.* The Muses.

l. 14. *Castalia's wimplin' streamies.* Castalia was supposed to be the fountain on Mt. Parnassus which Apollo and the Muses specially frequented. The 'wight of Homer's craft' in the *Jolly Beggars* found his inspiration in humbler and more convivial scenes :—

    'I never drank the Muses' stank,
       Castalia's burn an' a' that;
    But there it streams and richly reams—
       My Helicon I ca' that!'

l. 20. *They maun hae brose an' brats o' duddies.* His *Extempora- neous Effusion on being Appointed to the Excise* contains the same apology :—

    'Searching auld wives' barrels,
       Ochone the day

That clartie barm should stain my laurels !
   But what 'll ye say?
   These moving things, ca'd wives and weans,
   Would move the very hearts o' stanes ! '

ll. 29, 30. *why should ae man better fare, and a' men brithers ?*
The question was essentially characteristic of Burns's serious view
of society. The difference between the equality of mankind and
the inequality of fortune was to him a puzzling contrast. See
Epistle to Davie, A Man's a Man for a' that, &c., and *Letters passim.*
   ll. 31, 32. *Resolve, take thou the van, Thou stalk o' carl-hemp in
man.* The sentiment of these words is translated from Young—

'On Reason build Resolve
That pillar of true majesty in man,'

a passage which Burns inordinately admired, and frequently quoted
in his letters. 'Firmness,' he wrote (*Letter to Peggy Chalmers,*
March 14, 1788), 'is a character I would wish to be thought to
possess ; and have always despised . . . the cowardly feeble resolve.' Probably he admired it because he was conscious of his
want of it. Burns was ' wise to know.'
   ll. 39-42. The soundness as well as the sound of these lines has
been generally admitted and admired. The Epistle, taken altogether, is one of the best letters Burns ever wrote, whether in
prose or verse.

Elegy on Captain Matthew Henderson.

' A gentleman,' says Burns, in the strong language that was
characteristic of his praise, ' who held the patent for his honours
immediately from Almighty God.' Little is now known about
him. He was laird of Tunnochside (unidentified) ; had held a
Captain's commission in the army ; owned some property and
lived in Edinburgh ; and was buried in Greyfriars' churchyard
in that city on 27th November, 1788. For the rest, he was of an
unusually social and generous disposition, gentle and honourable
withal. Burns made his acquaintance during his prolonged stay
in Edinburgh, and was impressed with his many excellent qualities.
' You knew Matthew Henderson,' he wrote to his friend Cleghorn
of Saughton, near Edinburgh, ' he was a man ! much regarded.'
To another friend he wrote about the same time (summer of 1790)
—' You knew Henderson : I have not flattered his memory.' And

to Dr. Moore he wrote 'The *Elegy on Captain Henderson* is a tribute to the memory of *the man I loved much.*'

In this poem the imagination of Burns takes a sublime flight. Universal nature shares, or should share, the poet's grief for his departed friend. The death of his friend has changed the aspect of the world for him.

> 'The poets in their elegies and songs,
> Lamenting the departed, call the groves,
> They call upon the hills and streams to mourn
> And senseless rocks; nor idly; for they speak,
> In these their invocations, with a voice
> Obedient to the strong creative power
> Of human passion.'
>
> Wordsworth's *Excursion ; The Wanderer.*

The first stanza is hardly in keeping with the Elegy proper; and perhaps the last stanza, besides introducing in the first two lines an unnecessary discord, is an anti-climax of grief. These were probably the 'elegiac stanza or two' which Burns composed at the time of Henderson's death (Nov. 1788), but which, 'something coming in the way,' remained a fragment till July 1790. They were then incorporated with his later verses on the subject. (See *Letter to Robert Cleghorn*, 23rd July, 1790.)

ll. 3, 4. *Hawrl thee hame . . . o'er hurcheon hides.* Drag thee with a rough rope over hedgehogs to hell. Neither here nor in *Death and Dr. Hornbook* is Death regarded as a mere skeleton of bones. He is a skeleton in the original sense of the word—a *dried up* figure whose skin just covers his bones. But his skin is sensitive to the prickles of hedgehogs.

l. 5. *like stock-fish come o'er his studdie.* The figure of Death is here aptly enough (agreeably with the idea of it, as explained in the previous note) compared to a dried, or stock, fish, which is to be used hammerwise on an anvil in the infernal forge. To 'come o'er' is to thump or strike with full force. Cp. *Scotch Drink*—'Then Burnewin *comes on* like death at ilka chap.' Stock-fish is hard fish, 'stock' being akin to 'stick.'

l. 16. *Where Echo slumbers.* So high as to be beyond the reach of sounds.

ll. 39, 40. *Ye curlews calling through a clud, ye whistling plover.* 'I have some favourite flowers in spring, among which are the mountain-daisy, the hare-bell, the fox-glove, the wildbrier-rose, and the hoary hawthorn, that I view and hang over with particular delight. I never hear the loud solitary whistle of the curlew in a summer noon, or the wild mixing cadence of a troop of grey plovers, in an autumnal morning, without feeling an elevation of soul like the enthusiasm of devotion or poetry. Tell me, my dear friend, to what can this be owing? Are we,' &c.—(*Letter to Mrs. Dunlop*, 1st Jan. 1789.)

This Elegy in the sublimity of its discursive sweep suggests the similar exaltation of the genius of David as revealed in Psalm cxlviii. A remarkable feature of it is the accuracy of the numerous natural descriptions.

Tam o' Shanter.

The cottage in which Burns was born stands on the roadside a few yards distant from Alloway Kirk, the central scene of this inimitable tale of drink and diablerie. Now a roofless ruin, the Kirk was, even in Burns's childhood, hoary with age and super-natural associations. 'Many witch stories I have heard,' wrote Burns to Grose the antiquary, 'relating to Alloway Kirk.' These he doubtless ' owed '—it is his own word—to the ' old woman who resided in the family, remarkable for her ignorance, credulity, and superstition. She had . . . the largest collection in the country of tales and songs concerning devils, ghosts, fairies, brownies, witches, warlocks, spunkies, kelpies, elf-candles, dead-lights, wraiths, apparitions, cantrips . . . and other trumpery. This cultivated the latent seeds of poetry, but had so strong an effect on my imagination that to this hour, in my nocturnal rambles, I sometimes keep a sharp look out in suspicious places.' [Cp.

> 'Whiles glow'ring round wi' prudent cares
> Lest boglos catch [me] unawares.']
> *Letter to Moore*, Aug. 2, 1787.

Burns begged Grose, whose acquaintance he made in the sum-mer of 1789, to include Alloway Kirk among his pictured An-tiquities of Scotland. Grose agreed, on condition that the poet should purvey the letter-press in the shape of a witch story to accompany the engraving. Burns amply fulfilled the accepted condition, not alone by the metrical tale of *Tam o' Shanter*, but by a letter (first published by Sir Egerton Bry¹ges in *Censura Literaria* some years after Grose's death) in which he sketches three Kirk-Alloway legends. It is the second of these that Burns elaborated into *Tam o' Shanter*, and it may therefore be quoted here. But I may be allowed to notice in passing that the third of Burns's sketches doubtless gave Hogg, the Ettrick Shepherd, the groundwork for *his* metrical story of drink and diablerie—*The Witch of Fife.*

'On a market day in the town of Ayr a farmer from Carrick, and consequently whose way lay by the very gate of Alloway Kirkyard, in order to cross the river Doon at the old bridge, which is about two or three hundred yards farther on than the said gate, had been detained by his business, till by the time he reached Alloway it was the wizard hour between night and morning. Though he was terrified with a blaze streaming from the Kirk, yet, as it is a well-known fact that to turn back on these occasions is running by far the greatest risk of mischief, he prudently advanced on his road. When he had reached the gate of the Kirkyard he was surprised and entertained, through the ribs and arches of an old Gothic window, which still faces the doorway, to see a dance of witches merrily footing it round their old sooty blackguard master, who was keeping them all alive with the power of his bagpipe. The farmer, stopping his horse to observe them a little, could plainly descry the faces of many old women of his acquaintance and neighbourhood. How the gentleman was dressed tradition does not say—but that the ladies were all in their smocks: and one of them happening unluckily to have a smock which was considerably too short . . . our farmer . . . burst out, with a loud laugh, Weel luppen, Maggy wi' the short sark! and, recollecting himself, instantly spurred his horse to the top of his speed. I need not mention the universally known fact that no diabolical power can pursue you beyond the middle of a running stream. Lucky it was for the poor farmer that the river Doon was so near, for, notwithstanding the speed of his horse, which was a good one, against he reached the middle of the arch of the bridge, and consequently the middle of the stream, the pursuing vengeful hags were so close at his heels that one of them actually sprung to seize him ; but it was too late ; nothing was on her side of the stream but the horse's tail, which immediately gave way at her infernal grip, as if blasted by a stroke of lightning; but the farmer was beyond her reach. However, the unsightly tailless condition of the vigorous steed was, to the last hour of the noble creature's life, an awful warning to the Carrick farmers not to stay too late in Ayr markets.'

There is evidence both external and internal that *Tam o' Shanter,* like most of Burns's compositions indeed, was struck off at a heat —probably late in the autumn of 1790. The first authentic reference to its production will be found in a letter written by the poet to Mrs. Dunlop in November. 'I am much flattered,' he writes, 'by your approbation of my *Tam o' Shanter* .... 1 have a copy [of it] ready to send you by the first opportunity : it is too heavy to send by post.' By and by Grose sent him a dozen copies of the proof sheet of the poem, and these he distributed among his friends—Dr. Moore receiving his copy early in February, 1791, and the Rev. Archibald Alison, author of *Essays on the Principles of Taste,* his later on in the same month. To the latter he wrote —'[It] is my first essay in the way of telling a tale.' In popular estimation, and in the estimation of such critics as Scott and Lockhart, *Tam o' Shanter* is regarded as Burns's *chef d'œuvre.* It was the poet's own opinion : 'I look on *Tam o' Shanter* to be my standard performance in the poetical line.' (*Letter to Mrs. Dunlop,* 11th April, 1791.) Later critics, such as Carlyle and Matthew Arnold, rather give the palm to *The Jolly Beggars.* Carlyle goes the length of saying that 'it is not so much a poem as a piece of sparkling rhetoric.' 'The piece,' he goes on, 'does not properly cohere : the strange chasm which yawns in our incredulous imaginations between the Ayr publichouse and the gate of Tophet, is nowhere bridged over, nay the idea of such a bridge is laughed at ; and thus the Tragedy of the adventure becomes a mere drunken phantasmagoria or many-coloured spectrum painted on ale-vapours, and the Farce alone has any reality.' (*Essay on Burns.*) It was chiefly to decry Scott that Carlyle penned his harsh criticism of *Tam o' Shanter.* Scott had declared that 'no poet with the exception of Shakespeare ever possessed the power of exciting the most varied and discordant emotions with such rapid transitions.' The author of *Wandering Willie's Tale* (in *Redgauntlet*) was no bad judge of a tale of diablerie.

It has been attempted with indifferent success to discover in the land of Burns the prototype not only of Tam, but also of his 'sullen dame,' and his 'drouthy crony' the Soutar. Shanter is a farm on the Carrick, or southern shore of Ayrshire, and its tenant whilom was a Douglas Graham, who might have sat for Tam. But the type was common enough to be found in, or near, almost every market town in the Lowlands.

. l. I. *When chapmen billies leave the street,* i. e. when the sellers at the stalls and booths begin to pack up their wares, take down their stalls, and prepare to leave the market.

ll. 5-10. All this, by the use of the first personal pronoun, is in humorous sympathy with the hero of the tale.

l. 13. *This truth fand honest Tam o' Shanter.* Tam and the truth found each other. There is the suggestion of a regret on Tam's part at not starting for home earlier,—due partly to the 'lang Scots miles' with their evil associations with night, but chiefly to the domestic storm which was sure to burst at the end of the dreary night-journey. Shelley found home-going 'make the spirits tame'—so did Tam, for less ethereal reasons.

l. 19. *thou was a skellum.* 'Skellum' is the Scottish form of an ancient Anglo-Saxon word, the German form of which is almost identical, viz. *schelm,* a rascal. Some editors unwarrantably trans-late 'skellum' a wiseacre.

l. 28. *Kirkton.* The Kirkton is a common noun applied to any country town or village that boasts a parish church.

l. 38. *planted unco right.* 'Unco' is not an abbreviation of 'uncommon,'—though 'uncommonly' answers its meaning here quite well. It comes from Saxon 'uncuth'=unknown, from 'cunnan' to know. Tam's happiness on the occasion referred to was of a degree, though not of a kind, which he seldom experienced.

l. 40. *drank divinely,* i. e. went over like nectar. Said of 'swats'! But the palate was Tam's, and the company congenial.

l. 61. *Or like the snow falls in the river.* Supply 'that' between 'snow' and 'falls.' Cp.:—

> 'An' gied the infant warld a shog
> 'Maist ruined a'.'
> *Address to the Deil.*

ll. 77, 78. *That night, a child might understand, the deil had busi-ness on his hand.* An answer to Carlyle's criticism (quoted in the introductory note to this poem) that there is no bridge over the chasm that lies between the natural and the supernatural in *Tam o' Shanter.* See also ll. 31, 32. The idiom ' on his hand,' ' on my hand,' is preferred in Scotch to ' on hand.'

l. 84. *auld Scots sonnet.* A snatch of some old Scottish song or ballad. One is curious to know the character of Tam's lyrical lore. Cp.—

> ' He whistled up Lord Lennox' March,
> To keep his courage cheery.'—*Halloween.*

ll. 89-96. A doubtful tradition points out some of those places.
ll. 131-140. Cp. the incantation of the witches in *Macbeth*.
ll. 135, 136. The tomahawks and scimitars were no more out of
place on the ' holy table' in a Scottish ruined kirk than were the
contributions from Turkey and Persia in the witches' pot in a
Highland cave.   Both air and sea are the ready highway of
witches.

l. 154. *seventeen hunder linen*.   This is the trade name for fine
linen, woven in a reed of seventeen hundred divisions.

l. 158. *the bonnie burdies*.   The aforesaid 'queans a' plump
and strapping in their teens.'   'Burd' is for A. S. *bryd*, a wife or
woman.   Campbell has—

> 'By my word the bonnie burd
> In danger shall not tarry.'
>
> *Lord Ullin's Daughter*.

' Burd Ellen' is the title of an old Scots ballad.   And in *Early
English Alliterative Poems* (of the 14th century), edited by Dr. R.
Morris, 1864, we have in the poem on *Cleanness*, ' Thenne the
burde byhynde the dor . . . laughed' (l. 653), the reference
being to an incident in the life of Sarah, Abraham's wife.

ll. 159-162. Construe—' But I wonder that withered beldams,'
&c., ' rigwoodie hags that would have disgusted ' &c.

l. 164. *There was ae winsome wench and waulie*.   ' She was
a winsome wench and waulie ' is a verse of Ramsay's allegorical
poem *The Three Bonnets*, which had lingered in the memory of
Burns.

ll. 219-224. The tale would perhaps have been better wanting
this humorous moral.

Lament of Queen Mary.

This poem was composed during the last year of the poet's
residence at Ellisland, and probably early in 1791.   He wrote on
28th January to Dr. Moore—' The ballad on Queen Mary was
begun while I was busy with Percy's *Reliques of English Poetry*.'
About the same time he sent a copy of it to Mrs. Graham, of Fintry,
along with a letter, in which occurs the interesting remark—
' Whether it is that the story of our Mary Queen of Scots has
a peculiar effect on the feelings of a poet, or whether I have in the

R

enclosed ballad succeeded beyond my usual poetic success, I know not, but it has pleased me beyond any effort of my muse for a good while past.'

The scene of the ballad lies in one of the many places of captivity in England—some ten in all—in which Queen Elizabeth, for eleven years, imprisoned the fair but unfortunate Queen of Scots, who had fled to her for protection. The time is early in spring, near the close of the dreary period of Queen Mary's long imprisonment. Release came to her by the headsman's axe in Feb.. 1587. She was then only forty-four.

l. 11. *The merle in his noontide bower.* 'Merle' is here to be pronounced as a dissyllable. The merle (Lat. *merula*) is the blackbird—a French form. The merle and the mavis (the thrush) are all but inseparable with the old Scottish 'makkaris,' known and anonymous. Indeed the opening of this *Lament* is quite in the conventional style of the ancient Scottish descriptive ballad or poem. See Montgomery's *The Cherrie and the Slae*, Dunbar's *Goldyn Targe*, and the charming old ballad of 'minstrel Burn,' *Leader Haughs and Yarrow*, which Burns may have read in Ramsay's *Tea Table Miscellany*. It will be found interesting to compare the first stanza of Burns's *Lament* with the first stanza of Burn's Ballad.

ll. 19, 20. *The hawthorn's budding . . . and milkwhite is the slae.* True to nature. The sloe blossom is out while the hawthorn is only in bud.

l. 25. *I was the Queen o' bonnie France.* Mary was married in 1558 to the Dauphin—afterwards Francis II. He died in 1560.

l. 33. *thou false woman.* Elizabeth, from whom she expected protection.

l. 34. *My sister and my fae.* Sister is used here for kinswoman or cousin. Mary's grandmother was Elizabeth's aunt.

l. 37. *the weeping blood.* The sympathetic spirit, or tender disposition, common to women.

l. 39. *the balm that drops on wounds of woe.* The tear shed in sympathy, which consoles and comforts the mourner.

l. 41. *My son!* James VI and I.

l. 49. *O soon to me may summer suns.* This is a wish—not a fear.

On Pastoral Poetry.

This poem is undoubtedly Burns's. The only possible objection to his authorship of it must come from internal evidence, and to any man who can be said to know Burns's style, the internal evidence conclusively proves that Burns was the author. It was found among his papers after his death, and in his handwriting, and nobody would have thought of doubting whose production it was, had Gilbert Burns not expressed his dissatisfaction with it. Gilbert Burns probably knew less about his brother, either as a man or a poet, than many a stranger. Editors, however, have deferred to the superiority of his critical wisdom as established by kinship, and have, without a shred of external evidence, attributed the poem to Hamilton of Gilbertfield, to Fergusson, to Beattie, &c. As for Beattie, he did not possess that copious command of Scottish word and idiom which this poem reveals in every stanza ; at the same time his criticism of English poets would not have been so wide of the mark ! Fergusson, again, though his note was bold and mellow, was incapable of the concluding sentiment, and could scarcely have heard of Sappho-Barbauld. And Hamilton wanted strength to commit even the blunders of the poem. The '&c.' need not be disturbed in their obscurity. One point—it is the only one—in the internal evidence supposed to be against the idea of Burns's authorship, may be noted for its manifest absurdity, viz. that Burns never mentions Ramsay without referring to, and preferring, Fergusson; but that here the praise is all Ramsay's, and Fergusson's name never even hinted at. The first statement is false ; the second is true. And the reason of the poet's silence— if it be necessary to give a reason—is that the poem is *On Pastoral Poetry.*

ll. 1-6. *Poesie ! thou nymph reserved,* &c. This is Poesy in general. In the second stanza a particular kind of poetry, 'the shepherd-sang,' is selected as the main subject. With the whole of this opening stanza, cp. Goldsmith's 'Sweet Poetry . . . dear charming nymph . . . thou source of all my bliss and all my woe' (*Deserted Village,* ll. 407-414). Goldsmith was a favourite of Burns.

L 9. *sock or buskin.* Comedy and Tragedy—in short, the Drama flourishes.

ll. 13-18. This stanza refers to the four great divisions of poetry —the epic, the drama, satire, and song. It may be admitted that Burns's judgment of English poetry was not seldom at fault. To

R 2

compare Mrs. Barbauld to Sappho may have been a magnificent
compliment to the living poetess, but it was hardly criticism. The
stanza, however, may pass, if it be regarded as part of a poem
written in the character of a ploughman tinctured with English
letters.

l. 19. *But thee, Theocritus, wha matches ?* The question remains
unchallenged.

l. 20. *They're no herd's ballats, Maro's catches.* Virgil's *Eclogues*
are not the work of an ordinary versifier ; or, better, are not true
pastorals.

l. 21. *Squire Pope.* A mere amateur, or gentleman writer of
pastorals, with no practical knowledge of rural life and work.

ll. 21, 22. *busks his skinklin patches o' heathen tatters.* His
pastorals are only elegant imitations of favourite passages in the
classics, dressed up to pass as new and original. Cp. Horace's
'purple patch.'

l. 29. *the far-fam'd Grecian* is, of course, Theocritus.

l. 32. *honest Allan!* Allan Ramsay, author of the pastoral
drama *The Gentle Shepherd.* (See *Epistle to John Lapraik*, note,
ll. 79, 80, *ante.*)

l. 33. *Thou need na jouk behint the hallan.* Ramsay was by no
means unduly modest, or inclined to retire into odd corners at an
inspection of native ‘makkaris'; but he probably had no idea of
receiving so honourable a place in a review of the world's pastoral
poets. As he had not been known to claim equality with Theocritus, he is here invited to step forward beside him.

l. 35. *Tantallan.* A noted stronghold of the Earls of Angus on
the Haddington coast. ‘ To ding down Tantallan ’ was to perform
an impossible feat of strength.

l. 44. *bonnie lasses bleach their claes.* The second scene of the
first act of *The Gentle Shepherd* opens thus :—

> ‘*Jenny.* Come, Meg, let’s fa’ to wark upon this green,—
>   This shining day will bleach our linen clean ;
>   The water’s clear, the lift unclouded blue
>   Will mak them like a lily wet wi’ dew.’

l. 51. *Nae snap conceits*, &c. Neither extravagant sentiment, nor
elegant but empty compliment, but the sensible language of sincere
affection. (For ‘ bombast spates of nonsense ’ and ‘ snap conceits,’
see the addresses of Sir Piercie Shafton to Mysie Happer in Scott's
Monastery.)

THE SONGS.

The popularity of Burns rests mainly upon his songs. It was with song that his career as an author commenced, so early as his fifteenth year, and it was with song that it ended, in his thirty-eighth. Of the first fifteen of his poetical productions, only one is non-lyrical; and of the last fifty-two, forty-six are songs. His lyrics number altogether three hundred and nine—as against two hundred and fifty-four poems that are non-lyrical. It was during the latter half of his literary life that he composed the great bulk of his songs—and, indeed, of his poetry. Between 1785 and 1796 he produced no fewer than two hundred and seventy-nine songs; and 1795 was his most productive year, yielding so many as thirty-nine. Mere quantity, it is true, is not everything, but the thirty-nine include such popular pieces as *A Man's a Man for a' that*, and *The Braw Wooer*. The development of Burns's lyrical faculty was greatly encouraged by the inauguration in Edinburgh of two serial publications known as Johnson's *Musical Museum* and Thomson's *Select Collection of Scottish Songs*. To the former Burns was first asked to contribute when he was staying in Edinburgh in 1787, and the publication had at once his personal support and countenance. Writing from Edinburgh on October 25th, 1787, to the Rev. John Skinner, he describes his interest in it in the following terms : ' There is a work going on in Edinburgh just now which claims your best assistance. An engraver [Johnson] in this town has set about collecting and publishing all the Scotch Songs, with the music, that can be found. Songs in the English language, if by Scotchmen, are admitted, but the music must all be Scotch. Drs. Beattie and Blacklock are lending a hand, and the first musician in town presides over his department. I have been absolutely crazed about it, collecting old stanzas, and every information remaining respecting their origin, authors, &c . . . Your three songs, *Tullochgorum*, *John of Badenyon*, and *Ewie wi' the Crookit Horn* go in the second number.' Five years after he thus wrote to Skinner, he was asked by Thomson for contributions

to his venture. The letter which conveyed the request began :
' For some years past I have, with a friend or two, employed many
leisure hours in collating and collecting the most favourite of our
national melodies for publication '; and it went on, ' We shall
esteem your poetical assistance a particular favour, besides paying
any reasonable price you shall please to demand for it. . . . Tell me
frankly, then, whether you will devote your leisure to writing twenty
or twenty-five songs suitable to the particular melodies which I
am prepared to send you.' The reply to this request was characteristic : 'As the request you make will positively add to my enjoy-
ments in complying with it, I shall enter into your undertaking with
all the small portion of abilities I have, strained to their utmost
exertion by the impulse of enthusiasm. . . As to remuneration—
you may think my songs either above or below price, for they shall
absolutely be the one or the other.'

Burns's first poem was a song entitled *Handsome Nell*, written
in his fifteenth year. ' I never had the least thought or inclination
of turning poet,' he writes in his Commonplace Book, 'till I got
heartily in love, and then rhyme and song were, in a manner, the
spontaneous language of my heart.' He is more explicit in his
Autobiographical Letter to Dr. Moore : ' Among her other love-inspiring qualities [he is speaking of Nelly Kirkpatrick, his partner
in the harvest-field at Mount Oliphant] she sang sweetly; and
it was her favourite reel [*I am a Man unmarried*] to which I
attempted giving an embodied vehicle in rhyme,' &c. (See the
Letter.)

Burns's method of composing a song is thus described by him in
a letter to George Thomson of date Sept. 1793 : ' Until I am complete master of a tune in my own singing (such as it is) I never
can compose for it. My way is—I consider the poetic sentiment
correspondent to my idea of the musical expression, then choose
my theme, begin one stanza ; when that is composed, which is
generally the most difficult part of the business, I walk out, sit
down now and then, look out for objects in nature around me that
are in unison or harmony with the cogitations of my fancy and
workings of my bosom ; humming every now and then the air
with the verses I have framed.' This humming of the air he elsewhere calls ' *sowthing* the tune over and over ' : it was his invariable
custom from the very first when composing a song. He says
further—' Unless I be pleased with the tune I never can make
verses to it.'

Mary Morison.

Burns has referred to this song as one of his 'juvenile works.'
It was probably composed in the spring or summer of 1781, during
the Lochlie period of his life, and a few months before his
residence in Irvine. Mary Morison has been pretty conclusively
proved to have been a certain Elison Begbie, the daughter of a
small farmer near Galston. When Burns made her acquaintance
she was a domestic servant in a household near Cessnock water,
about two miles from the farm of Lochlie. He had previously
sung her praises as Peggy Alison, and the Lass of Cessnock banks.
She seems to have been a young woman of unusual intelligence and
refinement for a person in her station of life. That the poet was
deeply in love with her there can be no doubt. Her ultimate refusal of his addresses was a principal part of his misery at Irvine :
' To crown my distress, a *belle fille* whom I adored, and who had
pledged her soul to meet me in the field of matrimony, jilted me
with peculiar circumstances of mortification.' (*Letter to Dr. Moore,*
2nd August, 1787.) Hazlitt has said of this song that it belongs to
the class—pathetic and serious love-songs—which 'take the deepest
and most lasting hold of the mind.'

l. 10. *the lighted ha'*. Doubtless idealized from the village
dancing school at Tarbolton.

ll. 23, 24. *A thought ungentle canna be The thought o' Mary Morison.*
The same sentiment occurs in a love-letter to Elison Begbie :
' Once you are convinced I am sincere, I am perfectly certain you
have too much goodness and humanity to allow an honest man
to languish in suspense only because he loves you too well.'

An August Song to Peggy.

This was Peggy Thomson, with whom he first became acquainted, in his seventeenth year, at Kirkoswald, whither he had gone to
learn land-surveying. The first stanza of the song was composed
at that time. He returned to it on a return of his passion for
Peggy some eight years later, and finished the song as it now
stands. (See his *Autobiographical Letter to Dr. Moore.*'

ll. 23, 24. *The sportsman's joy, the murdering cry, The fluttering
gory pinion.* Burns omits no opportunity of denouncing sport.
Contrast this description, brimful of a genuine sympathy with the

lower animals, with Pope's description of the dying pheasant
in *Windsor Forest.* The only feeling in Pope's description is
the feeling of the mere artist.

My Nannie, O.

Who Nannie was is undecided. The Lugar, mentioned in
the first line, is a tributary of the Ayr, rising in Corsincon Hill,
and joining the main stream about two miles south of Mauchline.
In all editions of his Poems in his lifetime Burns printed Stinchar
for Lugar, but it was himself that proposed the alteration to Girvan,
or Lugar: Girvan 'suited the idea of the stanza best ; but Lugar
was the most agreeable modulation of syllables.' (*Letter to Geo.
Thomson,* 26th Oct. 1792). The song is written in the character
of a young ploughman in the service of a rich old farmer.

Rantin' Rovin' Robin.

Robin is, of course, Burns himself, born in the central division
of Ayrshire, Kyle, on 25th January, 1759,—the last year but
one of the reign of George II.

l. 13. *The gossip keekit in his loof.* To tell his fortune by
palmistry.

l. 20. *We'll a' be proud o' Robin.* Prophetic of the voice of
Scotland,—uttered in 1785.

Farewell to Ballochmyle.

Ballochmyle is about two miles from Mauchline, and was much
frequented by Burns, because of its fine scenery, during his residence at Mossgiel farm. The song was composed in 1785. About
that time Sir John Whitefoord was obliged to part with his estate
of Ballochmyle in order to meet liabilities which he had incurred
by the failure of a bank ; Maria is to be understood as his daughter.
The estate of Catrine adjoins that of Ballochmyle. The river Ayr
flows past both estates.

The time is autumn. The *Farewell* proper is contained in the
second stanza, and is supposed to be the farewell of Maria.

Meenie's ee.

Composed in the spring of 1786. The 2nd stanza is to be regarded as the chorus. Meenie is a diminutive of Marion. Jeanie was no doubt in the poet's mind, though he wrote Meenie. It was in the spring of 1786 that Jean Armour was advised to destroy his promise of marriage, and disown him.

l. 14. *the tentie seedsman stalks.* The sower carefully scatters the seed as he marches down the furrows.

ll. 21-28. Compare with these lines the 'hoary-headed swain's' description of Gray in the *Elegy written in a Country Churchyard.*

ll. 25, 26. *when the lark ... blythe waukens by the daisy's side.* Cp. the 2nd stanza of the *Address to a Mountain Daisy*—written about the same time : 'Alas ! it's no' thy neibor sweet,' &c.

Farewell the Bonnie Banks of Ayr.

This song was composed in the autumn of 1786, in the interval between the publication of the Kilmarnock edition of his poems and the poet's departure for Edinburgh. His thoughts at the time were reluctantly bent upon emigration to the West Indies, to which he expected to sail in a few days. The *Farewell* was to have been 'the last song he should ever measure in Caledonia.' The letter from Dr. Blacklock—one of the critics 'for whose applause he had not dared to hope '—made him, as has been noted above, alter his plans, and at least preserved him to Scotland. In Edinburgh, at the house of Dr. Blacklock, Burns recited this farewell song, preceding the recital with a short account of the scene of its composition. Professor Walker was present on the occasion and has reproduced that account :—The poet was on his way to Mossgiel from Dr. Lawrie's manse, where he had spent the day and the previous night. His path homeward was over a wide stretch of solitary moor. ' The aspect of nature harmonized with his feelings. It was a lowering and heavy evening in the end of autumn. The wind was up, and whistled through the rushes and the long spear-grass which bent before it. The clouds were driving across the sky ; and cold pelting showers, at intervals, added discomfort of body to cheerlessness of mind.'

ll. 13, 14. These two lines originally ran—

    'The whistling wind affrightens me,
    I think upon the raging sea.'—(*Stair MS.*)

Birks of Aberfeldy.

Composed while the author stood under the Falls of Moness, near Aberfeldy, Perthshire, on 30th August, 1787. Burns was then on a three weeks' tour in the Highlands.

To Clarinda.

Clarinda was Agnes Craig (Mrs. M'Lehose) a lady of moderate but independent means, and of the same age as Burns, with whom the poet became intimately acquainted during his residence in Edinburgh, winter of 1787-8. She inspired some of his best love lyrics, as well as a remarkable series of erotic letters. In his correspondence with her he figures as Sylvander.

Macpherson's Farewell.

The theme was got in the course of the Highland tour. Macpherson was a notorious freebooter, executed at Banff in 1700. He is reported to have been a skilful musician on the violin, and to have composed the rant or wild air for which Burns found vocal utterance in this 'wild stormful song'—as Carlyle calls it. It is wholly Burns's 'except the chorus and one stanza.' (*Letter to Thomson*, Oct. 19, 1794).

Of a' the Airts.

This is one of the most popular of Burns's songs, and was written at Ellisland, in honour of Mrs. Burns, in June, 1788. The poet was then preparing a home for her on his new farm in Dumfriesshire, while she was taking lessons in dairy management from his mother and sisters at the Ayrshire farm of Mossgiel. In the previous May his private marriage with Jean Armour had been formally acknowledged at Mauchline.

ll. 5, 6. *There's wild woods grow, and rivers row, And mony a hill between.* Cp. these with two very similar lines of a fragment, *My Jean*, composed nearly three years before :—

> 'Tho' mountains rise, and deserts howl,
>   And oceans roar between ;
> Yet, dearer than my deathless soul,
>   I still would love my Jean.'

The Lazy Mist.

This is less a song than a meditation on Time and its changes. It was first printed in Johnson's *Musical Museum*, 1790. It was composed in the end of autumn, 1788.

Auld Lang Syne.

This is the favourite re-union song in Scotland—but is almost invariably sung at parting ! There are various versions of it, differing chiefly in the order in which the stanzas are taken. Thus in Johnson's *Museum* the stanza beginning ' And there's a hand ' is taken last, while in Thomson's *Collection* the last stanza begins ' And surely ye'll be your pint-stowp.' Burns pretended that he had taken the words down ' from an old man's singing.' Allan Ramsay's song of *Auld Lang Syne* suggested nothing to Burns but the opening line and the title :—

> ' Should auld acquaintance be forgot
> Tho' they return with scars ?
> These are the noble hero's lot,
> Obtained in glorious wars ;
> Welcome, my Vara, to my breast,
> Thy arms about me twine,
> And make me once again as blest
> As I was lang syne.'

Go, fetch to me a pint o' Wine.

Enclosed in a letter to Mrs. Dunlop, 17th December, 1788. The first four lines are by Lesley (1636). The song is believed to have been suggested to Burns by a scene which he had noticed at Leith pier,—the parting of a young officer and his mistress, the former being ordered abroad with his regiment. It is to be regretted that Burns did not write more songs descriptive of battle and military bravery. ' The pomp and circumstance of glorious war ' were never more effectively presented than in the first half of the second stanza of this song.

l. 6. *the wind blaws frae the Ferry.* A west wind blowing from Queensferry down the Firth of Forth.

l. 7. *the Berwick-law.* A conical hill, rising from level ground, in the north of Haddington, so close to the shore of the Firth as to be a conspicuous landmark to sailors.

John Anderson, my jo.

This is the Scottish *Darby and Joan.* ' My jo' is a common term of endearment, meaning ' my joy.' Composed in 1789; printed in Johnson's *Museum* in 1790.

l. 5. *your brow is beld, John.* 'Beld' is not antithetic to 'brent' in the preceding line: it is not meant to be.

l. 13. *we maun totter down, John.* Not 'toddle'—as in some editions. 'Toddle' is said of infancy, not of age. Weakness and uncertainty of step are qualities common to both 'toddling' and 'tottering,' but the former word conveys also the idea of elasticity which is wholly wanting to the latter.

Willie's Browst.

Composed 1789; printed in Johnson's *Museum,* 1790. Burns has the following explanatory note : ' The occasion of it was this : Mr. William Nicol of the High School, Edinburgh, during the autumn vacation, being at Moffat, honest Allan [Masterton—who composed the tune] . . . and I went to pay Nicol a visit. We had such a joyous meeting that Mr. Masterton and I agreed, each in our own way, that we should celebrate the business.' Masterton was a writing-master in Edinburgh. Dr. Currie, the first editor of Burns's Works, says that the meeting ' took place at Laggan, a farm purchased by Mr. Nicol, in Nithsdale, on the recommendation of Burns.' There is some discrepancy here. Laggan was not bought till 1790, and besides it is not near Moffat, but near Maxwelltown.

ll. 13-16. A poetical paraphrase of the ' auld saw' (quoted in *Rob Roy,* chap. xxix.) ' It's a bauld moon, quoth Bennygask ; anither pint, quoth Lesley.'

To Mary in Heaven.

This and the companion song, *Highland Mary,* are the tenderest of all Burns's serious love-songs. There is some mystery about Highland Mary, which the poet seems to have—from no vain motive—encouraged. Her name was Mary Campbell, and she was employed as a domestic servant in some household not far from Mossgiel. Some time in the spring of 1786, he became acquainted with her, and by and by became her accepted lover. On the second Sunday of May, which they spent together ' by the winding Ayr,' they took a tender farewell of each other, pledging mutual fidelity in a manner peculiarly solemn, and—it is said unusually romantic. They never met again. Mary died, and was buried in Greenock in the autumn ; Burns in the interval had forgotten his vows. But he was ever afterwards remorsefully to remember them, as the anniversary of poor Mary's death came round. On the evening preceding the third anniversary of her death—that is, in September or October, 1789 —he was observed to ' grow sad about something, and wandered solitary on the banks of the Nith [at Ellisland] and about his farmyard in the extremest agitation of mind nearly the whole night.' It was in these circum-stances that he composed this pathetic song.

Banks and Braes o' Bonnie Doon.

The first sketch of this very popular song was made early in the spring of 1791. The song as it is now widely known first appeared in Johnson's *Museum* in 1792. The air to which it is inextricably set was the chance composition of an Edinburgh clerk, who, being ambitious to produce a Scotch tune, was directed to keep to the black keys of the harpsichord, and preserve some kind of rhythm. By so doing, he succeeded.

Oh for Ane-an'-Twenty, Tam!

First published in Johnson's *Museum*, 1790. It is sung in the character of a high-spirited young heiress, who will have the management of her estate and the disposal of herself at ' ane-an'-twenty.'

Sweet Afton.

Johnson's *Museum*, 1792. The date of its composition, and the heroine of it are equally doubtful. The Afton is a tributary of the infant Nith, flowing through the inland parish of New Cumnock in Ayrshire.

Song of Death on the Battle-field.

This was Burns's last composition at Ellisland. The date is
some time just before Martinmas, 1791. The song is thus pre-
faced :—' *Scene*—A field of battle. Time of the day, evening. The
wounded and dying of the victorious army are supposed to join in
the following song.' This is one of our poet's three best battle
songs. The subject was suggested to him by the title of a Gaelic
air—*The Song of Death.*

Parting Song to Clarinda.

See song *To Clarinda, ante.* These impassioned lines were sent
to the lady on 27th Dec. 1791. Lines 13 to 16 won the special
admiration of both Scott and Byron. Scott declared they contained 'the essence of a thousand love tales'; Byron prefixed them
as a legend to his *Bride of Abydos.*

The Lea-Rig.

Produced in Dumfries in October 1792. Suggested by a pastoral song in the 1st vol, of *The Musical Museum.*
  l. 20. *Alang the burn to steer.* That is, to stir, or move about,
angling. Hume in *The Day Estival*, published in 1599, has the same
form—

> ' Nor they were painted on a wall
>   Nae mair they move or steer.'

(This is Coleridge's ' painted ship upon a painted ocean.')

Highland Mary.

This and *The Flowers of the Forest* are the most popular of plaintive
songs among the Scottish peasantry. It was sent to George
Thomson for his *Collection* on 14th Nov. 1792. The rhymes are
faulty, but the popular ear is not fastidious if genuine passion thrill
along the lines. The Castle o' Montgomery is Coilsfield House,
then possessed by a family of the name of Montgomery.
  ll. 5, 6. Transpose to—' May summer first unfauld her robes
there, and may she tarry the langest there.'
  See note to *To Mary in Heaven, ante.*

Duncan Gray's Wooing.

This song was composed at Dumfries in 1792, for Thomson's *Collection.*

l. 11. Ailsa Craig is a rocky island rising from the firth of Clyde opposite Girvan on the Ayrshire coast.

l. 15. *Spak o' lowpin' owre a linn.* Committing suicide by drowning.

Braw Braw Lads.

The scenery of this song is on the Gala water, a tributary of the Tweed. Burns made his Border tour in May 1787. The song was written in Jan. 1793. It was suggested by the ancient song of the same name, and of similar chorus.

Wandering Willie.

Sent to Thomson in March 1793. Suggested by the old song of the same name and measure. There is no reason to suppose that 'Nannie' was Clarinda.

The Soldier's Return.

Sent to Thomson in April 1793. Lines 3 and 4 appeared in his *Collection* as—

' And eyes again with pleasure beam'd
That had been blear'd with mourning.'

They were his own; and he thought them an improvement. The 'improvement' was displeasing to Burns.

Bonnie Jean.

This very popular ballad was composed at Dumfries in June 1793, and sent to Thomson, who at first—and for a quarter of a century—refused it a place in his *Collection.* The heroine is not, as so many suppose, Jean Armour, but Jean, daughter of John McMurdo, Esquire of Drumlanrig. The poet sent a copy in July to Miss McMurdo with an accompanying letter in which he says : 'In the enclosed ballad I have, I think, hit off a few outlines of your portrait. The personal charms, the purity of mind, the ingenuous naiveté of heart and manners in my heroine are, I flatter myself, a pretty just likeness of Miss McMurdo in a cottage.'

l. 2. *At kirk and market.* These are the great gathering-places of the peasantry.

l. 5. *her mammie's wark.* Domestic work with her mother. The phrase was a common one.

ll. 21, 22. In his letter to Thomson, offering the ballad, Burns asks whether this image, as applied to what Coleridge has called 'love's first hope to gentle mind,' is not original. Coleridge's comparison, it may be added, is

'Eve's first star thro' fleecy cloudlet peeping.'

Coleridge wrote this in 1788.

l. 38. *to fancy me.* To love me. Fancy has often the same meaning in Shakespeare, e. g. 'Tell me where is fancy bred?' (*Merchant of Venice*).

l. 40. *to tent the farms.* To attend to the management of the farm. In the next stanza it is more poetically expressed—'To tent the waving corn wi' me.'

Scots wha hae.

The original title, *Bruce's March to Bannockburn*, applies rather to the tune than to the song. The words constitute an address which Bruce is supposed to have delivered to his troops just on the eve of the great battle of 1314. There is a graphic and circumstantial account of the circumstances in which Burns composed this patriotic war-ode, which has taken the popular and the poetic fancy, but which does not agree with the author's own unvarnished story. Carlyle caught at the romantic account and reproduced it in his own fashion :—'This dithyrambic was composed on horseback; in riding in the middle of tempests over the wildest Galloway moor . . . . Doubtless this stern hymn was singing itself as he formed it through the soul of Burns; but to the external ear, it should be sung with the throat of the whirlwind.' (*Essay on Burns.*) See also Syme's account quoted in Currie's *Life.*

Burns himself writes on the subject—' I am delighted with many little melodies which the learned musician despises as silly and insipid. I do not know whether the old air [it is said to be the oldest Scots air extant] *Hey tutti taitie* may rank among this number; but well I know that . . . it has often filled my eyes with

tears. There is a tradition which I have met with in many places
in Scotland that it was Robert Bruce's March at the battle of Bannockburn. This thought in my yesternight's evening walk warmed
me to a pitch of enthusiasm on the theme of liberty and independence, which I threw into a kind of Scots ode, fitted to the air,
that one might suppose to be the gallant royal Scot's address to his
heroic followers on that eventful morning.' (*Letter to Geo. Thomson*, 1st Sept. 1793.) It is certainly not impossible to reconcile
the two accounts.

l. 3. *your gory bed.* Thomson proposed ' honour's bed,' as ' gory '
was 'disagreeable' and 'discouraging'! 'I cannot alter it.' said
Burns promptly.

ll. 21-24. ' I have borrowed the last stanza from the common
stall edition of *Wallace* [Hamilton of Gilbertfield's—a mere travesty
of Blind Harry's]—

"A false usurper sinks in every foe,
And liberty returns with every blow;"

a couplet worthy of Homer.'—BURNS.

A Red Red Rose.

A simple, straightforward, impassioned love-lyric, conceived
with all the charming abandon of the old romantic ballad style.
It was probably written in 1794, and was first printed in Johnson's
Museum, 1796.

Ca' the Yowes.

A lovely pastoral song, set to an Arcadian melody. An earlier
version was composed by Burns (probably) in 1789, and sent
by him to the *Museum* (1790). The choral stanza is perhaps old.

l. 9. *Clouden side.* ' A little river so called, near Dumfries.'
(BURNS's *note*).

l. 13. *Clouden's silent towers.* ' An old ruin [Lincluden Abbey] in
a sweet situation at the confluence of the Clouden and the Nith.'
—(BURNS.) The ruin is on the Maxwelltown side of the Nith.

Snaws of Age.

Composed in the autumn of 1794. The lines seem to indicate
on the part of their author a sense of premature decay. He was

then barely 36. Compare with the sentiment of the two concluding lines that of the 4th stanza of *Man was made to Mourn*—

> ' O man! while in thy early years,' &c.

My Nannie's Awa.

Composed in the end of 1794. The heroine is almost certainly Clarinda. Here the poet remembers his promise (of 1788)
to 'let the scenes of nature remind him of Clarinda.'

A Man's a Man for a' that.

There is here an echo of one of the cries of the wild French
Revolution, which was in progress when, on 1st Jan. 1795, this
unique song was produced. He sent it to Thomson, but not for
his *Collection*,—' for the piece is not really poetry,' he wrote. If it
be not poetry—and Matthew Arnold, of all critics, alone agrees with
the author—it is something better.

l. 2. *That hings his head.* The antecedent of 'that' is understood.
ll. 15, 16. Cp. Pope's

> ' An honest man's the noblest work of God.'

l. 25. *A prince can mak a belted knight.* Cp. Goldsmith's couplet—

> ' Princes and lords may flourish or may fade,
> A breath can make them, as a breath has made.'
>
> *Deserted Village.*

l. 28. *he mauna fa' that.* Cannot make that happen. He must
not have the power of doing that allotted to him. ' Fa'' is 'fall to
one's power or lot.' The difficulty is with *mauna* : but the idea is
that Fate has not given a king such power. Perhaps *mauna* is for
may-na.

The Braw Wooer.

Composed, 1795.
l. 18. *the lang loan.* Originally, 'the Gate-slack,' a romantic
pass over the Lowther hills in Dumfriesshire.

l. 22. *the tryste at Dalgarnock.* The market at Dalgarnock, on
the Nith.

l. 33. A tart question, such as a woman can put, veiled under an
affectionate manner. The feet, of course, would not be described
at all in the question. Black Bess's feet were apparently a tender
subject.

In the Cauld Blast.

Composed by Burns in the last summer of his life, and while suffering from mortal illness. It was written, with some others scarcely less tender, in honour of Jessie Lewars, the sister of a brother-exciseman. This young lady came to assist Mrs. Burns with her household duties during the period of distress. Her gentleness and generosity helped greatly to enliven the domestic gloom. Mendelssohn's music for this song is well known.

ll. 9–12. Cp. Horace—

' Pone me pigris ubi nulla campis
Arbor æstiva recreatur aura,

.   .   .   .   .

Dulce ridentem Lalagen amabo,
Dulce loquentem.'—*Car.* l. 22.

Fairest Maid on Devon Banks.

This was not only Burns's last lyric, but his last composition. It was written at Brow on Solway Firth, 12th July, 1796. He died in Dumfries nine days later. It is an affecting appeal to Peggy Chalmers (Mrs. Lewis Hay), whom he had known at Harviestoun House, on Devon, in the happier days of 1787, and whom he sincerely loved, not to credit the slanders that were abroad about him, and that were making him lose so many friends.

GLOSSARY.

A.

A', all.

Aback, behind, at the back.

Abeigh, aloof; usually preceded by ' stand ' or ' keep '; O. Fr. *abois, abbay* ; equivalent to ' at bay.'

Aboon, above; A.-S. *abufan*.

Abreed, abroad, out.

Acquent, acquainted ; O. Fr. *accointer*. Cp. ' situate ' for ' situated ' &c.

Adown, down ; the prefix ' a ' is intensive.

Ae, one; intensive before a superlative.

Aff, off.

Aff-loof, offhand, freely, at once.

Afore, before.

Aft, oft, often.

Agley, asquint. To ' gley' is to squint ; to ' gang agley' is to go off the right or intended line.

Ahint, behind.

Aiblins, perhaps, possibly; from ' able.'

Ain, own.

Air, early. Another form is ' ear.'

Airn, iron.

Airt, point, or quarter of the earth or sky. Gael. *aird* (or *ard* , a height, a point (of the compass).

Aisle, or aizle, a hot cinder or ember; A.-S. *ysle*.

Aith, oath.

Aits, oats; from the same root as ' eat '; the original meaning is therefore probably ' food.'

Aiver, a horse no longer young ; a cart horse.

Amaist, almost.

Amang, among.

An, or gin, if; sometimes, though.

An', and.

Anathèm, anathematise, curse. Gr. *'and*, and *títheml*.

Ance, once.

Ane, pl. anes, one, ones.

Anither, another.
An's, and is; am.
Ase, ashes.
Asklent, aslant, to one side. Sw. *slant*, side.
Asteer, astir.
Aught, eight.
Auld, old.
Ava, a corruption of 'of all'; at all.
Awa, away.
Awee, a little.
Awkwart, awkward.
Awnie, awny, bearded (said of barley). Gr. *'áchna*, chaff.
Ayont, beyond.

<h2 style="text-align:center">B.</h2>

Ba', ball.
Backet, a small wooden square trough for holding coals, ashes, salt,
   &c. Fr. *bacquet*, a bucket.
Backit, backed.
Bade, past tense of bide, to endure; to abide; to await.
Baggie, stomach.
Bailie, a magistrate next in rank to the provost in a royal burgh; an
   alderman. From Fr. *baille*, an officer of the civil law. Lat.
   bajulus.
Bainie, bony, muscular.
Bairn, child. From 'bear,' Lat. *ferre*.
Bairn-time, or bairn-teme, all the children of one mother. From
   A.-S. *teám*, offspring.
Baith, both.
Bake, a small cake, or biscuit; a roll; any 'small' bread.
Ballats, ballads.
Ban', band.
Bands (of a minister), canonical neck-tie worn by Presbyterians.
Bane, bone.
Bang (of a gun), an imitative word.
Bardie, a poet—applied familiarly.
Barefit, bare-footed.
Baring (of a stone-pit), removing the turf, &c., and exposing the
   stones.
Barley-bree, the juice of the barley, fermented or distilled.
Barmie, fermenting, unusually active; barm = yeast; probably
   allied to *fermentum*.
Bashing (said of a reaper), striking, or knocking over the corn with
   his sickle.
Batch, a number of people of the same occupation; a baker's word,
   meaning all the loaves made at a baking.
Batts, colic.
Bauks, beams or rafters of a house.
Bauld, bold.

Bawseut, having a white mark on the forehead; having a *blaze,* with which word it is probably connected. There is also Fr. *balsan,* applied to a horse with a white mark on face or foot.

Bear, barley.

Beet, to add fuel; to kindle; to incite. Primarily to mend or repair, and thus probably connected with ' better.'

Beld, bald.

Belyve, by and by. In Ben Jonson's *Sad Shepherd* the form is ' by live.'

Ben, the inner or best room of a house. Used adverbially, it means towards or into that apartment. Compounded of ' be ' and ' in.'

Bere, barley.

Besouth, to the south of. Cp. ' benorth.'

Bethankit, thanks or grace after meal.

Beuk, book.

Bevel, slant. Ger. *bügel.*

Bicker, a short race; a wooden bowl for holding liquor.

Bide, abide, endure.

Bield, shelter; from the same origin as ' build.'

Bien (said of a person), well-to-do; (of a place), comfortable.

Big, to build.

Biggin, a building.

Bill, a bull.

Billie, comrade, fellow, young man.

Bing, heap. Probably allied to ' big ' = to build.

Birk, birch-tree.

Birkie, a lively young forward fellow.

Birr, an imitative word, same as ' whir.'

Bit, a diminutive.

Bizz, a bustling haste; also, to buzz or hiss.

Black-bonnet, the elder in charge of the ' collection ' taken at the church door.

Blate, bashful, sheepish.

Blaud, a large portion; also, to slap, or beat.

Blaw, to blow; to boast.

Blawn, blown.

Bleer't, bedimmed with weeping (said of eyes); blear-eyed.

Bleeze, blaze.

Blellum, a noisy prating fellow.

Blether, bladder; nonsense.

Blin', blind.

Bluid, blood.

Blink, glance; also the duration of a glance, a short while.

Blypes, peelings; primarily, coats (as of the skin).

Bock, to vomit; to gush intermittently; an imitative word.

Boddle, a copper coin of the value of two pennies Scots; a half-penny.

Bogle, a hobgoblin.

Bonnie, or bonic, beautiful, pretty.   Probably from Lat. *bonus.*

Boord, board.

Boortrees, elder trees or bushes.   They are common near cottages and farmsteads in Scotland.

Boost, behoved, must.

Bore, a hole, or crevice ; also a technical term in the game of curling. Lat. *foro.*

Bouse, to booze, to drink long and copiously.   From Du. *buis,* a tube.

Bow-kail, cabbage, so called from its round shape.

Bow't, bent, crooked.

Bracken, or brachen, a variety of fern.

Brae, a rising ground, a slope.

Bragged, reproached, defied, challenged.

Braid, broad.

Braik, brake, a large harrow to break clods after ploughing.

Braindg't, braing't (said of a horse), plunged, or rushed forward precipitately.

Brak, broke.

Branks, originally a bridle ; a kind of wooden noose like a muzzle.

Brash, a sudden and transient illness.

Brats, clothes in general ; aprons of coarse cloth ; covering.

Brattle, a short rapid race, accompanied with much clattering.

Braw, fine, gaily dressed ; worthy.   Same origin as ' brave.'

Brawly, very well.

Braxies, sheep which have died of a disease called ' braxy' ; from A.-S. *broc,* a disease or illness.

Breastie, breast.

Brechan, brecham, a horse-collar.

Bree, juice.   Allied to ' brew,' and ' broth.'

Breif, a spell.   A warlock-brief is a wizard's spell.   Lat. *brevis.* Literally a short writing on a piece of parchment of the nature of a charm.

Breeks, breeches.

Brent, primarily high, then smooth, unwrinkled.

Brisket, breast.

Brither, brother.

Brock, badger.

Brogue, a trick.

Broo, sap, liquor, water.   Allied to ' bree.'

Broose, a race on horseback at a wedding, from the church or bride's house to the bridegroom's.   It was engaged in by the younger part of the company, and the prize was a dish of *brose,* or pottage, made of oatmeal, butter, &c.

Brugh, burgh, town.

Brunstane, brimstone ; literally burn-stone.

Brunt, burnt.

Bughtin'-time, time at evening for penning the ewes to be milked. A bught (A.-S. *búgan,* to bend) is a wattled sheep-cote.

Buird, board.

Bum, to hum (of bees).
Bum-clock, the beetle, that 'wheels a droning flight' at evening.
Bunker, a bench ; a seat in a window, which may also serve as a
 chest. Probably from the same root as 'bench' and 'bank.'
Burdies, birds, small or young ; damsels ; young women. In the
 latter sense derived from bride, A.-S. *bryd,* a wife, a woman.
Bure, bore, past tense of ' to bear.'
Burn and **burnie,** a stream or brook. Allied to ' bound.'
Burnewin, corruption of ' burn the wind,' applied to a blacksmith.
Burr-thistle, the Scottish or spear thistle.
Busket, dressed, decorated. Cp. Ger. *butzen,* to decorate.
Buss, bush.
Bussle, bustle ; zealous activity.
But, without, or wanting.
By, beside ; for that. ' I carena by' = 'I care not for that.'
Byke, a hive, or wild-bees' nest. From ' big' = 'to build.'
Byre, cow-shed. A.-S. *bur,* a chamber.

C.

Ca', call ; drive.
Cadger, a carrier or travelling dealer ; a fish carrier.
Caird, a travelling tinker ; Gaelic.
Cairn, a heap of stones ; a Gaelic word.
Canker, a sore.
Cannie, cautious ; easy.
Cantrip, a charm, or spell ; an inexplicable trick.
Canty, cheerful, lively. Perhaps allied to Lat. *canto.*
Cape-stane, cope-stone, or top-stone. Allied to Lat. *caput.*
Carl-hemp, the largest or strongest stalk of the hemp-plant.
Carlin, an old, or elderly woman ; feminine of carl, a man ; from
 A.-S. *ceorl.*
Cartes, playing cards. Lat. *charta.*
Cattle, horses, as well as oxen. Low Lat. *capitale,* goods movable
 or immovable, but especially oxen.
Cauk, chalk. Lat. *calx.*
Cauld, cold.
Caup, a cup, a wooden bowl for holding either food or drink.
Causey, causeway. Norman *calsay*; Fr. *chaussée* ; from Lat. *calx.*
Certes, certainly.
Change-house, an alehouse,— 'change' meaning ' custom.'
Chanter, the flute of the bagpipe. Fr. *chanter.*
Chapman, pedlar, or merchant ; a seller at a market-stall. A.-S.
 ceáp, a saleable article ; price.
Chaps, fellows.
Chaumer, chamber. Lat. *camera.*
Chaup, a blow or stroke.
Cheek-for-chow, check-by-jowl ; A.-S. *cedce,* and *cedle* the jaw.
Cheeket, checked.

266   *SELECTIONS FROM BURNS.*

Chiels, or chields, young fellows.   Probably a corruption of 'child.'
Chimla, chimney.
Chittering, shivering (with cold)—to which it is allied.
Chows, chews.
Chuffle, chubby, fat-faced.   Fr. *jouc*; *joufflu.*
Clachan, a village or hamlet—a Gaelic word.
Claes, or claise, clothes.
Claiver, to talk idly or foolishly.
Clap (of a mill), clapper—a piece of wood striking against the
    hopper.
Clarket, written.
Clash, to gossip ; also gossip, or idle talk.
Claught, laid hold of, clutched.
Claut, to scrape ; also, a hoard or quantity scraped together.
Claw, to scratch.
Cleed, clothe.
Claith, cloth.
Clamb, climbed.
Cleeket, hooked.
Clink, chime or rhyme ; also to drop neatly, like a rhyme.
Clips, shears (for wool or weeds).
Clish-ma-claver, idle talk ; gossip.
Clock, a beetle.
Cloot, a hoof ; from the same root as 'cleave.'
Clootie, or **Cloots,** a ludicrous name for the devil, meaning—'you
    with the hoofs.'
Coble, a small boat ; a fishing boat.
Cock (a 'curling' term), the mark for which the curlers play,—
    the 'tee.'
Coft, bought.   Germ. *kaufte.*   From the same root as 'chapman'
    and 'coup' in horse-'couper,' i.e. 'dealer.'
Cog, a wooden dish.
Collie, a sheep-dog : probably from Gael. *culean,* a whelp.
Conveeners, conveners.
Convoy, to accompany a person part of his way homeward.   Lat.
    via.
Cood, cud.   A.-S. *ecowan,* to chew.
Coof, a simpleton, or fool.   Probably the same as 'chuff.'
Cookit, disappeared, hid ; appeared and disappeared by turns.
Coost, past tense of 'cast.'
Cootie, a kind of large spoon, or spade ; a wooden dish ; also,
    feathered at the ankle, or leg.   The 'coot' is the ankle.
Corbie, crow.   Lat. *corvus.*
Core, company.   Fr. *corps.*
Corn't, just fed with corn.
Couthie, affable, familiar, affectionate, comfortable.   A.-S. *cunnan,*
    to know.
Cowpit, overturned.   Perhaps allied to Ger. *kopf.*
Cowte, colt.

Cozie, comfortable, snug.
Crabbit, crabbed.
Crack, social and familiar talk. Ca' the crack = keep the conversation going.
Craft, croft.
Craig, a cliff, or steep rock; also, the throat.
Craik, the landrail, or corn-crake. An imitative word.
Crambo-jingle, rhymes, or doggerel verses, crammed together.
Crankous, fretful or faultfinding. Gael. *crioncan*, strife.
Cranreuch, hoarfrost. Gael. *cranntarach*.
Crap, crop.
Craw, crow.
Craze, weaken; connected with 'crush.' Crazy is weak of mind.
Creeshie, greasy.
Creel, basket.
Cronie, an intimate friend, or bosom companion. Perhaps from 'croon,' and 'crone.'
Crood, crowd.
Croon, to emit a humming or murmuring sound.
Crouchie, hunch-backed. From 'crook.'
Crouse, brisk and bold.
Crowdie-time, breakfast-time—used ludicrously. Crowdie is porridge.
Crummock, Scotch for the Gaelic word *cromag*, a staff with a crooked head.
Crump, short and crisp. From 'crumble.'
Cuif, same as coof.
Curchie, a curtsy. Fr. *cour*. Also a kerchief. Fr. *couvre*, and *chef*.
Curler, one who amuses himself by 'curling,' i.e. moving smooth heavy stones over ice to a mark.
Curmurring, rumbling.
Curpin, the crupper, or rump.
Curple, the curpin or crupper. Fr. *croupe*.
Cushat, the ring-dove.
Custoc, the heart of a stalk of cabbage or colewort.
Cutty, short; from Gael. *cutach*, short.

D.

Dad, father.
Daddie, father—more affectionate than 'dad.'
Daffin, gaiety, folly; also making sport. Connected with Ger. *tauben*.
Daft, foolish, giddy, sportive. Connected with 'daffin.' Chaucer has 'daffe.'
Daimen, occasional. Perhaps from A.-S. *deman*, to count.
Dales, deals, pieces of flat timber. A.-S. *dál*, a portion.
Darklins, in the dark.

Daud, lump, or large piece.

Daur, dare.

Daurg, a corruption of 'day's work'; a certain quantity of work.

Daur't, dared.

Dautet, doted upon, indulged, petted.

Daw, to dawn.

Deacon, master of an incorporated company.

Deave, deafen.

Deed, death.

Deil, devil.

Deil-ma-care, equivalent to 'no matter for all that.'

Deleeret, delirious.   From Lat. *de* and *lira*, a ridge; therefore to deviate from the right line.

Den, hollow, dingle.

Deposite, deposit.

Descrive, describe.

Devel, a stunning blow.

Differ, for 'difference.'

Dight, to clean, wipe, rub; also to sift (as chaff from corn).   A.-S. *dihtan*, to prepare; Lat. *dictare*.

Ding, to strike, beat, excel.   A.-S. *dencgan*, to beat.   The word occurs in *Piers Ploughman.*

Dinna, do not.

Dinsome, noisy, dinning.   A.-S. *dynnan* to make noise.

Dirl, or play dirl, to vibrate or thrill.

Dizzens, dozens.   In spinning, a dozen 'cuts' make a 'hank' of yarn.

Doitet, stupid, confused.

Donsie, stupid; perhaps restive and unmanageable (applied to a horse).

Dool, grief; to 'sing dool' is to lament.   Lat. *dolor*.

Dorty, saucy, nice, sullen.

Douce, or douse, sober, sedate, modest, gentle.   Fr. *doux*.

Dour, or doure, obstinate, severe, relentless.   Lat. *durus*.

Dow, can, may.   A.-S. *dugan*, to do, to be of service.

Dowff, dull, pointless.

Dowie, faded, or worn with grief, sad.

Downa, cannot.

Downans, grassy hillocks.   Sax. *dun* a hill, down.

Doylt, stupid (as from exhaustion after toil).

Doytin, moving stupidly.

Drap, drop.

Dreepin, dripping.

Driegh, or dreigh, slow, tedious.   Allied to Lat. *trahere*.

Droop-rumpl't, drooping at the crupper.

Drouth, drought.   A.-S. *drugian*, to dry.

Drumlie, muddy.

Drunt, pet; fit of sullenness.

Dub, a puddle.

Duddie, ragged.

Duds, clothes; especially coarse, or worn, or work clothes.

Dung, beaten, past part. of ding; exhausted.

Durk, dirk, dagger.

Dusht, pushed; perhaps overcome with fear.

Dyke, a wall (of turf or stone); in old Scot. and in Eng. a ditch. A.-S. *dic,* a mound, also a ditch.

E.

Earn, or ern, eagle, osprey, A.-S.

Een, eyes.

Eerie, having, or producing, a superstitious feeling of dread; dismal.

Eke, an addition. Lat. *augere* to increase. A.-S. *ican* to add.

Eild, old age.

Eldritch, or elritch, elvish; strange, wild, and hideous.

Eneugh, or enow, enough.

Entails, estate, or fee, entailed, i.e. limited to a particular line of heirs. Fr. *tailler,* to cut or notch.

Erse, Gaelic language. A corruption of ' Irish.'

Ettle, to aim, to try; endeavour, intention. Scan. *ettle* to endeavour; Icel. *aetla,* intend.

E'vndoun, or eendoun, downright.

Eydent, or cident, busy, diligent. The original meaning would seem to be ' constant.'

F.

Fa', share, or lot—what falls by fortune to any one; also to obtain, or have as one's lot.

Faddom, to fathom, to encompass with the extended arms. Icel. *fadma* to embrace. ' I fadmede . . . Denemark' occurs in *Havelok the Dane,* l. 1291, in this sense.

Fae, foe. A.-S. *feógan,* to hate.

Faem, foam.

Fain, fond, desirous, glad. A.-S. *faegen* to rejoice.

Fair fa', good fortune happen to;—an expression of well-wishing. Cp. the English song, ' Fair befall the dainty sweet.'

Fairin, a gift at or from a fair.

Fallow, fellow.

Fa'n, fallen.

Fand, found.

Farls, cakes; properly the fourth part of a cake, whether of oat or flour meal is a farl. A.-S. *feorth dál,* fourth part.

Fash, trouble or care; also to trouble. Fr. *se fâcher,* to grieve. The word was unknown in Scotland before the reign of Mary.

Fasten-e'en, the evening preceding the first day of the Fast of Lent.

Faulding, folding, enclosing sheep in a fold.

Fause, false.

Fau'ts, faults.

Fawsont, decent, respectable. Probably connected with Fr. *façon*; Lat. *facio*. It almost conveys the idea of 'fashionable,' 'genteel.'

Feat, neat, tidy. Fr. *fait*—with the idea of 'shapely.'

Fecht, fight.

Feck, vigorous; also quantity, number, value.

Feckless, (or fectless), feeble, producing no *effect*.

Feg, fig.

Feide, feud, enmity. From A.-S. *feógan*, to hate; and *had*, hood, state of being.

Fell, biting, strong (of taste); also a pasture hill; also skin.

Fend, to defend; to provide (in any way) for oneself. Lat. *fendere*.

Fere, companion. A.-S. *fera*, a companion.

Ferintosh, whisky; from the village in Ross-shire where a strong flavoured whisky was distilled.

Ferlie, a wonder; also to wonder. It occurs in Langland and Chaucer. A.-S. *ferlic*, wonderful.

Fetch't, pulled by fits and starts (said of a horse); also, to breathe audibly and with difficulty.

Fidge, to be restless or fidgety.

Fient, fiend, the devil. A.-S. *feógan*, to hate.

Fient-haet, fiend have it!

Fier, brother; also (joined with 'hale') sound, healthy.

Fissle, bustle or rustle. Probably from the sound.

Fit, foot.

Fittie-lan', the nearer horse of the hindmost pair in the plough. Literally 'foot the land.'

Flannen, flannel.

Fleech, to flatter (probably from the same root), to cajole, to beg persuasively.

Fleesh, fleece.

Fleg, fright; to frighten. Same as 'fley.'

Flichterin, fluttering.

Flingan-tree, flail. Properly the loose piece of timber which strikes the grain.

Flisket, capered, or fretted in the yoke.

Flunkies, liveried servants, footmen. Cotgrave derives it from Fr. '*flanquier*, to be at one's elbow for a help at need.' *Flanc*, a side.

Fodgel, squat and plump; fat.

Foggage, herbage, mossy grass.

Foord, ford.

Forebears, or forbears, ancestors. From A.-S. *fore*, and *beran*, to produce.

Forby, in addition. Literally, past before.

Forfairn, wasted or worn out. A.-S. *forfaran*, to waste or destroy.

Forfoughten, exhausted or fatigued with fighting.

Forgather, to meet. The prefix, *for*, is here intensive.   Cp.
  'forfoughten.' It is more commonly negative, as 'forbid.'
Forjesket, jaded with toil.
Forrit, a corruption of 'forward.'
Fou, full, drunk.
Foughten, fought.
Fouth, fulness or abundance : from 'full.'
Fow, a full measure (of corn), a firlot or bushel.
Fracas, (Fr.) uproar ; *fracasser* to break in pieces.
Frae, from.
Frater-feeling, brotherly feeling.
Freath, froth, foam.
Frien', friend.
Fu', full.
Fud, a hare's tail.
Fuff't, puffed, blew (said of a tobacco-pipe).
Furs, furrows.
Fyfteen, fifteen.
Fyke, trouble, fuss, restlessness.
Fyled, fouled, soiled.

G.

Gab, gob, mouth.
Gae, go.
Gaed, went.
Gaets or **gates,** ways. From 'go.'
Gallows-tree, gallows,—'tree' meaning 'timber.'
Gang, go.
Gar, make or cause.
Garten, garter. Allied to 'gird ;' Garter may be from W. *gar*,
    shank, or leg.
Gash, sagacious,—with which it may be connected ; talkative.
Gashin', talking freely and copiously.
Gat, got.
Gate, road. From 'go.'
Gaun, going.
Gawcie, large, bushy, full, stately.
Gawn, a corruption of Gavin.
Gear, riches, goods, tools.
Geds, pikes or jacks.
Geordie, guinea,—from the King's head on the coin.
Get, child. From 'beget.'
Ghaist, ghost.
Gie and **gied,** give and gave.
Gilpy, a young frolicsome person, boy or girl.
Gimmer, a ewe two years old.
Gin, or an, if.
Girn, grin ; also a snare.
Gizz, face. Perhaps from 'guise.'
Glaikit, thoughtless, giddy.

Glaizie, glossy. From ' glaze.'

Gleg, quick (of the eye or mind).

Glamour, effect of a charm or spell.

Glieb, a portion. The land attached to a 'manse' in Scotland is the 'glebe.'

Glint, to shine or sparkle.

Gloamin', evening twilight, dusk. From ' gloom.'

Glowre, to glare or stare.

Glume, gloom.

Glunch, to look sour.

Gos, the goshawk, or *goose*-hawk. The goshawk is the falcon, which was flown at geese, cranes, partridges, &c.

Gowan, the common, or mountain daisy.

Gowd, gold.

Gowden, golden.

Gowdspink, the goldfinch.

Gowk, cuckoo ; also a fool, or a person easily misled.

Grain, for grane, groan.

Graip, a three-pronged fork, used for cleaning stables.

Graith, dress or accoutrements.

Grape, to grope.

Grat, wept.

Grannie, grandmother.

Gree't, agreed.

Grousome, terrible, grim.

Grumphie, pig or sow. An imitative word.

Gruntle, snout.

Grushie, growing big, thriving. From Fr. *gros.*

Gude, or guid, good or God.

Guid-e'en, good evening.

Guid-willie, heartily with good will.

Gully, large knife.

Gulravage, hasty and riotous. Probably allied to ' ravage.'

Gumlie, muddy. To gummle, or jummle, is to shake so as to muddle.

Gusty, tasty. Lat. *gustus,* taste.

H.

Ha', hall.

Hae, have.

Haffets, the temples, sides of the head. A.-S. *Healf-heafod,* half-head.

Hafflins, partly ; also, lads not fully grown. *Half,* and -*ling,* indicating manner.

Hagg, a pit or break in a moss or morass. Connected with ' hack.'

Haggis, a kind of pudding made, in the stomach of a sheep or ox, of oatmeal mixed with various animal and vegetable ingredients, minced small. From ' hack,' to chop ; Fr. *hachis.*

Hain, to enclose as with a hedge ; to save or spare. Ger. *hain,* a hedge, or thicket ; *hägen,* to enclose, or keep.

Hairst, harvest. A.-S. *haerfest*; Ger. *herbst*.

Hairum-scarum, hare-brained, unsettled, like a person scared.

Haith, faith—for 'by my faith,' a minced oath.

Haivers, absurd talk, nonsense.

Halesome, wholesome. From 'hale.'

Hallan, a partition wall of a cottage intended to screen the apartment from the air when the door is opened; the door, in a general way. Probably a corruption of 'hall end.'

Halloween, 31st Oct., the evening preceding the feast of All Saints, 1st November.

Hamely, homely. A.-S. *hám*, a dwelling.

Han', hand.

Han'darg, the work of one's hand, daily toil.

Hangie, hangman—applied to the devil.

Hanker, crave after. From 'hang.'

Hansel, a gift bestowed at a particular season, as new year's day. From A.-S. *hand-sellan*, to deliver.

Hansel in, to introduce or initiate with a gift.

Hap, to hop; also, a covering.

Happer, hopper (of a mill).

Happing, hopping. Hap-stap-an'-loup = hop-step-and-leap.

Harket, hearkened.

Harn, coarse linen; the cloth made of the refuse of flax, called 'hards.'

Hashes, slovens, fools, asses.

Haud, or **hald**, to hold.

Hauf, half.

Haughs, low level land on the border of a river, usually fertile A.-S. *ge-heige*, a meadow.

Haurl, to drag roughly.

Havins, good sense, knowledge of decorum. From *hæf*, manners. The word occurs in Ben Jonson as equivalent to 'behaviour.'

Hav'rel, foolish in talk.

Hawkie, a cow with a white face; a familiar name for a cow.

Hech, an interjection expressing surprise and sorrow.

Hecht, called; promised. O. E. *hight*. From A.-S. *hátan*, to call.

Heeze, to hoise, or lift up. From O. Dutch *hyssen*, to hoise.

Herd, a shepherd; a pastor, or minister.

Hern, heron.

Herryment, ruin, devastation. From A.-S. *hergian*, to harry, or waste.

Het, hot.

Heugh, a ravine, hollow, or pit.

Hie, high.

Hilch, to hobble; also, to halt as if lame.

Hind, a peasant, a ploughman. From A.-S. *hína*, a servant.

Hing, hang.

Hirplin', crippling, or as if cripple; limping. Allied to 'cripple.'

T

Histie, dry, barren.   Perhaps for 'hirstie,' from 'hurst' a thicket. A.-S. *hyrst.*

Hitch, a loop, or knot ; also, to move by jerking.

Hizzie, hussy (housewife)—used contemptuously; but also, a strapping girl.

Hoast, cough.

Hodden-gray, a kind of coarse woollen cloth preserving the natural colour of the wool.

Hoddin', jogging, with the idea also of plodding.

Hog-score, the line drawn across the 'rink' in the game of curling, beyond which the stones must pass, or they are pushed aside.

Hog-shouther, to justle with the shoulder.

Hool, skin, husk, or hull.   A.-S. *hulu,* a covering.

Hoolie, softly, moderately, cautiously.   Usually conjoined with 'fairly.'

Hoordet, hoarded.

Hoosie, small house.

Horn, spoon—from the material; also, a mug or measure for holding liquor.

Hornie, the devil—because vulgarly imagined with horns.

Hotch't, shook ; bribbled.

Houlet, owl, owlet.

Howe, a hollow; also, in a hollow tone.

Howkit, dug.   Allied to 'hollow.'

Hoy't, urged, incited.   From O. Fr. *huer,* or *huyer,* to shout after. The same word occurs in 'hue-and-cry.'

Hoyte, to move clumsily.

Huff'd, checked, snubbed, disappointed.

Hughoc, little Hugh.

Hurcheon, hedgehog.   In Shakespeare, 'urchin.'   Fr. *hérisson.*

Hurdies, hips.

Hurl, to wheel or whirl.

I, J.

Jad, or Jaud, jade, a young woman (used familiarly); wench.

Jaukin', trifling, or wasting time ; dallying.

Jaups, splashes or flashes (of liquid).

Janwar, January.

Icker, an ear of corn.   A.-S. *acer,* ear of corn.

Jean, Jane.

Jee, (a verb of motion) to stir forward, to move forward.   To gae jee (said of a door) = to open.

Jimp, slender ; neat.

Jing, in the oath ' by jing,' or jingo.

Jink, dodge, or elude ; also, to turn or move nimbly, like liquids.

Jinker, one quick of motion (said of a race-horse).

Jirt, perhaps a sudden push, as a jerk.

Ilk, or ilka, each.

Ingine, genius; also temper or power of mind, native aptitude. From Lat. *ingenium*, native disposition.

Ingle, fireside; also, fire. Cp. Gaelic, *aingeal*, fire; Lat. *ignis*.

Ither, other; also used for 'each other.'

Joes, and Jo's, lovers, or sweethearts. Fr. *joie*, joy—a term of endearment.

Jokteleg, or jockteleg, a knife named from the maker, *Jacques de Liège.*

Jouk, to duck, so as to elude.

Jow, to swing and ring (said of a large bell).

Jundie, to push with the elbow; to justle.

K.

Kaes, jackdaws—named from their cry.

Kail, colewort; broth made with colewort; broth generally. Lat. *caulis*, a stalk.

Kail-runt, the stalk of the colewort, or cabbage. 'Runt' is probably allied to 'rind.'

Kain, or kane, duty (of fowls, corn, eggs, butter, or other produce' paid by a tenant to his landlord. It was probably a capitation duty, and the word was derived from Gaelic *can*, the head.

Kebbuck, a cheese. Gael. *cabag*.

Keek, to peep or peer; also a look or sly glance.

Keekit, peeped.

Keel, red chalk, ruddle. Gael. *cil*.

Kelpies, water demons or monsters that haunted fords and ferries, and at night or during a storm roared for their fated victim.

Ken, to know, to be acquainted with. A.-S. *cunnan*, to know.

Ken'les, kindles. 'Candle,' 'incandescent,' &c., are cognate words.

Kennin', slight degree (of knowledge), as much as to be known but scarcely more.

Kep, to catch (an object falling or thrown). Lat. *capio*.

Ket, a matted fleece.

Kiaugh, cark—accompanied by care.

Kilt, a loose petticoat dress worn by the Scottish Highlanders; also to 'tuck up.' Dan. *kilte*, to truss.

Kimmer, a female gossip, a married woman, a godmother. Fr. *com-mère*.

Kin', kind.

Kirk, church. Gr. *Kyrios*, the Lord.

Kirn, churn; also the feast of harvest home. Perhaps in the latter signification the word may be connected with 'quern,' the hand-mill, or with 'corn.'

Kirsen, christen, baptize; pour water on.

Kist, chest.

Kitchen, to give a relish to. Kitchen, besides meaning the cooking apartment, means anything cooked to be eaten as a relish to bread. From the same root as 'cook.' La.. *coquina*.

Kittle, to excite or stir up; also difficult, ticklish, apt.

Kittlin, cat-ling, a young cat, kitten.
Knaggie, full of knags, or projecting points.
Knappin', breaking at one stroke or effort. Shakespeare has 'to knap ginger.' A knappin-hammer is a hammer for making road metal.
Knowe, knoll. Cp. ' row ' for ' roll,' ' pow ' for ' poll,' &c.
Knurlin, a small dwarf. Connected with *cryle*, or *herle*, an imp.
Kye, kine, cows.
Kytes, bellies, stomachs. A.-S. *cwith*.
Kythe, appear ; literally to show. From A.-S. *cýthan*, to show. The word occurs in Chaucer.

L.

Lag, slow. The verb and noun only are in use in English.
Laggen, the corners of a wooden dish ; the angle between the side and bottom of a bowl, cask, or any wooden vessel. Allied to ' ledge.'
Laird, lord ; owner of land under the degree of a knight ; a proprietor. From A.-S. *hláf*, loaf ; and *weard*, ward.
Lairing, sticking in mud or mire.
Laith, loth, reluctant, unwilling.
Laithfu', bashful, backward of manner.
Lallan', lowland.
Lampit, limpet. Gr. *lepas*, a bare rock ; a limpet.
Lan', land. Cp. ' han', ' hand' ; ' win', ' wind,' &c.
Lane, self alone ; alone, or lonely.
Lanely, lonely.
Lang, long. Cp. ' strang,' ' strong'; ' amang,' ' among,' &c.
Langsyne, long since, long ago.
Lank, languid—a misuse of the English word.
Lap, leapt.
Lave, that is, or that are left ; the rest.
Laverock, lark.
Lays, leas ; fields.
Lea'e, leave. Cp. ' lo'e,' for ' love.'
Leal, loyal, true, trusty. Lat. *legalis*.
Lear, learning.
Lea-rig, land that has been ploughed but is now in grass. Lea is pasture land ; the rig, or ridge, is made by ploughing.
Learn, teach. It is used with this meaning in Shakespeare.
Lee-lang', livelong.
Leevin, living.
Leeze (me), or leeze (me on), dear to me is ; mine above everything else be. In Gavin Douglas's *Virgil* the form is *leuis me—i.e.*, probably, ' lief is to me,' dear is to me.
Leister, a spear with prongs like a trident, for striking fish.
Leuk, look.
Lift, sky. A.-S. *lyft*, the air. Hence our word ' to lift,' that is, to raise to the air. Lift, in the sense of sky, occurs in old English.

Lift (o' sense), a quantity, or load; to 'give one a lift' is 'to aid one.'

Lifted up, elated. 'Fu' liftit up with' is 'very much elated with.'

Like, about.

Limmer, a woman of loose, or too free, manners.

Linket, tripped along; arm-in-arm.

Linkin', tripping,

Linn, a waterfall.

Lint, flax. From this, linen.

Lintwhite, white as flax tow; also the linnet, or lintie,—receiving its name from feeding on the seed of the flax-plant. A.-S. *linet-wige.*

Loan, lane, or opening between corn fields leading to the farmstead, and left untilled as a path for the cattle home from pasture. Akin to 'lawn.'

Lo'e, love.

Lon'on, London.

Loof, the leaf or palm of the hand.

Loot, did let; also, to stoop.

Lough, loch, or lake, or arm of the sea.

Lowe, flame. A.-S. *lig*, a flame.

Lowin, blazing, or flaming.

Lowp, leap.

Lowse, loose.

Lug, ear. 'To lug,' meaning 'to drag,' is probably a derivative.

Lugget, furnished with a lug, or an ear,— or a handle.

Luggies, small round wooden bowls with a straight upright handle. They are made of staves, hooped together. A longer stave forms the 'lug.'

Lum, chimney.

Lunt, puff of smoke; emitting smoke. 'Lunt' or 'lint' was the match-cord with which guns were fired. Cp. 'The gunner held his linstock yare.'—Scott.

Lyart, having grey hairs intermingled; gray. The form in Chaucer is 'liard'—meaning gray (said of a horse).

M.

Mae, or mair, more. Lat. *magis*. The 'r' sound is occasionally also dropped in old English,—'mo,' for 'more.'

Mailen, a farm—so called because mail, *i.e.* rent, is paid for it. Gael. *mal.*

Mailie, or Maillie, a pet name for a ewe; Molly or Mary.

Maist, most. Cp. 'ghaist,' for 'ghost.'

'Maist, almost. The form 'amaist' is also common.

Mak, make.

Mallie, Molly, Mary.

'Mang, among.

Manteels, mantels, cloaks, coverings. Fr. *manteau.*

Mark, or merk, a piece of silver money, value 13*s*. 4*d*. Scots, 13⅓*d*.

sterling. The coin was probably named from the mark impressed upon it.

Marled, mottled, or variegated ; also, marvelled. O. Fr. *marellet* ; English *marbled.*

Maukin, a hare. Gael. *maigheach.*

Maun, must.

Maut, malt. Cp. 'faut,' 'fault' ; 'saut,' 'salt,' &c. In Scotch as in French the 'l' is frequently suppressed.

Mavis, a thrush. The old English name for the bird ; still in universal use among the peasantry of the Lowlands.

Mawin, mowing, cutting grass or corn with a scythe. A.-S. *máwan.* Cp. Gr. *amao*, I cut down.

Meer, or meere, mare.

Meikle, much. 'Much-el' is used by Thomson in *Castle of Indolence.*

Melder, the quantity of meal ground at the mill at one time. Ger. *mehlder* ; Lat. *molo*, I grind.

Mell, to mix ; associated. Fr. *meler*, to meddle, to mix.

'Meliorate, ameliorate.

Melvie, to soil (sc. with meal). A.-S. *melu* meal.

Men', mend ; reform, improve.

Mense, literally, manliness ; propriety of conduct, good manners. From 'man.' Cp. Lat. *humanitas*, from *homo.*

Merran, Marion.

Messan, a small dog ; a cur ; a lap-dog in Dunbar and Montgomerie. Derivation unsettled ; Jamieson (Scot. Dict.) suggests *maison*, with the idea of a house-, or lap-dog ; others Messina, in Sicily, whence it was first brought to Scotland.

Mettles, metals, different degrees of sharpness.

Midden-hole, hollow made for a dung-hill. A.-S. *myke*, muck, and *ding*, a heap.

Mill (in 'sneeshin-mill'), snuff-box. The tobacco-leaf was originally ground in the box.

Mim, prim, modest (with the idea of affectation .

Mind, remind ; remember.

Minnie, a childish or familiar word for mother.

Mirk, dark ; darkness. A -S. *mirc* ; Eng. murky.

Misca'd, calumniated, called bad names.

Mislear'd, unmannerly ; ill-bred, rude, mischievous. From *mis*, and *learned* ; therefore 'badly taught.'

Mither, mother.

Monie, many.

Moop, to nibble, associate with in eating. English *mump.*

Moorlan', moorland.

Moss-oak, an oak covered with moss, or that grows in a morass ; hence a stunted or rough old oak.

Mottie, dusty, full of motes. A.-S. *mot*, a small particle.

Mou', mouth. This is the only instance of the suppression of 'th' at the end of a Scottish word. To 'moe,' to make a mouth, occurs in Shakespeare's *Tempest.*

Moudiewart, mouldwarp, mole. A.-S. *molde,* mould; and *weorpan,* to cast. Shakespeare has 'moldwarp.'

Mousie, a mouse (which *is* little).

Moving, motive; strength of impulse.

Muckle, much; also, big.

Muslin-kail, thin broth, weak soup.

Mutchkin-stoup, a liquor measure to hold a 'mutchkin,' *i.e.* an English pint. Perhaps etymologically a 'meting' or 'measuring' can. 'Stoup' is from Icel. *staup,* a pot, or flagon.

N.

Na, no; not. It is much used enclitically with verbs, as 'canna,' 'winna,' 'dinna' = 'can not,' will not,' 'do not.'

Nae, no.

Naething, nothing.

Naigs, nags, riding horses; horses in general. From neighing.

Nane, none.

Nappy, or nappie, ale; strong (*sc.* ale). Skelton uses the expression 'noppy ale' in *The Tunnyng of Elinor Kummyng.*

Nearhand, nearly.

Neebor, or neibor, neighbour.

Neist, or niest, next or nearest. A shortened form of 'nighest.'

New-ca'd, newly calved. To 'ca,' is also to 'drive.'

Nick, notch; also a name ~~f~~or the devil. Ger. *nicks;* Dan. *nicken,* spirit of evil.

Nickie-ben, a familiar name for the devil, 'ben' probably conveying the idea of secrecy.

Nick-nackets, bric-a-brac, gimcracks, articles more curious than useful.

Nieve, fist. Dan. *naeve.*

Niffer, exchange; also to exchange in barter. Literally, to pass from one hand, or 'nieve,' to another.

Nines, in 'to the nines,' to perfection.

Nits, nuts.

No', not.

Nor (following a comparative) than.

Nowt, or nowte, nolt, cattle. A.-S. *neat,* an ox.

O.

Och! Oh!

Onie, or ony, any.

Or, ere, before.

O't, of it.

Ourie, cold, shivering; drooping.

Outler, an outlier, an animal on a farm not housed at night or in winter; outlying.

Owre, over.

Owrehip, over from the hip, *i.e.* with a full swing.

Owre-lang, over long, too long.

Owsen, oxen.   The singular, 'owse,' is to be found in old Scotch. Cp. the river names, Exe and Ouse, for the softening of *x*.

P.

Pack, intimately familiar.   Usually conjoined with 'thick.'   The original idea is 'closeness,' derived from the verb.   Lat. *pactum*, to fix; Gr. *pegnumi*.

Paidl'd, or paidl't, paddled.   Fr. *patouiller*, to 'work' with the feet (in water).

Painch, paunch; stomach; tripe (in the pl.).   Lat. *pantex, -icis*.

Paitricks, partridges.   Fr. *perdrix*.

Palaver, idle talk, merely ceremonious talk.   Fr. *palabre*, a word; Sp. *palabra*.

Pang, to pack or stuff.   Lat. *pango*.

Parritch, porridge (made of oatmeal).   Perhaps a corruption of 'pottage'; or from *porra*, a leek, from the principal original ingredient.   Cp. kail (from colewort), broth of any kind.

Pat, put; also, a pot.

Pattle, small plough spade or stick for cleaning the share.   Cp. Eng. 'paddle.'

Paughty, haughty; also petulant.

Pauky, or pawkie, sly but with intelligence and without harmful design.   A.-S. *pæcan*, to cheat.   From the original meaning would seem to come the use of 'packed' in 'a packed house, or jury.'

Penny-fee, wages paid in money; small earnings.   'Fee' is from A.-S. *feoh*, cattle, money, or property of any kind.

Penny-wheep, small-beer.

Pensivelie, pensively.

Pettle, same as pattle (given above).

Philibeg, or philabeg, a kilt.   Perhaps from Gael. *filleadh*, a fold of cloth, a plaid ; and *beag*, little.

Phizz, face; physiognomy.   Gr. *phusis* and *gnome*.

Phrasin', coaxing, flattering.   Gr. *phrazo*, I speak.

Pickle, few; a small quantity; a grain, or a few grains of corn. Probably from 'pick.'

Pit, put (present tense).

Plackless, penniless.   A plack was a small copper coin, value four pennies Scots,—⅓*d*. sterling.   A 'bodle' was half a plack.

Plate, in an especial sense the shallow vessel in which the 'collection' is taken at a church-door in Scotland.   Also called the 'brod,' *i.e.* the 'board.'

Platie, a small plate, such as is used with tea.

Plea, a law-suit.   Fr. *plaid*, speech of a pleader.

Plenished, supplied with the necessary articles (a farm with implements, a house with furniture); stocked.   Lat. *plenus*.

Pleuch, or pleugh, or plew, plough.

Pliskie, a mischievous trick. It is commonly used with 'play'—with which it is probably cognate.

Pock, pouch, bag. Same as 'poke,' or 'pocket.'

Poind (pronounce *pinn'd*), to seize (as for debt or rent, to distrain. A.-S. *pyndan*, to shut up. 'Pound' and 'pinfold' are cognate terms in Eng.

Poortith, poverty. The same affix, 'th,' is found in 'wealth,' 'health,' &c. Lat. *pauper*.

Pou, pull.

Pouk, pluck. A 'poukit hen' = a plucked hen. Said of hairs, feathers, &c.

Poussie, pussy,—a cat, or a hare. Gael. *pus*.

Pouther, powder. Fr. *poudre*; Lat. *pulvis*.

Pow, poll, head.

Pownie, pony.

Pree, or prie, taste. Another form is 'prieve,' which would connect the word with 'prove.'

Prent, print. Lat. *premo*, I press. Ital. *imprenta*, impression.

Prief, proof. Lat. *probo*.

Priggin', to haggle about a price, to cheapen; to entreat importunately.

Primsie, demure, prim—from which it is derived.

Propone, to propose, or lay forth. Propone as a legal term means to state, or advance. Lat. *pro*, and *pono* I place.

Proveses, pl. of proves or provost, the first magistrate in a royal Scottish burgh, corresponding to mayor in England. Old Fr. *prevost*; Lat. *præpositus*.

Puddin', pudding.

Puir, poor. Fr. *pauvre*.

Pund, pound. Lat. *pondus*, a weight; *pendo*. A pund Scots was equal to 1*s*. 8*d*. sterling.

Q.

Quat, quitted; also quit. Fr. *quitter*; Lat. *quies*.

Quaukin', quaking.

Quean, a young woman—used either familiarly or disrespectfully; a wench—with which it is cognate. A.-S. *cwén*. Cp. Gr. *gune*.

Quey, a young cow or heifer. Probably from 'cow.'

Quo', for quoth, said. A.-S. *cwethan*, to say.

R.

Rab, Rob, Robert.

Ragweed, the herb ragwort.

Raibles, holds forth in a confused chattering manner; talks nonsense.

Rair't, roared; also reared.

Raize, rouse, excite, madden. Ger. *rasen*, to rage. Chaucer uses the form 'rese.'

Ramfeezl'd, fatigued, exhausted.

Ram-stam, rudely and thoughtlessly precipitate. To 'ram' is to 'push'—like a ram. 'Stam' may be 'stammer,' or merely a kind of reduplication of 'ram.'

Ranks, right metrical order. Fr. *rang.*

Rape, rope. A.-S. *ráp.*

Rash, rush.

Rash-buss, rush-bush.

Ratton, rat.

Raucht, reached. Used by Chaucer. A.-S. *rácan*; Ger. *reichen.*

Raucle, rough, rash, stout. Chaucer has 'rakel hond,' with the meaning of 'reckless.'

Rax, reach; stretch.

Raw, row.

Ream, cream; also to froth or foam. A.-S. *ream.* Fr. *crême.*

Reave, or **reife**, to rob. A.-S. *reafian*, to seize and spoil. 'Bereave' and 'reft' are cognate.

Reck, care for and attend to.

Rede, advice; to advise. A.-S. *réd*, counsel.

Red-wat, blood. Red-wat-shod—having the shoes stained with blood.

Reed, pipe (said of a chanter, *i.e.* flute of a bag-pipe).

Reek, smoke. A.-S. *réc*; Dutch, *rook.* 'Rook' in Scotland means mist or fog.

Reestit, or **reistit**, smoke-dried (said of flesh or fish). Also, became restive (said of a horse).

Remead, or **remeid**, remedy. Lat. *re*, and *medeor* I heal.

Requit, requital, return.

Rief, or **reif**, plunder. A 'rief-randy' is a masterful and disorderly person who lives by robbery. A.-S. *reaf*, plunder.

Rig, ridge; a number of furrows taken together.

Riggin, the ridging or roof of a house; the back.

Rigwoodie, or **rigwiddie**, the rope of twigs or 'withes' that crosses the back of a horse when yoked. The 'woodie' also signifies the rope of a gallows. As an adj.—'tough, hard, and lean'; but perhaps 'gallows-worthy.'

Rin, run.

Rink, the course of the stones, in 'curling,' towards the 'ring.'

Rip, or **ripp**, a handful of unthreshed corn-stalks, or hay.

Risket, made a noise, in being severed by the plough-share, 'like the tearing of roots.' This is Burns's own explanation.

Rockin', a social gathering at evening of young people—who used to take their 'rocks' or distaffs with them. The wheel superseded the rock; but social meetings still were called 'rockins.'

Roose, praise; stimulate.

Roun', round.

Rout, route, road.

Rove, a roving or wandering (in search of unlawful pleasure).

Row, or **rowe**, roll.

Rowth, abundance. Perhaps allied to 'rough.' A rough house means a house where there is plenty of food freely bestowed.

Rowtin', lowing. An imitative word.

Rung, a heavy rough stick, a cudgel. The cross pieces of a ladder are called the 'rungs.'

Runkl't, wrinkled.

Runt, sapless hard stalk. See 'Kail-runt' above.

S.

Sae, so.

Saft, soft. Cp. 'aften' for 'often,' 'craft' for 'croft,' 'aff' for 'off,' &c.

Sair, sore, severe; also, serve. In the latter meaning cp. with it 'lea'e' for 'leave,' 'lo'e' for 'love,' &c.

Sang, song.

Sark, shirt. A.-S. *syrce*, from *sceran*, to cut.

Saugh, willow or sallow. Lat. *salix*.

Saul, soul. Also written 'sowl.'

Saumont, salmon. Also written 'sawmont.' Lat. *salmo*.

Saut, salt. Lat. *sal*.

Sautet, salted.

Sawin', sowing.

Sawnie, or Sandie, Alexander : a Lowland Scottish peasant : a Scotsman.

Sax, six.

Scar', scare. 'Scar' sheep are wild, readily frightened. From Icel. *skiar*, apt to flee.

Scaud, scald. Fr. *eschauder*.

Scaul', scold.

Scaur, or scar, cliff; also, easily frightened, or scared. With the former meaning, from A.-S. *sceran*, to cut; with the latter, see 'Scar' above.

Schachl't, or shachl't, shapeless, distorted. Allied to 'askew.'

Scones, soft round thin cakes of barley or wheat flour.

Sconner, disgust. A.-S. *scunian*, to loathe and avoid.

Scraich, screeching.

Screed, tear or rent; also to rattle off quickly; harangue. A.-S. *screádan*, to rend.

Scrievin', moving swiftly, tearing along. Dan. *skrav*, a stride.

Scrimpit, short of due allowance, the effect of parsimony. Ger. *krimpen*, to contract ; Eng. 'crimp.'

Scrimply, sparingly.

Second-sighted, possessed of the power of foreseeing disaster.

See'd, saw.

Seizins, investitures, possessions—a legal term. Fr. *saisine*, from *saisir*, to seize.

Sel', self. Cp. 'twal' or 'twel,' for 'twelve.'

Sen', send. Final 'd' preceded by 'n' is dropped as a rule; and 'win', frien', men', min', &c., are used for 'wind,' 'friend,' 'mend,' 'mind,' &c.

Settlin', settling.

Shaver, sharp dealer, rogue ; a humorous droll.

Shaw, show; also, a wood. With the latter meaning allied to shadow, and Gr. *skia*.

Shearing, cutting corn with a hook or sickle, reaping ; clipping its fleece off a sheep. A.-S. *sceran* ; Ger. *scheren*, to shave or cut.

Sheep-shank, anything feeble or unimportant ; applied to a person—thus ' nae sheep-shank ' is a person of some importance.

Sheers, shears. A.-S. *sceran*, to cut.

Sheugh, a ditch, trench.

Shirra-muir, Sheriff-muir, in Perthshire, where a battle was fought in 1715 during the Rebellion on behalf of the Stuarts ; any violent contest.

Shog, shake, jog.

Shools, shovels.

Shoon, shoes. A.-S. *sceón*.

Shore, threaten ; offer.

Shouther, shoulder.

Sic, such.

Sicker, sure. Cp. Lat. *securus*.

Sidelins, sideways, sidelong.

Siller, silver ; money.

Silly, weak—whether of mind or body ; helpless or defenceless,—said of the lower animals.

Simmer, summer.

Sin', since ; because.

Skaith, injure ; injury, hurt. Eng. scathe. A.-S. *sceathan*, to harm.

Skellum, a blockhead, a worthless fellow. In Low Germany, a rogue, *schelm*.

Skelp, slap; to move with a quick decided slapping step—as if barefooted. A.-S. *scylfan*, to tremble.

Skelvy, shelvy, laminated. A.-S. *scylfe*, a table or shelf.

Skiegh, or skeigh, apt to startle ; unmanageable ; skittish— with which it is probably cognate.

Skinkin', thin, liquid ; pouring out liquor. A.-S. *scencan*, to pour out. A ' skinker ' was a drawer or waiter.

Skinklin', sparkling; also, a small portion. In the former meaning, from A.-S. *scinan*, to shine.

Skirl, scream, shriek. Allied to ' shrill.'

Sklent, slant or slope ; strike obliquely ; glance ; to lie.

Skouth, room, freedom to range, scope.

Skriegh, shriek.

Slade, slided.

Slaes, sloes, sloe-berries. A.-S. *slá*.

Slap, gap, breach.

Slee, sly, clever, ingenious. Cp. Ger. *verschlagen*.

Sleeket, sleek, smooth and glossy.

Slypet, fell over slowly in a piece like a damp furrow from the plough-share. Eng. 'slip.'

Sma', small.

Smeek, smoke.

Smiddie, smithy. Cp. 'widdie' and 'withy.'

Smoor, smother, suffocate.

Smootie, smutty, sooty.

Smytrie, a lot of small individuals ; a smattering.

Snash, abuse, saucy and impertinent language.

Snaw, snow.

Snaw-broo, melted snow, snow-water.

Sned, cut, trim, prune. Ger. *schneiden*, to cut.

Sneeshin', snuff—a sneezing powder. From 'nose.'

Snell, keen, severe. A.-S. *snel*, swift.

Snick, a door-latch,

Snick-drawin', crafty ; stealing into houses ; removing the natural ridges on a cow's horns in order to conceal its age.

Snool, to keep under ; to submit tamely ; sneak abjectly.

Snoov't, moved smoothly or steadily.

Snowket, smelt about, snuffed at. Connected with 'snook.'

Snuggèd, made snug and safe.

Sodger, soldier.

Something, somewhat—*e. g.* 'something slow, lazy,' &c.

Sonsie, plump, good-humoured, well-conditioned ; 'having sweet and engaging looks,' says Burns.

Soom, or **soum**, swim. Cp. 'soote' for 'sweet' in Chaucer.

Sootie, one who is covered with soot like a sweep ; the devil.

Souple, supple or flexible ; swift. 'Souple scones' are *bannocks* (soft cakes of barley meal).

Souter, a cobbler ; shoemaker. Lat. *sutor*, one who sews.

Sow'ns, flummery—made of oatmeal flour steeped till it is sour.

Sowpe, (pl. **sowps**), spoonful, mouthful, a small quantity. Allied to 'sup.' Said of a liquid.

Sowth, to try over a tune, by humming or whistling low.

Sowther, solder. Lat. *solidus*.

Spae, foretell, divine. Dan. *spaaer*, to foretell.

Spairges, scatters, splashes, dashes, sprinkles. Lat. *spargere*, to sprinkle.

Spairin', sparing.

Spak', spoke.

Spate, flood.

Spavet, spavied, spavined. Ger. *spannen*, to stretch.

Spean, wean.

Speel, climb.

Spence, the inner apartment of a house in the country. Allied to 'dispensary.'

Spewing, being ejected.

Spier, ask. A.-S. *spyrian*, to inquire.

Spleuchan, tobacco-pouch.

Spouts, young fishes ; properly 'razor fishes.'

Sprattle, scramble and sprawl.

Spritty, full of rushes, or reed-grasses.

Spunk, spark of fire, a small fire ; spirit, mettle.

Spunkie, will-o'-the-wisp, *ignis fatuus*; also fiery, full of spirit. Ger. *funke*, a spark.

Spurtle, a stick used in stirring boiling porridge, broth, &c. A.-S. *sprytle*, a splinter or piece of wood.

Squad, a company, a set, or crew. Fr. *escouade*, a squadron or company of soldiers.

Squatter, to make a fluttering noise in water, like waterfowl disturbed.

Squeel, squeal. Allied to 'squall.'

Stacher, stagger, to walk as if about to fall.

Staggie, a young horse under three years old ; from Icel. *steggr*, a male fox, and indeed the male of several wild beasts.

Stan', stand.

Stane, stone.

Stank, a pool or pond   Lat. *stagnum*; from *sto*, I stand.

Stap, step.

Stark, strong, hardy. A.-S. *stearc*.

Starns, stars. Dan. *stierne*; A.-S. *steorra*.

Staumrel, bungling. Probably from 'stammer.'

Staw, stole ; also disgust, or surfeit.

Stechan, filling or cramming; gormandising ; also puffing and panting.

Steek, shut ; also stitch. Allied to 'stick,' to fix. Gower has 'stoke the gates.'

Steer, stir, molest ; move.

Steive, firm. Same as 'stiff'—A.-S. *stīf*, inflexible.

Stell, still—commonly illicit.

Stenn'd, bounded suddenly.

Sten's, leaps, springs unexpectedly. Lat. *extendere*.

Stents, taxes, dues, tributes. From *extendere* in its legal meaning of rating for assessment.

Stey, steep. A.-S. *steáp*, high.

Stibble, stubble. A.-S. *styb*, stub, or stump.

Stilt, limp like a cripple ; to halt.

Stimpart, half-a-peck ; 'eighth part of a Winchester bushel,' says Burns in his glossary. Fr. *huitième part* has been suggested as the origin of the word.

Stirks, young cattle, male or female, about two years old. Allied to 'steer,' and Lat. *taurus*.

Stock, a plant or stalk of colewort, a cabbage.

Stook, a pile, or shock, of sheaves standing on the field.

Stookèd, consisting of stooks, or shocks of grain.

Stoor, strong, harsh, deep (said of a voice).

Stoup, a deep narrow vessel for holding liquids, a flagon or pitcher.

Stoure, dust ; dust in motion ; also, a battle, or confusion.

Stow'd, stolen

Stow'nins, in a stealthy manner.

Strae, straw.

Straik, stroke.

Strang, strong.

Straught, straight.

Streekit, stretched.

Striddle, straddle. From 'stride.'

Strunt, strut ; also, spirituous liquor.

Studdie, anvil. Allied to 'stithy,' from Icel. *stethi*, an anvil. The form in Chaucer is 'styth.'

Stuff, corn.

Stumpie, short worn quill—consisting of only a stump.

Sturt, trouble, disturbance. Allied to 'stir,' and Dan. *styrt*, strife.

Sturtin, startled, frightened.

Styles, stiles, barred gates. A.-S. *stigan*, to ascend.

Sucker, sugar. Fr. *sucre*.

Sud, should.

Sugh, or sough, sigh long continued (as of wind in a wood).

Sumphs, blockheads without even obstinacy ; soft, spiritless fellows.

Suthrons, Southrons, Englishmen.

Swaird, sward of grass. A.-S. *swcard*, skin, surface, grass.

Swalled, swelled, swollen.

Swank, thin, agile, and vigorous. Ger. *schwank*.

Swankie, an active and clever young muscular fellow.

Swap, exchange. An old Eng. word. Dryden used it.

Swat, sweated.

Swats, new ale. A.-S. *swate*, ale.

Swatch, specimen.

Swirl, curl, curve. Allied to ' whirl.'

Swirlie, full of curves and contortions ; knotty.

Swither, state of hesitation. A.-S. *swæther*, which of the two.

Swoor, swore.

Syne, then ; also, perhaps, ' since'; ago.

T.

Tackets, small nails ; hobnails.

Tae, toe,

Tak, take.

Tangle, icicle ; sea-weed.

Tapetless, heedless ; pithless ; foolish. Perhaps from ' to-put,' like ' through-put.' The central idea of ' tapetless ' is want of energy.

Tarrow, delay ; haggle and hesitate ; murmur, complain.

Tassie, a small cup, or goblet. Fr. *tasse*.

Tauld, told.

Tauted, shaggy.

Tawie, tame, tractable.

Tawtit, shaggy.

Teats, or tates, small portions (as of wool).   Dan. *taer*, to pick wool.

Teen, anger ; grief.   From A.-S. *teóna*, vexation.   The word occurs in Shakespeare's *Tempest* ; and is used by Chaucer, Gower, &c.

Tent, attend to ; take notice of, observe.   Fr. *attendre*.

Tentie, attentive ; cautious, careful.

Tentless, careless.

Tester, coin—value sixpence ; so called from the impress, *teste*, a · head.

Teughly, or teuchly, toughly.

Thack, thatch.   Cp. Lat. *tego*, I cover ; *tectum*, a roof.

Thairms, intestines ; gut ; fiddle-strings.

Thane, title of honour corresponding to 'earl.'   A.-S. *thegen*, a servant (*sc.* the king's).

Thankit, thanked.

Thegither, together.

Thick, familiar, closely intimate.

Thieveless, without an object, unfit for action ; insipid ; trifling ; having no force of character.   A.-S. *theowian*, to serve.

Thole, endure ; tolerate—with which it is allied.   A.-S. *tholian*, to bear.

Thou's, thou art.

Thowes, thaws,   A.-S. *thawian*, to melt.

Thowless, unprofitable, useless ; having no force of character.   See 'thieveless.'

Thrang, throng ; busy ; in close numbers.   A.-S. *thringan*, to press.

Thrave, two 'stooks,' or shocks, of corn, consisting of 24 sheaves.

Thraw, twist or sprain ; also contradict.

Thrawn, twisted, sprained.

Thretteen, thirteen.

Through, to carry through.   To 'mak to through '=to 'make good.'

Throu'ther, through each other, promiscuously, confusedly.

Thuds, blows, dull heavy knocks.

Till, to, on to.

Tight, stout and active or smart.

Tinkler, tinker.   Named from the sound of his work.

Tint, lost.   To 'tyne,' or 'tine,' is to 'lose.'

Tip, tup, ram.   For pronunciation cp. 'bill ' for 'bull.'

Tippence, twopence.

Tippenny, twopenny (*sc.* ale).

Tirlin', unroofing, uncovering.   Allied to 'twirl.'

Tither, t'other, the other, another.   But 'the' precedes—'the tither day' = 'the other day.'

Titlin', tittering, laughing.

Tocher, dowry or marriage portion.   Irish *tochar.*   Cp. Lat. *donarium.*

Tod, fox.   Icel. *toa*, *tove*, a fox.

Toddle, to walk briskly with short, unsteady, and gentle springy steps, like a young child. Allied to ' totter.'

Toddy, a drink made by mixing whisky, sugar, and boiling water.

Todlin', moving gently, quickly, and unsteadily (like a young child).

Toom, empty.

Toop, tup, ram.

Toun, a farmstead. So used in Chaucer.

Tout, blow or sound. Said of a horn or trumpet.

Touzie, or towzie, shaggy, unkempt, disordered. ' Tease ' may be a connection.

Tow, a rope.

Towmond, twelvemonth, a year.

Toyte, to totter, or limp about. Connected with 'totter' and 'toddle.'

Transmugrified, transformed.

Trashtrie, a collection of trash. Icel. *tros* ; refuse, sweepings.

Trig, neat, spruce. Cp. Eng. 'trick '=to decorate. Milton uses 'trick.'

Trowth, truth. Used adverbially (with or without ' in ' preceding) to signify ' indeed.'

Trysted, agreed to meet at some particular place or time. From ' trust.'

Tug, pull.

Twa, two.

Twal, twelve.

Twins, loses, parts with. A.-S. *twaenian*, to separate ; from *twegen*, two ; *twynan*, to doubt. Cp. Lat. *duo* and *dubito*.

Tyke, a cur ; dog. Icel. *tyk*. The word is used by Shakespeare.

Tythe, the tenth part. A.-S. *teótha* ; Dan. *tiende*.

U.

Unco, unknown, strange ; rarely, unusually, very. A.-S. *uncuth*, unknown.

Uncos, news ; strange things, or persons.

Unfauld, unfold.

Upo', upon.

Usquebae, or usquabae, usquebaugh, whisky. Gaelic *uisge*, water, and *beatha*, life.

V.

Vauntie, vain, boastful, joyous. Fr. *se vanter*, to vaunt.

Vera, very.

Virls, small rings. Eng. ' ferrules ' ; Fr. *virole*, a little bracelet.

W.

Wa', wall.

Wabster, weaver. Cp. 'baxter' for ' baker.' A.-S. *wefan*, to weave.

U

Wad, would.

Wad, wager. A.-S. *wed,* a pledge. 'Wedding' is probably cognate. Cp. Lat. *vas, vadis.*

Wae's (me !), woe is me ! alas ! A.-S. *wa,* sorrowful.

Waesucks, literally 'woe is to us.' Sax. *usic* = us.

Waft, woof; the woven threads cast across the warp.

Wair'd, or wair't, laid out, expended. Icel. *veria,* to buy or sell. Eng. 'wares' is allied.

Wale, choose; also choice; also the best of its kind. Ger. *welen,* to choose.

Walie, beautiful; large. Also an exclamation of sorrow = alas ! With the former meaning it comes from A.-S. *wallig,* entire.

Wallop, to move strugglingly. Allied to 'gallop.'

Wame, belly. Eng. 'womb.'

Wanchancie, unchancy, unlucky. The prefix 'wan' (A.-S.) denotes deficiency.

Wanrestfu', unrestful, restless.

Wark, work.

Warl, world.

Warlock, wizard. A.-S. *wǽrloga,* traitor. Icel. *vardlokr,* an incantation.

Warst, worst.

Warstled, wrestled.

Wastrie, waste, reckless prodigality.

Wat, wet; also, know,—(from 'wit').

Waterfit, water-foot, *i.e.* the lower course of the stream.

Wattle, a twig or flexible rod, a few twigs twisted together. Allied to Lat. *vitilis,* plaited.

Wauble, to move from side to side with a weak wavy motion; waver.

Waught, or waucht, a copious draught. 'Swig' is probably cognate.

Wauken, waken; awake.

Wauket, thickened (said of the palm of the hand). A 'wauk-,' or 'walk-mill' is a fulling-mill.

Wauks, wakens. To 'wauk the night' is to 'lie awake the whole night,' 'to keep vigil the whole night.'

Waukrife, watchful, sleepless. A.-S. *wæcce,* watchfulness, and *ryf,* abundance.

Waur, worse; also, to worst, to baffle, or defeat.

Weans, little ones, children. Literally 'wee anes.' But perhaps from the verb 'to wean.'

Weason, weasand, windpipe; gullet. A.-S. *wǽsand.*

Wecht, weight; also a large round shallow vessel like a riddle or sieve, but without holes, used for winnowing corn and lifting grain.

Wee, small. Shakespeare uses it to describe Slender's face.

Wee-bit, very small. In the expression 'wee-bit hoosie' there are three diminutives.

Weeder-clips, instrument for cutting and removing weeds.

Weel, well.

Weet, wet, moisture (as of dew).

We'se, we shall or will.

Westlin, or westland, coming from the land westward, western.

Wha, who.

Whaizle, to breathe audibly like one troubled with asthma; wheeze.

Whalpit, whelped.

Whang, a thong of leather; a thick slice (of cheese, &c.).

Whare, or whaur, where.

Whase, whose.

Whatna, what or which (used adjectively). The form 'what'n,' or 'whatten,' is also used—with which cp. 'withooten' for 'without.'

Wheep, to whoop; also, beer—penny wheep = small ale.

Whid, a fib; also, to scud (said of a hare); playful chase or race.

Whigmaleeries, whims, crotchets; fantastical ornaments in dress, masonry, &c.

Whin-rock, whinstone, ragstone.

Whipper-in, one who whips in hunting dogs from straying; huntsman.

Whirly-gigums, petty fantastical decorations.

Whisht, be silent; hushed. To 'hold one's whisht' = to be silent. The form in Chaucer is 'huiste'; in Shakespeare, 'whist.'

Whitter, a hearty draught of liquor. Probably from the sound made in drinking greedily.

Whittle, knife. A.-S. *thwitan,* to cut. No connection with 'whet' (A.-S. *hwettan,* to sharpen) according to Prof. Skeat.

Whunstane, whinstone.

Whyles, at times, now and again; here . . . there.

Wi', with.

Wick (a term in the game of curling), to strike a stone obliquely. A.-S. *wican,* to fall back.

Wiel, a small whirlpool; a deep pool, or well. Allied to 'wheel.'

Wight, a person; also stout, enduring. A.-S. *wiht,* a creature. In the sense of 'strong,' it is probably connected with Lat. *vigeo.*

Wi'm, with him.

Winn, to expose to the wind or air in order to dry; to winnow.

Winna, won't.

Winnocks, windows of a cottage; windows.

Win's, winds.

Win't, winded (as thread).

Wintle, to stagger or reel; a staggering motion.

Winze, a curse or imprecation.

Withouten, without.

Wizen'd, withered and dry. A.-S. *wisnian,* to fade away, to dry.

Wonner, wonder. Cp. 'hunner' for 'hundred'; 'trem'le' for 'tremble,' &c.

Woo, wool.

Woodies, or widdies, withes; halters or ropes.

Wooer-babs, the garter knotted below the knee with two loops as worn by a wooer.

Wordie, small word.

Worset, worsted.

Wow! an exclamation of emphatic surprise or admiration; oh! I vow!

Wrack, vex; destroy.

Wrang, wrong.

Writers, attorneys.

Wud, or wood, mad.   Used by Chaucer, &c.

Wyle, to employ wiles, to beguile.

Wyte, blame.   A.-S. *witan,* to accuse or impute.   ' Wyte' occurs in Chaucer, Gower, &c.

Y.

Yard, enclosure; garden.   A.-S. *geard.*

Yealings, or eildins, individuals born at or near the same time. From ' eld,' old.

Yell, giving no milk.   From Icel. *gelld,* barren.

Yerkit, jerked.   A ' yerk' is a smart stroke.

Yestreen, evening of yesterday.

Yill, ale.   A.-S. *ealu,* ale.

Yill-caup, ale-mug.

Yird, earth.

Yokin', a pair of horses yoked to a plough; also a 'set to.'

Yont, beyond.

Younkers, young people.

Yowe, ewe.

Yowie, little ewe, or pet ewe.

Yule, Christmas.   A.-S. *geóla* ; *gýlan,* to make merry.   No connection with ' wheel,' according to Prof. Skeat.

THE END.